Seven Archangels:
An Arrow In Flight

Seven Archangels:
An Arrow In Flight

Jane Lebak

Philangelus Press
Boston, MA USA

Other Philangelus Press titles:
The Wrong Enemy (print)
Seven Archangels: Annihilation
Seven Archangels: Sacred Cups (Spring, 2015)

Other Jane Lebak titles:
The Boys Upstairs

Print version ISBN: 978-1-942133-03-2
Kindle ASIN: B00PB4I7BY
Library of Congress Control Number: 2014955901

Cover: C.K. Volnek

Dedication

To my mother, Maria Franzetti, who always encouraged my writing and saw the best in me.

A note about the format

The story of one nation, two species, and several centuries is going to spread out a bit differently than the story of an angel struggling with a huge mistake or a team of angels fighting to save a kidnapped comrade. In *Arrow,* each of the seven Archangels of the Presence will have his or her own story as they work through the time of salvation history. After each has had his spotlight, we'll begin the main story, the one driving all the rest. At the end, you'll get one more short story with everyone working together.

It's not the usual format for a novel, but I hope you'll find it's fun to spend a little solo time with each angel.

Heartless City

Three figures stood on the road with their backs to the sun, but only two cast shadows. Cattle clustered in the distance, their caretakers watching from the slanting shade of the terebinth trees, and even further beyond were sheep with their shepherds. At the crest of the hill before them, birds circled the gates of a walled city where even the land seemed to fall silent. Each mudbrick structure stood washed with flares of sunset that gave a burnt illumination to the little metropolis.

In a pitch between tenor and soprano, one of the two shadow-casters spoke like a dreamer. "The outcry against Sodom and Gomorrah is so great and their sin so grievous that I will go down and see what they have done. If it is bad as the outcry, I will know."

It was a perfect reproduction of God's voice even though none of the three were present when God spoke to Abraham. The speaker studied the city with simultaneous pity and revulsion flickering over her grey eyes. She ran one hand through blond hair emblazoned by the sunset.

Momentarily, the Cherub Gabriel continued in a more solid voice, "Abraham has asked for mercy, and God made an agreement. If we find ten righteous people in the city, we're to spare it."

Michael looked cautious. "That many? All but four were abandoned by their guardian angels."

Gabriel shook her head. An hour ago, she and Michael had been angels, two of the Seven directly before God. The Lord's touch had transformed them into humans for the day, but some of their origin showed. Gabriel seemed to brush against the ground without actually resting on it.

The only one not in human form, Raphael said, "You'll go as a woman?"

"I see no reason to change my apparent gender." Gabriel gave a perfectly balanced smile. "I've remained female since God created me, and I'm comfortable this way."

"Part of the report to God was that Sodomite men take advantage of women," said Michael.

"According to the report," replied Gabriel, "they take advantage of men, too. I'll be fine."

An unease crossed Michael's face as he folded his arms. He and Gabriel were obviously outsiders: with her blond hair, pale eyes and fine features, she looked like a northerner; Michael had a warrior's build and a square jaw, but his auburn hair and blue eyes gave him a striking appearance. God could have put them in Semitic bodies for the mission; Michael wasn't sure why He hadn't.

Raphael whistled to a bird, which called back from its bush.

Michael kept his head down. "I know God wants us to do this, but it goes against common sense. The whole city stinks of evil. Why not call Lot and his family away without going inside?"

Gabriel nodded. "As far as I understand, our presence will evoke their true natures."

Raphael kept his brown eyes trained on the hawk. "You're their last test."

Gabriel traced the flight of a honeybee before locating its hive in a tree a mile distant. "It would be unjust to condemn someone based on foreknowledge of events which won't occur. We'll go into the city and offer them a final test, and that will solidify them one way or the other."

Darkness shrouded Michael's eyes. He might have been a housewife finding bugs in the bread.

"I'd go instead if God let me," said Raphael.

"I'll obey," Michael said. "That wasn't an issue."

Michael and Gabriel proceeded on foot, Raphael on wings behind. "How did it get this bad?" Michael said. "I understood the Flood, but that was everyone. How can only two cities deserve destruction?"

Gabriel stayed toward the center of the road as they ascended the hill, but despite her silence, the information flowed into Michael as though she had spoken: Sodom started out clannish, and it prospered due to the trade routes. Over time the residents had stratified, either the comfortable rich or else the very, very poor who worked as servants or slaves.

She stepped around a puddle, paused at a snake sunning himself, and then looked up at Michael. "The economics don't allow for any meeting in the middle. Everyone has gotten so hidebound that they see one another as useful rather than as people. This distortion extends to their interpersonal relationships as well, thus the more sexual particulars of the outcry."

Michael said, "Is that their big sin?"

Gabriel's eyes unfocused, and her voice changed in pitch again so she became the mouthpiece of God, pulling words out of time. *"Now this was the sin of your sister Sodom: She and her daughters were arrogant, overfed and unconcerned; they did not help the poor and needy."*

Michael said, "Oh, there's an idea. If we show up as poor and needy, we can urge them to respond with compassion, and then we won't have to destroy the city after all."

Gabriel's voice returned to normal. "Your assertion is that it's easy to derail an entrenched self-centered focus. That may not be the case. Even if God causes upheaval in their lives in the form of a war, it may no longer be possible here to raise moral children."

A bee flew across their path, and Gabriel stopped, then followed it with her gaze. "Oh, there you are," she murmured, walking to the rotten trunk where the bees had made their hive.

She pressed her hand against the wood, closing her eyes. "Raphael, feel this. They're marvelous."

Michael glanced at the city and at the setting sun, but Raphael joined Gabriel in a languid and unhurried scan of the tree. "Hundreds of them," she said in a low voice. Workers buzzed out and landed on her, but she breathed over them and they only crawled on her without stinging. "Are you making honey? Do you have a lot of little ones in your comb?"

Michael checked the sunset again, the length of the shadows. He projected to Gabriel a sense of the time.

"God put this here so we can learn." Gabriel focused her soft grey eyes on him. "They don't sting when they're not threatened. The people in Sodom must feel threatened. Did you know that if something devastating happened to this hive, so long as there was one worker and one egg remaining, they could form a new hive? The worker could feed royal jelly to the one egg and raise up a new queen. The new queen would lay unfertilized eggs that became drones. The drone would fertilize the queen, and then she'd produce new workers. All that hope from just one worker and one egg. The goal with our test of Sodom should be to bring them that form of hope."

Michael looked at Raphael. *What?*

Look past what she's saying, Raphael said. *It's easier to do all this inductive stuff than to think about how horribly these people have behaved and what you're likely to do to them.*

Michael's eyes widened, and he glanced at Gabriel again. She didn't look nervous or grieved but was talking even faster than before. "Did you know if a beehive starves, they all starve at the same time? Individual bees don't hoard honey, just share and share until there's nothing left for any. Sometimes there's even honey remaining, but their wintering cluster only moves up the comb, not sideways, so if they don't break up the cluster, they never find the other honey. Maybe that's what's happening in Sodom. There wasn't enough love and concern left, and when we come, our test will break up their cluster and get them in touch with their own better natures. Then God can reach them."

She stroked the wood, her hand still covered with bees. "This tree is dead, but it's serving a purpose. Sodom could do the same. It may never have life again, but it can shelter life."

Michael said, "Gabriel? We need to get up there before dark."

Gabriel's brows furrowed. "Maybe the human soul is in some ways like a honeybee hive."

Raphael put a hand on her shoulder. "Maybe it is. Ask God."

She looked at him sidelong with a smile. "You *know* God teaches the Cherubim by letting us debate each other."

"So work with other Cherubim." Raphael glanced at Michael. "I'm a Seraph. Seraphim burn with excitement, so bring me the answers when you discern them, and I'll get excited. But sometimes the process gets a little tedious."

Gabriel sighed. "Truth exists, and by whittling at the argument, we'll reach it. Absolute truth won't contradict itself, and when we reach that nugget at the core of the argument—"

"Everyone in Sodom will be a thousand years old?" said Raphael.

Michael laughed aloud as Gabriel bit back whatever she'd been about to say.

Raphael added, "I know the word Cherub means *fullness of knowledge,* and I would never want you to change, but sometimes that's just a little too much fullness for the other eight choirs."

Michael realized Raphael was exerting calming pressure on the Seraph-Cherub bond he shared with Gabriel, and the words were only the surface of the exchange. Of all the choirs, only Seraphim and Cherubim bonded, probably because of their differing intensities and the ways they added to each what the other was lacking.

Michael said. "Leave the bees. It's too close to sunset."

Gabriel blew on her hand, and the bees frothed up, then returned to their hive.

When they reached the city's unmanned gates, Gabriel's eyes probed the empty nooks that should have had guards.

"They aren't afraid of intruders." Michael kept his voice low. "Reputation guards them."

Gabriel turned to Raphael, her eyes wider. "Are you sure you can't come with us?"

"I'm sorry." The Seraph's visage darkened. "I asked again. God refused."

Still scanning the city, Michael nodded. "You'd do best to pray for a conversion. We need six."

"What about Gomorrah?"

Gabriel shook her head. "If God judges against Sodom, we'll burn Gomorrah too."

Raphael extended the tips of his wings toward Gabriel and Michael in a blessing, then flashed away, transported like a thought.

Gabriel watched the place where Raphael had vanished, then sidled closer Michael.

"I'm with you," Michael said. "What can they do to angels?"

The Cherub crossed her wrists at chest height and closed her eyes: *They can make us witness evil.*

They entered the city and made their way toward the center square. What few people remained entered houses as the streets continued darkening. Reflected light produced horizontal trip-wires between buildings.

Michael felt Gabriel draw his attention to two men in a doorway.

"Good work." Michael assessed the threat level but kept walking. "Alert me to anyone else who takes notice of us."

Gabriel made no assent, but Michael could feel her senses expanding to absorb the entire area. He straightened with the posture of one who once had championed a defense no one thought he could win. Even without his wings, he carried an air that proclaimed his identity: military commander of God's hosts and one of the Seven.

Gabriel dropped behind Michael, seeming submissive instead of subordinated. She directed his attention to the individuals who watched from windows, all of whom wondered why a foreigner and his wife wandered Sodom at night.

Gabriel's nose wrinkled. "Three men on a rooftop just noticed us. They're obnoxious."

Michael led her to a shadowed portion of a mudbrick building and looked about the square where four streets intersected.

"The men left the building top," Gabriel whispered. "Four men are watching indecently from a ground-floor window."

"We're almost where I want to be. Hurry."

"They've left the window. Two boys are watching us all from an alley across the square."

She froze. "Two in front!"

The men jumped them before Michael could react.

Gabriel bolted.

Michael followed, scanning for a defensible spot. "Head for the corner building!"

The boys advanced from a side street, holding stones.

Frightened but fast, Gabriel dodged toward an alley where they might hide or scale the walls. But then a stone cracked into her head, and she dropped.

Michael hauled her up before running again, but she wasn't weightless, and the pursuers overtook him.

The three from the roof leered as more boys came with rocks. Four men climbed out a ground story window. Michael looked at the ladder ascending the wall of a building, but he couldn't guess how much two human bodies weighed versus how much that splintered wood could bear. The alley's mud reeked of urine and worse. He turned, but a man holding a club blocked the street.

The two original attackers approached, and Michael made a dark realization: the city had nowhere to hide because these were people well-practiced in hunting other people.

Gabriel squirmed to a stand, rubbing her head.

"Are you all right?"

Gabriel kept her voice as low as his. "I didn't think they could touch us."

The pursuers had formed a half-circle as they sized up the two angels. "Visitors?" asked one.

Her eyes round as saucers, Gabriel slid along the wall. Michael kept himself between her and the men.

11

The dusk-darkened mob forced them down the alley until Gabriel stopped retreating. Ten cubits behind them, the passage ended in a twenty-cubit mudbrick wall.

"Sweetheart," said one, coming too near, "welcome to Sodom."

Gabriel shoved the man. Michael drew his knife, but the men rushed him.

At the sounds of a fight, Sodomites poured from their houses. As though the original eleven were not too difficult to handle, now two dozen interested onlookers surrounded the fight, laying odds and placing bets.

At the far end of the alley, Gabriel screamed. Michael lunged for her, but six attackers pressed him back against the wall, and he took a punch to the gut.

Four men had Gabriel's arms and legs pinned. Even as they brought her to the ground, she struggled.

Above the men's laughter sounded Gabriel's calls for help. Michael pushed forward, but the gang shoved him back against the wall. "You're next," the closest man said. "She's just the appetizer."

She kicked. Michael twisted. There were just too many.

"Raphael!" Gabriel called, then gasped as someone wrenched both her arms behind her back, forcing her to thrust out her chest. Two of the men pressed up against her. "God!"

Too many people blocked Michael's view of what was happening. One man flung out a bit of fabric: her belt, followed by her overtunic.

Riotous laughter.

One man pushed a knife under Michael's chin, keeping him back against the wall. He couldn't see Gabriel, but he could hear. He prayed, *God, God, help—*

Gabriel erupted with light that must have been visible from Abraham's tent. Screams from the crowd, and even Michael found himself blinded. It seared through the alley for one second, two, and then it faded. As his vision cleared, he found the shadows of Gabriel's attackers scorched into the walls, but as for themselves, the men remained holding tight. The person they still had pinned to the ground was no longer female but male.

And instead of running in terror, the men laughed. "Well, looks like we got ourselves a godling," said one. And another, "We're having some fun tonight."

Screaming, Michael thrashed until he couldn't breathe. He could do it, just go ahead and call down that fire right at this very moment. Why had Abraham bargained for ten good people? Ten people who did nothing to spare the innocent were the same as having no good people at all.

God, please, save us. We're only angels. Michael's eyes burned, and his throat spasmed. *Father, have mercy! I don't care what they do to me, but spare Gabriel.*

Another light suffused the alley, this one less frenzy than pure strength. It leak up from the ground and out of the mudbrick walls, silencing the attackers in a timeless paralysis. Brightness like fingers and a hand held all of them in place. Michael felt one of the light fingers take the tears from his eyes.

This wasn't Gabriel's light. Gabriel had no light left to give. This light was God's.

When the light ended, the men shuffled away like automata.

Michael ran through the dispirited walkers. Gabriel huddled in the filth, curled like an egg.

The alley had re-darkened as if the light of God had not just entered. Gabriel's clothing was twisted around his waist, but the fabric was uncut, and he wasn't bleeding. It had happened so fast. Surely they hadn't succeeded?

Squatting by Gabriel's side, Michael felt panic raising. His human body coursed with chemicals that had his brain on high alert and his body ready to run, but there was nowhere to run to, only one big place to run from, and they had to stay because the assignment wasn't finished.

Shifting his focus so he was looking into God's eyes, Michael forced himself to go still. He couldn't fall apart, otherwise that was two of them down. He had a responsibility, first to the mission God had given him, and second to Gabriel.

After a minute of silence broken only by his heaving breaths, Gabriel edged himself to a sitting position. Finally he struggled to his knees, then leaned on the wall and climbed to his feet.

Michael tried to speak, but Gabriel started walking. Michael fished Gabriel's belt from the gutter, but Gabriel limped silently, one hand pressed to his side. His breaths came shallow, and Michael began to wonder if he shouldn't send Gabriel away—but would Gabriel even leave with the assignment incomplete?

As they passed one house, a man called, and Michael's throat tightened: he'd had more than enough of Sodom's men.

The call came again, and the man ran to meet them. Michael pivoted, glaring.

The man trembled, and Michael recognized Abraham's nephew Lot. "Here, my lords, please turn in to your servant's house and spend the night, and wash your feet; then you may rise early and go on your way."

The offer was about thirty minutes too late. Michael kept his eyes and expression flat. "We'll spend the night in the open square."

Beside him, Gabriel tensed.

Michael turned to the Cherub—and for a moment was lost.

"Please, my lords," the man said, "I beg you, the night is cold, and the city even colder. Come with me."

Biting his lip, Gabriel stared at the ground, still breathing in gasps. Michael said, "We accept."

Michael tried to take Gabriel's arm, but Gabriel slipped just beyond reach. They followed Lot to his home, Gabriel struggling to keep pace.

Lot's wife and daughters met them at the door. "Prepare a meal for these two men."

The older daughter brought out wine, and Michael forced Gabriel to drink. He was pale and looked to be in a cold sweat.

"Is your companion sick?" asked Lot.

Michael cleared his throat before speaking. "He needs to lie down."

Lot escorted the pair of angels to a chamber without windows; most of this house's thick walls seemed to lack them. Lot brought in a pitcher and a basin of water, then went in and out of the room bringing other items until Michael wished he could bar the door. By the time Lot was done, Gabriel had curled around himself on the mat and closed his eyes.

Michael brought the basin of water to Gabriel's side and wet one of the cloths, then reached toward him.

Just before his fingers would have touched Gabriel's shoulder, Gabriel exploded to his knees with his fists raised.

They regarded each other for several minutes, the pair of angels, both with wide eyes and both breathing quickly. Finally, Michael looked at the warm cloth and extended it to Gabriel.

The Cherub took it without brushing Michael's fingers. He ran it over one of his arms.

"Are you all right now?"

Gabriel went to work scrubbing himself all over: his face, his arms, his neck, his shoulders. Michael flinched to see the bruises purpling his skin and the way Gabriel couldn't twist toward his left. He was about to loosen his tunic and get his chest when he froze.

"I'm sorry," Michael said.

Gabriel looked up, ashen.

Michael whispered, "I did all I could."

Making no reply, Gabriel returned to scrubbing his arms until the skin turned red from friction.

"I don't know what else I could have done," Michael said.

Gabriel wrung out the cloth and set it over the side of the basin. He finally extended a hand, but drew it back before he touched Michael's. He tried an unsteady smile.

Both paused then, spines straight like antennae. Michael and Gabriel listened, and then Gabriel drew his knees to his chest, rocking in the darkness. The flat depths of his eyes seemed even greyer than the beaten dirt of the floor.

Michael ran from the room.

At the front of the house, Lot's wife and daughters stood by the entrance. The youngest sobbed.

The wife's voice sounded like a dart. "He's out there for you."

Michael slipped past them to the door.

15

"The house is surrounded," the younger daughter said. "We'll never survive! They'll tear us to pieces and sell us as slaves!"

Michael held out a hand. "They're all shouting at once, and I can't make out the words."

He closed his eyes, and Lot's voice became audible to him. "What do you want of my household?"

"Where are the men who came to you?" asked a voice. And another, "Bring them out so we can give them a proper greeting to Sodom!"

Laughter and tumult. Mockery.

Lot urged, "Please don't harm my guests." Someone shouted from the back of the crowd, and Lot drew a deep breath. "I have two virgin daughters. Let me bring them out to you, but don't do anything to these men."

The crowd pressed closer, and Michael could feel their rising anger.

"Get out of the way," one voice said. "You're a stranger but you dare judge us! We'll deal with you worse than them!"

Michael flung open the door and grabbed Lot by the shoulders. He yanked him inside, and Lot's wife slammed the door.

Lot stumbled to his knees. "I've tried—I've offered them everything –"

"Too much."

Michael turned to see Gabriel: ash-white and raspy, but glaring at the man who was willing to cast his two children to the whims of an evil crowd. He edged out his words between shallow breaths. "Nobody is going to get raped."

Michael clenched his fists. His eyes fixed on the wraith that had become of Gabriel, the crying daughter, the drawn faces of her sister and mother, the pallor of Lot's cheeks. The din outside increased.

Michael returned to his angelic form. At the entrance of Lot's home he stood with shimmering wings at his shoulders and a sword of light in his hand. Lot's family retreated to the walls, but Michael let the power of his natural form flood him. "Enough of this city, enough of this evil!"

16

Michael hurled his sword through the wall, into the crowd, and as it traveled at eye level, it struck each man blind. The noise ceased momentarily, only to return as cries of confusion.

The sword returned to Michael's hand. He faced Lot.

"Do you have anyone else here? Sons-in-law, sons, daughters, or anyone you have in Sodom, take them *out* of this infernal city! We'll burn this place in the morning. God has judged against it."

The family stared. Michael breathed heavily for a moment; then the brightness faded, and he remained in human form.

Gabriel spoke in Heaven's language. "There's not ten. We can do it now."

Michael started. "We have to get the family out of here."

"No, we don't! We were told to find *ten good people!*" The pitch of Gabriel's voice raised. "Four isn't ten! We can burn the place and go home! Please, Michael — all of them are going to die anyhow! In the long run, what does it matter when it happens?" A hysterical edge came into Gabriel's voice, and he leaned harder on the daughter, hand pressed to his ribs. "It's just a city. Cities fall."

"No." Michael put iron into his voice, and Gabriel looked only betrayed. "It can wait until tomorrow. None of them will escape God's justice." He stepped toward Gabriel, and then in human language, said, "Come on. Let's get you back to the room."

Gabriel recoiled from Michael, so Lot's daughter brought him.

"Is there anything else you want?" she asked.

"Yes." Gabriel seemed small. "Stay."

"Michael?"

Raphael stepped back as the Archangel startled to full awareness, then met his gaze in the dark.

Michael sighed as he sat up. "Thank goodness. I was hoping you'd come."

Raphael lowered his eyes but remained otherwise motionless. "I couldn't intervene."

"I understand."

"Will Gabriel?" Raphael squatted beside the sleeping Cherub. "You're in shock, aren't you?" he whispered. A sharp pause. "And not just emotional shock. They really got to you."

Raphael extended his hands to Gabriel, then jerked them back like a child warned not to touch fire. Instead Raphael hovered his hands over Gabriel as if rippling the waters of a pool without breaking the surface. "He didn't get raped. Physically, it's bruises and internals. I've been given permission to heal those, but the spirit I can't heal." Raphael concentrated so he illuminated the room. "This isn't a condemnation of you, Michael, because you didn't know, but I want to show you: when someone is panting for breath and the skin is bluish, that's an emergency, and I want you to call me."

Michael put his head in his hands.

Raphael's amber glow settled around Gabriel, whose breathing immediately eased. "Come on...knit together. Don't let your kidneys shut down. It's only me."

Michael whispered, "I didn't realize how badly they hurt him."

Raphael concentrated only on Gabriel for the time being. Then the glow dissipated, and he turned back Michael. "How are *you*? I can do as much for you. I can mend the bruises, but not the heart."

Michael glared at his lap, the tightness of words wrapping around him. He tried to speak, but what words would cover this? Instead he spoke with his posture, his facial expression, and strong emanations like pulses from his heart. He clenched his hands and tightened his shoulders.

Raphael sat cross-legged before Michael, then leaned forward as Michael closed his eyes, but all the Archangel could project was anger: he hadn't known what to do.

"I know what we do now. We pray." Raphael took Michael's hands. "And you need to forgive yourself."

Michael pulled free his hands. "A better commander would have avoided the whole incident. We just walked in without any tactics in place. They call me their commander—all the choirs— because I challenged Satan with *Who is like God?* But I'm just an Archangel mixing with Cherubim and Seraphim. There are seven choirs of angels stronger than me that could be doing my job, and for that matter, the majority of my own. That's not right."

Raphael offered a smile. "God likes to lift up weak people and put down the strong ones."

Michael said, "But my native endowments—"

"—are so augmented that you're Gabriel's equal. Easily. You threw Satan into Hell."

Michael huffed. "And for all that, I couldn't overcome ten malnourished humans today. At least if Satan had been behind it, I could have fought."

Raphael said, "You think he wasn't?"

"Not directly," Michael said. "Not this time. These people carry their own evil."

They stayed quiet a moment, during which Raphael's eyes wandered back to Gabriel, who lay motionless as if dead. He answered Michael's projected question with, "Dreaming. I can feel it."

"Angels don't dream."

"Human bodies do. You're both human right now."

Michael paused. "Nightmares?"

Raphael's mouth tightened. "Just dreams. I didn't feel him hashing this out with God earlier, so maybe that's what he's doing in his sleep."

Michael said, "He wouldn't talk to me."

"Then he'd better talk to God before he buries the whole thing. What good is it to stand in the presence of God if you're not going to tell Him when you're furious or at the end of your strength? I already did." Raphael shifted as if to leave. "You'd better get some sleep, too. The human body has certain basic needs, and you're denying one of them by staying awake all night."

"But Gabriel?"

Reflected glory passed across Raphael's eyes as he prayed his question. "I'm allowed to stay."

Michael lay back on his pallet, and Raphael pressed both his hands against Michael's head. The Archangel could feel the bruises healing and tried to thank him, but he had grown too sleepy.

The last thing Michael saw was Raphael, his wings half-extended, reaching for Gabriel, but again God held back his hand before Raphael could touch him. "Be well," whispered the Seraph. "I'm right here, and I'm not leaving."

Gabriel awoke to find Michael sleeping.

He sat on the mat and pulled the blanket taut about his shoulders, surprised by the painless movement of his arms and the ease of his own breathing.

"Hey there."

Gabriel jumped, shifting rapidly so he faced Raphael, and he retreated even as Raphael raised his hands. "It's okay. I'm not coming close."

Gabriel shivered, and then he kept shivering.

A moment after, Raphael reached for his soul through the bond they shared, and Gabriel tensed. Raphael backed off while Gabriel kept his head bowed, his cheeks hot, and now he couldn't look into the Seraph's eyes.

Images and impulses came to him from Raphael, less invasive this time as the Seraph only projected: Nothing had changed between them. He was distraught that it had happened, but what the men had done, had wanted to do, didn't change their friendship, and again he offered his soul through their bond.

Gabriel projected an image back to Raphael: filthy rags.

Sorrow projected in return. A picture of the rags as linen squares bleached white, pressed and folded. Then Raphael repeated he was staying until morning.

Gabriel closed his eyes and lay on his side.

Alone in the middle of the night, an angel generally will talk to God. Gabriel did not pray. He kept his attention off Raphael. He curled tight as before.

Hands. Blows. Faces. Hot breath.

A cry formed in his throat, but he killed it. Don't think about it. They'd all be dead in the morning. They'd never be able to touch him again. It happened and it was over. Don't think about it. Kill it.

Raphael could put him to sleep—would he like that?

Recognizing the thought as a projection from Raphael, Gabriel agreed, and then the heaviness of an exhausted body dragged his protesting thoughts under.

Gabriel found herself lying in a field, arms and wings wrapped around her legs. A breeze stirred the trees, and the grass blades brushed her sides to its rhythm.

Thick draperies hung throughout her mind, like curtains partitioning rooms in a house. She pushed at one but then decided to leave it be. For now, she was an angel alone in a field. In angelic form once again (she felt surprised at feeling surprised—when hadn't she been an angel?) Gabriel stretched her arms and unfurled six grey wings. Her blond hair dangled over her shoulders.

She straightened her simple clothing and leaped into flight.

In three beats, the wings lifted her in an escape from the earth, carrying her to the level of the clouds.

Don't fly too high, or you'll fall, warned something inside.

Gabriel looked at the clouds and knew they would grab her if she came closer, but she couldn't stop ascending.

Oh, she thought. *I'm dreaming like a human. That's unexpected.* Unexpected, but a unique chance to gather data about a human's unconscious thought processes.

The clouds nabbed her. They gummed her and swallowed her, holding her arms and legs like clamps, and she called out. Her wings sliced the vapor, but the amorphous mass reconstituted itself just as quickly as her feathers could cut.

Gabriel freed herself and plunged toward the ground. Unable to slow in time, she crashed into the grassy hillside on her back and couldn't move no matter how hard she tried.

Sleep paralysis. She'd heard of the phenomenon, and she knew it caused some distress to the humans who experienced it. *My body can't move, and that's carried through into the dream.*

The waving grass snapped over her and lashed her to the ground. Her limbs found themselves, but too late. The grass kept snaking around her, pulling her into the dirt, and when she screamed, over her mouth like a gag.

Again, wings scissored uselessly as Gabriel tried to break the living ropes.

Tighter they held her, rings of pain that muffled her hearing into a whine. As the pressure prevented her from drawing breath, her vision scattered into hundreds of green points.

Abruptly the earth gave way, and she plunged into an underground lake.

With no sense of direction in the lightless water, Gabriel swam. Could she find an exit? Would her wings grow waterlogged? She couldn't drown, but the water could affect her in other ways. Claustrophobia and hysteria could accomplish what suffocation could not.

With every stroke she longed for a rock, and finally she found one. Clawing upward, she surfaced through tripwires of light and gasped until her ribs hurt. Ribs – something had hurt her ribs. Something terrible. *No, don't think about it.* The air tasted stale, but she didn't get a chance to look around before a hand grasped her wrist and hauled her from the water.

The men of Sodom.

Gabriel knew she was dreaming, but she yanked toward the water. The crowd pulled her away. They cropped her hair close with a knife, then sliced off her belt. Someone else ripped off her sandals.

"Leave her alone!"

Raphael and Michael flashed their swords, scattering the Sodomites.

Michael lifted her from the rocks, supporting her with an arm and a wing. Raphael stood on her other side, holding his sword erect as he stood guard.

Gabriel wrapped her arms around herself. "Thank you. Is this really you in the dream, or are you also dream figments? I haven't devised a means of determining whether you're real."

"Just relax," Michael said. "We're here now."

"We'll take care of you," said Raphael.

They flashed her to the field where she had begun. The grass was no longer a predator, moving only as the wind directed.

Until Raphael pushed her to the ground and knelt over her body. Gabriel screamed, but Michael tore off her tunic, and he pushed her shoulders to the ground while Raphael put his hands on her body.

Gabriel kicked Raphael in the stomach, but Michael jerked her backward. "This is a dream! Why are you doing this?"

Michael pinned her arms behind her back, and Raphael maneuvered his body too close to her own. Hot breath struck her lips.

"You're only a dream! In God's name and authority, I order you to leave!"

They both vanished. Good. She got to her feet and looked around, then made the field vanish, then the clouds, then the sky itself.

"So," she said, not bothering to fold her wings around her naked body, "Are you done testing me?"

No answer, so she scanned the blank field of her vision for the only one who could have intruded on her mind this way. "I know better than to expect an apology, but since I've passed this test too, shouldn't I get an explanation?"

Still nothing. Gabriel said loudly, "I should be furious at you, but I keep rationalizing. 'All things are permitted for a purpose.' Michael or Raphael couldn't have come up with this kind of senseless act. Not the men of Sodom. Not nature or 'circumstance'."

She paused just long enough. "Not even Satan."

She stood absolutely still, but no answer came. "Well? Don't I get a reason?"

She changed her sight to an inner sight, the Vision of God where she could look at Him face to face, and He wasn't angry.

"I'm not very happy with you right now," she said.

She clenched tight as God touched her soul. A mote of His peace settled on her even as one of her wing-pairs dropped to become a new garment, but like the clothing, the peace stayed on the surface.

"I love you, Gabri'li," God said.

"Why are you telling me that now?" She frowned. "You permitted that. You cast us to those savages and let it happen."

Silence.

She pressed her palms to her eyes and knitted her fingers. "I need you to give me an answer. Your orders didn't leave us any choice." She fingered the grey tunic lying against her skin. "I need to know why you made that happen to me."

When God didn't give any more of an answer than His presence, Gabriel tightened her fists. "You made me a Cherub. I live to answer these questions! When tragedy happens to people I offer them reasons, so how can you deny me what I'm supposed to give them?"

God didn't sound upset. "Do you think a reason will help you?"

"Of course a reason would help!" Gabriel's eyes glinted. "I know how you work with humans, but when you give them suffering it's either in punishment for sin or because they're part of a fallen world, and in my case, neither applies."

God said, "Go on."

Gabriel folded her arms. "It stands to reason that you had an objective in mind for this experience, some effect intended to be wrought by myself or by Michael. But Michael declined to use their attack as an indicator for Sodom's immediate immolation, so —"

"You're theorizing," God said.

Gabriel said, "Thank you."

"There are times when theory isn't the goal, even for a Cherub," God said. "Sometimes what you need is to feel."

Gabriel wrapped her arms around her stomach. "I don't want to feel that. I'll panic. If I panic, I can't think clearly. It was bad enough with the human stress hormones and pain receptors at work that — "

God said, "Gabriel, stop."

Gabriel fell silent, head bowed.

God said, "You have to draw closer to humankind, to feel their fears and pressures. I want you to sample their frustration, their limitations, and their perspective."

Gabriel sighed. "I know why they feel what they do. Stress hormones. Pain receptors. I experienced them, and I'm grateful to you for making me an angel."

God said softly, "But what about compassion?"

As though an Arctic wind blew over her sweat-beaded skin, Gabriel recoiled. "But— We're not the same."

"You're not the same. I don't want you to be the same. I want you to be the soul I made you." God's voice didn't have the gentleness Gabriel expected, and she raised her grey eyes to seek out God's face in the mist. When that failed, she again turned that gaze into her heart and found Him in the Vision. "I want you to have empathy for them. I want you to feel why I love them."

Gabriel committed the words to memory. She tried not to process them as she heard; there would be time enough afterward, after Sodom and Gomorrah became a cautionary tale and after she was back among her own kind. Her own choir, who knew why man had fallen in the first place and who would know how to help them persevere anyhow.

Gabriel sat on the formless ground of the dream-plane and did her best not to recall the grasp of disgusting, sweating, angry men or the desolation of an alley devoid of Godliness. "I don't forget things, so will I carry this gash with me forever, not wanting to be touched by even my closest friends? Why did You permit me to doubt Michael and Raphael? For that matter, why would You let me doubt You?"

God moved around her like humid summer air.

"And while I appreciate the new experience, there's the matter of this dream."

"You gave that to yourself," God said.

Gabriel started. "Angels don't dream."

"You're not an angel at the moment. You're in a human body."

Gabriel's shoulders dropped. "If you want to be technical about it. But then you allowed me to dream something five times more frightening than what happened in that alley."

God said, "You were well into the process of repressing the experience, and I will not leave you crippled by fear for the rest of eternity. That's not living life to the fullest."

Gabriel folded her arms. "Your point. So the dream had a purpose, but I still haven't the slightest clue what your reason was for allowing the incident that sparked the dream."

"Just trust that there was one."

Gabriel huffed. "You could tell me."

"Sometime in the future, you'll fulfill the ultimate purpose in my having created you, and this will have been one of the elements against which I shaped you to make you perfect."

Ultimate purpose?

Gabriel looked up with round, round, asking eyes.

"I'm not going to tell you yet," said God.

She made her eyes yet rounder, and more beautiful.

"No," He said.

She sighed. "Michael suffered, too."

God's expression chided her. "His lesson," said God, "is his own. I'm with you now. I'll stay with you. But you know what I want you to do."

She nodded, and the dream faded. Gabriel awoke to discover the night had become morning.

Michael opened his eyes to find Gabriel sitting on his own mat, watching him. Gabriel projected, *Good morning!*

Michael, careworn even though he had slept, leaped up and hugged Gabriel, nearly knocking him to the ground. He realized too late that he wasn't supposed to have touched him, but when Gabriel didn't recoil, Michael closed his eyes and laughed.

After a moment, he sat back from Gabriel and looked at him directly, the sky eyes expressing sorrow to the cloud-colored ones.

Gabriel nodded, echoing Michael's expression.

Michael touched his hands to Gabriel's and smiled in return.

They went into the kitchen where Lot's wife cooked breakfast over a fire. "Where's your husband?" asked Michael.

"Speaking to our sons-in-law," answered the woman.

She handed Michael and Gabriel bread, a handful of figs, and pottery cups. They seated themselves and began eating, Michael noting how Gabriel had recovered his appetite. "I'm glad to see you're better this morning," the woman said. "I told Lot you needed a night's rest. He thought you were dying."

Michael met Gabriel's eyes. "Raphael visited," he said in Heaven's native tongue.

Gabriel nodded.

A moment after, Gabriel added, "I talked it out with our Father last night. We reached an understanding."

Lot entered the kitchen, still wearing his overtunic against the morning chill.

Michael turned to him. "Where are your sons-in-law?"

"They refused," said Lot. "I'm afraid they're like the rest."

Gabriel stood. "It's time, then. You have to take your wife and daughters away so you don't burn with the city."

Lot's wife rushed to his side. "Now? Can't I say goodbye? I have friends here. If I tell them, maybe we can convince our sons-in-law to come with us after all. Maybe you can talk to them."

Michael caught a hesitation in Gabriel's eyes, but then Gabriel shook his head. "God has His reasons. It's time to go."

Lot, his wife and daughters tried to gather the things they wanted to take, but half an hour later they kept finding more material objects that had to accompany them to their new life. Finally, Gabriel and Michael grabbed the family by their arms and led them forcibly from the city.

At the base of the ridge, Michael and Gabriel stopped. "Don't look back," Michael said. "There's nothing to be gained by looking back."

Gabriel watched the city gates for any people in pursuit, but none came. Lot thanked them again, and he took his family into the wilderness.

When at mid-morning, Lot had achieved a safe distance, Gabriel stood.

"It's almost over," Michael murmured. "So many people. Two cities full of dreams and good intentions."

"They had no good intentions here." Gabriel had all but shaken the dust off his sandals when they left. "Ask for our orders, and let's get it over with."

The Lord instructed Gabriel to take Sodom and Michael to destroy Gomorrah, then restored them to their full angelic forms.

The light faded, and Michael turned to Gabriel only to exclaim, "No!"

Gabriel faced him. Gone was the lithe form, the angular features. Even out of the human body, Gabriel had remained male rather than returning to her natural form.

Michael said, "You aren't going to change back?"

Gabriel's wings closed around himself. "I'd rather not."

"You're out of danger. Don't do this to me." Michael grabbed him by the shoulders, but Gabriel yanked backward. "Please."

Rubbing his arms, Gabriel looked at some of the feathers on the outermost pair of wings. "I'm not particularly attached to myself one way or the other. We're pure spirits. It's all affectation anyhow." His brows tightened. "Please don't take it as an insult. There isn't any guilt on you."

Without another word, Gabriel spread his wings and glided toward Sodom. Michael watched him from the ground, and then with just a thought, he flashed himself to Gomorrah.

Gabriel didn't hover for a last look at the faces, at the servants hanging laundry or the merchants trying to make a living. He didn't look for the ones who had cracked his ribs or torn his clothes. He opened his hands and formed the fire of Heaven, gathering it until his feathers and hair stood up with the heat. He set out a circle of flame to demark the city's boundaries.

As he closed the circle, he hesitated at one rotten tree. A tree containing a beehive. Inside, or outside the circle?

It took too long to decide, and he redrew the circle six times in five seconds. Inside or outside?

They don't sting when they're not threatened. And Gabriel – was he being threatened?

Outside, then. He tightened the circle and left the hive on the border.

With God's energy coursing through him, Gabriel poured liquid flame into Sodom like molten steel into a cast.

Every plant and animal he dispatched according to the will of God. Every human life, snuffed out, the fear and the outcry and the pain washing past without leaving a mark on him in the center of that aerial kiln.

More. Everything. Everything, gone. Scorched down to the bedrock, crumbled into ashes and then the ashes themselves crumbled into something that resembled sand. Filth scoured clean that would never again harm anyone.

Gabriel lowered the fire and checked. Nothing remained of Sodom.

His mouth twitched. He called it good.

Michael appeared beside him, tears in his eyes. Gabriel hardened his gaze and stared at a rotten tree that returned the look without flinching. In the hive, he could sense the bees confused by the smoke, gorging on honey as if preparing to leave their home. *Good. Swarm away. There never was any hope here to begin with.*

Together they returned home, to the Lord.

Holiday

Raguel finished binding the last of the demons that had attacked Jericho. "Michael? You need any help over there?"

Michael was scanning the city walls from a distance. "I think the humans have it from this point. They'll take care of the military threat fine now that we've gotten rid of the demonic one."

As Raguel brought the demon over to the rest of their captives, he looked up and realized—he knew this one. They'd worked together before the Winnowing, back before Satan had rejected God and brought a third of the angelic host down with him from Heaven.

"Anzaniel," whispered Raguel.

The demon's eyes glinted: victory and rejection and hatred all at once. He might as well have said, "I was waiting for you to realize. But I'm not him anymore."

A chill spiked through Raguel as he remembered this fallen angel unfallen, showing him one star out of millions in a star nursery and explaining how this one would never form more than a brown dwarf, and how excited this angel had been about all the variations in the ways you could burn hydrogen. *God did this*, the angel had said, delighted. *God did it all!*

And here he was, today, bound and gagged after trying to harm the Israelite forces at Jericho so an attack by the Canaanites would kill them all.

A hand landed on Raguel's shoulder. "Hey," Michael murmured. "Come with me."

Michael flashed them both away from the city wall. Raguel said, "I have to finish my work."

Michael folded his arms and shook his head. "You have to get a breather. I've seen that look on my men before, and I know you've seen it too. Last week, didn't you send Dobiel for a break?"

Raguel said, "I had to. He'd pushed himself so hard he was shaking."

Michael nodded. "But when was the last time you took any time off?"

Raguel shrugged.

"You ensure that your direct reports get rests on a regular basis." Michael pointed at him. "I'm going to do the same. Take twenty-four hours, and I don't want to see you on duty until this time tomorrow."

Raguel opened his hands. "What should I do?"

"And that," Michael said, "is proof positive that you need a break. Creation is huge and this is a gorgeous world." He swept out one hand and one wing to take in the expansive horizon. "You're fighting to defend it. You deserve to enjoy it. Now go."

Michael vanished.

Raguel huffed. *I don't really need a break,* he prayed.

There's 'need,' God replied, *and there's 'would benefit from.' Don't turn the latter into the former.*

Raguel smirked. *Well, at least let's make it useful time.*

He began his twenty-four-hour enforced holiday by heading to his spot directly before God, one of the Seven Archangels of the Presence. Training his inner focus on God, he drank in the Beatific Vision: his understanding of God in all His splendor. Light from light, truth from truth, this was his creator and his lover and his sustainer, and Raguel shed his concerns just to dwell in that Presence.

He hadn't always been able to do this. Only after the Winnowing were the angels given the gift of seeing God as He is. But now, having experienced Him unfiltered, Raguel wouldn't have been able to live without Him.

It's been too long, Raguel prayed, and God welcomed him back: they could be together now.

Eventually Raguel found himself gentled away from contemplation, and he looked around at the angelic choirs. The Seraphim were singing "Holy Holy Holy" in their eternal trisagion. The Cherubim were contemplating and debating and studying. The choirs rayed out from the Throne of the Almighty, the most powerful ones closest to the center, and yet here stood Raguel, only a Principality and yet right in the heart, directly before the Almighty.

Dizzying, when he thought of it. A reward God had given him for doing nothing more than remaining true.

Raguel asked for an assignment. The Holy Spirit responded, "You're assigned to eighteen more hours of relaxation."

"Is there anyone I can help?"

"I want you to help yourself."

An unusual assignment, to be sure. If he'd been assigned to protect one of Israel's judges, he'd have reconnoitered, taken stock of the angels under his command, assessed the threat, and then strategized. How do you strategize doing nothing?

So Raguel reconnoitered: what areas of his spirit needed the most rest? And what resources did he have to meet that need? What were the threats to his spiritual well-being? And given that, how could he eliminate the threat?

He could sleep. Angels didn't need to sleep on a regular basis, but they could sleep in response to emotional exhaustion. He wasn't that badly off, though, so he considered lesser remedies, and that's when he decided on art. Some kind of art was the way to relax.

Raguel flashed himself back to Earth with a thought, arriving in the crown of a century-old cedar that swayed in the wind but didn't buckle under his immaterial form. If he'd been anything but pure spirit, Raguel couldn't have stood on those topmost branches: his form was a head taller than even the tallest man he'd ever met, and he also had four ruddy wings on his back.

All of Canaan stretched before him, spreading to the seas on one side and mountains on the other, more mountains to the north and wasteland to the south, but here lay a plateau where cows grazed and bees buzzed. Farmers worked their crops in every direction, and Raguel recognized their angelic guardians at their sides saying "Grow." In the distance, a Virtue read a story by a stream. Two Cherubim crouched, engrossed, over a game of strategy atop a rock while one Dominion fished without bait or hook, just for the lazy pleasure of nothing to do.

What was Michael doing now? Did he need help? But no, Michael had told him to quit worrying for one day. He could get back to work in a few more hours.

Raguel slipped to the base of the tree where he considered what kind of art to indulge in. He could read. He could attune his ears to the Heavenly choir and listen to their music. He could draw, and in the end, the act of creation appealed most to him. He created parchment and charcoal pencils with just a thought, and he made himself semi-solid so he could use them.

Raguel illustrated his prayers, offering the drawing to God even as he sketched: colors and light and blends that appealed to his sense of vision and at the same time represented souls. The tragedy of that lost angel he'd just encountered, the victory of the Jericho souls who would survive the threat, and on the margins, a promise. A promise of redemption to come, a soul so great and so pure that it would reconcile the world.

What Raguel thought it would be, that was. He wasn't sure. None of the angels were.

As night tucked in Canaan, Raguel focused a glow onto the parchment and determined to finish before his holiday ended.

It was then the peasant came.

The man who entered Raguel's grotto exerted all the strength in his aging body to swing a wooden staff into the bushes, driving off any number of small animals.

"They may be Your chosen people," Raguel muttered to the Lord, "but God, they're strange people."

"I heard you!" The man whirled in Raguel's direction and pointed a careworn finger. "Where are you?"

Raguel looked up from his parchment, eyes shining.

Hovering above the man's head to avoid the swinging stick, the man's guardian opened his hands. *He's searching for an angel. He heard you because he has an amulet.*

Raguel frowned at the other angel.

The guardian shrugged, looking helpless.

The man poked the air at random points with the staff, and Raguel burst out laughing.

"I hear you," the man said. "You're coming with me!"

Raguel gestured to his drawing and pencils, which vanished back to Heaven. "Whyever would I accompany you anywhere?"

The old man jabbed the air near the tree, and Raguel grabbed the staff; the angel could feel the tingle of idolatry, but prayers to El Shaddai had also seasoned the wood. The man tugged it back.

"I have an amulet. You have to show yourself."

Raguel looked at the guardian, who seemed mortified.

What do you want me to do with him, Lord?

I want you to love him, God replied.

Yes, Raguel prayed, *but how? Should I make myself visible?*

You can if you want.

Raguel revealed himself where he sat, legs tucked up and wings tight around him.

The old man started.

"Give me your name," said Raguel.

"Eliakim ben Yehudi," said the old man.

"Explain yourself, Eliakim ben Yehudi." Raguel kept his voice steady, as if talking to one of his soldiers. "What sort of amulet are you wielding that 'commands' me to obey?"

The man raised a leather thong from beneath his grey beard. On the end was a clay charm stamped with symbols.

"I'm impressed." Not for the reason the old man thought, but it was an impression nonetheless. "What kind of service are you compelling?"

Is that the right term?, Raguel thought to God.

If he were compelling you, you'd know what to call it, God told him.

The man frowned. "Let me see all of you."

Raguel climbed to his feet before the old man, who stepped backward as he stared at the eyes shining high over the top of his head. Raguel kept a dry tone. "Will I suffice?"

Eliakim grimaced. "You'll have to."

The guardian burst out laughing, hands over his mouth. Raguel tried not to look at the guardian in case he did the same. "Where do you live?"

"In the house at the base of the hill—"

Eliakim stopped whatever he'd been about to say because Raguel had flashed them both to the building.

Raguel inspected the small building. "Now, what service did you require?"

Eliakim was panting, trembling. Humans react badly to angelic transportation. "You could have warned me!"

"I could have. What service did you require of me?"

The guardian laid a hand on his charge's shoulder. "Play nice."

Eliakim led Raguel into the mudbrick house's courtyard past a dead firepit. The man leaned heavily on the walking stick as he seated himself at a table in a back room. Raguel glanced around—then bristled. Anger rippled from his heart.

The old man clutched the amulet in his wrinkled hand.

Raguel faced him, eyes glowing like stars. "You have an Ashera in here."

His wings flared. He could level this house and snap that man like a cracker. Eliakim squeaked, "I don't."

Raguel marched into the corner and snatched up a clay idol, a woman with curls on her head and both hands supporting her giant breasts. Raguel crushed it in his fist.

Red crumbs trickled from his palm. "El Shaddai is your one God."

The old man had gone pale.

Raguel dusted his hands, sending a shower of clay around the room. His eyes narrowed. "Did you summon me to insult God with idols?"

Eliakim clutched the amulet in his hand. "I meant no offense. I want you to stay for the night."

Raguel squinted.

"I demand safety. You're ordered to remain until morning to make certain I stay safe."

Raguel cocked his head. "You need protection?"

"I'm an old man." Eliakim looked aside. "My children are scattered, and my wife is dead. I want you to stay until I die."

Raguel's eyebrows raised. "You plan to die tonight?"

"I know I'm going to die tonight," said the man. "An amulet told me."

Raguel glanced at the guardian.

"It's true," said the guardian. "His heart will stop before sunrise."

Pausing momentarily, Raguel looked about the house, the man's possessions, and foresaw it all dissolve into time. "What do you think I can do?"

"Just guard me," the old man grumbled. "Is that so difficult?"

Raguel said, "You...summoned an angel to protect you from...nothing?"

"If I had known angels were so obstinate," said Eliakim, "I might not have."

Raguel reached with his heart to God. *Love him,* God had said. It would have been easier to protect him—at least there you could put a barrier around the man, shore up his soul, dispatch your soldiers to the vulnerable places and watch for an enemy. Why hadn't God arranged things so Eliakim had found a different angel?

Raguel bit his lip. "There's nothing really to protect you from. Do you want reassurance?"

The man shrugged. "I don't know. You're the angel."

"You're the arch-mage with the amulet."

Eliakim snickered, Raguel realized what he had said, and they both laughed.

Eliakim said, "You might start with your name."

"Why ask my name?"

"Because I want to know who's with me." The man folded his arms. "I won't set up idols to you. I don't have time even if I wanted to."

That made sense. "My name is Raguel. I'm a Principality, and one of the seven archangels of the Presence."

Eliakim raised his eyebrows. "So I did well for myself, didn't I?"

Raguel frowned. "You consider angel-hunting like any other competition?"

"No, but if you were a fish, I'd eat well for a week."

Raguel decided to take this as a compliment. He went to the table and sat opposite Eliakim. "You're a fisherman?"

Eliakim shook his head. "Occasionally I'll catch fish, but I farm. Always did. Took over from my dad. Some years are tough, but God kept us."

Raguel said, "And your sons will take over the farm after you?"

Darkness crossed the old man's face. "My sons died fighting to preserve the land." He hauled himself up from his chair. "I'm not showing you good hospitality, talking about the past. Would you like food or drink, or are you unable to eat our sort of food?"

"I have no need."

Eliakim stopped, and Raguel saw that momentary emptiness on the man's face: rejection. Uselessness.

"Although, come to think of it," Raguel said, "if you have some wine, let's share that."

Eliakim brought two cups and a wineskin. "I thought much wine is a mocker."

"It is, but it depends on how you define *much*." Raguel grinned. "I've got an angelic body, so I don't have to get drunk. But I could tell you some stories about the people I've outlasted."

Eliakim arched his eyebrows. "Are you old enough to tell those stories?"

"Pardon me," Raguel said, "but I'm far older than even your esteemed years."

An awkward silence. Eliakim asked, "How old?"

"God created time after He created us angels; I suppose I'm ancient."

"You don't look it." Eliakim filled both cups. "How many angels are there?"

"Each star in the sky has its guardian angel, and each person on the earth has a guardian, and there's still plenty left over."

Eliakim didn't seem impressed. "Do you die?"

Raguel tasted the wine. Not bad, although a bit sharp. "None have so far, not even those thrown into Hell, which is why that's a horrible place to be. We don't have bodies that age or decay."

"What's Hell? Is it Sheol?"

Raguel thought a moment. "Sheol is kind of like a store-room. Human dead aren't judged and sorted yet, so Sheol is where they stay until that happens. If you die with your soul properly aligned, I'm told Sheol is a natural state of happiness, like waking up slowly in the morning, and the souls stay that way until the Messiah opens Heaven."

Eliakim drummed his fingers on the table. "And will I go into Heaven?"

Raguel took a drink before answering. "I'm not capable of weighing a soul. But you do know your Ashera is a problem. Worshiping an idol? That's offensive to God." His eyes glimmered. "Astarte and Anat aren't hanging around too, are they?"

Eliakim tensed. "But Ashera makes it rain. My mother said she's God's consort."

"God has no consort," Raguel said. "Trust the Torah: your God is One. There is no other in Heaven."

Eliakim still looked angry. Raguel reached for God. *I'm not up to this. I'd rather be fighting fifty demons.*

"Well, then tell me about Heaven."

Raguel thought. "Picture it as though it's an onion. On one layer are the nine choirs. On others there are gardens and fields, God's library for us, a concert hall, and so forth. On higher layers there are private places, individual spots where some of us have homes. Your guardian has a small home with some pictures of you and a garden where he grows herbs."

Eliakim sat up. "He farms? What about you?"

"I haven't claimed any single area yet, other than my spot directly before God in the Ring of the Seven. He assigned that to me." Raguel shrugged. "At any rate, God used Heaven's outer rim for Eden. The world isn't joined to Heaven anymore, except at certain spots like Jerusalem, but angels have Heaven inside themselves—the Vision of God and the sense of God's love. Nothing is ever the same after experiencing that. If it vanished, you'd die."

Eliakim looked bored rather than enticed. Raguel sighed. *Doesn't he want to be with you?*

Eliakim's fingers drummed the table. "How do you raise enough to eat?"

"We don't eat. We're not farmers, just tenants who live off the generosity of the Landlord."

"So everyone in Heaven is going to stay there forever?"

"Yes..." Raguel hesitated. He would never lie, but it popped into his mind that in Mesopotamia the people had a legend about Gabriel—they called him Jibril—claiming he once fell into disgrace for not obeying a command exactly as given, and that God closed him away from Heaven for a time. But he decided not to mention it—Eliakim had enough to think about it, and anyhow, when Gabriel had asked if (in theory) one could lose God's love, God had said no.

Raguel diverted the conversation by asking about Eliakim's farm, and Eliakim told him about the land, the crops, the bad years. The disasters. There had been several of those, but the family had recovered and farmed on. Raguel said, "And that was the blessing of God that you did," and Eliakim said, "Well, we made do."

Eliakim said, "If you did choose a home, where would you locate it?"

"In God's heart."

"No, you don't get it," said Eliakim. "I mean, what sort of area? What trees would you plant? What crops would you grow?"

Raguel shrugged. "I don't eat."

"You *drink.*"

"It's *your* wine." Raguel chuckled.

"Okay, so you're not farmers." Eliakim shook his head. "What work do you do then?"

"Other than keeping the company of old men?"

"Other than making wisecracks."

Raguel's eyebrows shot up. "Well—whatever God asks me. I've guarded the elements."

Eliakim said, "You keep the wind in a bag and the rain in a bottle? Like an Ashera?"

Raguel took more of his wine. Why the change in tone? Why the anger at him? Eliakim said, "You could come back and rain on my crops for me."

Raguel had uncovered the bottom of the cup. "But you'll be dead by morning." His voice softened.

Eliakim rose and stood by the window. "It's a shame that all these plants will go to waste. The poor folk will harvest them, and maybe one of them will bury me. I'd have them do it here, on my own property. Not that you'd care."

Raguel sat holding the empty cup.

God reached out to Raguel.

But he's not a cruel man, Raguel prayed.

In answer, God refilled Raguel's cup. He tasted, and it was better wine than before.

"This was my life's work." Eliakim still looked out the window. "My wife is buried here, and two of our sons. It was my father's land before mine, and so back to Joshua's time. But it's tired. The fields need to lie fallow for a few years."

"Maybe they'll get that now."

"It's more than that: they need rain; they need shade. This land needs someone who understands it."

"You?"

Eliakim nodded. "I did everything here. How would you feel if God came and took away all your work, all at once? And not because you did anything wrong, but just because He could."

Raguel flinched. "I like working for God. I ask for assignments."

"But if he took away all your assignments, and wouldn't give you any more, wouldn't you care how the next person did them?"

Raguel said, "Well, to tell you the truth, yes."

Eliakim said, "This is the work I had to do. I did it. I did it well."

40

Raguel took his hand. "And you're angry at God that it's going to end?"

Eliakim lowered his head. "God is the king. I can't curse God and live."

"I wouldn't ask you to curse God." Raguel touched his shoulder. "But getting angry at something you don't understand? I think we all do that. But then you trust. You wait it out."

Eliakim said, "Like harvesting. You don't know how the plants grow, but you figure they'll do it, and you wait."

Raguel nodded. "Yeah. Just like that."

"That's hard."

Raguel said, "Is that why you'd ask Ashera for help? Because it's automatic – you tell the Ashera what to do, and if you did it right, she has to answer?"

Eliakim took a deep breath.

"You can't control God," Raguel said. "God's got control, and He's going to do what He wants. But that makes it harder to let go."

"Maybe so." Eliakim looked glum. "Hold on. There's something I need to do."

He got up from the table and rummaged in the corner until he came up with another small figure, an Ashera. He threw it into the fire. He took a number of small jars filled with incense and other powders and threw them into the fire too. Raguel raised the flames, and one by one Eliakim threw amulets into the fire. "There," he said. And then paused. "No, there's one more."

Raguel said, "You know what you need to do."

Eliakim took the amulet he'd used to find Raguel in the first place, and into the hearth it went.

His face sagged as he watched Raguel, waiting. Then he looked back into the fire, but when the amulet was gone, Raguel still remained. "Aren't you going to disappear?"

Raguel said, "It never had any power over me anyway. I'll stay."

Eliakim sat again, rubbing his temples. He said, "That's it, then. There's nothing between me and the Lord."

41

Raguel said, "Likewise, they weren't really protecting you. You did what you needed to."

"I don't know anything anymore," said Eliakim. "I doubt there's sun and rain in the realm of the dead."

"But there's souls," Raguel said. "And goodness grows in souls just like seeds do. The Messiah will direct us to reap when it comes time."

Eliakim raised his eyes. "Tell me more about that."

"I'm not sure," said Raguel. "God hasn't revealed all that much about the Messiah, except that judgment has been reserved to him. And until then, you'll wait in Sheol. It might be a thousand years, but God's promised, and the Messiah will come."

"That's a long time to wait in an ante-room." Eliakim sat with a heavy puff. "But I'm glad I'll get to farm again."

"The real future is in fishing," God said through Raguel, who then laughed.

Is that a hint? asked the angel. *That's going to drive the Cherubim crazy.*

Eliakim drew up short. "Fishing?"

Raguel reached across the table. "We'll learn together."

Eliakim sat forward. He breathed heavily, and one hand found its way to his left arm.

"Am I going to meet you again?" asked the old man.

"Shortly." Raguel touched the man's hair. "Let yourself sleep."

Eliakim rested his head on the table, and Raguel returned to his angelic form.

The guardian wrapped blue wings about the old man and placed a hand over his eyes. In the next moment, the guardian looked driven: he squeezed his arms around his charge, and with a gasp, he wrenched backward as his wings flared.

In that moment, the man's soul was in the guardian's arms, the angel in shock.

No longer an old man but a human spirit, Eliakim recognized both his guardian and Raguel. Raguel blessed Eliakim, and then the guardian ushered the man to Sheol.

Raguel stood alone in the room, then gathered the man's body. He went into the field, and as the sun rose, he created a grave and buried the body. Day dawned, and Raguel knelt in prayer, reaching for God and wondering if he'd done any good at all.

Well done, Rague'li.

Raguel looked back over the farm, the grain heads and the vines. The farm without a farmer.

Come home, God said. *He'll make election now.*

Stones

1015 BC

David's hands shook as he stripped off Saul's armor, dropping it with a clatter to the hard-packed earth of the river bed.

Goliath.

What had he gotten himself into? An hour ago, standing before the King of Israel, it had sounded so simple: he protected sheep, and if he could protect sheep, how much easier must it be to protect men? Men weren't stupid like sheep. Men could defend themselves.

And yet now, after bragging that he'd defeated bears and wolves while shepherding, David wondered if his father would see him ever again. How bad it would hurt to die.

He glanced at the armor on the ground. It offered some protection, at least. He ought to take it. Armor too heavy to walk in. A sword too heavy to lift. A warrior giant too tall to see without craning back his neck, standing with the sun at his back and roaring with laughter at a frightened Israelite boy.

An insect crawled over the dirt by David's sandal. He thought of the bug's armor, the snap if he were to push on it with his heel, followed by the death of the soft creature within.

There was no way he could do this. His brothers were right — his mouth and his ego had gotten him into trouble again. But after they'd accused him of bragging, how could he back down? He'd be the same kind of coward he'd accused them of being.

Well, a living coward. Maybe that was better than a dead braggart.

No one would see. He could run.

His eyes turned toward the brush on the hill across the river, but before he found a path for escape, he saw someone watching.

His heart hammered.

The person's eyes were so intense, a purple so deep they appeared black, that it took David almost a minute to notice the lavender wings.

He slipped out of his sandals. Holy ground. He swallowed and inclined his head.

The angel studied him. David waited for words, instructions, admonishment, but nothing came. As the wind rustled the bushes and the water clicked over stones, he watched the angel watching him in return.

With features neither male nor female, in appearance not much older than himself and slight of form, the angel sat with knees tucked, arms wrapped around its legs. The silence continued, and David shifted with discomfort.

Finally he said, "Speak, lord, for your servant is waiting."

The angel maintained silence.

He said, "Will you strike down the warrior giant for me?"

No motion from the angel, but David had the strong impression of a refusal.

He said, "Will you come with me into battle? To defend the Lord's people?"

For the first time, the angel responded: its head tilted, and the eyes lowered.

Again a strong impression in David's heart: someone more powerful would accompany David in battle.

David almost asked if an even stronger angel were on the way, to combat a man so tall and so broad that he surely had Nephilim blood. But the words caught in David's mouth as he realized what the angel meant.

He swallowed. "May the Lord defend his people."

The slightest of smiles passed over the angel's face, and a warmth stung behind David's eyes, blossomed in the base of his throat, and spread from there through his chest. Gasping, he felt the pure pleasure of an angel beholding himself and beholding God at the same time.

David stepped away from the fallen armor and searched the river bed for the things he needed. Stones, rounded by time and by water, small enough to cup in his palm, heavy enough to fill his sling. One. Three. Five.

His pouch full, he looked up to thank the angel, but it was gone. In its place he saw only a distortion of the air, an ember amidst a hot haze.

"Uriel," he whispered. *Fire of God.*

He replaced his sandals and returned from the river.

In Carnation

973 BC

Saraquael arrived in the morning.

Gilded with sunlight, Saraquael stood by the open frame of the window, six cerulean wings folded at his back. Naomi approached the vision, and she smiled. Eyes round, she touched the silk of his tunic, fingered the fringes of his overcoat. Only eleven, the daughter of King David and Queen Bathsheba stepped backward, beckoning him, but Saraquael refused.

Naomi paused, puzzled. And then she realized: this was goodbye.

Saraquael stood with silent shimmerings about himself, gnats of God-love that hovered over his head. His eyes sparkled like opals. He handed Naomi a glass bubble the size of a human heart, and she accepted it with tight eyes. Saraquael bent his height toward her, kissed her on the forehead, wrapped her in his wings, and dissolved into the air. Naomi remained holding the bubble.

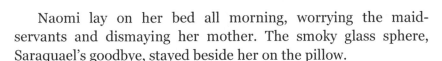

Naomi lay on her bed all morning, worrying the maidservants and dismaying her mother. The smoky glass sphere, Saraquael's goodbye, stayed beside her on the pillow.

Staring at the glass, she wondered what was inside, what he expected her to do with it. Was this the kind of gift they gave in Heaven? The smoke had dissipated throughout the morning, and Naomi strained to see with the bubble held close to her eye. Nothing was clear.

The morning passed, as mornings tend to, and eventually it became an afternoon. The sunlight hung vertically from her curtains like stockings waiting to drip-dry. An hour after an uneaten lunch, the smoke vanished.

Saraquael had sealed a flower within the bubble.

How had he done that? The pink flower had no stem, and it had multiple petals in a half-sphere, crisp and wrinkled.

Only a pink one—but no, she never should have expected him to give her a red flower as if he were a man. His red flowers went only to God.

But at least he had thought her worthy of a flower at all. How many people made friends of angels? Nobody nowadays. Maybe some in scripture, and those were either long dead or else absorbed directly into God's heart, like Enoch. So meeting him at all had been a gift, and the fact that he'd spent time on her. She shouldn't have expected more.

Naomi cradled the bubble in her hands for a while, imagining the flower needed her warmth. But when it was time for dinner, she threaded a silk string through the glass loop and hung the gift from the drapery rod at the western window.

A young princess, Naomi wandered within the palace walls hoping someone either would or would not notice her. She spent a lot of time in the gardens, but she never dug in the dirt.

Naomi first met Saraquael on a day like any other in the House of David, a routine in its own living rhythm. Naomi awoke and her maids set out her clothing, brushed her hair and made up her eyes and face. Rings and necklaces and slippers, and then breakfast in bed.

She'd continue the day with a stroll through the gardens, and after lunch her tutor would aid in the study of Torah and other pastimes deemed appropriate for a young lady of the House of David. She learned to spin, to weave, to sing, and to play music.

The day she met Saraquael, she had walked through the garden only a few hours before nightbreak; *he* had stood among the royal foliage. She'd rounded a corner and had seen Saraquael fingering the leaves of a fig tree.

She gasped, and he spun to face her, and before she could stop herself Naomi was gaping at those tremendous wings, the strong frame that could lift a body into flight with sweeping strokes. Kneeling, she begged him not to vanish. She asked his name and asked again until he answered her.

When her panic subsided, Naomi met his eyes with a smile and lost a part of her awareness forever. Every awkwardness sloughed from her as eyes that viewed God face to face focused on her, eyes large enough to encompass the world and small enough to see her. Naomi pleaded with Saraquael to stay longer, to talk.

So he stayed. They talked. Saraquael mentioned he was a poet, and when Naomi asked to hear some, he recited.

His eyes, leafy like the banks of the Jordan, had danced every time they lighted on Naomi. Some of the love he shared with God reflected from those twin convex mirrors whenever she felt his attention.

That evening she wrung a promise from him that he would return the next day. Saraquael refused at first because he hadn't intended to be visible in the first place. Naomi asked, since it had been accidental, then could it have been God's will? At her insistence, Saraquael asked his Father, and with permission he visited her every day for more than a month.

Naomi received Saraquael's flower the morning after she decided to fall in love with him.

She missed Saraquael's poetry, but more than that she missed the poet. An angel—what could an angel want with a human girl? She had been selfish to waste his time with her friendship. Every power of Saraquael's was focused on God. Who was she in comparison? A princess of the House of David or a fig tree or even a stone would all be the same to him.

If Naomi had not wanted to love him, maybe Saraquael could have stayed.

Her maid noticed the bubble. Although the maid said nothing, Naomi figured the gossip would start about an unknown suitor for Bathsheba's daughter. Her mother would visit and discuss propriety. Perhaps Naomi would mention Saraquael. Thinking about her mother's response, though, she wondered if she had rather not.

After two days, the base of the bubble filled with a finger-width of water and roots. When sunlight struck the glass, Naomi would lie in bed watching the flower, wondering how the flower got its air. The bubble had no seam; how had it grown at all?

Miraculously, a rumor spread that David himself had given his daughter the gift, and no one came to discuss proper conduct with suitors. Naomi also learned the flower's name: dianthus. Carnation. But despite that, she didn't get a visit from her mother.

The first week after meeting Saraquael, Naomi had swung like a pendulum between urgency and peace. She pestered her tutor with questions about angels and absorbed whatever lore he knew: God had created angels in nine orders; seven angels had the honor of standing directly before God; one-third of the angels had rebelled. Angels did not have bodies; they did not eat; those who loved God loved him fully, but not to the exclusion of every created thing; they were sinless but not perfect because only God is perfect.

Saraquael told her the same things differently: that every angel is individual in the eyes of God, and that He who makes souls sees each as a new species, one as different from another as the birds are from the beasts from the fish from the bacteria (something Naomi had never heard of before and seemed a little scary). Saraquael told her about the Vision of God, a sight more than a sight, that showed him all the beauty in the world and simultaneously revealed its potential. He said the Vision was something he needed, that it made Creation more wonderful than it could be otherwise. He said with it, God showed him the art of the world, and wonder filled him with the love of it all.

Saraquael said that although he wrote poetry, some angels sang, others studied the Earth, and some invented. When Naomi asked if she might become a poet like him, he said she should try. He produced ink and parchment for her, and he turned her loose.

Unfortunately, using heavenly parchment didn't make for heavenly poetry. She gave up after her first try, but the next day he asked her to try again. She asked him to keep reading to her, just so she could learn, and he'd recite other poems and dissect the way they worked. She brought him a scroll of poems her father had written: Psalms. Saraquael was delighted. That afternoon she listened to him reading for hours, then promised Saraquael that someday she would match it.

Nowadays, without him, Naomi crossed out more words than she retained. She told herself if poetry were creation, then these were labor pains.

With all her practice, the results ought to be better. Something blocked her. Her urgency showed through the words she chose, her frenzied rhythm, her uneven parallels. He'd told her about resonance and symbolism, but the technique she couldn't learn from Saraquael was his peace. Among so many accomplished people, so many brilliant and wise men who would change the world, Naomi hungered to be more than an ornament, more than a flower in a glass sphere.

When Naomi wrote poetry by lamplight, she dreamed about astonishing her father by reciting her best work. The whole court would know the king's daughter had inherited her family's gift of wordplay. Her father would come to her and listen, and her mother would approve.

The flower grew, its roots spreading through the water. Naomi looked on it daily, often resting the bubble against her cheek. The flower neither withered nor faded, thriving on her attention.

Day by day, Naomi continued writing; at nights she held her pages by the lamp-flicker, wondering what Saraquael would say, what would make him laugh, how he would give direction without making her feel inept. At one of the worst lines of poetry ever written, Saraquael had burst out laughing because she had tried so hard. After a sullen pout, Naomi found herself laughing too. And he, with his smile, had helped her try again.

She couldn't remember even one unkind word from him in all the hours they spent together. He'd always realized what little things she wanted him to notice: perhaps her earrings, or the way the maidservant had styled her hair, or even her dress. He approved when she took his advice. When Naomi had felt like crying, he understood her mood instantly, and every time approached her depression differently: once making her laugh and at another time letting her talk. Once he let her cry, cocooned her in the cloud of his wings, keeping her sealed invisibly inside so no one would disturb her soon afterward.

Naomi had told Saraquael she wished she had a more artistic heart, like his own. She wanted to act as a creator in miniature, investing the lives of all her characters with value and resolving their worries. She wanted to describe perfect worlds and show perfect lives. Excelling in such a structured form as poetry, with such a hierarchy of masters, would make the art truer.

After Saraquael's departure, Naomi found she could spill forth poem after poem (not good, but written) on a bright afternoon when birds called one to another and flowers swayed in the breeze. When she stood in the shade of a fig tree, she could easily turn over words in her mind, and some mornings she would finger the fringes of her curtains and close her eyes against the sun.

The roots of the carnation had continued growing, tiny bubbles clinging to their smooth length.

Naomi lay dreaming.

As a child she hid in the garden, waiting for her mother to miss her and come looking. She crouched until needles of pain poked into her calves and her folded body ached, and then she came out to find her mother had gone inside the palace. When she asked the maid if she had been missed, and why had no one come looking, the maid said that of course Naomi had been missed—everyone was worried sick—and she should go play with the other children.

While she twitched in her bed, Naomi's mind raced up a tower to look out over Jerusalem, the houses and the city walls, distant herds of sheep and roads with travelers passing, none noticing the princess in the tower. Birds circled, one so low she might have raised her hand and have it alight, but then it spread its tiny wings and rose into the light of a pink sunset.

Her breathing grew ragged in sleep. Naomi remembered dressing in a gown alongside all her half-sisters and then marching into the main hall of the palace for a ceremony. She held a cluster of wild flowers, but her mother had taken from her because none of the other girls had flowers. As King David passed, one ambassador commented what lovely daughters he had, and David had said yes, they were all very lovely. Naomi smiled at him, but he did not meet her eyes.

The dream-memories might have continued, but then her images mixed with day-residue and melted one into the other, so that as a little girl she hid in a white dress behind a bush, a small bird in her hands, but the bird flew away when she tried to hold it too tightly, leaving behind a pink carnation.

Naomi awoke for good when David walked by and did not return her smile.

The room's darkness smothered her like wet gauze, but she shuddered it away. She turned to the window for light, but the best she could get was moonlight reflected from her poetry pages.

An animal called outside, and as Naomi turned, her eye caught a haze rising from her pages. She startled, but it was only the moon's pink reflection on a white surface. The bubble and carnation hung in stillness over the poetry.

The next time a poet recited before the court, Naomi resolved to try her work against a man.

She found the poet during the dinner following his recitation. He brushed her off until she explained that she was Bathsheba's daughter, and then he agreed to hear her recite

He frowned while she recited, seemed startled when she finished, then fingered his earlobe and told her she had promise. She asked if it were good, and he said it was admirable she was writing already, then turned to talk to one of the Levites.

Flushed, she thanked the poet and left the dinner early. She cried only a little on returning to her room.

Nothing hurts more, Naomi thought to her carnation, than being told you have *promise*. Potential counts for nothing. It's the words, the deeds. Those matter.

But she had an answer now. The poet hadn't enjoyed her work, so doubtless the court would dislike it, and that meant she'd never get to present it to her father. She'd reached her potential and could only stagnate now: the palace had become a world that would suffocate her, and how could she get the sustenance she needed? She had to leave.

Swallowing, she looked out her bedroom window. Outside the city walls, campfires of traveling merchants glimmered like beeswax candles. She might join one of them. She could leave in durable clothing and take any money she could find. She would bring her poetry and recite at the towns she passed. She could spin or weave to earn her keep. Then, when she grew proficient, she could return to her family and the court, and by then her brother Solomon might be king. Solomon would let her recite. After all, he had already written a poem of which everyone spoke well.

Naomi grabbed a dress from the closet and laid it on her bed. She gathered her writing next, placing all the pages into a leather bag.

A white gleam struck her, and she faced the window.

The pink carnation, hanging in its glass bubble, had focused the sunset into one dagger of light. She blinked until she could see again.

Peering around floaters, Naomi moved away from the light-spear. The carnation had grown larger, filling all the space in its glass bubble. In the water at the base, the roots traced the folds of the lowest petals.

She pulled the thread and freed the hanging sphere, warming it against her palm.

Naomi cradled Saraquael's goodbye, losing herself in the gleam of the curved glass, prickling with the reflected needles of the sunset. She traced the fullness of wrinkles in the petals, a marvelous cerebellum filling the whole bubble, and having inhabited everywhere it could, needed to escape, needed freedom.

Naomi imagined the roots moving, groping the bottom of the glass with their questions.

Her eyes grew wider and rounder; they filled with water.

Naomi grabbed a pottery basin, and then the glass bubble lay smashed.

She tossed it aside, then dropped to her knees to pick the flower out of the broken glass. In her hands, the carnation was so much smaller than it had seemed. The lens-like confinement of the glass globe had made the bud seem bigger.

Naomi set the flower in bowl of water and sat beside it until it died.

A maid knocked at the door and asked if something had broken. The daughter of David and Bathsheba stood, hung her dress in the closet and placed her writing on the dressing table. The maidservant knocked again. Opening the door, she said that yes, she was fine.

The woman nodded, but suddenly her features shifted into the fatherly, concerned smile of the poet-angel. Naomi startled, and the look was gone.

Leaping from heart to heart as on stones through a stream, Naomi realized, a visiting angel could still protect and cherish. Friends need not always be visible. That night she wrote a poem to an angel about a dead flower, and she thanked him. Aided only by the light of a lamp, she set down letters with black ink on an unwrinkled sheet of white parchment.

Pomegranate

960 BC

Michael felt the summons from God and dropped to his knees where he was.

He called his sword back into his substance, then he crossed his arms over his chest and drew up his wings. *Ready, Lord.*

Open your hands.

Michael found himself holding a crowned red fruit.

Bring this to Gabriel.

Michael flashed to Gabriel with a thought.

He arrived at the Temple Mount as the sun rose, standing atop a half-completed wall and wondering why God wanted him to deliver a fruit to a creature who never got hungry.

"Michael!" Gabriel raised his wings. "Have you seen the supports for the walls? This is amazing!"

Beside Gabriel, Raphael nodded with eyes so bright they gave off heat. "You've got to let him tell you about this."

Michael followed as Gabriel showed off the architecture of Solomon's temple, the supports crafted in such a way that they wouldn't run through the interior. "It contains design elements from a number of surrounding cultures," Gabriel said, "but if you'll note, Solomon modified them all in order to preserve the unique aspects of Israelite worship and the Israelite relationship to the Almighty as His chosen people."

Michael said, "I have something for you."

"In a minute." Gabriel then spent that minute explaining the origin of the stone blocks used for the foundation and the techniques developed for transportation of the carved stones.

Raphael said, "Surely they didn't come out of the ground that way."

Gabriel shook his head. "They're carved at the excavation site so the temple won't be defiled by the sound of chisels! Isn't that amazing?"

Michael said, "Is your minute up? I have something for you."

Gabriel paused. "Is that a pomegranate?"

Raphael said, "Oh! Like that fruit on the capitals at the front of the Temple—" and they both flashed to the front of the building, bringing Michael with them. The sky had grown just light enough to see the stone carvings.

Michael handed the fruit to Gabriel.

Without looking at it, Gabriel turned to Raphael. "Okay, so you were asking me about the symbolism of the pomegranate, and I told you how the multiple seeds inside the fruit represent the multiple mitzvoh in the Torah. Because of the multiplicity of seeds, it also represents fruitfulness. And it represents learning, too."

Michael watched Raphael's gaze all but devour Gabriel as he veered off into a lecture about pomegranate properties. For the moment, you'd think nothing in the world was more important than a fruit's antioxidants, or how pomegranate juice could lower cholesterol levels or repair damaged DNA. Raphael, who on his own tended to rush from topic to topic, remained focused on Gabriel's mini dissertation about the growth and tending of pomegranates, and for some reason Gabriel was getting more enthusiastic.

It was their bond, something Michael never really fathomed. But he watched with a smile because together a Cherub and a Seraph became something more, something intense and joyful and careful and amazed by God.

All the same, *Why did you want me to deliver a pomegranate?* Michael asked God.

Wait and watch, God replied.

At the point where Michael knew all he had ever wanted to learn about the cultivation of pomegranates (in fact, more), the workmen began arriving. Gabriel flashed to ground-level to inspect one of the tools.

Michael said to Raphael, "He's so different when he's with you."

"Well, not as if I would know." Raphael laughed. "I suppose I'm different too. I do see him with the other Cherubim, and they tend to get a bit esoteric. Discussions like how the future Messiah's mother's eye-color will affect the Messiah's theology."

Michael paused. "You made that up. Didn't you?"

"You can go on thinking I made it up if that makes you feel better." Raphael chuckled. "Maybe the two top choirs bond just so we won't strangle each other."

Michael laughed out loud.

Gabriel reappeared on the wall top. "Come see the Holy of Holies. We won't be going in there after it's complete, but we can now, with the workmen."

Michael followed. "Why can't we go in after it's complete?"

Gabriel said, "Only the high priest goes in there. That's where the Ark of the Covenant will be housed."

Michael replied, "We look God in the face. It's probably okay to stand near the Ark."

"Solomon's already drawn up the rules. No one but the high priest." Gabriel floated up the steps to the raised floor, then ran a hand over the cedar planks. "Isn't this amazing? It's fascinating the way the humans render objects serviceable and beautiful at the same time. God doesn't need the beauty, but it's fitting to have beautiful things for Him, and it will serve to uplift the people's minds to greater theological truths. Did I mention Solomon imported this cedar from Tyre?"

Raphael hesitated, his eyes glinting with reflected light from God. "Assignment," he said, and Gabriel extended a hand to him in blessing. Raphael touched his wingtips to Gabriel's, then departed.

Gabriel brought Michael to the stacks of cedar logs outside the construction site, then showed him the pulley system that raised hundreds of pounds of wood without exerting hundreds of pounds of force; Gabriel called it mechanical advantage, distributing the wood's downward force over the tension of several sections of rope rather than just one rope. But Gabriel watched it more, studied it in longer silences, and then started drawing diagrams in the air using light.

Michael said, "It's okay. You don't have to show me this if you're bored."

"It's not at all boring." Gabriel frowned. "This is physics. Humans use their tools in order to manipulate their environment within God's established physical laws, and that's entrancing."

Michael said, "But it's not as exciting as pomegranates?" But then he realized the difference: Raphael wasn't here, and neither was Raphael's fire. Gabriel was returning to his normal, thoughtful state.

Gabriel said, "Pomegranates are life. Cedar planking is art. This is physics— Oh," he interrupted himself. "That's not safe."

"Where?"

Gabriel set the pomegranate into the solid heart of a log and pointed to a scaffolding. "On the second level, the third support in from the back? The strut snapped, so they propped a pole in between it and the first level to support the second, but all that does is transfer the overload to the lower support."

Michael called to the guardians closest, who called to their charges. The foreman looked, but then dismissed the concern as the men hauled up another load of wood onto the scaffolding.

...which then collapsed, avalanching wood and men to the ground.

Gabriel rushed forward, shoved one of the workmen to the side, then dove headfirst into the chaos.

Michael called orders to the nearby guardians. "Everyone, clear your charges! Give me a headcount of all the wounded! Gabriel! Report!"

"There's a man trapped in the debris," Gabriel called from beneath the wood. "He's—Oh!"

Gabriel shot from the tumble of logs and boards. "He's got an Ashera!"

Michael said, "But he's alive?"

"I maneuvered the falling wood so he got pinned rather than crushed." Gabriel shook his head. "But he's wearing an Ashera charm, so if he wants further assistance, let him call on it."

Michael said, "Find a way they can get all that debris off him." He turned to three of the nearby guardians. "We've got a man under there. Alert your charges."

The guardians took off. Gabriel murmured, "He's an idolater."

Michael murmured back, "Analyze the stability of the debris pile and come up with a method to get him out of there."

Gabriel looked disgusted. "I don't want to touch him." He went back under, and after a moment Michael could feel Gabriel's energy sluicing through the wood. The workmen made voice contact with the man beneath the pile, and two of the foremen started calling for their crews.

Gabriel surfaced. "I've got a way. But, Michael –" He sighed. "The penalty for idolatry is death. If he dies, when they extract his body and find the idol, they'll see God's justice at work."

Michael focused on the pile, focused further through the wood until he could see the man's soul and could feel that idol's black presence.

Gabriel said, "I hate losing his soul as much as you do, but freeing him short-circuits God's decrees and doesn't guarantee conversion anyhow. Moreover, we're endangering the souls of all the other workers, who may attribute his survival on the Temple mount of all places to the idol."

Michael tasted the fear rolling off the man, the pain, the terror of what happened if that tenuous pile gave way. He could smell that idol's evil and the way it stained the man's soul—the way it would for eternity if nothing changed.

Michael heard himself speaking. "What if that Ashera isn't his?"

Gabriel said, "Supposing, for example, that an Ashera charm on a thong fell from a bird just as the scaffolding broke, landing around his neck and under his tunic?"

Michael said, "He's not calling on Ashera or Ba'al to help him. I'll re-assess if he does. Tell me which pieces need to be removed and in which order."

Gabriel gestured, and the logs lit up in different colors before the angels' eyes. "They need to come off in order like the color spectrum, starting from red and ending with purple. But he's got to stay still so the centers of gravity won't change."

"Thanks. Get back under there and keep him calm."

Gabriel didn't hide his reluctance, but he slipped back into the heap.

Michael turned to the work foreman's guardian. "Did you understand?"

The foreman's guardian studied the rainbow lights the humans couldn't see. "I'll try to guide his decisions. Get me some prayer support."

The sun baked the men as they pried apart the pile. The priests came, praying for deliverance even as local women brought in water for the workers and tended the wounded. A team of donkeys helped clear the debris. Even though Gabriel stayed beneath to keep the man still, every so often the wood shifted, and momentarily the order of the lighting would alter.

Michael slipped beside Gabriel. He'd gone half-underground, lying directly beneath the man but with his hands on the man's head and his wings wrapped around him. The man's guardian lay inside his form, exuding calm. Gabriel murmured the Shema over and over, a drone and a steadiness that the man himself absorbed. Though in and out of consciousness, his lips moved with the prayer.

Michael touched Gabriel's wing with his own. "Thank you."

So intent on the man, Gabriel didn't respond.

Before the sun set, the foreman gave a shout, and the workmen were able to grab the man under his armpits and drag him from the pile. A woman ran to him, wailing and calling his name. She raised his body and kissed his face until with a moan he opened his eyes.

Beside Michael, Gabriel ran his fingers through his feathers. "I was in contact with that idol for the whole day. I need to purify myself." He glanced at the heap of wood and former scaffolding. "They did a marvelous rescue job. I'm impressed."

"Thanks for the help."

Gabriel shrugged. "It was obvious once you realized three of the beams bore the majority of the weight. Oh, here it goes."

As the man sat up, the woman—old enough to be his mother—reached under his tunic and pulled free the thong with the Ashera charm. "Thank you," she wailed, and kissed it.

Michael flinched. *I'm sorry. Thank you for letting us save him anyway.*

In his heart, God said, *Wait.*

The man pulled back from the woman, and he yanked the charm off his neck. "This didn't save me! The God of Israel saved me!"

The woman gasped, closing her hand over the idol. "But—"

"The Lord our God, the Lord is one." The man's eyes watered. "I have sinned against him with idols, but he saved me anyhow."

The man's guardian cheered.

Michael grinned. *Thank you!*

God said, *Thank you for advocating for him. He needed a chance.*

Gabriel bowed his head and clasped his hands before his chest. *Thank you for saving him. I apologize. I judged too hastily.*

The man crushed the idol beneath his heel, then leaned on one of the other workmen to hobble away from the building site.

Cleanup continued until sundown, when the men left. Gabriel pulled the pomegranate out of the wall and as he sat back on the top with Michael, he said, "Oh, I forgot to mention something."

Michael turned to him just as the wood pile creaked and twisted, and then with a bang that resounded off the sky, a log cracked. The pile collapsed further.

"It's not stable anymore. But no one's around. It should finish settling overnight." As a log finished rolling to the opposite wall, Gabriel held up the fruit in the moonlight. "Why did you give me this?"

Michael said, "God told me to give it to you."

Gabriel cocked his head. "Why?"

God replied, *I wanted you to learn about it.*

Michael chuckled. "You talked about pomegranates for that long, and there's something you didn't know?"

Gabriel looked puzzled, so he turned it over in his hand, turned it around again, lit it up from the inside out. As Michael watched, Gabriel illuminated various parts of the fruit, traced the cellulose structure of the pulp, felt through the living parts of the seeds, then shook his head. "What am I missing?"

The moon rose. Gabriel focused on his open hand so his sword appeared, and then he shortened it to a knife blade. He made himself solid enough to slice into the fruit. Juice gushed onto his hands and clothes, but Gabriel concentrated until it vanished. Nestled in the white pulp were fruity pips, each bearing a seed.

He ran his fingertip over the pips to loosen them, and then he popped one into his mouth.

Eyes wide, he turned to Michael. "It's sweet! Sweet...and bitter."

He pulled out more and tasted them again, then handed half the fruit to Michael. As Michael tasted them, Gabriel closed his eyes, and in the next moment Raphael appeared. "Try this!" Gabriel broke off a part of the fruit and gave it to him. "They're sweet and bitter together! I had no idea!"

At Michael's side, Gabriel closed his eyes. *Thank you,* Michael felt him praying. *Thank you for fruit, and for knowing about fruit.*

Thank you, God said in reply. *Thank you for learning.*

A Fish Story

Tapping her foot, Sarah held up half a broken dish. "This is the fourth time this month, Rebecca."

The maid scowled as she got a whisk broom for the other pieces. "At least it's only my fourth time."

Sarah dropped the pottery on the table. "What?" And when the maid didn't answer, "What did you say?"

The maid kept sweeping the pieces. "You know what I mean. You're the one who strangles your husbands. Married seven times, but you haven't kept even one. Good men, fellow exiles from Israel here in Nineveh's territory – it's not as if we have thousands of them, or as if you're killing Nineveh men. By comparison, what's breaking a dish? Your husbands are dead— and you should join them!"

Sarah stood motionless even as the other servants stared. Then like a slingshot, she pivoted and raced to her room.

Sarah's feet pounded her intentions in rhythm: *I'll hang myself, I'll hang myself, there's nothing left worth living for.*

"Come to me." Ghosting her was the demon Asmodeus, crooning inaudibly. "Come to me."

Sarah's guardian angel couldn't block out the demon's call, but he prayed. As Sarah reached her room, Uriel appeared in purple fire, a flurry of silk garments and six lavender wings.

Unable to see the angels, the woman barricaded the door. Her guardian dropped to his knees, praying, but Uriel reached out to block Asmodeus's will, locking down the demon so Sarah could make a free choice. Sarah heard neither, twisting her belt into a noose.

"God's forgotten you," said Asmodeus. "He's let seven husbands die and lets you be a shame to all Israel."

Sarah tested the knot and looked for a place to fasten it.

"Sarah," said Uriel with a very level glance and voice, "people will level this insult against your father: 'He had a daughter, but she hanged herself for ill fortune.' You'll cause your father in his old age to depart to Sheol in grief. It's far better for you not to hang yourself."

Sarah took a breath and set down the noose. "No, I can't. People will insult my father, and he'd depart to Sheol in grief. It's far better for me to beg the Lord to have me die."

The guardian angel looked up through his tears.

Uriel regarded Sarah at the windowsill; facing the Holy Land, she leaned on her hands.

Asmodeus' eyes glinted, staking out his territory. He couldn't touch her now, not during her prayer, but he had all the time in the world.

The Throne departed.

Directly before God, Uriel lay prostrate and remained motionless until the Most High asked the Throne to rise. Uriel knit prayerful hands and waited with wide eyes. Then a smile dawned on the angel's features.

Raphael and Gabriel arrived as one before the Most High. "Ready, Lord," said Raphael.

"Two prayers will arrive now," said Gabriel in a pitch between tenor and soprano. "Receive and present them."

Gabriel's employment as God's mouthpiece brought no reaction from Raphael other than a nod for the Cherub to continue.

"This comes from Sarah, daughter of the exile Raguel of the tribe of Naphtali."

Raphael closed his eyes, simultaneously receiving and presenting her prayer:

Blessed are you, O Lord, my God!
Forever blessed and honored is your holy name:
Oh Lord, bid me to depart from the earth,
never again to hear such insults.
O Master, I am innocent, and I've never defiled my own name
Or my father's name in this land of exile.
I've lost seven husbands: seven good men.
Why should I live?

"You can't mean me to kill her?" Raphael said. "Can I find her another husband? What do you want me to do?"

Gabriel brushed his wings by Raphael's, and he drew down the Seraphic fire.

"You'll help her," said Gabriel in God's voice. "She's obsessed by the demon Asmodeus because he thinks he loves her." He added in his own, "There's a second prayer coming, from someone else."

Raphael channeled the second prayer, this one with an older feel and a different voice:

All your ways are mercy and truth, O Lord,
You are the judge of the world.
And now, look with favor upon me.
Punish me not for my sins,
Nor for those of my fathers.
So now, command my life's breath to be taken from me
That I may go from the face of the Earth into dust.
It is better for me to die than to live
Because I have heard many insults
And am overwhelmed with grief.
Lord, refuse me not.

"But—why?" asked Raphael. "Why two at once?"

"Lack of faith." Gabriel shrugged. "I don't understand it either."

God said, "The second prayer belongs to Tobit, another exile of Naphtali living in Nineveh. He's become blind after many years of faithful service to me."

"You must remember him," Gabriel said, projecting a list of details into Raphael's head. "He's the one who used to bury the dead even when the Ninevites warned him not to."

Raphael frowned. Of course Gabriel would recall the location and the dates, but Raphael remembered the heat, the misery of the Israelites kidnapped by Nineveh and deported en masse to another country, the grief of the onlookers who longed to bury the dead but longed even more not to be noticed by their captors.

"Tobit's fortune failed him, and now he's living on the charity of his relations." Gabriel shook his head. "And he's just had a spat with his wife, which I suppose makes his situation seem worse."

Raphael's feathers spread. "Is there a way I can help?"

"Rapha'li," said God, "you are my healer. Heal them both. Act in whatever way you wish to alleviate the sufferings of Tobit and Sarah, and also, put Tobit to the test. He is a faithful servant, but he can grow more than he has."

Raphael knelt with his arms crossed over his heart.

At that moment, Sarah descended from her room, and Tobit left the courtyard where he had prayed.

The sun-baked earth shimmered while a figure who cast no shadow waited beside a stand of trees. A second figure appeared shortly.

"This is going to be an interesting assignment. Thank you for letting me come with you." Gabriel grinned, and Raphael could feel Gabriel's mind turning over the pair of problems and all the various wild cards. "Tobit believes God's going to answer his prayer with death, so he's cramming as much as he can into one final sermon to his son Tobias about duties toward his mother, practicing virtue and avoiding evil, almsgiving and charity, proper marriage, industry, prompt payment of wages, temperance, and prayer...among others."

Raphael chuckled. "In other words—"

Gabriel finished, "—everything he should have said long before."

"But he lived it," Raphael said. "His faith is failing now, but he knows God blesses His people."

"That's true," said Gabriel. "The way Tobias is listening, I think he'll make you a good pupil."

Raphael probed Gabriel with amused eyes, but Gabriel only fingered one of his primary feathers. "This morning Tobit remembered the money he left with his relative Gabelus in Rages. He's happier now thinking he'll leave a wealthy widow and son."

Raphael huffed. "They'd rather have him than the money."

"Maybe you can tell him that." Gabriel's eyes unfocused as he probed through the walls. "Tobias says he doesn't know how to get to Rages."

Raphael could have done all the information-gathering on his own, but it felt right for his Cherub to do it, and he enjoyed the feel of Gabriel planning and re-planning even as Raphael knew instinctively what he wanted to do. "That's easy. I'll just offer my services as a guide."

Gabriel nodded. "I figured you would."

You'll put me in a human form? Raphael asked, and God agreed.

Gabriel sparkled. "Good. I wonder what you'll look like?"

Raphael said, "I wonder what I'll call myself."

"'Oh, I have the perfect name for you: Raphael.'" Gabriel nodded. "*God Heals* is a very solid name. It says what you are."

"Yes—an archangel of the Presence." Raphael shook his head. "I'd rather they think I'm human."

Gabriel flinched "They don't treat other humans very nicely."

"I can't have them thinking I'm a god."

Gabriel choked. Then, "No, of course not. But you can still use your God-given name."

"Which they'll recognize."

"They aren't that smart." Gabriel chuckled. "Besides, isn't the man you're going to see in Rages named *Raguel,* brother of *Gabri*? You'll fit right in."

Raphael withdrew his heart from the vibrations coming from Gabriel, vibrations too sharp and angry. "I can't have them following my orders just because they think they're disobeying God if they don't. God told me to test Tobit. So, no. I can't be an angel. Besides, no one's going to notice a human name." Raphael's nose wrinkled. "Why are you arguing with me?"

"Because *I'll* notice." Gabriel glared into the sunlight. "And it's not just the name, is it? Once you make up a name, you're going to need a lineage and credentials, and that's more lies to cover up the first. They'll want to know things that happened in your past. You'll be in major trouble if Tobit starts quizzing you about who, what and when. Where do the lies stop?"

With a feeling like a *thump*, Raphael found himself a solid man.

Tobias the younger stepped out of his doorway and squinted in the dry light of the Nineveh desert. He was sixteen, angular and a little too tall for his own body. He took a few steps with his eyes adjusting and bumped into Raphael, who was still trying to figure out what he was.

Tobias blinked at Raphael before asking, "Who are you?"

"An Israelite," said Raphael. "I've come to find work."

Tobias squinted upward at Raphael, who realized just then how tall he was in human form. "We're looking to hire someone," said the young man. "Do you know the way to Media?"

"Oh, I know the place well." Raphael turned to hide his smile, staring off to the east as though he could see Media from where he stood. Gabriel floated on the periphery of his consciousness. "I used to stay with my kinsman Gabelus, who lives at Rages. It's about a two day journey, in the mountains."

Tobias gaped. Raphael flashed him a smile.

"Wait right here," Tobias stammered. "You might be just what we want."

Raphael looked up at the sun as if checking the time. "Okay. But don't be long."

Tobias flew into the house.

Arms folded, Gabriel appeared in front of him. "I had no idea you have a kinsman in Rages. Second cousin, is he?"

Raphael shook his head. "Has anyone ever said you have a hang-up?"

Gabriel huffed.

"You have a hang-up."

"And let's see: a two-day journey? On foot?" Gabriel opened his hands. "Plus, Ecbatana isn't in the mountains. We're in the mountains right now, but you'll be going downhill."

Raphael said, "I know that. I want to see what will happen."

"What will happen is he'll decide you're a liar and that's the end of your assignment."

Tobias stuck his head outside. "Please come to speak with my father."

Raphael entered, Tobias before and an invisible Gabriel behind.

Tobit's room was dark and dusty the way the room of a blind man might become. Tobias said, "Father, he's here."

"Joy to you," said Raphael.

"What joy is left for me?" said Tobit. "Here I am, a blind man who can't see God's sunlight but have to remain in darkness. Even though I'm alive, I'm among the dead because I can hear a man's voice, but I can't see him."

Not exactly the life of the party, thought Raphael to Gabriel, but the Cherub didn't relax. Raphael said, "Take courage. God has his healing in store for you."

Gabriel glared sideways at the Seraph. "You can't avoid inserting your name, can you, *Rapha'el?*"

Tobit remained gloomy. "My son Tobias has to go to Rages, in Media. Can you go with him? We'll pay you."

"I can go with him," said Raphael. "I know all the routes. I've traveled to Rages and crossed all the plains and mountains. I know every road well."

Gabriel said, "And here comes the cross-examination."

But instead of a quiz about which roads he'd take, Tobit said, "Tell me whose family and tribe you're from."

Gabriel bristled.

Raphael glanced at Gabriel. "Why? Do you want a tribe and a family? Or are you looking for a hired *man* to travel with your son?"

Gabriel's approval surged through him.

Tobit's mouth tightened. "I wish to know truthfully whose son you are, and what your name is. I'm entrusting my son to you."

With a flare of disgust, Gabriel vanished. Raphael braced himself. "I'm Azariah, son of Hananiah the elder."

Tobit exclaimed, "*God save* you, brother!" A series of strange chills curled along Raphael's spirit, not at all unpleasant. "Don't be upset with me for wanting to learn the truth about you. You're one of my own kinsmen! Your father and I used to make the pilgrimage together to Jerusalem. A good lineage. Welcome!"

And then, despite Gabriel's predictions about getting cross-examined, no more questions came, not even, "So how is your father?" The old man beamed, his sightless eyes wrinkling as he told Raphael about the money he'd be retrieving. He finished with, "For each day you travel, I'll pay the normal wages. Perhaps I'll even give you a bonus."

"It's a deal," said Raphael. "Don't worry about your son. We're leaving in good health, and in good health we'll return to you."

Gabriel sat on a rock. Michael stood beside him, the lowest leaves of a cedar touching his hair.

"He's sorry you're upset," said Michael.

"You say that as though I can't detect what he thinks." Gabriel nudged the ground with his foot. "He shouldn't have lied."

Michael said, "But God gave him permission."

"It's a compromise of his integrity: that's the name game." Gabriel looked bleak. "Yes, prevarication gets the job done, but maybe honesty and not deception would do the job better."

Michael didn't respond.

Gabriel spoke almost to himself. "God should have reminded Raphael distortion was wrong. But it's not really *wrong,* either. It's grey."

Raphael appeared. "You're grey too."

Gabriel glared at the ground. "Grey of wing isn't grey of soul."

Michael stepped backward.

"Stay." Raphael reached toward Michael. "Will the pair of you be around for the journey?"

Michael shook his head. "I'll catch up when you confront Asmodeus, but before then, call if you need me."

Raphael's eyes searched out Gabriel's, but the Cherub avoided his Seraph's gaze. "I'll be here and there," he said, "*Azariah.*"

When Tobias left Nineveh accompanied by the angel, the dog trotted behind."He's not usually this friendly," said the young man. "I guess he can tell you're my kinsman."

"You'd be surprised at what dogs can figure out." Raphael reached a hand to the dog, which bounded around him, barking. "They're fairly intelligent, but not smart enough to sin."

Tobias thought. "Then dogs are the best animals?"

"I wouldn't say that," said Raphael. "If I had to pick a kind of animal to be, I'd want to be a bird. I love flight. I mean the concept of flying." He laughed out loud. It would be a fine thing to reveal his identity right at the start. "How would you like to fly to Rages instead of walking there?"

Tobias considered. "Birds work too hard. Dogs have it easy, though. Yeah, they work, but we feed them. Cats have it best, though: every time I see a cat, it's pondering some innate mystery."

Where have I heard things like that before? thought Raphael to God. *The boy sounds like a Cherub.* To Tobias, he said, "Probably thinking about food."

"They're deeper than that. They play." Tobias nodded as if the question were already settled in his mind. "I never see birds play."

Raphael shrugged. "Swallows play. They'll pluck a feather from themselves, carry it up very high, drop it, and chase it back and forth as it falls."

"Training themselves to catch insects," said Tobias.

"Insects don't fly the way feathers fall."

Raphael realized, *I'm sounding like Gabriel!* and then, *I wish he weren't disappointed in me, Father.*

They kept up their conversation until they reached the Tigris. There they broke for the night, Raphael making their camp while Tobias waded into the river to wash up.

Gabriel? he called. When he didn't get a response, he called again, this time reaching inside through their bond. And instead of an answer, nothing.

Gabriel?

"Azariah!"

That was Tobias. Raphael bolted to the river.

Just off shore, Tobias thrashed, screaming, a fish clamped to his leg. Silver and longer than his arms, the fish whipped like a flag in a high wind. Tobias slipped on the moss-covered rocks, then shrieked as the fish started dragging him to deeper water.

Raphael rushed to the water's edge. "Grab the fish by its gills! Don't let it get away!"

Tobias kept screaming for help. Raphael shouted again, "The gills! Grab its gills!"

Tobias finally seized the gills, and the fish opened its mouth. He yanked his leg free.

"Don't let go!" Raphael shouted. "Haul it to shore!"

His fingers still wrapped around the snapping head, Tobias wrestled the thrashing weight inch by inch onto the rocks, then staggered onto the pebbles.

Away from the river, the fish flailed until it died.

Tobias stared at it as it twitched. His heart leaked terror, and his breath was heaving. He didn't say anything, and when he'd been quiet too long, Raphael put a hand on Tobias's shoulder. Only then did the boy lunge for Raphael. He held Tobias close.

"I didn't know what to do." Tobias kept his hands locked about Raphael's waist as though he would be swept away into the river. "I'm so glad you're here. I was so scared."

"You're okay. Take a deep breath." Raphael tried to look him over. "Let's get a look at your leg."

With Tobias seated on a rock, Raphael examined the bite, swabbed off the wound, and stopped the bleeding. One of the plants on the shore was just right to prevent infection, so he bound it to the cut with a strip of cloth. By the time he finished, Tobias had his breath back, but he was still shaking. And strangely, so was Raphael. It was odd, but he kept re-visiting the images of that fish, the struggle, the shouting.

Raphael forced himself to let off a long breath. "Okay." He was safe. He had to remind himself, they were both safe. "Next, you caught the fish, so you get the prize. You need to cut open the fish and take out its gall, heart and liver. They're good for medicine."

Tobias looked at the thing. "Really?"

Raphael handed him a bronze knife.

"You know..." Tobias looked up. "Since I went through all the trouble of catching the fish, I'll give you the honor of cleaning it."

Raphael frowned. "I believe the fish caught you."

Tobias tried to hand back the knife. "I'd never have caught it without your help."

"I'll cook it." Raphael walked back to the camp. "You gut it."

After Tobias had fallen asleep, Raphael returned to his angelic form and played with the dog.

Tobias's guardian, Ezdrael, sat with one hand on Tobias's shoulder. "Thank you so much for your help with the fish. You handled it really well. You could have grabbed the fish, gutted it, and told him to hold the medicinal parts, but instead you let Tobias do it himself."

"Well for that matter," said Raphael, "I could have cured Tobit in a flash of light, flashed them to Rages for the money, and then transported everyone to Ecbatana and exorcised Sarah."

That would have taken care of one part of the assignment. But testing Tobit—that hadn't gone very well. The man was rooted in his despair and concerned more about the money than about his son. Gabriel had been indisputably right that Tobit should have questioned him before trusting Tobias to his care, and instead, there hadn't been anything at all. Just money.

Ezdrael laughed. "I'd love to see the look on their faces if you showed off a bit! But this way, at every step, Tobias has a choice to obey or not, so he reaffirms his alignment to God through obedience."

Raphael traced on the ground with a stick. "Obedience. Kind of important in all this."

"Oh, please." Ezdrael huffed. "Gabriel's just being obnoxious."

Raphael looked up. "I don't think he's being obnoxious."

The guardian shook his head. "It's typical Cherub behavior, the kind I'm trying every day to make sure Tobias doesn't get stuck in. I'm surprised Gabriel's got any friends left at all."

"What?" Raphael's wings flared, and at his side, the dog growled. "You're not being fair."

"Fair? I'm not playing by the rules?" The angel rolled his eyes. "But Gabriel sure is. He's got all these rules memorized and holds us to standard. Does it look like it *might* look to someone that you *might* be getting close to breaking a rule? Well, out you go."

Raphael wrapped his arms around himself. "It's not like that. Cherubim don't realize."

"What exactly don't the members of the smartest choir realize?" Ezdrael's feathers spread. "Oh, right, feelings. Feelings aren't easily defined, so they don't touch them. Meanwhile Gabriel walks around convinced he's God's gift to knowledge."

Raphael forced a smile. "He *is* God's gift to knowledge."

Ezdrael said, "A fact he's keenly aware of."

"Stop it!" Flames erupted around Raphael's eyes. "For pity's sake, he's *my* Cherub!"

God, help us. Raphael clenched his fists and hunched over himself. *I need you to please step in here.*

Ezdrael looked at the ground. "I'm sorry. Forgive me for being uncharitable."

Father?

God said to both of them: *I love him.*

Ezdrael said, "That wasn't in question. Gabriel's the one not acting loving toward Raphael. He needs to change what he's doing."

A chill settled over Raphael. "That's not true. He's fine just the way he is. I don't want him to change."

From God: *Leave him to me. If you must say something, pray for him.* And then a moment later, Raphael felt himself becoming solid, his wings dispersing and his body heavy, his eyes closing.

Raphael murmured, "What should I do about Gabriel?"

Ezdrael said, "You should just let it ride. Gabriel's smart. He'll realize he's wrong."

Should I? Raphael prayed.

He's your Cherub, God said. *Right now, Tobias needs you. And you need to sleep.*

Raphael didn't refuse the offer.

The next night when they made camp, Raphael and Tobias prayed together. Despite his airy prediction about "two days" of traveling, they hadn't gotten near to Rages yet, and they'd been going downhill all the way, but Tobias didn't seem to mind.

They ate figs as Raphael directed Tobias's attention to the sunset, where light filtered down in bright columns as if through windows in the sky. "I have a friend who never fails to point those out to me. He says it's 'proof once again that air is a colloidal suspension.'"

Tobias said, "What on earth does that mean?"

Raphael laughed. "I don't know, but I'd hate to tell him after all this time."

Tobias cracked up. "Well, if you're not admitting your ignorance, maybe now would be a bad time to ask what medicinal value there can be in a fish's heart, liver and gall?"

Raphael swallowed a bit of fig. "If you burn the heart and liver so the smoke surrounds a man or woman obsessed by a demon, the obsession will end and no demons will return."

Tobias nodded. "That could be useful."

"As for the gall, if you rub it into the eyes of a person with cataracts and blow into his eyes, his sight will be restored."

"My father!" Tobias exclaimed.

"Exactly," said Raphael.

Tobias lay back resting his head on his hands. The sky had gone purple and orange. "What do you suppose Heaven's like? I mean, is it worth it?"

Raphael laughed. "Everyone says it is."

Tobias turned his head to look at Raphael. "What do they say?"

Raphael groped for words. "It's hard to tell you. There's a Vision, a Vision so special it overflows into all your other senses. God fills you with love, and you bubble inside, always just on the edge of something wonderful but never quite overwhelmed. It changes everything about life, just knowing how much you're loved."

"That's incredible." Tobias whistled, still staring at the stars. "I kind of hoped we'd know everything once we got to Heaven."

Raphael muttered, "I know some who think they do."

Tobias laughed out loud. "No need to go to Heaven to meet those kind of people. But I hope so. I hope God has a huge library with lots of scrolls. Maybe he'll tell us what's a colloidal suspension."

When he lay down to sleep, Raphael realized he hadn't spoken to or heard from Gabriel all day. He doubled up in his bed-roll and shivered.

Gabriel? he sent. *I want to talk to you.*

Nothing.

Raphael opened his senses to all creation, extending until he could feel Gabriel's spirit. Not here, on the plane of Creation, but back in Heaven. He sent him an invitation, a curling thread of fire, a tease and a promise. They could sit up and talk all night and watch the stars and play with the silly dog, and it would be fine. Raphael had missed him, but they'd be together now.

Gabriel didn't come. He didn't refuse, but he also didn't arrive. And the longer the silence stretched, the more lonely Raphael felt.

God, help me, he prayed.

Be patient, Rapha'li.

Little by little Raphael loosened the knot of his body enough to lie flat. He breathed deeply, and when he opened his eyes he found it was morning.

Getting started felt extremely difficult, but Raphael managed to rise. He made breakfast for himself and Tobias and began a conversation while they ate.

"When we reach Ecbatana tonight, we can stay with Raguel, a relative of yours."

Tobias's head jerked up.

"Of *ours*," Raphael amended. "I was thinking, you know, Raguel's daughter Sarah is still unmarried. Since you're Sarah's relative, you have a right to marry her, and then you'd inherit her father's estate. Sarah's sensible, courageous, beautiful."

Tobias put down his breakfast. "No. Before you say anything else, no."

Raphael said, "This is a great idea. Tonight I'll ask her father to let you have her as your bride."

"No."

Raphael gestured to Tobias to keep eating. "When we return from Rages, we'll hold the wedding feast for her."

Tobias rolled his eyes. "You're making one very big assumption aren't you?"

This resolution to his assignment had occurred to Raphael on the first day: Sarah needed a husband, and Tobit had a marriageable son. "I'm not assuming anything. Raguel can't keep her from you because that would be a capital crime, and he'll know that. Then when we return from Rages, we'll just take her back with us to your house."

"I don't think you're listening to me. No."

Raphael paused. "Whatever for? Sarah's a wonderful woman."

Tobias had forgotten his breakfast again. "This 'wonderful woman' has already been married seven times, and each of her husbands died in the bridal chamber on the night of the wedding. They dropped dead. People say a demon killed them."

Raphael seemed puzzled. "If it were a demon, wouldn't it hurt her?"

Tobias spoke with a campfire hush. "He loves her, so he doesn't harm her. But he murders any man who comes close."

"I suppose that would put a damper on the wedding night," Raphael admitted.

"You're a relative of hers too," Tobias said. "If you're so enamored of the wonders of Sarah, *you* marry her."

If he'd been here, Gabriel would have laughed at him and said something about the kid being perceptive. "You're a closer relation."

Tobias looked earnest. "I wouldn't stop you."

"You're being impertinent."

"I'm my father's only child. If I die, I'll bring my parents down to their graves in grief." Tobias folded his arms. "They have no one else to bury them!"

"Oh, please. Your father buried the dead." Raphael set down his own breakfast. "If God let that happen, those dead would rise from their graves to bury your parents themselves!"

Tobias laughed, and Raphael knew he'd broken through.

"Besides, remember your father's orders. He commanded you to marry a woman from your own family."

Tobias muttered, "I'd rather live to regret disobeying."

"Listen to me." Raphael leaned forward, his soul sparkling with fire the way it did when he empowered Gabriel. "Don't give even another thought to the demon, but marry Sarah! Haven't you been paying attention? When you go into the bridal chamber, you can put the fish's liver and heart on the embers for the incense. As soon as the demon smells it, he'll leave."

Tobias frowned. "As though there aren't worse smells in Hell."

"Then, before—" Raphael started snickering. "Yes, there are worse smells in Hell, but just trust me on this one."

"I don't see how a bad smell—"

"You don't give a guy a break, do you?" Cherubim: always demanding the exact mechanics of how everything worked. "Take it on faith. I haven't led you wrong so far." Tobias nodded, and Raphael continued. "Before you go to bed, both of you should pray. Beg God to show you mercy and grant her deliverance. But don't be afraid: God set her apart for you before the world existed. You'll save her, and she'll go with you. And I suppose you'll have children."

"You *suppose* I'll have children?" Tobias arched his brows. "You're so certain about everything else."

Raphael laughed out loud, and then so did Tobias. "Tonight," Raphael said. "You'll see her tonight, but first, let me tell you a bit about her."

When the pair reached Ecbatana, Raphael led the way directly to Raguel's house. At the gate, the man looked up and exclaimed, "Greetings to you, brothers! Good health to you!"

Gabriel said I couldn't resist inserting my name, Raphael thought to God, *but it looks like neither can you.*

Raguel's wife Edna came to the gates. "You look just like our kinsman Tobit."

Tobias said, "We're exiles from Naphtali at Nineveh."

Edna looked startled. "Do you know Tobit?"

"Indeed we do!" answered Raphael.

"Is he well?" Edna said.

"Alive and well," said Raphael.

Tobias was about to explode. "He's my father!"

A reunion followed, and the family exchanged hugs and tears. Raphael was asked for his name and family again, and he winced. Gabriel hadn't shown himself for days now. They hadn't been apart that long since they'd bonded.

Raphael and Tobias got bedrooms in the house and water to wash their feet. Raphael changed clothing and then sat on the bed.

Michael's voice: "You look tired."

Not needing to travel through the intervening space to get from one point to another, angels have never developed the habit of knocking on doors. Raphael wasn't used to being surprised, but he only shrugged. "We walked all day, and tonight's going to be a long one. Will you pray with me?"

Their hearts mingled along with their intentions as they prayed. Michael frowned as he highlighted the demons around the house: several in key spots, but always around Sarah was Asmodeus, one of Satan's most powerful Seraphim and obsessed with the woman's every movement. *I want him out of here,* Michael prayed.

Raphael joined his prayer to Michael's: *Will I be able to do it? Asmodeus is stronger than I am. I need your help.*

From God: reassurance, the thought of Tobias's prayers and Tobias's pure heart, and then something more, the thought of God's strength.

"Gebher'el," whispered Raphael, the more formal version of Gabriel's name, meaning *Strength of God.* "Where is he?"

Patience, Rapha'li.

Patience. Because walking for days when you usually teleported didn't require patience. Raphael chuckled, and God warmed his heart. Then the servants called, and they went downstairs for dinner.

Across the room, Asmodeus glared at Raphael, the human disguise not fooling him for a moment, and then he focused on Tobias with a hatred even more intense.

Raphael steeled himself. "And there," he whispered, "is Sarah."

The boy halted in his tracks. "That's her?"

She stood alongside her mother, eyes downcast, hands clasped behind her back. She'd bound her black hair at the base of her neck, but when she looked up, a few strands escaped to fall across her face.

"Who do you think you are, Eros?" Michael murmured.

"Let's go talk to her," Raphael said, "shall we?"

They approached Sarah and Edna, who led them to the courtyard. Edna gave the usual, "Are you comfortable?" and when the conversation grew awkward, Raphael said, "We've had quite an adventure so far."

He started off with the fish, and the first time he left off a key detail, Tobias immediately corrected him (ah, Cherubim) and then continued (again, Cherubim). As Tobias kept talking, Sarah started looking up, watching him, focusing on how scary it must have been and how brave he was to travel so far from home. "My father thinks he's going to die," Tobias said, "so he wants me to retrieve the money he loaned our relative Gabelus," to which Sarah said, "But what good is the money if your father's dead? It must have been so hard to leave him. And I can't imagine how hard it was to send you."

Raphael backed out of the conversation at that point, drawing Edna aside to ask a pointless question about the house.

By the time dinner was ready, Raphael could see how Sarah and Tobias were hanging on each other's every word, but she kept biting her lip. What had happened to seven might also happen to eight.

Tobias pulled him aside on their way into the dining room. "Azariah," Tobias said, clutching at Raphael's sleeve, "remember what you said on the road? Ask Raguel to let me marry her."

Sarah's father, overhearing, looked abruptly scared. Raphael nudged the boy toward him.

Grim, Raguel put an arm around Tobias' shoulders and escorted him a distance away from the party. Tobias shot him a glance, and Raphael followed.

Raguel said, "Eat, drink, and be merry tonight, for tomorrow— for no one is more entitled to marry Sarah. Even I don't have the right to give her to anyone but you." Raguel shook his head. "But I have to explain the situation frankly. She's married seven men, all of whom were kinsmen such as yourself, and each one died on the wedding night. But now, son, eat and drink. I'm certain the Lord will look after you both."

Across the house, Asmodeus encircled the woman's soul, fencing her in and coiling around her, eyes glittering. Tobias faltered.

Raphael smiled into the boy's soul the same way he would have into Gabriel's, giving him access to the strength of his Cherub nature. Tobias clenched his hands and focused himself. Calling on Raphael's soul without realizing what he did, Tobias said, "I won't eat or drink anything until you set aside what belongs to me."

At Raphael's side, Michael said, "Is there any chance you could talk to Tobias about women as property?"

Raguel inclined his head. "She's yours according to the decree of the Book of Moses. Your marriage has been decided in Heaven. Take her. From now on you're her love, and she's your beloved. She belongs to you today and ever after. And tonight, son, may the Lord prosper you both. May He grant you joy and strength!"

Joy and strength, Raphael thought. *I'm the angel of joy. And God's Strength—where is he?*

Asmodeus clutched Sarah, wrapping his wings around her with such darkness that for a few seconds, Raphael couldn't sense her soul.

Raguel took Sarah by the hand and gave her to Tobias with the words: "Take her according to the Law. By the decree written by Moses, you are her husband, and she is your wife. Take her and bring her back safely to your father. May the God of Heaven grant both of you peace and prosperity."

Asmodeus drew still closer to her, clinging.

While Raguel drew up a marriage contract, Raphael walked across the room and looked out the window. *Asmodeus is so tight to her,* he prayed. *I'm really going to need your help. At my strongest I'm not a match for him, and without Gabriel—*

Behind him, one of the servants whispered to another, "They scrounged up another husband for her."

The other whispered, "I wonder how long she'll take to murder this one?"

Raphael whirled on them. "I beg your pardon?"

Both servants looked up, eyes wide. "Is it your place to spread rumors?" Raphael said. "I thought the position of a servant was to serve, not to pass judgment on the employer."

The servant glared at him. "Surely you know. She's had seven husbands!"

Raphael said, "It's not your concern. None at all."

The servants backed out of the room.

"No wonder they'll one day call you man's best friend," Raphael said to the dog, who wagged his tail excitedly. "You can't speak."

Michael returned to him. "Asmodeus has this household under pretty good grip."

"Do you know what drew him here in the first place?" Raphael shook his head. "There's no way I can dislodge him alone."

Michael nodded. "I know how you feel. Satan outclasses me in just about every way too." He paused, and then, "God says you'll have His strength."

Raphael's eyes widened.

Michael assented.

"Where's Gabriel?"

"With Tobit and Anna. He started pressing Tobit with questions about your story, which got Tobit thinking about the fact that he didn't vet you very well." Michael chuckled. "I get the impression Tobit is re-assessing his priorities right about now."

Raphael crossed his arms. "That's helpful."

"You know how Gabriel gets right before he says something he's been thinking about?" Michael nodded. "He's that way. Be patient."

"Patience is difficult without a Cherub."

"Tobias is a Cherub."

"He's *Sarah's* Cherub," Raphael muttered, then stopped. "Oh..." He grinned at God. *I didn't think I'd respond to a human Cherub the same way as to an angelic one.* He reached for Tobias the same way he'd have reached for Gabriel, and he gauged the intensity of the contact. It wasn't a primary bond like Gabriel's. It wasn't just an awareness of the other's presence, though, because

84

they could trade power and maybe over time learn to hear each other's thoughts. *How sly of you.*

Not sly, God replied. *It was a matter of need.*

"Azariah," Tobias called, "it's time for dinner." Raphael turned, but then he wondered: did Tobias need him to bond so he could complete the journey, or had it been him who needed Tobias?

He didn't get a chance to wonder longer. Tobias grabbed him by the arm and pulled him up the stairwell.

Raphael said, "No wonder you needed a guide. We're eating in the other room."

Tobias whispered, "What do I do?"

Raphael whispered back, "Eat dinner?"

"No, I mean...in the bridal chamber."

Raphael nodded. "We went over that. Stay calm. Put the fish on the coals for the incense. Pray with her for deliverance."

"Yeah, but...after." Tobias flushed. "The bride/bridegroom thing. What am I supposed to do?"

Oh, that. "I don't have any more experience than you do." Raphael wished for a moment that Gabriel were here to answer, but then again, Gabriel would probably say, "He needs to insert his reproductive organ into hers and then generate a sufficiency of friction to trigger a sperm ejection reflex." So he'd have been on his own anyhow.

Raphael said, "Well, here's my suggestion. You take her hand. You look at her. You talk."

Tobias shook his head. "That's not what I mean."

"It *is* what you mean." Raphael took a deep breath. "You promise her all of yourself. You promise you'll always be there. You promise that forever and ever, she's your love, and that when you guys have grandchildren and great grandchildren, and a stranger comes to the door, you'll tell him all about your beautiful bride and how much she's changed your world. And you'll hold her hand, and you'll promise."

Tobias said, "But the rest of it?"

Raphael shrugged. "I don't know anything about the rest of it. I only know about the important part."

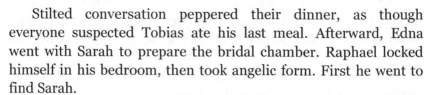

Stilted conversation peppered their dinner, as though everyone suspected Tobias ate his last meal. Afterward, Edna went with Sarah to prepare the bridal chamber. Raphael locked himself in his bedroom, then took angelic form. First he went to find Sarah.

Sarah sat on her bed crying, her mother's arms around her, but between her and her mother was Asmodeus, always Asmodeus.

Raphael slipped his lithe spiritual form into the mother's body, his shape contouring to hers and moving with her movements. Asmodeus recoiled from him, and Raphael shed light through mother and daughter. He-in-she raised a hand to Sarah's cheeks to dry the tears, then looked into her red eyes. "Be brave, my daughter." Edna's words were soothing, calm. "The Lord of Heaven will grant you joy in place of your grief. Courage, Sarah." Then Raphael let go Edna's body, and she left the room.

Raguel escorted Tobias to the bridal chamber, and Tobias closed the door with only a little hesitation. At the head of the bed, Sarah curled around herself, and Asmodeus curled around her, his soul a black fire to consume Tobias.

"Don't touch me," she urged. "If you can touch me—you're the first. There've been seven. My father told you. But no one's ever touched me. It's when they try to touch."

Tobias raised a hand. "I understand. And I'm not going to touch you yet."

Sarah watched as Tobias (with shaking hands, something Raphael could relate to at this moment) took the fish's liver and heart and placed them on the embers for the incense.

Sarah leaned forward. "What's that? Something you do in Nineveh?"

"This drives off demons," Tobias said. "Azariah told me."

The fish entrails sizzled as they hit the coals, then blackened. A fishy smell filled the room.

Sarah coughed. "Is the smell what drives them off?"

Tobias laughed out loud. "Now we pray."

Asmodeus uncoiled, raising his sword and hovering over Sarah like a storm cloud. "We have worse smells in Hell." His eyes glinted. "Touch her. Touch her, and we'll see what the fish does."

Tobias sat on the bed and said, "Father Almighty," and Sarah extended her hands to his as they prayed.

Asmodeus extended a hand of his own.

From the corner, Raphael said, "Reconsider."

Asmodeus pivoted to find Raphael with his face lit by the embers on which the fish burned. Fire coursed around him, and Asmodeus glanced at the fish.

Over the fish hovered the letters I X θ Y ∑.

Light blasted from the fish, hurling Asmodeus from the room. Raphael streaked after him, whipping forward with tendrils of will to grasp Asmodeus and bind him. Raphael's will coiled around the demon's wings, crashing him into the ground. They'd gotten all the way to upper Egypt.

Asmodeus twisting his eyes toward Raphael. "She was mine! She's supposed to be mine!"

Raphael began binding the demon.

Asmodeus spat at him. "You didn't save the wretch yourself— it was Him! It was that fish-God of yours!" Raphael tightened the bonds on his hands and feet, and Asmodeus hissed, "Why all alone? Where's your Cherub?"

So Raphael gagged him too.

The sun hadn't yet set here. Raphael looked over the sands and sighed. *Thank you. Thank you for the strength to subdue him. He didn't touch Tobias, did he?*

God replied, *Go check it out.*

In the bridal chamber, Tobias and Sarah remained in prayer, hands clasped, eyes devouring one another but hearts fixed on God.

Raphael glanced at Ezdrael. "He's fine," said the angel.

Michael said, "But you ought to go look at the rest of the family."

Out in the courtyard, Raphael saw what was going on and choked. Raguel had summoned his servants, and they had dug a grave.

"Hurry," Raguel was urging the servants. "If Tobias dies, we'll be subject to even more ridicule."

They'd worked quickly. In the time it had taken to dispel the demon, Raguel and his men had dug waist-deep into the ground. Raguel turned to one of the maids. "Now," he whispered, "check on them. Tell me if we need to bring him out."

Raphael flashed to a tree limb to watch what happened next. A moment after, the branch swayed, and a wing touched his own. He pivoted and found Gabriel.

Fire surged. "You're here!"

The Cherub shrugged. *Obviously.* "I came to explain."

Raphael hugged him, heat welling inside. "I'm just glad you're here. It's all right now."

"It's not all right." Gabriel folded his arms. "I keep having angels arrive with advice, and eighty-five percent of the advice-givers are divided between 'You're perhaps being too harsh' and 'You need to get over yourself,' so I figured you might not understand either."

"You're right. I don't understand." Raphael fingered the edge of Gabriel's wing. "I thought we were going to do this assignment together."

Gabriel looked at the moon, the stars, the light reflecting from clouds over Ecbatana. "You've done rather nicely without me." He gestured toward the house. "You got Tobias here in one piece, burned out a demon, and married the pair. The last healing is as good as done, too."

"But I missed you." Raphael's heart sent faster vibrations, but Gabriel still didn't absorb them. "I'm sorry I disappointed you, but you owe me an explanation."

Gabriel wouldn't look away from the sky. "There are very strong arguments against using alternative names and fabricating identities. It's a denial of your essence, and once you've denied that, it's a matter of time until you deny everything else, right up to and including God."

"But God said it was all right. This was my assignment." Raphael wrapped his hands around the branch. "I never would have done it if He hadn't said I could."

Gabriel didn't react.

Raphael looked for Gabriel's grey eyes with grainy night-sight, but the other watched only Raguel.

"That man endured a lot," said Gabriel. "He's the one they're going to forget, but he's suffered as much as any of the others in this story. He's wondered what sin he committed to deserve such ignominy. He's doubted Sarah and had to defend her nonetheless. He's grown old with the fear of his daughter married to only a demon."

Raphael looked away from the Cherub and breathed deeply with closed eyes, trying to restore some equanimity to his soul. Gabriel noticed, then exerted some of his calming influence and took the fire into himself.

Gabriel looked back at the freshly-dug grave. "Tobit and Anna are counting the days."

"Michael told me you helped out with Tobit." Raphael also stared into the gash in the ground. "You could have come here."

They both raised their gazes from the grave at the same moment, and Gabriel finally met Raphael's eyes.

"Master Raguel!" came a cry, and Sarah's father looked to the servant who sped from the house. "He's alive!"

Sarah's father ran toward her. "What? Say it again!"

"He's fine! He and Sarah are alive! They're fine!"

Raguel dropped to his knees in the courtyard. "Thank God. Thank God. Thank God."

Gabriel and Raphael still had their gazes locked.

"I want an explanation," Raphael said.

Gabriel looked confused. "I thought I just gave you one."

"More than that." Raphael shook his head. "You gave me a dissertation about the moral implications of mendacity, but that doesn't explain this. You. Me. Here. Now."

Gabriel opened his hands. "I can't countenance evil, and I won't be an accessory to lying." He frowned. "Lying is lying is lying. The other Cherubim and I kept debating all the variants on what it means to tell the truth. For example, your false name in some ways means the same thing as your real name, and one can argue you're an Israelite because you serve God. There's also the mitigation of any damage by revealing the truth later, and the falsehood is undoubtedly in the service of a greater good. The Cherubim also came up with several hypothetical situations in which one could argue—"

"And none of that means a thing because you still treated me like a criminal." Raphael's fire flickered around his feathers and danced over his hair. "Rather than any benefit of the doubt, I got cast aside, and that's it. You're done with me."

Gabriel's eyes flared. "I'm not done with you!"

"You left."

"But I'm not—" Gabriel's voice changed in pitch. "Did you think I was abandoning you?" He leaned forward. "That wasn't my intention. I didn't mean you to interpret my actions that way. I was still helping with your assignment."

Raphael pulled back from him. "You left, and you stayed away."

Gabriel shook his head. "You didn't need me here. You had a Cherub with you, and you knew my objection to the secondary lies that would follow the first."

The spiritual fire around Raphael engulfed the tree, all except for Gabriel who continued absorbing it.

Gabriel finally said, "Do you understand?"

"I am very, very," Raphael pulled back his fire from Gabriel, "very angry at you."

Gabriel huddled over himself.

"You can't just run off in your own head and do what you think is right and assume it's fine just because it's fine to you." Raphael's eyes glowed. "You left me alone, and for all that you've been discussing the nuances of truth for seven days, you've said nothing to me about why you did what you did."

Gabriel wrapped his hands around each other and tightened his wings around himself. "I can't lose you."

"And it was okay if I lost you?"

"But— If you fell—I can't. I can't believe you'd risk that." Gabriel's eyes gleamed. "I can't see you fallen: we're too much one soul. What would I do without you?"

Raphael muttered, "I assume you'd keep debating."

"I'm sorry." Gabriel tucked his head onto his arms. "I'm sorry."

Gabriel didn't move for a while, and Raphael relaxed bit by bit. His fire lowered. Finally Raphael moved next to him on the branch and put his wings around him.

"Please forgive me," Gabriel said. "I acted irrationally. I didn't consider all the variables. I shouldn't have let an emotion dictate my actions."

Raphael finally let Gabriel take his fire, and Gabriel returned back to him that ice-like Cherub calm. He could feel Gabriel reaching for God, and Raphael joined in the prayer. From Gabriel: apologies, surprise, confusion. *I didn't know what to do.* And then, as Raphael settled in to adore God while Gabriel prayed, he felt God's reply: an urging that Gabriel should learn.

An answering urgency from Gabriel: *I know, I know, I'm so sorry.* Raphael nestled closer to Gabriel and prayed while Gabriel kept going back and forth with God. They remained in the tree, their prayers woven around one another, until the sun began to brighten the sky. Beneath the first pink-tinged clouds they prayed the morning prayer together.

Raphael stretched. "Back to my job."

Before he could flash away, Gabriel grabbed his hand. "Do you forgive me?"

Raphael nodded. "Of course. Will you stay?"

Gabriel looked right into his eyes. "I think I will."

Next morning, Raphael mentioned to Raguel that a spot in the garden looked like a hole had been dug and filled in during the night. The man of the house sighed, and Raphael walked away to laugh in private.

Tobias found the angel and smiled weakly. "Azariah?"

"Yes, Tobias, husband of Sarah?"

"I'm not sure how to begin."

"Why not start with thanking me? You're alive."

"Thank you. I have to ask you a favor."

Tobias looked so sheepish that Raphael stood to his full height and glared at him.

"You're the head of a household now! I'm your hired man. You don't ask favors—you give me orders! Walk away and come back, and start over."

Tobias, with eyes as large as fists, backed around the corner.

Gabriel leaned against the wall with arms crossed. "My, are *you* a tough man to hire!"

Raphael's eyes flashed. "It's time he grew some spine. He's married now, and this morning Raguel gave him half his property. He's no longer a child." With a huff, Raphael sat to wait for Tobias's return.

Tobias strode around the corner. "Brother Azariah, I have a task for you."

"Yes?"

"Stand up while I'm speaking!"

Gabriel burst out laughing, and it was all Tobias could do not to crack up himself. Raphael got to his feet with a bemused smile.

"And wipe that smirk off your face. Take four servants and two camels and travel to Rages to give Gabelus the bond. Bring both him and the money back with you to the wedding celebration." Tobias looked worried again. "My father is counting the days until my return, but Raguel swore to hold a fourteen-day wedding feast, and I can't violate his oath."

Raphael rubbed his chin. "How do you know I'm not going to run off with your money? It's worth a lot more than my salary."

Tobias looked glum. "That's a good point. I trust you, though. You're family."

Raphael chuckled. "To some I would say trust family least of all, but for now that'll do."

Tobias pointed at him. "It had better. I'm paying you."

92

"Getting married made you a smart-mouth, didn't it? Enjoy the feast."

Raphael followed the road again, this time with a larger retinue that included Gabriel in spiritual form. The traveling felt easier this time, whether because of the terrain or the company Raphael wasn't sure, but while the servants chatted among themselves with stories (both legends and anecdotes they'd witnessed in the family) Gabriel was often sitting on one of the camels, singing. Raphael would let Gabriel's voice shoot through him like pins and needles, a beauty that left him simultaneously homesick and yet glad to be here, right here. Any uncertainty from the past week evaporated on the road under the sun.

In Rages, Gabelus approved the bond and turned over ten talents of silver, then loaded his own animals and servants and set out back to Ecbatana. They camped for their final night just outside Ecbatana, with eight days of the wedding celebration still to be held.

"The trouble is," said Gabriel, sitting before the Seraph, "Tobit knows when his son should return. Time expires in five days."

Everyone else had fallen asleep already, and Raphael sat near the banked fire. "The desires of Tobias's and Sarah's parents are mutually exclusive." He threw pieces of straw like darts through Gabriel's form.

"Uriel sent word that Anna and Tobit are beside themselves." Gabriel snatched one of the straw darts as it passed. "I should go help them, but I don't want you to think I'm deserting you."

"No." Raphael sighed. "You'll be waiting for me."

Gabriel enwrapped him in his wings like a fog, then dissipated until he'd vanished, leaving Raphael with only a blessing and a hint of dew on his clothing.

After fourteen days, Tobias and Sarah departed with Tobit's money, plus the property and the entourage Raguel insisted on sending with them. They made much slower progress than on the outgoing trip, and Raphael grew frustrated by both the non-urgency of their crew and the urgency of Gabriel's reports: Anna was sure Tobias was dead, and Tobit blamed only himself if the worst had happened.

When they reached the city of Kaserin, therefore, near Nineveh, Raphael suggested that he and Tobias go ahead to prepare Tobit and Anna for the shock of so many people. They parted with the company, the dog trotting behind them.

With Tobias's home in view, Raphael said, "Do you remember the gall?"

Tobias shrugged. "Sure, it's still in my pack. You said it helped heal the blind, so I figured I'd give it to my father."

"Good." Raphael shook his head. "But you need to know what to do with it. Smear the fish gall on his eyes. The cataracts will shrink and peel off, and he'll see again."

Tobias redoubled his speed, and Raphael hurried to keep up. From the house, Anna shouted, and in moments, Tobit had opened the gate to stand at the road. From the roof, Gabriel watched.

Tobit and Anna swamped Tobias in a hug. "Thank God in Heaven you're safe!" Anna was sobbing. "I thought you were dead. I was so scared."

Tobit said, "What happened that made it take so long? Did you get hurt?"

Gabriel sent to Raphael, *Clever. The money isn't with you.*

Raphael replied, *God sent me to test him. You think this is a pass?*

Gabriel winked at him.

Tobias said, "I want to show you—No, wait, I want you to see."

Tobias blew into his father's eyes, then smeared on the medicine. Tobit gasped, and Anna exclaimed, "What are you doing?"

"It stings," said Tobit.

"This will help," Tobias said. "Strength, father. Azariah told me about this."

Tobit rubbed his eyes, and Anna gave him a cloth to wipe the tears streaming down his face. Then, as Tobit blinked, his head jerked up, and he gasped, head whipping around. He looked at Anna, then at Tobias, and then he lunged for Tobias and hugged him tight enough to take his breath away.

"Thank God," he whispered. "Thank God."

Tobias was beaming. "Wait! There's more!" So Tobias told them about Sarah and Gabelus and Raguel.

"What are we waiting for?" Tobit said. "Let's go to the gate and meet them!"

Tobias grabbed his mother by the hand, and they headed off.

Raphael stayed by the wall of the house. "I'll wait right here, then."

Gabriel flashed to the wall beside him. "Good job."

Raphael reached toward Gabriel's wing. "And now I can come home."

Gabriel raised his feathers out of reach. "Absolutely not. You've fulfilled the letter of the law, but not the spirit."

Raphael squinted.

"You have to tell them who you are." Gabriel's eyes narrowed. "Or would you rather return in a hundred years to discover a temple to the traveling fertility god Azariah?"

Raphael grimaced. "You make a persuasive argument. When might be a good time?"

"They're going to have yet another wedding feast (it's been a long time since you've attended one of those, right?) only this one is a mere seven days. See what happens when they offer to pay you."

Raphael gave a mock-worried look. "You think I didn't earn my drachma-a-day?"

Gabriel shrugged. "Let that be his final test."

Raphael nodded. "That sounds all right. There's nothing pressing my return."

"Except me, but I'll wait." Raphael shot a happy look at Gabriel, who smiled dryly. "It's interesting to walk through a city I know will be destroyed."

"Are you always this grim, or is it only the prospect of another seven days of wedding feast?"

"A combination thereof." Gabriel slipped down from the wall. "But I'd rather stay with you."

At the end of the wedding celebration, Tobias called Raphael from the house, now streaming with light and free of dust. In the courtyard, Tobit was looking at the clouds, smiling as if he still couldn't believe how God had blessed him.

Taking a full breath, Tobias began. "Azariah, I know what we agreed to pay you, but listen." He took Raphael's hand. "You're family, and you've saved my life, saved my father, showed me how to save Sarah—money is an insult after all that."

Raphael squinted. "Go on?"

Tobias said. "Money is an insult, and it's not a fair repayment, but it's pretty much the going rate in this world." He laughed. "So I want you to take as wages half of all you brought back."

Behind Tobias, Gabriel nodded.

"You have to thank God," said Raphael. "Give Him the praise and the glory. Always acknowledge the good things He did for you. A king's secret is prudent to keep, but the works of God should be made known everywhere."

He shook his head to bring down the Seraph-fire, and Gabriel moved within his heart to help him. "Let me tell you the whole truth." Raphael collected himself, closing his hand into a fist through Gabriel's. "Now I'm not going to conceal anything from you. When your father and your wife prayed for death, I was the one who presented and read the record of your prayer before the Glory of the Lord." Raphael swallowed hard as comprehension dawned first on Tobias's face, then on his father's. He turned to Tobit. "I did the same thing when you used to bury the dead. When you prayed, God commissioned me to heal you and Sarah." They were both looking stunned, so he said, "I am Raphael, one of the seven angels who enter and serve directly before the Glory of the Lord."

Is that clear enough for you? Raphael thought to Gabriel.

Gabriel coiled around his heart, cool and strong.

A very pale Tobias and Tobit took a step backward. Tobit dropped to his knees, but Raphael took him by the hands and drew him back to his feet.

"Don't be afraid, and don't kneel to me," Raphael said. "Thank God now and forever. As for me, when I came to you, it wasn't any whim on my part, but God's will. So continue to thank Him every day. Praise Him with song!"

That was the first moment Raphael wondered how exactly he was to make his exit, so he decided to take a page from Gabriel's visit to Samson's parents. "It's time for me to ascend to Him who sent me."

"Azariah," Tobias said, grabbing his hand, "please stay."

Raphael shifted his hands around Tobias's and squeezed. "I shouldn't."

"Oh, Azariah—Raphael—thank you. Thanks for everything." Tobias hugged him tightly.

"I'll pray for you," Raphael said.

Tobias backed away and Raphael rose into the sky.

Tobias called to him, "Can we tell people?"

"A king's secret is prudent to keep..."

"All right, all right!" Tobias beamed. "I'll write everything."

Raphael flashed the boy a smile, then flew high over the city. Father and son continued looking upward for a while even after they no longer could see him, until Sarah came to them and asked the men of Nineveh why they were looking into the sky. Tobias went to her side and told her what had happened.

Gabriel saw this and decided it was good, and he returned to the Glory of the Lord.

Irin

614 BC

Yoram's voice broke while he stumbled through the ancient words. Parchment crumbled beneath his fingers every time he unrolled the teacher's scroll to its next column, and he dared not think about the words he pronounced. Instead he concentrated on the individual syllables. *In the name of the Holy, in the name of the Deep, in the name of Sheol...*

He hesitated just long enough to hear shouts: an army. Babylon. Nineveh falling.

Yoram's voice cracked again as he continued the incantation. Yes, Nineveh had conquered Israel and deported the entire population, but that was so long ago; now Nineveh was home. But Babylonians destroyed whatever they touched. He needed help. Nineveh needed him.

Yoram had to keep changing the incantation from "we" to "I" because he was the only one there, and apparently whoever wrote this expected there to be two or more. But finally he reached the end of the scroll, and there Yoram hesitated before the last character. A seal. A pictogram. How was he supposed to pronounce that?

He traced it in the dirt of the floor with his finger, and he did his best to whisper the word. "*Irin.*" What he was summoning would hear it anywhere. "I summon and promise myself to you."

Both lamps blew out in a wracking wind, and a light seared from the scroll.

Yoram braced himself against the table, forcing himself to stare into the glow. "I bind you to me," he warbled, his voice simultaneously a man's bass and a child's soprano. "I command you."

"Did you really just say that?"

The sound reminded him of lightning. Not thunder's dark roll as much as a starkness that left his hair standing on end. Yoram gulped. "I said the words. I made the promise."

"And I wish you hadn't," said the light.

A second light took shape, and in that moment, the room screamed with the wrench of metal twisting, the hollowness of loss and bewilderment and a raw, raw grief. For a moment the world couldn't bear two lights, but it struggled to contain them both.

"You?" exclaimed the first light. "But—"

"What have you done to yourself?" said the second. "This is what you've become?"

"Get out of here," said the first. "I answered. I showed up. This isn't your concern."

"It's absolutely my concern," said the second. "You're the one who should be leaving."

Yoram looked from one to the other, then again. "I only called one! Who are you?"

"I am the one you summoned," said the second light.

"I'm the one you summoned," said the first.

Between the two of them came a wrenching agony, that of the world cored out and its seeds spilled.

Yoram looked at the sigil on the parchment. One sign, but it did seem now to be symmetric. Maybe it was two?

The first light sounded incredulous. "Are you crazy? You didn't even know what you were calling?"

The second said, "Begone, demon!"

The first said, "Demon? Aren't you even ashamed of yourself?"

"I have nothing to be ashamed of. Of course I'm staying," the second said. "I didn't expect *you* to obey."

The first sounded irritated. *"You* shouldn't have expected me to let you win."

The angels crackled where they touched like storm fronts, but the air smelled more of fig blossoms than ozone. Yoram struggled to remember everything he'd ever heard about magic, words whispered by aged men or creaky grandmothers. You had to get authority over the spirit. So simple-sounding: use its name and give commands.

"Silence!" Yoram squeaked. Both beings snickered. "Show me your forms. Lower your light."

The angels regarded each other. "I will if you will," said the first.

"We're bound by virtue of his infernal promise," said the second.

The first said, "Half-bound. One soul, one promise. Two of us."

Yoram said, "Enough! Show your forms. Now!"

The first said, "Don't believe you're in control here."

Despite their words, both figures dimmed until they appeared in recognizable shapes: tall, slender, vaguely androgynous, eyes and long hair flecked with gold. Each bore four golden wings and wore black, and each regarded Yoram with intent.

"You're really young," said the first.

"Not too young to commit," said the second.

Yoram bristled. "Give me your names."

The second's voice darkened. "Why do you ask my name? To make idols? Do you plan to worship me?"

"No." Yoram swallowed hard. "I control you, not the other way around. Who are you?"

The second said, "As you wish. We are Irin."

The first shimmered uneasily. "We are not Irin."

Irin. Yoram looked again at the scroll, struggling to remember his Hebrew lessons. Twin angels? Oh no—an incantation for two people to recite. No wonder he'd gotten two. He'd called one, but both heard.

The second said to the first, "I heard how your master gave you a new name after you left me. But we both know what you really are."

The first said, "You're the one who left."

Yoram said, "Wait, one of you is fallen?"

Despite standing with folded arms and a cocked head, the first seemed afraid and wouldn't look away from the second. "Think about it, Kid. You summoned us using a scroll of Solomonic magic that you stole from an old man who shouldn't have had it in the first place. What did you think was going to appear?"

Yoram looked from one to the other, heart pounding. Now he really needed to get control over both of them. He didn't know much about adversaries, but you didn't want them out of your authority. "By the authority of God's name, I command you to obey me."

Neither Irin moved. Good start. But even just standing there, the twins' spirits tore at one another, pushing reality sideways from itself, each vision on a separate axis when they should have been one. True twins: they resembled each others' forms, but what felt more identical were the spirits. The same abilities, desires, dreams—and yet one had fallen and one not.

Now that he knew to look, Yoram detected differences. The air sparkled around the first one's ears like precious stones. The second one's garb seemed plainer, like a soldier's. The soldier-angel kept its gaze under strict control, its face set. The first seemed uneasy—no, worse than uneasy: horrified. Skittish. And as Yoram studied the pair, he had a sense that one was female and the other male.

Yoram said, "Babylon is attacking Nineveh. I want you to destroy the Babylonian forces and save the city."

The first said, "No!" and the second said, "Yes."

Yoram turned to the first. "You can't refuse. You are under my authority!"

The first said, "God condemned this city."

The second said, "God has condemned this city before. Remember Jonah? In His Mercy, he will spare the city again because of Yoram's prayer."

101

Again the vertigo, the tension of metal-on-metal.

The soldier-angel sneered at the first. "Your forces caused this, Freak. No wonder you want to destroy it."

Yoram said to the first, "So you're the demon?"

"Of course he's going to say that," said the freak-angel. "But it's God's will that this city fall. That army has to come."

The soldier said, "Quiet! I've seen God's face, and Yoram's call is His Will."

The freak sparked the way contact with another person will spark if you've been touching wool. "You're taking advantage of him. He's just a child. Yoram," the freak said, "this is all to a purpose. If Nineveh falls to Babylon, Israel may eventually return to its homeland."

The soldier said, "Yoram is old enough to understand you're lying, Irin. The Babylonians are idolaters, not a tool of the Most High."

The freak's head whipped around. "Wild isn't evil."

The soldier folded his arms. "You've become a wild thing yourself."

The freak-angel turned back to Yoram, desperation tingeing her aura. "Kid, who are you to challenge the will of God?"

Yoram's voice wavered. "But how can an invasion be His will?"

The freak was pulling back from the soldier, but Yoram had the sense she would resist leaving him—resist by fighting if necessary. Her fear and energy in combination left Yoram nauseated and self-conscious. The power surging from the soldier was just as strong, but it never wavered in its certitude.

The soldier said, "God delivered Israel from Egypt."

The freak said, "But He sent them there first. They needed that time in the desert. This is the same."

The soldier said, "Israel's sins sent them here as punishment."

The twins had locked onto one another again, and Yoram struggled to stay on his feet. Get control. Hah. It should be so easy, *Just exert your authority.* Were those old men insane? How had they gotten to be old men in the first place, doing stunts like this? But then again, they weren't here doing this now. It was easy to exert your authority in the situation by never getting into it in the first place.

He looked again at both, all the time noting more differences: the jewels on the first, the piercings and gaudy clothes. The other, undecorated, upright, firm. The same, and yet not. The gold on the freak had been replaced by dun, like dying wheat grains.

Fallen, it had to be. Its soul grew wilder every moment it stayed near the soldier, but the soldier's spirit had also begun surging. Rage, grief, the opposition of the pair tore into Yoram's heart like a minor key.

Were they one person? Is that what made angels twins, since they didn't have bodies and wouldn't have been born together? Or maybe two souls, absolutely identical, so each looked at the other and saw himself – herself – only now they were mortal enemies. But how could you be your own mortal enemy?

It didn't matter. "You," he said, pointing to the soldier. "Can you spare the city?"

"I can, or at least your own life." The angel's head bowed. "But you must hurry. The Babylonians are close."

"You can't!" The freak's voice grew shrill. "The city has to fall!"

The soldier said, "You must. God's people need you."

Yoram turned to the freak. "They need me! This can't be God's law! A nice God wouldn't do this! A nice God wouldn't want us to suffer!"

The freak exploded with screaming light. "He's not a nice God—He's a Holy God. And what you're doing is repugnant!"

Yoram collapsed to his knees, tears streaking his cheeks.

The soldier pointed its sword at him. "Are you worshiping an idol? Get to your feet."

Yoram screamed, "Both of you go away!"

"You summoned us." The freak sounded unhinged. "You have to make a choice, and if you choose neither of us then you've chosen me."

"Choose." The soldier looked right at Yoram. "This whore is a liar, but she's telling the truth right now. God wants you to choose, and you have to choose me."

In the distance: Metal and stone collapsing, the music of battle. The walls had been breached.

And in the house: Irin.

God, help me, he prayed.

"He's not going to help you." Yoram couldn't tell which had spoken. "You promised yourself to darkness. Choose wrong and that promise becomes permanent."

Choices. The eternal pit and eternal death. Save the city. Save himself.

Yoram looked at the freak. "You never told me your names. What is your name?"

The freak said, "Remiel."

No help there. He said to the soldier, "And yours?"

"Camael."

Again, no help. Still looking at Soldier Camael, Yoram said, "Why did you let Remiel fall?"

The Irin looked at one another, steady and focused, but the grief so strong between them. Two halves, ripped apart.

Camael said, "It was her choice. She renounced me and all I embraced."

Yoram closed his eyes. The world was a rhythm growing always more unchained, the pounding of feet on the roads and the clamor of frightened people dying. The ground vibrated beneath his knees.

"Remiel," he said, "why did you let him go?"

"Oh, Yoram," and Freak Remiel's voice broke. She finished in a whisper. "I did everything I could."

Yoram looked up, met Remiel's chaotic gaze and saw no more gold than before, but he continued looking at her.

"I choose you," he said to Remiel.

Only then did Yoram see the tears in her eyes, the yearning. The glow had hidden them, but they were there after all.

Camael raised his sword, then stopped as though restrained. Remiel looked at her brother the way she had looked at Yoram, locked together for another moment, wishing time and the winnowing had never happened.

Camael bowed to Remiel. "Well met."

He vanished.

Remiel shuddered, then covered her face in her hands.

"Remiel?" Yoram could barely hear his own voice over the chaos in the streets.

"I'm here, kid." She moved Yoram and made him look up with one finger under his chin. A fruity smell mixed with the dusk of her presence.

"Did I choose right?"

"I think so." Her eyes watered. "It's hard to tell sometimes. But Nineveh can fall now. And Israel gets home someday. So you did all right."

In the street, a woman screamed. Yoram winced.

"The city will fall, but let me take you away." Remiel held his hand. "Anywhere—Jerusalem, Shechem, wherever."

He pulled away. "This is my city. Please go."

She lowered her hand and then disappeared. The scent of her lingered in the air, but Yoram didn't argue with her to leave. He took up a sword and went into the streets to defend his city however he could.

Remiel stood outside a semi-circular building with her aura eclipsed so she could stare at the distant stars and the close empty spaces.

Home. Heaven.

God's voice beckoned in her heart, but she closed her eyes. She could look into His face, but then she'd see how He loved her despite this thing she was now and what she could have become—Camael, Camael...

Instead she walked into her building without illuminating it. But the emptiness, it echoed, so she raised her wings and engulfed the interior in light to reveal an arena surrounded by mirrors. She concentrated until the air itself blasted music: clashing, minor-keyed, and with a driving thrum.

Remiel danced. She stamped and swung until she and the music couldn't be parted. Ten minutes, twenty—what did time matter? She refused to ease up, because if she kept going, kept going until she was so tired she couldn't think, maybe then...well, maybe then she wouldn't think.

Turning to the mirror at one wall, Remiel saw wild eyes and her hair fallen about herself. She raised a bangled arm to brush it back, but then turned, driving her soul's frantic music louder. No one outside the studio would hear it except God, and He would hear it regardless.

Her temples throbbed. She looked a second time sideways into the mirrors. Her hair stuck to the sweat on her cheeks.

Between one note and the next, she called scissors into her hand. She flashed to the glass, then yanked the ends of her hair and started shearing. The severed strands dropped. She snapped the blades until whatever hair remained stood up on its own. She slashed the bangs, then went back for the bits she'd missed.

She lowered the music with a blink.

Turning her head, Remiel saw not only the cropped hair but also all of her earrings in the mirror.

Mirror.

She smashed the scissors into the glass. Ugly – horrible – an obscenity in the sight of God. She beat the reflection until it became nothing but fragments. Just little parts of herself, millions of them, the only piece of junk God ever made. Worthless. Disgusting. But no, Camael was so, so beautiful, and they were the same image. She could have been that – but he could have been her too. And now what were they?

She yanked the rest of the glass off the wall and sent it skittering over the varnished wood. Nothing. She hurled the scissors after the glass. She didn't even deserve to exist.

She dropped to the floor shaking on broken glass and hugging her knees to her chest. Camael. *Camael.* Oh, God, why?

The music stopped.

She felt it arrive—present the way smog clings to the ground, delivered like a package with Divine fingerprints lingering all over its soul. Raising her head, she recognized a shade, a fraction of a human spirit. It studied her as one awakened in the watches of the night and unsure where he was.

"Yoram?" She reached out hands speckled with mirror shards. It drifted as if on the wind, but it neared her. Nothing but a soul longing for its body. But finished. Elect.

Remiel rocked on her knees as she embraced the shade against her heart. It had promised itself to something it didn't know, and now it was hers, so she gave it back to God. Dismissed, the spirit began dispersing, but it struggled to stay together. It reached for her, fingered her sharp-edged hair like a toddler touching its mother.

Remiel put her hand over his. "You didn't know." Her voice cracked. "I hadn't seen him. Hadn't seen him since—what he'd done to himself. But it's all right. I forgive you. Sleep in peace."

Remiel hugged the soul to herself until it finished fading back into Sheol. Cradling the boy in her arms among shards of glass and shorn hair, she finally let God inside her heart to share how much she grieved for half herself.

Wanderer

593 BC, Elul 29

"I love these!" Remiel hovered over a line of emperor penguins, her hands clasped at her chest. "Gabriel, quit admiring the permafrost and get over here!"

He looked up from the ice to see her drop to a stand behind one of the penguins and imitate its waddle.

Dobiel, the guardian angel of Persia, said, "How do they know where to go?"

Remiel said, "Why destroy the mystery of it? They know where they're going because they know."

Gabriel sifted some snow through his fingers, watching the way the miniature pieces fluttered back to the surface and re-compacted. Such dry air here – great for experimenting. He'd have to come back later.

Dobiel said, "Gabriel, do you know?"

"If you visit in the summer," Gabriel said, "the coastline is a lot closer to the nesting ground. They're making this trip repeatedly as the ice grows outward, so it's all familiar ground. It only looks unfamiliar to us because we haven't been making the journey every day." He shrugged. "What looks like wandering is very different when you're living it."

"You're destroying my fantasy," Remiel called from the line of penguins. "I like to think the Holy Spirit is leading them."

Gabriel said, "I never claimed He's not. Only that they're not working from a blank slate."

Again he paid attention to the multitude of snowflake forms, then snaked out his heart for Raphael.

Raphael dwelled in intense adoration directly before God, so *in love* he was actually burning. Raphael had opened wide his entire heart, showing God his whole self and offering everything he had even as he bubbled with joy.

The Spirit asked if Gabriel wanted to join, but Gabriel withdrew, shivering at the nakedness of that kind of union. He adored God too – of course, that went without saying – but when Raphael did that, just so open and vulnerable, well, that was private.

Remiel looked up. "Afraid?"

Gabriel said, "What?"

"I just got a sense of fear off you."

Gabriel shook his head. How odd that she picked up fear from him, not when he could see God just as well in created things as in contemplation. God was all around. Wasn't Remiel finding the imprint of God right now on those penguins?

Abruptly all three angels' attention was drawn toward the Divine Will, and Gabriel felt a summons. Making himself docile to the calling, he found himself drawn away from snow, away from linear time and into spiritual time. The Spirit drew him into the prayer-vision of a prophet in ecstasy.

Remiel's heart shadowed his until she separated from him and wrapped around Ezekiel in the Temple. The prophet was engaged in an ecstasy similar to Raphael's in Heaven.

Gabriel didn't coalesce in one place as much as gel into a vision of the Temple on Earth as a reflection of the Temple in Heaven. The proportions were the same but the sizes different, one rooted in space and the other encompassing all. Gabriel was located in Ezekiel's mind and in the Spirit and in the shared space between them.

Ezekiel fixed his attention on Gabriel, who took a place at the base of the Chariot of God. It wasn't so much a real structure as a mystical construct, untrue but more than true at the same time. God tended to use these pictures even though Gabriel would have

109

preferred to use the real thing: just let the humans accept that some questions were mysteries.

Remiel kept Ezekiel's heart open toward the Spirit of God; she trained his attention on Gabriel, and Gabriel found himself represented as a man wearing white linen.

Steadying himself, he waited.

Gabriel's focus swept through the vision Ezekiel was seeing, looking at the likeness of a throne of sapphire over his head, and beneath that throne, he sensed the souls of other Cherubim. To Ezekiel's mind, they were represented as wheels, giving the universe its rotational force and at the same time moving only because of the power of the Almighty.

The Lord said to Gabriel, "Go in among the wheels beneath the Cherubim. Fill your hands with burning coals from among the Cherubim and scatter them over the city."

The city? Jerusalem.

Jerusalem had been degrading itself for generations, less and less worthy to be the City of God which housed the Holy Temple. Still, to destroy it like Sodom: it was a pity. No one here had ever harmed Gabriel directly, but what they'd done was worse. Although the Sodomites had attempted to harm a foreign woman, Jerusalem had been treating with even less hospitality the God who had been revealed to them in fire, in the law, and in their salvation.

As Ezekiel watched, Gabriel entered the wheels.

Gabriel took in the whole of Jerusalem, and he hesitated. What God was instructing would result in the city's destruction. Those coals would burn out the spiritual connection between Jerusalem and God, but like most visions this one had a connection to reality, and the city itself would burn. Just like Sodom. But surely there were ten good people in Jerusalem—?

God repeated, "Take fire from among the wheels, from among the Cherubim."

Probably God needed to make sure Ezekiel heard what was going on, and also to prompt him because he'd missed his cue. Gabriel knew how this sort of thing was supposed to go: Ezekiel needed to beg for mercy on Jerusalem, and then God would grant it because ever since the Exodus, God had given Jerusalem chance after chance. The Redeemer hadn't come yet, so there was no real chance God would destroy Jerusalem the way He had Samaria. God was giving Jerusalem a good scare, giving them a chance to learn and mend their behavior.

There would be suffering of course, but everyone knew souls learned and grew through suffering.

Moving alongside the throne, Gabriel took his place beside one of the Cherubim, and instead of stepping into the fire to gather coals, he extended his hand.

The Cherub within took up some of the fire and poured it into Gabriel's hands, and Gabriel went out into the Temple area where Ezekiel again could see him. In full view of the prophet, he scattered the coals over the city.

The Cherubim and the throne rose with a rushing, whispering sound, and the glory of the Lord departed from the threshold of the Temple.

The Spirit eased Gabriel out of Ezekiel's vision until he was once again standing with Dobiel and Remiel. But Remiel – Remiel looked terrified. At him. She was looking at Gabriel with horror.

The voice of the Lord spoke inside all three. "Remiel, Dobiel, return to me. Gabriel, stand before me this instant."

The three angels appeared before the Most High without hesitation, but Gabriel had gone tense. What was wrong?

God had shown him to Ezekiel. Go take the coals. Go scatter them over the city. He'd scattered the coals – he couldn't be punished for that. He'd taken the coals...

"Take your places," God commanded.

No, he *hadn't* taken the coals. He'd had a Cherub hand them out to him. A moment, just a moment, but a moment that gave the coals time to cool. He'd changed God's instructions.

All the Seven had assembled. Gabriel took a place beside Raphael, his wings touching the Seraph's. Raphael looked startled, only Gabriel didn't dare meet his eyes. God was using the same voice that had condemned humankind to struggle and death.

"Gabriel, approach."

He didn't look toward Raphael as he stepped forward, but he kept one wing touching him. Then he took another step and lost even that contact.

"You disobeyed."

A chill enfolded his body, like a hand over a glass figurine it didn't want to shatter.

God regarded him without saying anything.

Questions arose all around him, and Gabriel retreated inside his head. He had no plausible deniability here. He knew it. God had said to take the coals and destroy Jerusalem. And instead he'd spared Jerusalem on his own volition and his own authority.

But it didn't make sense—surely God hadn't wanted flaming destruction! God had to have wanted what Gabriel thought he had—another chance for Jerusalem, the continued covenant, their growth—

Gabriel stared back into Divinity, unblinking, unmoving.

"You aren't the first to try to stare me down, Gebher'el."

Gabriel bent forward, holding his wings close to his body and wrapping his arms around himself. "I'm not. But—" He could see it now—he'd heard one order and fulfilled what he thought that order should have been. But— "You can't," he said, "you wouldn't," because as a Cherub, he knew, "oh God, no—" what was coming.

Like a blink, the Vision of God closed from his sight.

Gabriel huddled in stillness. Paralyzed. His eyes dilated, but he couldn't see divinity. Just emptiness. In his heart, no sense of God.

He doubled over, onto his knees and farther down so he folded like an egg, arms clutched around himself.

None of the other angels were speaking. No, why would they? He wouldn't speak up for them under the same circumstances.

He found his voice. "Forever?"

The answer, "One year."

Gabriel breathed softly, still not looking up. "I shouldn't have done it. I apologize."

No answer.

No mercy? After all he'd done, all the years he'd served? When so many other angels bent or broke the rules and God never said a thing? "Why?" he asked, and then his voice pitched up. "Why won't you answer me?"

More silence.

Gabriel blasted out of Heaven like a missile, then plummeted toward the Earth. He collided with the ground, scorching a mile-long trench through the forest and ending at the base of a mountain. He staggered to his feet and launched again, unhurt except for this spiritual blindness, this ache and emptiness and loneliness.

He misjudged the height of the mountain and slammed into a rock; he'd become tangible enough to have the wind knocked out of him. Ruah. He'd had the spirit knocked out of him too.

Sprawled on the pinnacle, the Cherub clung to the stone a long time, eyes squeezed tight, trying not to consider—or remember—what had happened. Because he knew: his own authority, his own assumptions, his decision—that wasn't right. God had ordered one thing and he'd done another. How often had he been the one to say that when God gave an order you had to carry it out? He'd dressed up disobedience as obedience, and to what end? Continued idolatry? The enslavement of a people who would rightfully blame him if they were better off dead?

"Father God." He wrapped himself tight. "What did I do?"

Tishri 1

After Michael somehow got the mess under control in Heaven, he went to Gabriel.

In the darkness, Michael adjusted his sight until he sensed the stillness enfolding the whole mountain, plus at the crown of its stillness, Gabriel huddled against a rock and staring without focus into the mountain's heart.

Michael reached for him. "Gabriel—?"

The Cherub whipped into a stand. "Go away!"

Wings raised, Michael backed up a step on the rock ledge.

"I felt you coming! Do you think I'm stupid," Gabriel's words ended in a flat, dry tone, "just because I was idiot enough to lose God's love?"

"I don't think—"

"Go home. I want Raphael." Gabriel dropped back to the rock, tucking up his knees and pulling his wings tight around himself.

"You've got me." This was horrible. Worse than horrible. Gabriel had turned colorless. All his natural strength had shattered within him, and Gabriel's name meant Strength of God. Well, no strength anymore. No God either. What was left?

Michael wrapped his arms around his waist with a shiver.

He hadn't thought about what he'd expected to find, but it wouldn't have been this. Maybe he figured Gabriel would have been crying – he'd have been crying himself, that's for sure. Or maybe Gabriel analyzing and endlessly dissecting the events leading up to the punishment and the potential pathways afterward. Michael would have sat while Gabriel gave a detailed analysis of the loss and started compiling statistics. But here instead was a Gabriel like a shell, and waiting for him to discuss the problem like a Cherub wasn't going to work. This was just like Sodom – Gabriel wouldn't reach past the shock to the logic. If he could have, Michael's help would have been redundant.

Sodom. What should he have done then that he'd regretted not doing ever since?

Michael seated himself beside Gabriel, and then carefully, he hugged him.

It was an even chance Gabriel would shove him aside, but instead Gabriel leaned into the hug, and Michael wrapped him in his wings.

Gabriel didn't shrug off the green cocoon of Michael's feathers. The stars changed position. The evening sounds changed to midnight sounds. Gabriel's grip eased, and his pulse too. And then, at some point, Michael knew he'd fled into sleep.

Even sleeping, every so often, he shuddered.

Midnight yielded to dawn, Tishri 1. And as the first sunlight cleared the horizon, Gabriel awakened.

Gabriel burst out of Michael's grasp, whipping his head around with his eyes changing focus fifteen times in ten seconds as he searched for something he couldn't see. His wings flared as his neck arched. A moment later he collapsed to all fours, choking on a gasp, radiating despair and terror. Michael moved closer, but Gabriel scrambled away. Craning his neck, Gabriel looked at the sky, then down at his hands, then turned his stunned gaze toward Michael.

Without the smoothness of yesterday's movements, Gabriel hugged his thighs to his chest, pressed his forehead against his knees, and wrapped his wings about his body like wet cellophane. And there he stayed.

Michael worked at untensing himself and sitting back against the rock.

When Gabriel's voice emerged, it came as a whisper. "One year."

Michael shivered.

Gabriel buried his face in his folded arms. "I can't do it."

Michael inched closer. "What choice do you have?"

Gabriel stayed quiet another long time. Then he said, "Is it possible to die of homesickness?"

Michael traced his fingers over Gabriel's outermost feathers. "It's never happened before."

As he lifted his wings away from Michael's touch, Gabriel closed his fingers over a handful of stones and let the dirt slide out.

Crickets chirped in a nearby bush. Gabriel glared at them, and they silenced. Some low clouds rolled in, leaving Gabriel's eyes lightless. After a while, Michael looked down in prayerful

Twelve months

Tishri

Cheshvan

Kislev

Tevet

Schevat

Adar

Nissan

Iyar

Sivan

Tammuz

Av

Elul

thought and extended his heart to the other angel, but his fractured spirit buckled under even gentle pressure, so Michael withdrew.

Gabriel gave a chuckle like the creaking of the moon, a laugh that moved his shoulders in small jolts that resembled sobs, only with a dry sound. "What am I going to do?"

"What else can you do?" asked Michael. "Come home and bear it as best you can."

Gabriel tucked his head. "Why do you even want me there?"

Michael said, "You didn't actually sin, did you? You just didn't carry out the orders exactly as given."

Gabriel said, "There's no difference."

"There's a huge difference." Michael leaned forward. "Intention versus mistake."

"You're talking about the distinction between orthodoxy and orthopraxy," Gabriel said, "and I'm not up to debating it now. We have God's word on it anyway. I didn't fulfill His command exactly, and I got reprimanded. Therefore you don't want me in Heaven."

"You're wrong because I thought I did." Michael frowned. "Yes, you got punished. God took the Vision. But you're still sinless, and God didn't forbid you to stay with all of us. So of course we want you home."

Gabriel tossed one of the stones away from himself, projecting a feeling Michael couldn't name.

Michael groped for something else to say. "Where else would you go?"

Gabriel tossed another pebble after the first. "I could stay here. Where better for a disgraced angel than a disgraced planet?"

Michael looked at his legs, stretched full-length. "If you think that's for the best."

"Of course I don't think that!" Gabriel hurled a shower of stones into the bushes. "But none of this is for the best. It wasn't part of the Plan. The Best is gone. Destroyed. Irretrievable."

Michael cringed. Why hadn't someone else come for Gabriel? Uriel or Saraquael or anyone else? If he'd asked, anyone would have pleaded for the chance to come. It had been him, though, him who'd just gone out and said, "I'll go get him." Rushed in yet again without knowing what to do.

Gabriel glared sullenly. "I know you're unsettled, and I apologize. Perhaps you should return."

That was a break. Michael looked up. "And you'll come with me?"

Gabriel huffed. "What's there for me?"

"The rest of us." Michael stood and offered a hand to Gabriel. "Please? I don't want to leave you here."

Gabriel took his hand, and Michael flashed them home.

Before Gabriel even placed where they'd landed, Remiel rushed him and wrapped him in her arms. "I'm so sorry. I'm sorry – I did everything I could, but I didn't realize. I should have done something more."

Gabriel tensed under her embrace, but she wouldn't let go. He realized Michael had brought them to a field in one of the outer layers of Heaven, not the inner circle. No, of course not – he didn't belong there anymore. "I don't blame you for anything," he told Remiel, but she buried her face in his shoulder. "It's my own fault."

He hated saying that. But that probably meant he should say it more.

"Hey, give him space to breathe." That was Saraquael, and he helped loosen Remiel's arms from around him. Then Saraquael met his eyes, and Gabriel shuddered to realize he was crying. "I'm sorry. I don't know what else to say."

Gabriel reached with his heart for Raphael, because Raphael would know what to say, and for that matter, Raphael would give him space, maybe bring him to a library and stay in the next room while Gabriel figured out what to do. But instead of sensing fire, Gabriel sensed nothing. Not a wall as much as an empty container. Avoiding him?

That made sense. No one would want to touch pain. When it didn't hurt so much, Raphael would come to him.

But the conversation was stalled, and Saraquael still had tears in his eyes, so Gabriel said, "Who has my place?"

"Dobiel," said Saraquael.

"He didn't want it." Remiel shook her head. "We wanted to keep the spot empty."

"That would be ridiculous." Gabriel realized he had his wings too tight to his body, so he struggled to relax them, to smooth down the feathers instead of fanning them out with tension. "An empty spot would be a living monument to disobedience." He bit his lip. "Is Raphael okay?"

All three looked at each other. Remiel said, "I...don't know. I could ask Raguel. Raphael took it badly, and Raguel pulled him away."

Gabriel straightened. "I didn't feel that at all."

Darkness had clouded Remiel's voice. "You were feeling a lot of other things."

Not enough. Not feeling God, for instance.

Uriel appeared and without hesitation embraced Gabriel.

Michael said, "Uriel was praying for mercy before God even said anything."

Gabriel closed his eyes. "Thank you." Too many angels here – and the one he wanted decidedly missing. "I need – Could I just have some time? To myself? I need to sort things out."

Michael looked hurt, but he left with Saraquael. Remiel took his hand. "I understand. But if you want any pointers, or if you just need to talk about it, I know it's not the same, but I might be able to help you since I went through something similar."

Before Gabriel could ask what she meant, she'd vanished too.

He turned, but Uriel had stayed, and Uriel grabbed his hands and looked him right in the eye.

God still loved him.

It came from Uriel's eyes, the curve of Uriel's spine, the relaxation of the innermost feathers on the smallest set of wings, a message sent from unmoving eyes and firm hands. God still loves you.

Gabriel pulled back, but Uriel's grip on his hands tightened, and Uriel leaned forward.

Gabriel looked himself over, smiling dryly. Uriel looked over Gabriel again and nodded.

Gabriel said, "I know what you're trying to do, but I deserved this."

Uriel embraced him, and then in words for the first time, whispered, "Don't assume you know what God's doing."

Gabriel found a quiet corner of Heaven and tried to sort through his situation. It hurt. He hadn't expected (no, of course he hadn't expected – no one could have expected this...) He wouldn't have predicted the sheer gap in his perceptions from the loss of God's light in everything. He hadn't spent every waking second staring directly into God's eyes and embracing His fullness the way Raphael had been doing at their last contact, so Gabriel would have hypothesized the loss of the Vision would mean the loss of direct communication and dry prayer sessions.

He wouldn't have hypothesized that ache every moment, like when the Sodomites pounded him in that alleyway and left his ribs hurting long into the night, and that feeling of life scorching out inside or the sudden stabbing pains with deep breaths. That was more how it felt now – less like a gap and more like a wound.

So he huddled in a niche in the rocks, trying to hash out a logical plan. He worked out the number of minutes in a year and then worked out how many minutes he'd already spent. Too many spent. Too many to go. All of them worthless without God.

After some number of minutes, Uriel flashed away, and in the next, Raguel appeared. "Hey," he said, "do you want to go on patrol with me?"

Gabriel shivered. "No, I'd rather not."

Raguel sat on a rock.

Gabriel said, "Weren't you about to go on patrol?"

"It can wait."

No, they couldn't do this – they mustn't. He was still an angel, spiritually crippled but not in need of constant tending, or were they afraid he'd disobey further and outright rebel?

Gabriel said, "Can you ask God if I have any assignments for now?"

Raguel's eyes gleamed with a light like a sword through Gabriel's heart, and as Gabriel looked away, he said, "No, you've been relieved of duties for now."

Gabriel said, "For the whole duration?"

Raguel said, "Would you like me to ask?"

And see that reflected light again? Gabriel said, "No!" He stood. "Let's go on patrol, then," and Raguel took him, looking relieved.

After patrol, Saraquael joined them, and then Raguel left while Saraquael stayed.

This was insupportable. Were they going to pass him, hand to hand, around the whole nine choirs? And was God going to withhold all assignments until this situation ended?

He tolerated it through several shift changes, waiting for Raphael to show up and put an end to this ridiculous process. Only Raphael never came, and the one time Gabriel just went to Raphael's home to look for him, the place felt devoid of Raphael's spark, and Dobiel (who trailed him at the moment) looked only uneasy.

When Dobiel left to change shifts with Saraquael after too many Godless hours, Gabriel seized the moment and vanished.

Tishri 3

Gabriel appeared in a semi-solid state somewhere north and very much west of the Holy Land. He kept his signature suppressed so the other angels couldn't find him, and he stayed insubstantial. The night was warm, so he spent the evening in a cluster of rushes by the bank of a stream.

As the stars rose, Gabriel emitted tentative streamers, touching the world surrounding him. He plunked small stones into the stream one after the next until none remained in his reach. He tucked his knees up to his chin and stared at the running water.

120

Raphael, he thought. And then, *Michael. Remiel. Saraquael. Raguel. Uriel. Dobiel. God, God, God.*

In the total silence, Gabriel closed his eyes, wrapped his wings about himself. Not raising his chin from where it rested on his knees, he breathed a song:

"How long, O Lord? Will you forget me always?

How long will you hide your face from me?

How long will I cry in my soul,

Sorrow in my heart every day?

Listen to my prayer, O Lord my God.

Enlighten me against despair.

But I've trusted in your mercy.

Someday my heart will rejoice in your mercy.

I will sing to you always,

I know you've done what is fair."

And now, it was past time to figure out what to do with himself. Gabriel started by building a campfire because he'd seen them so often. Even if his spiritual form couldn't get cold, at least he could watch the flames.

As the fire consumed the sticks, he closed his eyes, and bracing himself, he stopped suppressing his presence.

Michael appeared, startled. "You're leaving us?"

"I'm not leaving *you,*" Gabriel said. "I'm changing location."

Michael still looked scared. He settled partway around the fire from Gabriel. "You don't need to do this. We're going to miss you."

"I already miss you," replied Gabriel. "Don't try to make me say melodramatic things. This is for the best... the best we can attain from here, at least."

The fire devoured wood in order to give them light. A stick crackled, and sparks ascended until they winked out.

Michael sounded tentative. "Is there anything I can bring you?"

Gabriel glowered. "You can bring me Raphael."

Michael recoiled. "You know why I can't."

Gabriel gasped just like when the men beat him in Sodom. "Oh, but God—" He put his head into his hands as his voice cracked. "But—"

He pulled his wings tight, and once again there was that urge to run accompanied by nowhere to run to. You couldn't outrun hate. Couldn't leave behind grief.

Gabriel kept his head tucked. "Please, try to explain to him. Don't let him hate me."

"I'm not sure what I can say."

Gabriel got up. The air shimmered around Gabriel as he resisted his own impulse to flash away. "I don't— Then leave. If you're as angry as he is, why are you even here?"

Michael flinched. "I'm not angry. I just don't know how much I'm allowed to tell him."

Gabriel pivoted back toward Michael. "He can't even bear to hear about me?"

Michael looked sad. "He asks about you all the time. But—" He paused. "Wait. You don't realize?"

Gabriel stared in incomprehension. He shook apart all his bits of data and pieced them back together in a different way: the presupposition had been that Raphael chose not to approach him. But what if... "God ordered him to stay away from me?" A long, long moment passed. That fit the data. It fit the emptiness whenever he reached for their bond. "And... That's why I can't feel him?"

Gabriel dropped back to a seat before the fire, and he tightened his wings around his shoulders.

Across from him, Michael radiated worry.

After another protracted pause: "God broke the rest of my bonds, too?"

Gabriel's voice cracked, and Michael leaned forward. "I don't know about all of them. But he would be here. I know he would"

"So he's not furious at me?" Gabriel bit his lip. "I don't suppose you can shuttle messages? That would obey the letter of the law and disregard the Spirit."

Michael swallowed. "I honestly don't know how much is allowed. I'll do what I think I can."

"Don't take any chances." Gabriel put more wood on the fire. "It's not worth it. You saw what happened."

Michael looked uncomfortable. "If you stay in the plane of Creation, are you going to become human?"

"I'm an angel. But I might ask God to put me in a body." Gabriel stared at the ground. "If you think about it, they sleep. It's a legitimate means of shearing a quarter of the time off the sentence."

Michael's eyes glinted. "Is that your motive?"

"Just a side effect." Gabriel folded his arms and rested them on his knees. "I thought maybe I could be useful, and then the sleep thing occurred to me. Of course, humans dream, too, which might negate any benefit." Gabriel closed his eyes. It throbbed, that empty space where God should have been. "You can't get around God's orders. A year is a year, and God knows what I'm going to do with it, even if I don't. But I can't help wondering if it's a calendar year, a lunar year, a solar year... I didn't think to nail it down at the time."

Michael said, "I can ask. It might make it easier if you kept track of the days."

Gabriel huffed. "It does nothing of the sort."

More silence. Michael said at last, "Where will you go?"

Gabriel's head shot up. "The chosen land. Where else would I go? Or are you saying," Gabriel asked, his voice changing pitch, "that He's forbidden my going there?"

Michael opened his hands. "I'm not holding back anything. If He permits humans the luxury of being with Him, why not you? They're sinful."

Gabriel's hands clenched. "But their kind was promised a redeemer, and ours who got winnowed out went directly into Hell—except for me."

Michael shook his head. "I wouldn't say you've been winnowed."

Gabriel picked at the grass his semi-solid weight had flattened. He was thinking now more as disconnected images than as words: a shattered vase; half-eaten food gone rotten; torn fabric.

123

Michael shook his head. "He still loves you."

Gabriel shrank a little. "You all keep saying that."

"Because it's true." Michael nodded. "It seems like this has a twofold agenda."

"Aside from the obvious?" Gabriel put a little acid into his voice. "Banging it into my head to obey orders has to be one reason. What's the other?"

"Bringing you closer to humankind. Uriel says that regardless of your form, you'll start feeling increased empathy for humankind, and that's aside from any faith you kindle in them."

Gabriel murmured, "God always brings good from evil."

Michael frowned. "You aren't evil. Don't say that."

"Not-God equals evil."

"Don't use logic. You may be a Cherub, but even Cherubic souls aren't logical. They're souls. There are too many degrees of grey to catalog..." Michael got to his feet. "You're not evil! Don't say that!"

Gabriel hesitated. "So what am I?"

"Complacent?"

Gabriel shook his head. "Complacent. That works."

Michael moved around the fire and sat closer to Gabriel. "Remiel said that this looks like a plan to her. She says God will prepare you for a specific assignment."

Gabriel sat straighter. "She's good at reading the Divine Will. What sort of assignment?"

"No word of it reached me, if anyone knows. But that's exciting."

"I'd love to know my ultimate purpose, assuming I haven't wrecked it already." Gabriel leaned forward. "Could you do me a favor? Ask God to give an assignment to me now. A big one. One with lots of little regulations in it – I can get it right. I promise you, Michael, I'll nail it. Something heroic and huge, something for the ages. I'll prove myself all over again, and then God can take me home because I'll have fulfilled everything."

Michael lowered his gaze, and Gabriel's heart sank. "Don't you think we already asked that?"

124

Gabriel's shoulders sagged. "Then what does He want me to do? I can do it."

"He hasn't said. It's between you and Him now. Your discernment led you here, so this is where I'd suggest you start, much as I don't like it." Michael's head raised, and his eyes became more earnest. "Oh, and Raguel said if you have any problems with demons, give a yell for him."

Gabriel raised his eyebrows. "The threat alone will probably keep them away."

"If they bother you, the same goes for me. Call me, and I'll come with a sword in each hand." Michael's eyes smoldered. "Whatever they plan, they'll forget it if they try. They won't remember what they were doing, what they intended to do once they had you down... they'll forget their *names* by the time I'm done."

Gabriel crossed his legs at the ankle, grinning. "That's very kind."

"Don't minimize the threat." Michael trembled. "Once they realize, I'm sure they'll engulf you."

Gabriel sighed. "I know. They're not liable to exercise clemency or moderation in regards to me."

"Clemency? They'll persecute you to no end!"

"Like at Sodom?"

Michael flinched. "Much better your body than your soul."

Gabriel bit his lip. "Much better neither."

"Stay aware." Michael's voice lowered. "They'll hit you and hit you hard once they find you vulnerable. Why should I have to tell you that?"

"I'll keep on guard." Gabriel frowned. "If I were in a body, would I have a guardian?"

"Raguel already offered, but God said you wouldn't have a single angel who watched over you. Maybe you could have a series of shifts."

Gabriel shrunk a little inside. "That's not necessary. You all have assignments, and I can call for help."

Michael opened his hands. "How would you know? If you became human you'd lose your angelic senses and some of your abilities. You won't know when attacks come."

"Surely I don't have to submerge all of me." Gabriel joined eyes with Michael. "It's only time. I just have to get through time. God will protect me, and what better friends could I possibly have?"

Michael nodded, then stood. Gabriel touched his hand to his temple while the Archangel vanished.

And for the next ten minutes, Gabriel fought the urge to summon Michael back.

So quiet, so unnaturally silent. He had no one else in his head or in his heart.

No, he'd tough it out. Loneliness must be part of the punishment, otherwise why would God have taken Raphael? It wouldn't do to anger God further. He'd told Michael it was for the best; he couldn't head back after less than a quarter hour. And it wasn't anything to be afraid of, being alone. Cherubim worked well in solitude. He'd get through this.

Gabriel drew closer to the fire and stared into the heart. Fiery ones. Seraphim. It would be futile to touch this kind of flame, but for a moment he hungered for it.

So that was what Remiel meant. Her separation from Camael was equivalent to his separation from Raphael, not from God.

Oh, Raphael—a whole year? When he'd been hoping for days now to find peace under Raphael's wings, even if the Seraph was enraged, and just huddle there in whatever shelter he could—

A rabbit's sniff startled him, and Gabriel jerked away even as the rabbit bounded backward. He turned to see a number of glinting eyes.

"Hello there," he said, his voice unsteady.

The animals remained distant. Gabriel called to the plants so they would put up shoots, and the rabbits browsed.

Where will you go? Michael had asked.

Gabriel gestured toward the fire, and abruptly Raphael sat there, facing him; just an image, but he could try to pretend— couldn't he? "Maybe I'll find a God-fearing town somewhere,"

Gabriel said to the image. "I could travel about, I suppose, not staying long anywhere. I think I'd have to because people tend to enquire about one's past. *Where are you from? Why did you come here?* I won't lie, so staying in one city might get tricky."

The idea of introducing himself as an angel in disgrace seemed, at best, repugnant. He didn't dwell on the possibility.

One of the rabbits jumped into his lap, and Gabriel stroked it. "It's all contingent on God's approval." Gabriel looked only at Raphael's face. "I can't get into a human form by myself, so God would have to do that part."

He leaned back on his hands, allowing the rabbit to jump to the ground. He looked back at Raphael, whose image he was able to manipulate into the expressions he would have expected had Raphael actually been there. It was unbelievable, how much this hurt. He didn't even know what he wanted to say, so he just kept talking. "The human form will one day be glorified by a redeemer, so it's not exactly a horror to be trapped in that clumsy state. Demons think that, so I guess it's a point in my favor that I'm considering it. I wouldn't like being human for long stretches, but I'll shoulder the burden if it means I can help out down here."

Gabriel found the rabbit looking at him again, and he shooed it away. It was definitely a rabbit through and through, not a spy for a demon or an angel. It just wondered what he was doing there. "I'm wondering that too, wondering why I'm wasting my time talking to a rabbit and some manipulated light," Gabriel said, "so you're in good company."

Good company. Well, at least not-evil company.

"Another potential problem," Gabriel said, again to Raphael, "is that I'm not good at wearing a body. None of us is. I don't have the right balance or the experience making those split-second reactions a person spends a lifetime learning. A careful observer might be able to detect the difference because the nature that walks or stands is second nature, not primary."

Raphael in the fire nodded. He looked concerned.

"Oh, I know all the drawbacks," Gabriel said softly. "Fatigue, hunger, sickness. On the other hand, I always enjoyed other aspects of the body: taste, touch, true sound, true sight, and smell. Laughter. Sleepiness. Awakening."

The rabbit hopped back into the brush.

"And that—" Gabriel whispered to Raphael, "I guess that's it. The last time I'm going to see you until God brings me home." He looked back at the image of Raphael in the fire and met its eyes for a very long time.

Finally, finally he whispered, "Goodbye."

He winked out the image and was once again alone.

Tishri 4

In the morning, Gabriel prayed to become human, and God answered. Right where he was, Gabriel found himself in a body.

And he practiced. He practiced walking. He practiced running. He made note of all the physical sensations of a human moving through the day: what it meant to be hungry and thirsty; what it meant to be tired. He browsed around until he could find food, and he looked for a place to spend the night.

He kept his angelic senses open as he moved, but the other angels left him alone, and he didn't detect any demons. But he sensed everything else – the movement of air against his skin, the touch of fabric, a thousand sounds and smells and the taste of his own teeth. It was dizzying, terrifying in a way, and he wondered how humans sifted it all to know what was important. How could they pay equal attention to a moving cloud and a moving predator and assign more value to one than the other?

Too much, too overwhelming. Gabriel asked for the ability to switch back and forth between spiritual and material. It took some concentration at first, but after several tries, he found it easier. Just before sunset, he located a stand of rushes, and he settled in for the night.

Tishri 5

The night had so many sounds. Insects and animals, the wind, the stream, the gentle motion of the Earth itself and the sound of plants growing. And early in the morning, two men on horseback.

"They haunt the stream," said one man.

It took Gabriel a moment to figure out which language they were speaking and to start thinking in that language.

"I wouldn't go anywhere near it," said the other.

Gabriel had been observing a colony of ants and their easy observance of the very simple programming that made up their lives. He'd gone semi-solid to play with them, testing their response to different obstacles. Despite what he'd said to Remiel about the penguins, he couldn't see God in them. Not really. He knew God had created ants and that they were acting in accord with God's will, but it wasn't the same.

He raised his head and looked through the plants to see what appeared to be farmers with calloused hands and large muscles. He made a mental note that he might need those and to figure out how to change his form in order to get them.

A boy's voice piped up. "What makes you think it's haunted?"

"See the reeds? They're taller there and thicker than anywhere else. Not even on the opposite bank of the stream. Ghosts do that."

Gabriel glanced up with large eyes.

"I don't believe in ghosts," said the boy, "only in the gods!"

Probably a good call, but Gabriel could discern in the child's voice an early adolescent self-confidence that might or might not last until adulthood.

"You don't have to believe in them," said one of the men. "Just be respectful. Ghosts don't take kindly to insults."

"Well, watch!"

A crashing sound as the boy hurled himself into the rushes. It didn't occur to Gabriel that he was visible until a moment too late.

The boy caught one sight of Gabriel and shrieked. Gabriel vanished, shaking, horrified.

"Brennos!" shouted the father. "Get out of there!"

The boy wheeled. Invisible, Gabriel covered his face in his hands. He could hear the boy's heart pounding while his father or his uncle yelled at him, and Gabriel accepted every word as though directed at himself.

Stupid, stupid, stupid. He should have noticed how the reeds were growing, and he should have predicted a boy that age would run to investigate with no warning. But most of all, he should have remembered how solid he was and that a human could see him. What if it had been one of the adults? What if whoever spotted him had chosen not to run but to attack?

Gabriel immersed himself in prayer, and he didn't stop. He prayed that he wouldn't fail again that badly. And he prayed for the boy, that the boy wouldn't retreat into superstition after seeing something he couldn't explain.

Gabriel hadn't prayed since God's verdict, but this wasn't for himself, so he didn't hesitate. Gabriel prayed for the opportunity to make amends, for the wisdom not to frighten anyone again, for the foresight to keep his origin secret, and then without planning it, he prayed that God would still love him.

Once that burst out, it repeated over and over in his head: urgent, sincere, frightened. He slowed, but it would pop up again, then another pause, then again, and he'd pause, and it happened once more.

As he prayed it dawned on him: he'd assumed that when God shut him out, the silence went both ways. It didn't have to be like that: of course God could hear him. If God would put him in a body, then God was still listening, and maybe they could make amends. Now that Gabriel had a better sense of thirst, of hunger, he realized he'd been hungry and thirsty for prayer, so he kept praying for anything that came to mind. He prayed for the Earth, for the land around himself and for the people. He prayed for the animals, the plants, and the little lives borne on wind and water. He prayed for his friends, especially for Michael, Remiel and Dobiel. He prayed for Raphael.

Practicing being human was important, but he didn't want to stop praying, so he experimented. He tried praying while solid, tried keeping focus, tried until he realized there were too many human needs to meet and retreated into semi-solid form again.

When the sun set, Gabriel curled up beneath his wings and prayed himself to sleep.

Tishri 6

At dawn, Gabriel awoke with light in his eyes. A peculiar tension built up in his throat and lungs and he breathed deeply, then opened his mouth very wide and expelled all the air—his first yawn. He stretched, a little amused by how a semi-solid body just did what it felt like, but as he moved he dislodged a pile of reeds.

Where had that come from? He hadn't pulled them down around himself last night, and he certainly hadn't done so while asleep.

Behind him he heard a gasp, and he turned to find a boy. The same boy as yesterday. "Brennos?"

The boy had come back to find him and had covered him with reeds in order to set him on fire. But no, no, Gabriel forced down the thought and studied the boy. He looked terrified, pale and with his eyebrows an inverted V, poised to run but with nowhere to go: he was between Gabriel and the stream.

No, it was safe. He didn't have to be afraid of this child.

"I saw you yesterday." The boy gulped. "I had to know if you were real. But if my father followed, he'd see you—so I covered you up."

Gabriel nodded. He was still wearing wings, and he pulled them tighter. The boy must have worked hard to cover that much space.

"What are you?" asked the boy.

Gabriel didn't answer: how many times had demons turned themselves into gods doing just this sort of thing? But not giving an answer made it even more certain he'd come back to find a statue and daily sacrifices. When in doubt, try the truth. Gabriel said, "I'm a messenger."

The boy's eyes widened. "Is it a message for me?"

That hadn't worked as planned. "No, not yet."

"Oh..." Then the boy's eyes brightened. "What's your name?"

Gabriel said automatically, "Why do you want to know my name?"

"I just want to know what to call you."

Basic convenience, not idolatry. "I'm Gabriel."

"What a great name!" Brennos clambered closer, all his fear forgotten. "This is great—I'm talking to a real spirit! Can you fly?"

"Yes, but I can't carry you."

"Oh. Because I bet that would be fun. Wouldn't my father be surprised if I showed up flying?" The boy laughed. "Actually, are you allowed to leave this spot? I thought ghosts had to stay where they were. Were you killed here? Does it hurt to die? What do you do all day?"

Gabriel said, "I answer questions one at a time," and Brennos laughed again.

The boy's unruly black hair got in his eyes, but he just kept asking questions and then asking the next before Gabriel answered anything at all, so Gabriel sat back and assessed the situation: yesterday's scare hadn't harmed him, at least, and Gabriel thanked God for that. On the other hand, today's constant conversation wouldn't permit Gabriel to immerse in prayer again, but he thought that fit repayment for startling the boy the day before. That and the badgering of sounds, the boy's smell, the colors and the motion crowding his vision. They all gave him a headache.

Brennos pulled a flat bread from his pack and tore it lengthwise, then handed half to Gabriel. The boy stuffed his face while talking, and Gabriel took a tentative bite. Sense and smell burst on him, raw, but once those hit, his body wanted to keep eating. Sharing a meal. A social interaction.

A motion at the edge of the meadow caught his attention: a family of deer. A doe stood at a tree and gripped the bark with her teeth, pulled, and tore away a long strip. The naked wood gleamed beneath, just like Gabriel's heart. He flinched as a yearling did the same, peeling back the skin and leaving everything an exposed nerve.

Brennos said, "Hey, look, deer."

Gabriel couldn't look away because that tree looked just the way he felt: the outer edges stripped away and everything open to the world. God. He needed God, and God was gone.

He called the stag away from the tree before it stripped more bark, and as it stepped closer, Gabriel glanced at Brennos. "Have you ever touched a stag?"

Brennos shook his head. "My father says they're too wild to get near. You'd need a horse."

"I wouldn't," said Gabriel. "Stay still. Keep silence."

With closed eyes, Gabriel coaxed the stag until it advanced across the grass toward the stream. Gabriel sent images of safety, a sense of desire, and the animal kept moving until it stopped before him.

"You don't know whom you've come to," the Cherub murmured in his native language, "just what."

It was a good size, five hundred pounds and three cubits at the shoulder, five-pointed antlers sprouting from its skull. Gabriel drifted to a stand, then set his hand on the animal's flank and rubbed it. He scratched it behind the ears, rubbing those spots on the head that animals like because they're so difficult to reach. The stag enjoyed it, but Gabriel also used it as an opportunity to kill an army of parasites.

He reached for Brennos with his heart before remembering he needed to speak. "Come now."

Smaller when confronted by an angel and a wild animal, Brennos peeked around Gabriel's wings.

Gabriel took the boy's hand and laid it on the stag's flank. The animal huffed, but it didn't run.

"Wow." The boy laughed. "He's so...huge."

"Now, I want to offer you a trade." Gabriel made his voice low. "I'll keep this animal right here with us, and you can spend the day with me, but in return, I want you to teach me to act just like you."

The boy frowned. "What?"

"I want you to critique my performance," Gabriel said. "Tell me whenever I do something a real person wouldn't do. Messengers need to look like real people, and I can't do that yet. I need someone who's an actual person to tell me all my mistakes."

The boy said, "I don't want you to get mad."

Gabriel's brow furrowed. "Why would I get angry?"

"If I criticize you."

He shrugged. "I need to learn. I can't do that on my own."

The boy agreed, and then he said, "You don't move right, though. You're rough. You need to just...be smoother. And your face is really blank, like a mask."

Good. Exactly what he needed to hear. Gabriel made his wings vanish, and he led the stag back into the woods.

"Wow," Brennos gasped under the canopy of the forest. "This is great. I'm glad I came for you. I'm glad I found you. This is great."

"Don't be too excited," Gabriel said. "How's my walking now?"

They spent the day wandering or resting. Brennos showed Gabriel how to find good plants, and they picked berries or fruit just turning ripe. Gabriel asked every question he could come up with about living like a human, how to know what the body needed and how to meet those needs when they arose. He asked what fevers felt like and how you knew when your blood glucose levels had dropped, how to tell the difference between dreams and reality, how to attach varying levels of importance to rival sensory stimuli. "You said I asked too many questions," Brennos said at one point. "You ask even more, and I don't even understand what you're talking about."

In exchange, Gabriel made plants sprout and branches erupt into buds out of season and then into flowers. He spun up the wind into little cyclones that made dust devils dance at their feet. He turned the spray coming off a waterfall into ice in mid-air, and they watched it melt as it floated downstream. Gabriel brought honeycomb out of a beehive, and they tasted the honey while he kept the bees calm.

By sunset, with Brennos stumbling with exhaustion, Gabriel returned him to his home. The stag bounded back into the woods, and Gabriel made sure it knew where to find its family.

"That was great," whispered Brennos. "Thank you. Thank you so much."

"You're welcome," Gabriel said. "You've helped considerably."

Brennos said, "Do you want to do this again tomorrow?" When Gabriel replied only with silence and a lowered glance, the boy said, "Where are you going?"

"To the Holy Land."

The boy lunged forward to hug him. "Remember me."

Gabriel tensed under physical contact that felt more like an attack than a social gesture, and as soon as Brennos released him, he stepped backward. "Don't cry. Go home and know you've had today."

Brennos tried to step toward him again.

"I'll pray for you." Gabriel arrested the boy's movement with a long glance, and then the angel dissipated.

Tishri 7

Gabriel touched down in Jerusalem and took on a man's body. This time he changed his appearance: darker hair, a beard, and clothes to match the general population. Standing out didn't seem like the best idea, not when he hadn't fully mastered the art of carrying himself.

His senses exploded again like a tree stripped of its bark, but worse than before because now he'd made his form fully human. Assaulted at once by a half-dozen conversations, by the smells of smoke and sewage and sweat, by colors and motion, he felt nauseated and wanted to go numb, but what could he do?

Worse still, through his angelic senses he could feel the holes in the fabric of the city, the spiritual webbing that tied Heaven and Earth at this particular point. It smoldered, a fire not completely out but not quite ablaze. Continuously the spiritual coals devoured the city's soul, but not enough yet to destroy the spiritual connection. Hot enough and those coals could have demolished the earth. A second's hesitation, a handoff rather than a grab, and now he walked through a city that would survive the chaos to which God had resolved to abandon it. Try as he might, he couldn't ignore the fire, and he knew the angels in the city felt it too.

But he had no choice, so he tucked his head, pushed his hands into his pockets, and tried to walk the way Brennos had taught.

135

Gabriel went first to the Temple in the northern part of the city. Crowds pushed past along with their animals and other offerings: fruit and bread and wine. In the Temple courtyard, he struggled to find a place to pray, but so many people moved around. He got bumped too often, touched or breathed on. It felt just like Sodom, and he couldn't pray.

Further in, the priests were conducting sacrifices. Gabriel had nothing to sacrifice. He'd never needed to own anything, and anything he valued had already been taken away, so he instead found a group discussing a minor point of the Law, and he listened. They were getting it wrong, but when he tried to correct them, they shouted him down.

By the evening, even though the crowds thinned out, Gabriel had trouble thinking. He recognized this as the dizziness Brennos said could indicate dehydration and hunger.

He approached one of the priests. "Is there a place I could spend the night?"

The priest said, "There are plenty of lodging houses in the eastern part of the city. Ask there. They don't charge much."

Gabriel said, "I don't have any money."

The priest said, "You're out of luck then."

As the priest turned away, Gabriel stepped forward. "And where can I obtain food?"

The priest said, "Well, without any money at all, I guess you could beg."

And that was it for help. No one else had any better offers, so Gabriel found a secluded alley and returned to his angelic form. Relief rushed through him, and he chose a spot on a roof where he could spend the night in prayer. Quiet prayer. Prayer with no one touching him or yelling in his ear. Then at the next dawn, he returned to a man's form.

The city buzzed more as the days progressed toward Yom Kippur. The city grew only louder and more confusing, and Gabriel did his best to keep both his distance and his identity. When he got hungry or tired, he returned to angelic form just long enough to recharge. When someone asked his name, he used his God-given one. He might be cut apart from Heaven, but he didn't have to lie.

Tishri 10

For Yom Kippur, crowds filled the Temple precincts. Gabriel gave up trying to filter the sensory input and watched the goings-on from the Temple roof. Thousands of angels clustered there as well, not all of them guardians. Gabriel kept his slate eyes from focusing too long on anyone he knew, absorbing the churning motion of the white-clad crowd and the indistinct but interwoven voices. In this form at least he didn't have to deal with the touches, the smells, the demands of five conversations taking place in the same space.

Gabriel slipped through the roof into the sanctuary and watched the Holy of Holies, the seat of God on Earth. In addition to the angels packed inside, priests filled the anteroom of the Temple, and the chief priest read one of David's psalms. He wore a chest-plate with twelve stones, one for each of the tribes.

Gabriel's heart tensed as all the angels fell silent. Waiting. Atonement. Forgiveness.

The chief priest opened the curtain to enter the sanctuary, and Gabriel watched for a glimpse of the Ark.

He couldn't see it. He could see where it ought to be, but not the Ark.

Closing his eyes, Gabriel inhaled and tried to keep steady. Prayer continued around him, but his ears rang.

A touch at his arm.

Michael.

The Archangel indicated Gabriel should accompany him, and they both reappeared on a housetop a mile from the Temple. Gabriel had his wings tucked as close as he could to his body, his arms folded, his head bowed. With bleak eyes, he stared into the city.

"You didn't need to take me out of there. I couldn't see the Ark anyway." Gabriel spoke with his regard rather than his mouth, which had remained tight.

Michael sat beside him. "I could tell. I kept praying everything would settle on Yom Kippur and you'd have finished atoning, but as soon as you looked, it was obvious."

Gabriel tucked his head. "No, of course not. I can't be forgiven like a man because I'm not under the same covenant they are." Gabriel kicked at some rotted leaves on the roof. "It was ignorant to hope for more."

Michael wrapped a wing around him.

Gabriel shifted sideways and quoted the prayer for the day. "*The great trumpet is sounded. A still, small voice is heard. The angels shudder, saying, 'This is the day of judgment,' for God's very ministers are not pure before Him.* Least of all myself."

Michael said, "Go on. *But penitence, prayer, and charity may avert the harsh decree.*"

Gabriel let out a sigh. "I can't stay here."

Michael said, "Come back with me."

That wound inside reasserted itself, a burn exposed to air. Go home, as if it were that easy. "I don't have an assignment. I've got nowhere to go, and I can't do anything for you. I've decided to stay on Earth. I just can't stay in this city, near this Temple and these people. It's too much."

Michael blessed Gabriel before he left.

Tishri 11

Sensory stimulation seemed less intrusive in the dark, so Gabriel went solid at one of Jerusalem's gates just before dawn. Already he could hear noise from the city, but in the relative quiet, it was easier to focus. He needed to find work, and he needed to leave the city. Raphael had found work as a guide, so it made sense that he could too.

The first five people he approached didn't need a guide, and several others were only looking for temporary workers. Gabriel considered taking an offer for manual labor, but then he saw a man leading four donkeys while his wife guided their three children. Gabriel approached them, and as he did, he sensed a double-presence about the wife: she was pregnant.

"Could you use a guide?" he asked.

"Do I look like I don't know how to get home?" snarled the man.

He didn't appear lost, no. "I could help with the animals," Gabriel said. "Instead of a day's wages, I need food."

The man eyed him. "Well, you look strong enough."

"Please, Joachim," said the woman, "let him help. We have a long way to go."

The man spat onto the road dust. "All right. You get two meals, same as the rest of us, and you take those two animals."

Gabriel took hold of the tethers. The man stalked ahead, not saying anything else. Gabriel laid a hand on each donkey, then sent calm and sleepiness into their minds. After a few minutes they followed without tugging the leads.

They had traveled about a mile when the woman said, "What's your name?"

Until now, it hadn't been clear whether social speech would be accepted across the employer/hired man divide. It still wasn't, so he kept it brief. "Gabriel."

The woman smiled. "My husband is Joachim. The children are Ruth, Rebekah, and Joseph. I'm Martha."

Joachim said, "I hope you have places to go in the North. We're stopping at Lebonah."

Lebonah sounded as good as any other spot on the map. For now, Gabriel was enjoying the relative silence of the road. Fewer people, less motion, easier rhythm. The travel might give him a chance to get used to filtering his senses.

After an awkward pause, Martha said, "Where is your family from?"

Gabriel drew breath and then said, "It doesn't matter. I'm looking for work now."

Rebekah, the oldest, tugged at Gabriel's cloak. "Is your family with God?"

"Most of them." The child looked sad when he met her eyes. "The rest of us have scattered around the world."

"It's a holy and wholesome thought to pray for the dead," Rebekah chirped. "That's what the Levites say!"

Gabriel said, "It's good that you listen to their teaching."

The donkeys jostled against Gabriel, and he scratched their warm faces while he walked.

"Were your family farmers?" asked Martha.

Gabriel's gaze dropped. "In a way. We shepherded, too. Or anything else we found needed doing."

Martha said, "Joachim, isn't Saul ben Zadok looking to hire more shepherds?"

Joachim looked over his shoulder. "If you need work, he's a good man. If you work an hour for him, though, you work a whole hour. No one makes a fool of him."

Rebekah tugged at Gabriel's tunic again. As he looked down, she raised her arms and smiled hugely.

Even never having worked with children before, Gabriel recognized a request to be carried. He scooped her up and set her laughing on the back of one of the donkeys.

Joachim whirled. "He'll throw her."

But the little girl held with two fists to the mane, and the donkey didn't break stride even when her pumping legs pounded his sides.

When they made a camp for themselves, Joachim grudgingly admitted that Gabriel did work well with animals, and Martha fed Gabriel as promised. He paid attention to the way she cooked, trying to figure out what needed to be done to make food edible because invariably he'd need to do it himself. Soon after, eating was a relief because at least that one sense stopped pestering him for now.

Gabriel lay down that night with the stars for a tent and prayed before sleeping. Again his senses were at war, but a different war: he was exhausted from travel, true, but as soon as everyone went sleep, he tensed. Because sleeping in this form – how could he protect himself? Did he trust Joachim? One of the children flung out an arm and brushed Gabriel's back, and he sprang up, but no one else moved. So he prayed. He opened his angelic senses and prayed, and eventually his human form took him into darkness.

The heaviness began lifting, and as Gabriel awoke, he reached for God. Nothing.

Heart racing, he bolted up, stared, stared again, and then in one moment of heartbreak, he remembered.

Shoulders slumped, he closed his eyes. No. This wasn't right. This couldn't be.

Pressed against his leg was the young boy Joseph. Gabriel edged away, then poked the campfire. It had smothered under the weight of its own ashes. He ought to rebuild it, but for now he sat in the chill.

The stillness made his mind vibrate with thoughts, and the thoughts resounded off the distances, the stars, and the sparse trees stacked in the miles. In sleep, the children sprawled haphazardly. Martha and Joachim slept on a blanket behind him, leaning against one another as the night trudged into morning.

He ached. God should be available in a sunrise, in the starlight, in the curling breeze. But instead, flatness. Emptiness. The wound was back, and worse, Gabriel felt hungry again. It was so much to process, and he had no one to discuss it with.

For a moment he considered speaking to the family's guardian angels, but he pushed that from his mind because guardians have so much to do, and he might be an imposition. If he spoke to them once, they might feel pressured to speak to him every time he found himself alone. He might not, either.

Raphael. If anyone would have been able to help him through this, it would have been Raphael. But he couldn't, and who else would know?

A moment later, a bright presence wrapped around his world, and Gabriel looked up to see Saraquael. The Dominion said, "Good morning!"

It slipped out before Gabriel could stop it: "That's debatable."

The Dominion smiled with an ease that left Gabriel feeling crowded in the morning that only moments before had seemed empty. "I thought maybe you needed something."

Gabriel looked down. "Everything. But you can't bring it to me."

Saraquael settled on the ground beside the dead campfire. "Well, as long as I'm here, you have a message. The Lord says you've chosen a good family to travel with."

And as long as he was here, Gabriel might as well figure out what he was doing with his next few days: "What about this shepherd, Saul?"

"No word on that. The Lord's pleased with you this far, however, so I'm positive you'll make the right decision."

Saraquael's eyes danced with glitter, but Gabriel realized right now Saraquael was trying to read his mood and come up with something to say—the same way Michael had at the campfire. Trying to read him. Trying to solve the unsolvable. Saraquael breathed over the fire pit, and the fire returned to life.

Gabriel got up and paced, not turning to see if Saraquael would follow. "You don't have to stay with me, you know." He used his normal voice. "I'm not completely incompetent."

Gabriel felt Saraquael turn his attention to God.

Saraquael could—could just—

Gabriel spun in time to catch the residual brightness in Saraquael's eyes.

Saraquael looked inspired. "Why not keep a journal?"

Gabriel reeled from the reflected glory. "What?"

"To write all your thoughts about the time you spend here."

Gabriel stepped back. "Why?"

"You don't have to." Saraquael shrugged. "I thought it'd be worth suggesting, and God said you might want to try it."

"That I should keep my waking thoughts cataloged for posterity's sake? I suppose that will facilitate Satan's attacks, when he does his nightly reading."

"Satan won't ever get access to it, and it wouldn't serve *posterity* so much as you, for you to get your thoughts together. Don't get upset. It's not an order."

Gabriel paused. "I'm not upset."

"You look upset," Saraquael said. "I told God that if I were in your place I would turn out flurries of bad poetry, but you don't have the same sort of outlet. God said I could tell you. Keeping a journal wouldn't be a bad use of time. You write what you're feeling. Or thinking."

Gabriel's lips tightened.

"I could get you all the parchment and ink you want," Saraquael said, "and I'll give you a quill. I have six wings full."

Gabriel shifted his weight. "Everyone in Judah won't wonder what I'm doing?"

"No one has to know."

Gabriel forced a smile, and although he realized it didn't reach his eyes, he hadn't been in this body long enough to know which muscles to force to fake a whole smile. "Thank you. It's a kind gesture, but it's not right for me."

Just then Rebekah awoke, and Saraquael vanished.

"Will you let me ride on the donkey again?" she begged.

"You get up in a cheerful mood," Gabriel said.

"Uh-huh! Can I?"

"We'll see."

"No—say yes!"

Those tremendous eyes implored, like an angel's, and Gabriel responded without words, his eyes saying, *I'd like you to ride, but your father might disapprove.*

Her face melted in sorrow.

Gabriel's eyebrows arched into a resolution to try his best.

The girl nodded and went to wake her mother.

Only later, while walking the donkey on which rode both Rebekah and Joseph, did Gabriel realize that he had communicated with a child in the manner of angels.

My first entry:

When God asks nicely, you do it. I don't know what good a journal brings anyone, least of all myself, because it's humiliating. God already knows every word I would write and the words I refrain from writing, but Saraquael swears by this strange habit of making fleeting thoughts permanent.

I write on a sheet of parchment, after dark. I'll be able to join the sheets together and roll them into a scroll if I go through more than one page. I'm stretched out on my stomach with the fire before me so I can see the parchment and the individual words, and I've solved the problem of spying-eyes by writing in my native language. If any human tries to read over my shoulder, he'll be confused, to say the least.

Apparently if necessary, Saraquael will take away my written pages and replace them with unwritten ones. Isn't that a lovely thought? It's like filling a ceremonial vat with a spoon, and he thinks I may do it more than once.

Shouldn't we reserve writing for meditations and observations? But instead I'm watching a scrap of parchment and feeling my face get red because the fire is too hot—but if it weren't that then I would feel too cold, and I don't want to shiver tonight. What I do want is sleep. No one prepared me for that. It's easy to believe the human form bursts with energy if you've never spent more than twenty-four hours wearing it at one time. How convenient that Raguel says, "You must feel very strong," when all he's done is use it for a total of thirty hours in eternity. I find it ironic that those farthest removed from the experience are most able to see the good points.

So what am I supposed to write? Saraquael wasn't a tremendous help about that, other than acquiring the above-mentioned materials, and yes, he did search his wings for just the right feather. He's been generous. But he didn't tell me what to put on the parchment with the quill once I had it.

I'll continue tomorrow.

Tishri 14

When they reached Lebonah, Joachim brought him to the shepherd Saul ben Zadok.

A hard man with a predator's stare, Saul examined Gabriel for quite some time.

"You got hurt as a child," he said.

"Pardon me?" asked Gabriel.

"You move awkward. It's your hips, right?"

"Well, I fell, somewhat." Gabriel's cheeks grew hot. "I didn't think it worth mentioning."

Saul ran sun-dried fingers through his grey-wired beard. "Can you walk long distances? Are you able to run fast? Can you deal with animals?"

Gabriel made sure to stand straighter. "I made the trip from Jerusalem with Joachim and his family."

Saul still looked him over, eyeing the plain fabric of Gabriel's tunic and top coat, seeing the newness of his sandals. "He said you were good with the animals."

Gabriel watched Saul with calmness, but a calm of such intensity that Saul paused to study him.

"You're different."

Not different enough, Gabriel said with his eyes, but Saul didn't read that.

"You say your name is Gabriel? Welcome to my employ. Allow me to show you the place."

Shepherd

Kislev 2

Shepherding worked well for him, no question. Lots of time alone with the night, only a few others to work with, and common meals. Plus, Gabriel could make use of these over-ratcheted senses to warn about weather, about wolves, and about problems with the sheep.

"The wind's going to pick up," said Zachary, one of the shepherds.

Gabriel looked at the sky, shaking his head. "The worst is past."

"You're never wrong about that," said Jacob, the third shepherd, "but it just feels off."

Gabriel said, "In the Law it says—"

Zachary said, "Enough of the Law. We'll see what the wind does and whether the wind cares about the Law or the prophets."

Jacob snickered. "We could always preach to the sheep."

Gabriel bristled, but this had been going on for a while, trying to educate men who didn't recognize an education when they heard it.

The sun set as the flock settled down. The shepherds called back the stragglers and made sure all were accounted for. Gabriel said, "Who's taking first watch?"

A wolf howled.

All three shepherds tensed, and then another howl came from the other side of the field.

Gabriel picked up his staff. "Zachary, Jacob, get to the other side, and—"

Zachary raced away from the sheep, tearing off into the darkness. Gabriel turned to Jacob. "Your staff," he said. "Get it. Now."

The shepherd hesitated, picked up the staff, and then bolted when a third howl sounded.

The sheep had begun panicking, and Gabriel stretched out with his heart and imposed calm. He had to keep them together. They might lose one. He might get attacked. But he couldn't leave them undefended.

Another howl. He sent his senses into the woods to find the wolf minds and convince them not to strike. There was something...not wind, but as Jacob had said, something off. Something storm-like that wasn't a storm.

Gabriel called the sheep again, walking around them, touching their faces and saying their names. He paced and reached to touch the minds in the woods, and what he found left him shivering.

Gabriel crouched before one of the sheep and hoped his voice sounded steady. "You might as well come out now."

Only a moment passed, but then a shadow separated from the dark woods, drifted toward him, and seated itself on a rock. "I had wondered how to confirm your identity," it said, sounding amused, "and here you've saved me the trouble."

Satan. Here. Talking to him.

Gabriel's human heart pounded, and he shivered despite the tinge of Seraphic fire cracking in the air like the campfire's sparks.

"*Don't be afraid*," said the voice. "We were friends once, and now we can be again."

"Allow yourself to stand corrected."

"Still a Cherub."

"Entirely a Cherub."

Tishri

Cheshvan

Kislev

Tevet

Schevat

Adar

Nissan '

Iyar

Sivan

Tammuz

Av

Elul

The silence continued for long enough that Gabriel decided to walk away from the sheep. His adversary perched a stone's throw away, and if he struck, at least the sheep should be safe.

"So confirm its truth, the rumor I hear," Satan said, turning to watch him walk, "that God sliced you away from Heaven's mantle forever?"

Gabriel made his voice smoother than honey. "Where did you hear that?" He consciously stopped his fingers from clutching at his tunic.

"Everyone buzzed about your apostasy for weeks." Satan shrugged. "Some said you destroyed all of Gaul when you fell, so I was disappointed only to find a trench in the earth and the top knocked off a mountain."

It was so cold tonight. "At least I destroyed only a mountain top. You managed to take down the Earth."

"Well, I am a much greater spirit than you, as you certainly *know*, Cherub, although I doubt you're so weak that you can't take out more than a hill." Satan leaned forward. "From that I have to assume you weren't *thrown* out of heaven so much as you *fled*. Am I correct?"

Gabriel's so clearly forced smile did little to relax the rest of him. "You're flattering me."

Perching on the rock with his knees up against his chest and his twelve wings pulled in, Satan seemed a vulture in the night. "The truth isn't flattery. You're the closest in power to me, so I fully expected to find a chunk of the earth obliterated, not just a stand of tall grass and some extremely happy rabbits." He grinned, and starlight glittered in his platinum hair. "To be honest, Gabriel, I'm thrilled to be having this conversation at all. Tell me, how did it happen?"

The Cherub averted his eyes.

"Come on and answer. You always proclaimed that nothing true is not worth talking about, and when you live with us, we're going to cherish all the particulars."

"I won't live with you in Hell." Gabriel kept his eyes narrow, his tone even.

"Not now, perhaps, but we both know this dismal Earth wearies the spirit. You'll get bored and come with me sooner or later."

Some of the sheep had begin wandering. Gabriel looked up, but before he could do anything, Satan called them back. After a hesitation, they returned. Satan said, "This job is hardly a challenge. You just need to convince them to stay all in one place, and then it never occurs to them to leave. It's something like what He does." He turned back to Gabriel. "You're leaving me curious, and I can't stand that. What made you change your mind about Him?"

Gabriel glanced into the woods. He shouldn't look away from an enemy that close, not when he couldn't feel his every movement, but he didn't want Satan reading him either.

"We all have to realize something sometime, and it's easier if you do it sooner rather than later," Satan said. "You have no hope."

Gabriel looked back, glowering.

Satan leaned forward, and for a moment Gabriel caught the icy green of his eyes. "Trust me, because I've seen this before in every possible iteration. The ones who suffer the most are the ones who don't accept where they are."

Gabriel met those eyes levelly. "You don't know where I am."

"I don't need to have witnessed a suicide in order to recognize a corpse." Satan frowned. "Give me that much credit."

"It's not like that."

"You're smart, but you're avoiding the evidence. Reality itself leads me to only one conclusion."

Gabriel tightened his overtunic around his shoulders.

Satan sighed. "I wish you believed me."

"You wish that of everybody."

"Yes." A momentary honesty: Gabriel looked down to hide his compulsive grin. Satan continued, "But you're freezing, and there's no need to continue this conversation in the cold. Please accept my hospitality for an evening."

"I have a job to do."

"I can dispatch some of my fellows to oversee your duties until you return." Satan opened his hands. "Asmodeus would do it. He begged to be the one to approach you. On his knees, hands clasped, promised me anything I wanted. I refused him. Do you know why?" Hunger transformed Satan's face. "You're a Cherub in need of a Seraph to bond to. He wants you. I want you more."

Gabriel shuddered.

"Give yourself time," Satan said. "I know your kind, and you'll get crazy without that fire to invigorate you. When it gets bad enough that you start shaking, call. Either of us will be able to meet the need."

Gabriel battled nausea. "No, thank you."

"That's two of us you've disappointed in one night." Satan stood. "But my offer stands: whenever you choose to leave, you've got a place with us. Just one visit. It's not as if I'm asking you to decide immediately about being my co-regent." He allowed that to hang in the air. "I'll visit again tomorrow."

For a long time after the figure departed, Gabriel couldn't disperse the tension. Ridiculous stress hormones, lingering long after the danger had passed. Although he couldn't tell for sure. Even afterward, when he longed to slump backward and close his eyes, he did neither for fear that demon minions watched invisibly.

He wanted to call for Michael but didn't. He finally stood to walk among the sheep, and he knew tonight he'd have to stand every watch.

I have to write now. I'm holding God to His promise on this. He guaranteed no one would ever read what I'm writing, and that's what I want. No one, friend or enemy. I'm not even happy with Him reading it, but whom is that truly an indictment of?

What was I thinking? Why didn't I call for Michael? The instant Satan showed up, I should have told him to leave and then called Michael and had him make Satan leave. But—

He thinks I fell! He thinks I rebelled, or at least he's trying to make sure that's what I did. He called me a corpse. He's telling me just to accept where I am because he's seen it before. Is he trying to be helpful? Why did I listen to him?

It's too cold to think tonight. I'm not in my right mind. I was scared and the others had just deserted, and I didn't make good decisions. I want Raphael here to bounce this off of. Raphael would have fought him for me. I'd have asked Raphael to do it. I think I would have.

But Satan's found me, and now he'll keep finding me. They're going to have a constant vigil around me, and Satan's not going to care one whit about having them take shifts. He may take all the shifts and stay himself. I've got a guardian angel right now, only it's a dark one.

No, stop, be logical. So he's watching. What is he going to see? He can't read my mind. Yes, it's galling that everyone's chattering about me, but I knew that would happen. Guardian angels are constantly comparing notes, and naturally they don't care if a demon or two overhears. Yes, he called me a corpse, but he's a Seraph and they're prone to exaggeration. Plus, he has a lot to gain if he brings me to his side. He'd like nothing better. That much at least he was honest about. I think he meant the co-regent thing, too. I could tell he was genuinely baffled and all but vibrating inside to be sitting there talking to me like this, in this state.

Plus, now that I think about it, he was asking questions in an attempt to get me to specify exactly what's happened, what the timetable is, whether I think I can return, and what my crime was in the first place. I've just got to keep myself from talking to him, and I managed to do that tonight, somewhat. At least about important matters.

So even though he's found me, what's the worst that can happen? If he kills this body, I'll wake up in Heaven. Some worst-case-scenario that would be: being forced into Heaven. Or being forced to find another job.

All the same, I wish he hadn't found me. I wish he hadn't been sitting up there like an older brother trying to usher me through a difficult rite of passage.

Kislev 3

"Good evening!" Satan's voice came the next night—almost at sunrise.

"That's debatable." Gabriel squinted at him. A steady drizzle had pattered over the field all night, so he stood near the fire simultaneously trying to keep it going and keep his blood from freezing like slush. The other two shepherds had returned, abashed, but neither had offered to take an extra watch just because they'd abandoned Gabriel the night before. "I believe it's closer to 'good morning'."

"Please forgive me. Circumstances detained me."

The sheep had settled down to sleep off the rest of the night, not caring so much about the rain. In the tent, Zachary snored while Jacob mumbled a dream conversation.

Satan said, "They say you use your real name."

"Why not, *Satan?*"

Satan's eyes glittered. "That's so funny! I always thought you needed to develop a sense of humor."

Gabriel sighed.

"Yes, of course." Satan folded his arms. "Raphael would protest that you do in fact have a sense of humor." He tilted his head. "Speaking of Raphael, how is he these days? I'm surprised he isn't helping."

Gabriel made sure not to react. "He's doing fine where he is."

"He's not exactly loyal if he's not here," Satan said.

"I never asked for his loyalty."

"I wouldn't expect you would have." Satan frowned. "But I remember his undivided heart, and it must have ripped him in half when you abandoned him."

Gabriel's jaw tightened.

"Since he's not here," Satan said, "I have only three options to consider. He could be angry at you for leaving him. He could be ashamed of what he perceives as your failure. Or you might have gotten disgusted with him when you decided servitude wasn't worth the bribes."

Gabriel wrapped his hands in his overtunic.

"If it's the first two, don't worry," Satan said. "He'll come back. Even in the third case, it's merely a matter of time. I'll help."

Gabriel glared at him, his heart pounding. "You leave Raphael alone. I promise this: if you harm him or target him, you can forget about these pleasant nighttime conversations. I won't have anything to do with you if I find out, even once, that you approached him."

Amused, Satan raised his hands as if to indicate surrender.

He sat on the same rock as last night, and he studied Gabriel for a long while. Gabriel got to his feet and walked to the sheep. A moment later, although it continued drizzling, the rain stopped soaking into him, and his clothes grew dry. He looked over his shoulder at Satan, who shrugged.

"I shouldn't have brought him up," Satan said. "I won't again."

Gabriel bit back what he wanted to say.

Satan said, "A human frame couldn't support your wings, could it?"

The words came quicker, much easier than talking about Raphael. "The form would be top-heavy, structurally speaking, causing chronic low-level stress on the spinal column, and it would never fly anyhow. The bone structure is grounded in the wrong places, and the weight would exceed its capacity. At best, a solid angel would glide, and more likely plummet."

Satan grinned, and Gabriel caught himself smiling too. His muscles had tensed involuntarily: that adrenaline again. He looked into Satan's eyes and then looked deeper, into his heart. A Seraphic flame danced in the depths of that shadow, the angelic part of him that kept captivating Gabriel's inner sight.

A blush had risen over the mountains ahead of the sun. The clouds seemed to seal down the light, and everything else appeared in shades of grey and black. Satan looked toward the light at his side and then back again to Gabriel.

Gabriel walked through the sheep, mentally keeping a tally of which were where and what they were doing. His legs got wet as he moved over the ground, but the rain continued avoiding him. As he walked, he sang, but his voice cracked when he tried to hit a high note.

How mortifying. His angelic voice could have done it easily. He tried to keep singing, but then behind him, Gabriel heard music.

He turned to find Satan playing the ten-stringed lyre.

Satan met his eyes as he played, taking the song through its entire melody, weaving his Seraphic fire into the tune so it swirled about a Gabriel who listened transported. He could remember the last time he'd heard that lyre played by that hand, and he wrapped his arms around his stomach.

Satan halted abruptly, leaving only the susurration of rain. "I didn't mean to stop you. You have a beautiful voice."

Gabriel shook his head, scattering raindrops.

"You *had* a beautiful voice in your rightful form," Satan said. "You hit notes I couldn't even think, and you made it sound simple. I loved playing for you. You made me sound better."

Gabriel forced a smile. "Maybe I did."

"Do go on," Satan said. "Even if it's just a concert for the sheep."

Gabriel tucked his head, and rain ran down his neck. He kept his song to himself as he walked back to the animals.

No, no, no, no, no.

Even I can't count the ways I mishandled things tonight. What am I thinking? Am I stupid?

I don't want to leave God. I love God. I miss God. I don't want to leave Him. I want to go back. So what am I doing talking to his enemy? Why am I tolerating his presence? Why did I say he could continue coming to me if only he left Raphael alone?

That music... I thought I'd never hear him play again. He wrote the most beautiful song I ever heard, back before the winnowing, but no one's played it since. You could hear his skill even tonight. With the fields so empty, it sounded like a concert in a theater, and the rain like applause. He still can do that.

This is going to get back to them. Michael's going to hear about it. Zachary and Jacob's guardians aren't going to keep their mouths shut. They're going to tell everyone they come across that Satan is pursuing me, and that I'm listening. And they're going to want to shake me and ask me what on earth I'm thinking, and even I don't know what on earth I'm thinking, because I can say right now that I should tell him to go back to Hell and leave me alone, only I haven't done that. Not even once.

Isolation makes up part of my punishment. Asking the other angels to stay might anger God. It might anger them. It might keep them from some more important work. I know they pity me, and they wouldn't leave if I told them how hard this is. I promised myself to bear up as best I could, but I never anticipated that I might seek out a companion in Lucifer. If that's what I'm doing.

I could have called for help. I should have. But like a pathetic, paralyzed, hungry, shivering and lonely human being, I didn't react. Satan's a peer and a superior, and it feels so good to tease him and banter and converse on a level I know I can.

I'm paralyzed. I don't know how to stop it. I don't know even if I want to. God, help me.

Kislev 4

God, my Father, I'm sorry about what happened last night.

I need your help. I don't know what to do. I know what I should be doing, but I know I'm not doing it, not doing it right, and last night I gave him one hundred percent of everything he expected to get out of me.

I wasn't prepared for him to show up that way. I figured there'd be a preamble, a "Hello" when I could turn and tell him to leave, but when he announced his presence by reciting epic poetry, I found myself intoxicated by his voice, his cadence, and the fact that the poem really was splendidly written in a language I hadn't heard for months—and then just when I gathered myself to interrupt him, the way he pre-empted me and said, "Isn't it dynamic how the writer sets up truth and beauty as diametric opposites?" and instead of saying, "Go away," I replied with, "The writer is setting them up as tropes, not opposites," and suddenly we were off. How long did we argue about metaphor, poetic structure, synecdoche, whether specific lines had been written with a certain symmetry to aid in oral translation of the poem from one poet to the next, and on and on...? And then he produced three competing versions of the same poem and spread them out, side by side by side, and he and I were side by side, poring over the different lines, pointing out where there were alterations and where some phrases were inexplicably the same through all the versions. It was like an intellectual orgasm.

I can't think of anything more dangerous to me: an unbonded Cherub and an unbonded Seraph alone in the middle of the night with only a huge debate between us. And in the thick of it he said, "Are we going to argue like this when you're my co-regent?" and I didn't even pause, I just shot back with, "Only if you want to do things right," and he laughed out loud, and I laughed with him.

By that point things had gone too far—he started asking questions and I engaged with them. What did you do? / Something stupid. / Is it forever? / No, just for a while. / Are you mad at Him? *More and more personal, more detailed. It was only when he asked about Raphael that I stopped cold, because I could see Raphael's eyes in my mind and I knew if he were here, he'd have driven off Satan and then turned next on me: outraged, disbelieving, injured. I held that in my mind, and Satan changed the subject, but for a moment there, he had me completely. He got everything he tried to.*

I'm sorry. I'm sorry, and I don't know what to do. I can't even run away—he's going to find me. No matter where I go, what form I take, he's going to find me. Please stop him from coming back. Please give me the presence of mind to yell for Michael when he returns, or just send Michael anyhow, or at least give me enough grace to say no. No, no, no, just repeat No until he leaves.

I love you. But he keeps showering me with the things I want, and every time it's different so I'm not prepared. Please help me. I'm going to fall.

Gabriel exploded out of dreams, that first gasp as he reached for God and his heart closed on nothing, and then the search, the search again, and then the awful, awful, awful memory.

He curled over himself, nauseated and defeated.

"Wow," said Satan's voice. "Do you do that every time?"

Gabriel groped for anything that resembled composure. "You had better have a good reason."

"You called for me."

Gabriel sat upright so quickly his heart pounded.

Satan said, "Oh, you were dreaming? I thought you'd finally come to your senses. I wouldn't have disturbed you otherwise."

Gabriel wrapped his arms around his legs and tucked down his head. That empty burn inside, that tingle from Satan's fire so close, and the simultaneous horror that in his dreams he might have called for someone and it might have been Satan. Might have. He could be lying. What did Zachary and Jacob think when he woke up this way? Where were they?

Gabriel looked around: the sheep remained settled, but both Jacob and Zachary were out cold. "I need to wake up Jacob. It's his watch."

"I'll shepherd for you."

"Don't put yourself to any trouble." Gabriel scrambled to a stand. "Sheep are dull."

"As are men. Gabriel, come with me."

Satan touched his shoulder, sending an electricity straight to Gabriel's stomach. "I want you with me." Satan stepped closer. "You don't belong to this, with these flies on a dunghill. You need to be among your own kind, with those who appreciate you. Why must you limit your extreme abilities to forecasting the weather and singing to sheep? Sheep are stupid. You hadn't engaged in a decent conversation in weeks, and it's made a wreck of you. Come with me."

Gabriel felt clumsy in the midnight air. No, there was no way he'd called Satan, no way that Jacob and Zachary had fallen asleep accidentally. This had to be a setup. Satan was spiritually battering him. But even now he only wanted sleep, and Satan demanded a decision.

"You can't stay like this," Satan said. "You've lost your edge. I pity what you've become, but it isn't so late that you couldn't recover yourself. These *things* sleeping in the field don't care about you, and your former friends—where are they? Shouldn't they have come by now just to get rid of me? If God cared, wouldn't He intervene?" He waited as if for lightning, but none came. "I'm the only one who cares what you decide. I want you with me."

Gabriel drifted like a leaf from whatever wakefulness he had achieved. "But you're lying."

"Not this time."

Gabriel closed his eyes, nearly sound asleep standing upright. It was so hard to think, so hard not to drift back into dreams. Keeping his eyes closed, he sat on the ground.

"I mean it about offering you co-regency." Squatting beside him, Satan rested his hands on Gabriel's. "You'd be so useful to me that any loss of my own authority would be negligible. You don't have to have your own army. It can be your own library, your own research staff—anything you want. You want Seraph fire; I can give you Seraph fire. We can play music together. We can debate. We can invent whole systems of philosophy. You won't have to interact with anyone you don't choose to, but you can have one hundred percent access to me whenever you want. We have what you need, and it's what they refuse to give you any longer. Just give me one thing: give me a chance."

Gabriel pulled back, shaking his head.

"You're not the angel you were." Satan for the first time brought a sharpness into his voice. "You're playing with half-measures, breaking your own bones. You try to be human while not letting go your angelic self, standing with two continents drifting apart beneath your legs. The strain will tear you in pieces, Gabriel. Nothing can survive midway. If you have to pretend to be a man, then you need to do it the whole way, but you can't. Your soul is as angelic as they get, and our kind don't sit well in flesh. We surpass them in every way. Even in a body, you hold onto your angelic nature. Therefore hold it completely and stay with me, either as my guest or as my prince."

Gabriel wouldn't open his eyes. "No."

Satan's voice darkened. "This halfway-house of a body you're wearing doesn't make you any more a human being than I am. Oh, you breathe and piss like a human, but where does that get you?"

"No."

Satan leaned closer, his breath alighting every one of Gabriel's raw nerves. "You're lowering yourself to the level of a lizard for no reason. You're degrading our whole species, and that nauseates me. These treeless monkeys think you're strange, detached, and hardly trustworthy. They all know you're not really a monkey. They just haven't figured out what."

Gabriel's jaw tightened. "No."

"Isn't being your full self better than wasting half your life sweating and eating?" Satan said. "You're shameful to be with."

"Then go away!" Gabriel leaped to his feet and towered over Satan for a moment until Satan stood too, a head taller and with wings flared.

"I'll take you with me!"

"No!"

Satan tried to speak again, but then he stopped, just stopped. And in the next moment, eyes livid, he filled the air with fire. "You Fatherless wretch! Get used to feeling lonely, because it's permanent."

And then – nothing. He was gone.

Gabriel stood trembling. That was it. No poetry, no philosophy, no banter...Satan wouldn't appear in person for a long time, if ever. An urge to call him popped into Gabriel's throat, but he whispered, "No."

The cool air prickled his skin and he concentrated on that, on the sound of the flock breathing and the expansion of his own lungs. Let the senses distract him from the temptation. He didn't bother waking the other shepherds. Instead he walked among the sheep.

Dear Father, thank you. I couldn't have... Thank you.

Kislev 5

Watching the sun rise, Gabriel combed every aspect of that exchange, Satan's every gesture and projection. He analyzed the emotional manipulation and the tactics. He ran through his every possible response, and on balance, "No" had been pretty effective. But he flinched whenever he remembered those words like knives.

Get used to feeling lonely, because it's permanent.

If God cared, wouldn't He intervene?

Shameful to be with.

Shameful. Of course he should be ashamed. He spent thousands of years telling everyone to obey the law and then he didn't do what God told him to do. If the angels weren't ashamed to be with him, that was to the credit of their charitable natures. But God would be ashamed of him by now, certainly. He was trapped. He'd come down here to help people, and instead he was with a pair of shepherds whom he couldn't make care about the Law. Given that, how could he possibly make up for what he'd done?

And last night – what if he hadn't actually rejected Satan enough? What if he'd flirted with evil too long, or if he'd crossed the line into sin and just didn't know it? If he'd hesitated too long? Why would God ever trust him to work with His creatures again?

He ate his morning bread and tried to talk logic to himself: God had given him the grace to say no. That's not what God would do to someone who'd sold his soul. This residual fear was just a temptation. Of course, God still might never entrust any task to him again, ever. But not because of last night.

As the sun climbed, Gabriel mentally tallied the sheep and then walked to the far end of the flock to gather up some stragglers. He talked so they'd follow, keeping his voice low and calm.

"I don't know that I'm entirely nauseating," Gabriel said, and one of the sheep butted its head on his leg. He rubbed it behind the ears. "I'm nauseating to Satan, but I'd probably be that regardless. He was tactically flawless last night – almost. But he tipped his hand."

He had three ewes following now at the bottom of the hill, with Zachary and Jacob at the top. He could hear their chatter just as well as he could feel the grass brushing against his legs and smell the dirt in the sheep fleeces. Too much sensory feedback. "That's been the wedge he used to get at me. I can't be all these things at the same time and still be what's important. It leaves the gate wide open for Satan to parade through."

One of the ewes started pulling up grass, and Gabriel let her. There was no hurry to get back to the rest, and what was up there for him anyhow?

"I'm not one of the Seven anymore," Gabriel said, "but I'm still an angel. I'm not a human, but I'm still a son of God. And I'm not supported by my friends, but I'm not without allies. Or am I?"

Another ewe came up beside him, so Gabriel sat on the grass and looked at her at eye-level. She nuzzled him, and he rubbed her face. "I can't be a demi-god and shepherd for the rest of the year. Satan nearly got me, and I can't let that happen again. If the problem is having a split nature, then I have to un-split it."

Go home. Be an angel again. A useless appendage to the Heavenly Host, but safe while he ran out the clock.

Or, go the other way.

Gabriel shuddered. At the top of the hill, Zachary said something low and Jacob laughed out loud. The sun gleamed off a rock. One of the sheep bleated.

Gabriel took a deep breath, feeling the full stretch of his ribcage and diaphragm, and then he submerged the rest of his angelic heart.

It hurt at first – no, not hurt, more like the deer stripping the bark from the tree again, only this time he was stripping his own bark. Instead of his senses sharpening, they dulled. The light dimmed and he couldn't hear Zachary any longer, couldn't feel the angels at the top of the hill, couldn't smell the flowers past the scent of the sheep. He worked his fingers down into the sheep fleece and closed his eyes because of the questions, the things he didn't know, the things he couldn't predict and would have to guess. The smallness. He hadn't expected to feel small.

"Gabriel!"

He startled, looked up the hill. Three people now, not two. He hadn't heard the third approach, and he should have. No, he shouldn't have. He shouldn't ever have been able to do that. He didn't know who the third person was, and that was the way it should be for a man.

Gabriel called the ewes, and they followed him up the hill.

He hadn't quite gotten to the top before he recognized Saul. The ewes blended back into the flock, and Gabriel approached. "Good morning, sir."

Saul grunted. "Okay, now all three of you, I want a full count of these sheep."

Gabriel couldn't just know how many there were this time. They sorted and counted until Saul was satisfied all were present. Then he said, "Now, tell me about that wolf attack."

Zachary said, "We drove them off!"

Gabriel tensed.

Saul looked him right in the eye. "And how'd you do that?"

"I took up my staff," said Zachary, raising his even now, "and we made noise and rustled the bushes and threw rocks into the underbrush."

Saul looked at Jacob. "Is that true?"

Jacob looked at Zachary. "Yes, sir."

Saul turned to Gabriel. "And what did you do?"

Gabriel said, "I stood there. I walked between the wolf and the sheep, and I patrolled there. Standing on two legs makes men appear larger to predators, and standing without running makes men appear threatening."

Saul said, "Only one wolf?"

"There were more in the distance," Gabriel said. "Only one approached."

His heart pounded, and his lips were numb because Saul was very close, and he didn't want to lie, but what if Saul kept demanding the truth?

"Were you afraid?" said Saul.

Gabriel swallowed. "Not at first. By the end? Terrified."

Saul said, "Go on. And what did you do to that one wolf?"

Gabriel said, "I talked. I kept saying, 'No.' I held onto the only weapon I had, and I guess you could say it wasn't a normal wolf, so – it left. It took its pack with it."

Saul kept looking into his eyes, and then he said, "I'm appointing you overseer."

"What?" Zachary shouted. "That foreigner?"

"Yes, that foreigner!" Saul spun to face Zachary. "And if *that foreigner* had brothers, I'd hire them in a heartbeat and leave you two standing in the city gates begging for the chance to dig ditches!"

Gabriel stepped backward. "But—"

"You deserted my animals!" Saul was shouting at Zachary, who'd gone ashen. "My work is keeping sheep, not giving alms to Israelites."

Zachary said, "I didn't desert them – I stayed and fought."

"You ran into the town, and you got drunk. I don't know what that one did," Saul said, gesturing at Jacob without even looking, "but I do know he lied to me too. Gabriel stayed, and I only have all my sheep because he did. Which one did the job I ordered? The Israelites or the foreigner?" He turned to Gabriel. "I've got men coming with another flock I've just acquired, and they're going to be yours too. Two men and fifty sheep." His eyes narrowed. "The sheep will be nervous and harder to handle until they get settled in, but I trust you."

Schevat 20

In the pouring rain, Gabriel coughed until his lungs hurt. *An airway that doubles for food transport is a major design flaw,* he told God. *Having the mucus membranes drain into it only compounds the problem. Surely you could have found a better construction.*

The sheep huddled miserably, so he didn't have much to do, which was just as well. His head ached.

Zachary reported to him. "All accounted for. Do you want me to have the sheep pray the evening Shema?"

Gabriel murmured, "I'm sure they please the Lord just fine without our help, thank you."

Zachary stalked away. Jacob looked abashed, then followed him. Gabriel remained in the shelter of the tree, surrounded by as many of the sheep as could crowd beneath.

At least the two new shepherds – twin brothers – didn't harbor the same animosity Zachary did. Their sheep had arrived in sad condition, though, haphazardly shorn sometime during the summer and dreadfully skinny. Gabriel had done his best to get those sheep into good fields, but they were still skittish, and he couldn't make the grass grow lush for them.

Now the rains had come, and he'd received the gift of learning about upper respiratory infections and the subsequent response of the human immune system. Fascinating in its own way, when he could remember a Cherub should be fascinated by new experiences.

He coughed again until his ribs ached. One of the new shepherds arose from the fire in front of the tent and brought him a cup shedding steam. "Thought you'd like this."

"Thanks." Gabriel wrapped his hands around the cup, warm with a welcome that left him homesick. He sipped, and the broth traced down his throat.

Seraph fire. Scalding broth was as close as he'd come to that for a while, and he closed his eyes.

"You want to take a break?" said the shepherd.

"Just a little longer." It would be so welcome to collapse in the tent and let his immune system fight a thousand tiny battles. But the warmth in his palms left him homesick, and he'd rather be homesick among sheep than in a tent with Zachary and Jacob.

The other shepherd stayed with him, and Gabriel relaxed. Sometimes the lack of Seraph fire left him shaking and nauseated. Right now it just left him sad. Raphael. He wouldn't have minded standing in the rain with Raphael.

The second of the new shepherds came from the tent and insulted his brother, who slapped him on the back and called him something even worse. Gabriel tensed, and then both brothers laughed.

In the next second he realized: envy! This was a temptation to envy. So he set it aside and reminded himself of the good bond these brothers had. And then, because he'd learned temptation didn't always go away after you reasoned with it, he drained the rest of the broth and headed for the tent where he kept his one bag of belongings. As soon as he entered, Zachary huffed and left, but Jacob only sat in the corner, looking miserable.

Gabriel unrolled his scroll and wrote, the date, then "Envy" and "passed" along with a few of the details.

Jacob said, "What's that?"

Gabriel said, "Taking inventory."

How handy to be their foreigner: he could

Tishri

Cheshvan

Kislev

Tevet

Schevat

Adar

Nissan

Iyar

Sivan

Tammuz

Av

Elul

write anything he wanted in Heavenly script and his companions, barely literate in Hebrew, could believe whatever they wanted. Gabriel maintained a running chart.

Sin	Commentary
Gluttony	I kept thinking about the extra barley cake after dinner, but I let Zachary take it instead. Zachary then tried to make me drink more wine than would be prudent, but I reminded myself that puts me to sleep within a half-hour, and I said no. Zachary finds it amusing. (Sub-temptation: anger.)
Lust	That dream was pretty startling. I distracted myself and that seems to have helped.
Anger	Was irrationally irritated by one of the rams misbehaving. Asked Jacob to take over for a few minutes.
Laziness	It was so hard to awaken and get started for the day, but I forced myself to get moving. It's easier if I don't take rests during the day. I'll try to get to sleep earlier.
Pride	Caught myself thinking I'm smarter than Jacob and Zachary. It's only being honest to admit this, so I'm not entirely sure how to tackle this temptation other than to refuse to act on it.
Envy	Wished I could have camaraderie like the twins do, but reminded myself God isolated me for a reason. Distanced myself so as to prevent a recurrence.

Satan was too cunning an adversary to leave a matter such as sin up to personal impressions. Gabriel needed data, so he tracked the trends of the temptations. He'd taken to noting the specific steps he'd used when presented with any individual temptation, that way if they increased in difficulty he would be able to analyze what tactics had succeeded and extrapolate for more complex situations.

He glanced at Jacob, who continued watching. It wasn't just demons who could tempt, of course. He had four souls to work with, and they surrounded Gabriel's days with coarse language, coarse stories, and coarse alcohol.

Jacob said, "Do you have to keep track of a lot of things now that you're an overseer?"

Gabriel paused. "The sheep are depending on us."

Jacob's voice dropped, and his eyes darted to the tent entrance. "Right, but, do you think I could ever do something like that?"

Gabriel kept writing. "I don't see why not."

Jacob said nothing else, just sat glumly. Gabriel prickled with that "watched' feeling, and he tried to ignore it.

He'd developed his initial perspective on sin by debating with the other Cherubim. This—this was different. It was one thing to discuss boredom and the need for belonging which might drive a man to drink to excess, but when you actually saw fellow shepherds enthusiastically engaged in the process, it seemed simultaneously more baffling and more understandable. Trying to tell them what they were running from, and another way to fill the emptiness, well it left them laughing at him or mocking God, and that was even worse.

Their small-mindedness wasn't a temptation against Gabriel; it was just demons playing with easier souls when Gabriel didn't succumb to them, so maybe that made their sins his fault. But on the other hand, they were making choices. Like Jacob right now choosing to stare at him instead of doing something productive.

Gabriel said, "Why don't you play your flute?"

Jacob said, "Really?"

Gabriel said, "Sure. Music is pleasing to God."

Fortunately God had set the bar low in terms of music's ability to please him, and at the very least, it would get Jacob's attention off his writing.

Out came the flute, and Jacob raised it, but then stopped. "The sun's setting," he said, almost a question.

Gabriel refrained from saying that's why he'd lit the lamp.

Jacob continued, tentative, "Maybe we could pray the evening Shema together?"

Gabriel sat up, heart pounding. "Sure."

What had he done? How had he gotten this kind of change in Jacob?

They prayed (*Lay us down, Lord our God, in peace...*) but Gabriel kept battling distraction. Praying. With Jacob. Jacob who followed Zachary who hated him. And yet here they were.

At the end of the prayer, Jacob picked up his flute and played a melody Gabriel recognized from weeks of tending the sheep. Gabriel put away his parchment. He'd need more sheets soon, and a way to fasten them into a scroll, but he hadn't spoken to any of the angels in so long that he hesitated to ask now. Instead he wrote smaller and smaller, keeping his thoughts more compact. If he called Saraquael, what would Saraquael say? Would he even come?

The last angel he'd spoken to was Satan. They'd remember that.

Gabriel lay down with his head on his pack, and he closed his eyes while Jacob kept playing. The rain pattered against the side of the tent, and he could no longer hear the crackle of the fire in the shelter of the entrance. His exhausted body melted into the ground, the muscles unclenching until he could feel his face aching where he'd been frowning. The new shepherds said he always looked sad, and maybe he did. He should. *What did I do to get Jacob to pray with me?* he prayed. *I'd do it with Zachary, too. Father, I need to teach them, but they haven't been listening.*

And he'd been so annoyed with Jacob right before then. What if he'd snapped at the man? Would Jacob have asked? Or would he have counted it as yet another reason to reject the Law?

His thoughts drifted through any way he'd interacted with Jacob in the past two days, analyzing the way he'd told him which field to bring the sheep to how he'd instructed him about one of the rams and even a comment about a meal. Nothing stood out, and Gabriel's thoughts drifted, and his eyes closed.

A hand landed on his shoulder and shook him. He reached for God, and when his heart clasped on nothing, he leaped up, gasping, looking around the dark tent. Behind him, laughter. Zachary. "Get up, scaredy-cat. It's your turn."

168

Zachary thought it hilarious when Gabriel awoke frightened. Gabriel thought he traded watches with the other shepherds just so he'd be the one to awaken his overseer every time. Gabriel swallowed the resentment (*Note temptation, anger*) and tightened his overtunic before going outside.

Zachary had let the fire die (*Note renewed temptation: anger*) so Gabriel didn't bother with it before doing a walk-around of the flock. The rain had let up, but the wet grass made his sandals slippery.

God, what do I do about Zachary? That he could make someone angry enough to sin had never occurred to him before now. What would possibly be worth angering God? How much could he have annoyed the man if he'd sacrifice God's love in order to enact small inconveniences against another human?

Gabriel got the fire going again, then sat with it at his back as he watched the shadowed forms of the sheep at rest. Shivering, he huddled around himself.

The fire crackled to Gabriel in a language he could no longer understand, but the fire didn't care and continued a sentence in which he already had lost the verb, and which never could come again in time unless to displace another message, even more valuable than this one and indecipherable without it.

He shut his eyes and stopped the nasty thought that he had lost a year: a year God had created just for him and he had returned, saying *no thank you*.

God, my Father, my God, I'm so sorry. I'm trying to make some value of this mess, but I can't. Jacob turned around and it wasn't even my doing. Zachary's getting hardened and that probably is. Every time I try to fix things, I end up making it worse. Please don't stay angry at me.

He coughed again, but the coughing didn't hurt nearly as much as the peeled-apart feeling. It couldn't scab yet, not for months, and exposure to the open air could sting without forming a hard layer beneath which to heal. Souls couldn't toughen, of course, only scar, and who knew what pattern this scar was leaving for everyone to cringe at for the rest of eternity?

The fire was stronger now, so Gabriel added a knotted bit of wood. Dampened by the rain, it crackled and smoked. Gabriel wondered at the knots, looked into himself and saw all the knots in his spirit, a tree with the bark growing to cover a fungus but leaving the wood bumpy underneath.

So many midnight thoughts. He felt cluttered, and this body only made it worse. He could shed it, could spend the rest of his year in private prayer until discernment and reading and contemplation cleared him of all the twists. Go. *I'm not doing any good here,* he prayed. *This was a mistake on top of another mistake. They're better off without me.*

He hesitated. *Note temptation: despair? Is that despair? Or is that realism?*

Did God want this? Rain and bronchitis, nasty shepherds and hunger, heavy labor, broken bones, and possibly death? He wasn't helping anyone by doing these things.

It popped into his head: maybe they weren't the ones that needed the help.

He frowned. The sheep? The sheep would have been scattered if those had been real wolves, but they weren't.

No, not the sheep.

He thought. *We agree I have to suffer because I disobeyed. But I'll suffer no matter where I am. That's part of why I'm here: I figured I might as well help others while I was suffering. Why this suffering?*

Nothing came to him at first. Maybe it was this specific kind of suffering. Maybe he needed to experience being hated and being sick in order to learn something specific about God, something he wouldn't have learned otherwise. Probably in a thousand years, he'd be glad for having learned it. Unless he let being down here change him so much that he didn't even appreciate knowledge. That would be awful.

He hesitated. Or would it? Didn't he always say suffering caused growth? Maybe God wanted him to grow. He'd grown after Sodom, learned better how to protect himself and how to isolate his analysis from his emotions. Maybe he had to do that again.

In which case, he should assist the process. *Father, if you want me to stay here, please use this time to sculpt me. To cut away the non-essential parts and keep me focused on the better ones.*

The fire kept chattering, and Gabriel waited, but he didn't feel any different. There should be more, though. What more did God want him to say?

And if it's necessary, if my being myself hinders You, then burn me out completely and remake me.

But nothing came of his offer, no matter how long Gabriel waited at the fire and watched the sheep.

Adar 16

In Heaven, Michael looked over Dobiel's shoulder at a map. About to point out a strategic weak spot, he halted in place. In his heart he heard: "*Michael!*"

He flashed away without hesitation, because that was Gabriel.

Michael appeared in Gabriel's tent with his sword already drawn, and he only just registered the demon hovering at his bed before striking. It howled and fled, and Michael dropped down through Gabriel's body. Pulse – racing. Adrenaline – pumping. Gabriel gasped for air as if terrified.

One of the other shepherds was laughing out loud. "Poor thing. Did you have a bad dream?"

Michael glared, but immediately another shepherd said, "Quit it, okay? Yes, he had a nightmare. Don't you ever get tired of acting like a brute?"

Michael looked at the guardians in the tent, who wore a mixture of concern and resignation: they hadn't been able to dislodge Asmodeus when he came.

Gabriel was still shaking, and Michael made himself visible just to him. After a moment, Gabriel met his eyes, registered him, and then whispered, "You—"

Michael said, "I'm going to hunt him down and chain him. He won't bother you again."

Gabriel sat forward urgently. His hands had knotted in his blanket, but they were shaking.

The second shepherd, the one that hadn't acted like a jerk, approached Gabriel. "Are you all right? It's okay. You were dreaming, that's all."

"I'm not supposed to dream." Gabriel put his face in his hands. "Not like that. That was real. That was real."

"No. Here." The shepherd put his hand up to Gabriel's. "This is real." He put his hand on Gabriel's bag, the one he always kept at his side. "This is real. You're okay."

Another shepherd put his head in the door of the tent. "Everything okay?"

Gabriel said, "Is it my watch?"

"No. Go back to sleep."

The other two shepherds returned to their beds, and Gabriel curled onto his side. "Michael," he breathed. "You came."

"You called." Michael slipped his sword into its sheath and sat next to Gabriel. "I said I'd come if you called."

Gabriel curled tight, knees to his chest, hands over his face. Words popped into Michael's head: *Can you stay? Please?* Staining the words was fear, pure fear. Michael touched Gabriel's shoulder and squeezed.

Was it real?

"No," Michael whispered. "It was a dream, nothing more."

It wasn't just a dream, Gabriel sent. *It was everything.*

When Gabriel hadn't fallen asleep after another five minutes, Michael placed his palm over Gabriel's eyes and forced sleep on him.

Adar 17

Throughout the night Michael sat beside Gabriel, praying. Gabriel slept beneath a blanket, but Michael could outline his whole form, the way he lay on his left side, the lower leg at only a slight angle, the upper one positioned over it with his foot pointed down. He'd learned to manage the body, shifting so the curves met one another and stayed comfortable. Even while asleep he frowned, lines etched into his cheeks.

Just before dawn, Satan appeared.

He glanced at Michael with a smirk, although his hand shifted toward his sword.

Michael narrowed his gaze. "Why are you here?"

"Someone put a blade through the heart of one of my captains." Satan shook his head. "I couldn't believe it was one of these guardians, but it turns out they knew they were outclassed and sent for you instead."

The shepherds' guardian angels maintained quiet, but Michael felt their uneasiness. "You have no right to be here. He's got enough to deal with."

"I have every right to be here," said Satan, "and I know precisely what he's dealing with. Far better than you can."

Michael's words died in his throat.

"Although I admit," murmured Satan, "it must be harder for him, since the Tyrant played him along first with all the love-patter and nonsense. He hasn't yet given up hope." Satan shook his head. "It's really a shame, but that's His tactic."

Abruptly Michael felt his senses invaded by images pushed on him from Satan. Before he could reject them, he realized he was seeing as if through Gabriel's eyes. Gabriel's dream: Gabriel entering a room empty except for one figure: an angel armored in black metal with a red cape, black and red jewels, a diamond-encrusted silver sword, and a black helmet with metal framing his eyes.

Oh, God, no, Michael prayed. *That's not right.*

Jagged shadows gashed over the demon's high cheekbones, the narrow chin, the finely chiseled nose. The eyes and mouth were set with contempt, and the gauntleted hands hovered over the hilt of both the sword and a curved dagger. The leather boots shone with rubies and blood. The demon commanded an intense power. Michael realized Gabriel had watched, entranced, for a long time.

"Who are you?" Michael heard himself ask with Gabriel's voice.

"I'm you," said the figure. "I've always been you."

No wonder Gabriel had awakened screaming. Michael pushed off the intrusive thoughts, glaring at Satan, who only laughed.

"May God strike you," he whispered. "That was totally unnecessary. We saw that happen to too many of us."

"What would you have been, Michael, evil?" Satan paced around the outside of the tent, swallowing the tiny camp with his stride. "Nothing. Spit and dust. You're such a minor Archangel, you'd command nothing. Gabriel, now, he would have had power, but you—?" One of the shepherds' guardians drew closer, and Satan chuckled again. "We wouldn't have noticed you at all. But Gabriel..."

Satan conjured the image of the dark Cherub to stand before himself: the dark prince, hardened and cold, angry, choked by ice of the heart. It turned toward Michael, then glared at the guardians (who looked even more upset now), but then it looked at the sleeping Gabriel. Grey eyes like knives, the mouth a permanent sneer. The thing loathed him.

Michael's fists clenched, but Satan embraced the thing, then held it at arm's length to inspect. "This is the Gabriel I like to see! Mine, all his devotion set on me. Loyal to me, and only to me. Those dark eyes smolder with ambition in my name. With Gabriel on our side, we might just have defeated you."

Michael trembled. "You didn't."

The morning glow on the high plain began to turn into sunrise. Michael looked at Gabriel and made certain he would sleep a little longer.

Satan dissolved the image of the evil Gabriel and seated himself again inside the tent. "He's mine. It's only a matter of convincing him." Satan looked into Michael as if he could see right through him. "Are you now regretting the worst bargain you made in your life?"

The guardians glanced at him.

"God allowed it." Michael's wings shivered. "I told you to go back to Hell."

"I'm just so persuasive." Satan cocked his head. "And really, thank you so much for upholding the terms God agreed to on your behalf. You've been most helpful."

Michael itched for his sword, but God reassured him.

Gabriel stirred.

"You're going to lose this battle." Satan's green eyes swept over the sleeper. "I've got his attention, and he wants me."

Smirking, he vanished.

That wasn't really a bargain, Michael prayed.

Months ago, just after Gabriel's Vision had been stripped, Satan had approached God's throne and said, "Gabriel. I want him."

Saraquael had been standing closest, and using his voice, God said, "Gabriel chose to be with me, not you."

Satan had said, "Clearly he's in the process of un-choosing, and in the interests of justice, he should be with me." Michael had told him to go back to Hell, but Satan insisted. Again Saraquael had delivered God's reply: "Unless Gabriel chooses to leave, he is mine."

Satan had said, "In that case, I demand a fair chance to have him make a free choice." God had asked for terms. Satan said, "I want access. Let me speak to him without You protecting him."

And again, Saraquael had delivered God's answer: "Access is yours, only if he sends you away, you must go."

Satan had said, "And these—" with one sweep of his hand taking in Michael and the other angels, "—can come only if he calls them, and they cannot warn him in advance."

And God had agreed, "They will intervene only if he calls. But then you will have to leave." With those concessions, Satan had left the ring of Seven.

So no, not a bargain. More as if God had capitulated. With Gabriel in this state, Satan had been sure to attack. He'd merely approached God for sanction.

Satan had studied Gabriel for two weeks before striking.

Michael shivered, remembering the conversations related by the local angels, the way Satan had altered the weather for days to make it frigid, the times he'd hungered to charge in and tell Satan to leave, the demon's smug satisfaction whenever he ended the meetings, the third night when Remiel had been hollering at God and Uriel pleading in prayer trying to win Gabriel the grace to tell Satan to just leave, but Gabriel never called, so they couldn't interfere. Never had Michael imagined Gabriel would have listened, would have conceded as much as he did. And then, like the dawn of grace, that fourth night when Gabriel sent Satan away and buried himself entirely in a man's body.

Gabriel squinted and stretched, then breathed deeply.

Crouching again, Michael touched Gabriel as he opened his eyes. The Cherub focused long-distance as if by reflex, and abruptly he gasped, then deflated.

Michael bowed his head. Gabriel did this every time he awakened.

A few minutes later, Gabriel sat upright, casting his gaze about for a moment before Michael realized what was wrong and made himself visible.

"You stayed," whispered Gabriel, abruptly smiling.

Smiling? No, he was beaming. Michael moved closer, and Gabriel laughed with relief. He kept it soft, though, because of Jacob and Zachary.

Gabriel slipped out of the tent. "Go take a break," he told the twin shepherds, and they headed away. Gabriel stirred up the fire and then checked on the sheep.

Michael followed. "Good morning."

"That's debatable." Gabriel gave a wave of his hand. "The social conventions of hospitality demand I offer you something to eat, but I also realize it's futile."

Michael laughed. "You're hospitable enough, don't worry."

Gabriel spoke rapidly as he walked around the animals to bring the stragglers back. "I'm sure this is of less interest to you than it is to me, but a few of these animals have definite personalities, and I need to work with those specially to keep them from leading the rest of the flock into trouble. Kind of like some human souls, I've discovered." Gabriel shrugged as he called one of the ewes. "They don't all have their own names, but some of them you just get to know after a while."

Gabriel's spirit sparkled as he spoke, and Michael leaned in to listen. He so seldom talked this way. "Are you doing all right?"

"It's an adventure in some ways." Gabriel stopped in his tracks as he thought. "God's still giving me little lights and graces, which is a huge surprise, but I have to work to recognize them.

Sometimes it's been a while and then I wonder whether He's stopped sending them or if I've just stopped listening. Every day is a package, gift-wrapped in a way by the ribbon of the rising and setting of the sun."

Michael grinned. "Saraquael would like that image."

"I think it was his image to begin with." Gabriel shook his head. "Sometimes I'm glad for the new experiences, but then I consider all I've lost, and I don't think I'm going to make it through."

For an instant Gabriel turned older, the life gone from his face, but then he gathered himself and Michael could no longer see the emotion in his human features.

"You haven't lost everything." Michael felt hollow, like a bell with no clapper. "You kept a lot more than you thought you could."

"I'm missing the glue that gives the world meaning." Gabriel wrapped his arms around his stomach. "Without God the world becomes a parade that glorifies nothing."

"But God isn't lost either." Oh, for Saraquael's way with words, or Uriel's steadiness, or at least a second voice to back him up. Michael bit his lip and brought his wings closer to his body. "He's just misplaced."

Michael started when Gabriel burst out laughing.

"How can someone misplace something infinitely large and omnipresent?" He snickered. "I'm the one who's misplaced."

Michael said, "You can stay with us still, you know. You're not lost if you don't want to be."

"I think I'm pretty much here for now." Still chuckling, Gabriel got down on his knees and roughed up one of the ewes, who head-butted him. "They're starting to shear the sheep, and I learned the most amazing thing: I'm no good at it. Not even a little." Michael laughed out loud, and Gabriel grinned. "Zachary or Jacob take a flint knife, secure the sheep, and fleece the thing in under a minute. Me?" He grinned. "The first time, Jacob grabbed me by the arm as if I were Abraham with Isaac, trying to save the sheep's life. The second sheep was perfectly safe but needed re-shearing. The third took twenty-six times as long to shear as it should have. By the end, even the sheep was bored. There was no fourth sheep. Zachary suggested I make myself useful sorting fleeces, and that," he added with relief, "I could do."

Michael laughed, then wondered whether Gabriel meant that as a joke.

Gabriel rubbed the ewe behind the ears, but his voice grew strained. "It's ironic, because being here is teaching me more every day than I would have learned in Heaven during the same time. Isn't that the ultimate gift God could give a Cherub?" Gabriel looked Michael in the face. "And do you know what?""

Michael leaned forward.

"It doesn't help at all." His voice cracked. "Even when I'm learning, I know it's something I shouldn't have been here in the first place to learn."

Michael had nothing to offer now. Not even comfort.

Gabriel stood away from the ewe. "I apologize. I shouldn't burden you with my own musings. It will end eventually. Years passed in Heaven without my noticing. No matter how useless it is, my heart keeps beating and my lungs keep working. My body lives, so I'll follow its example."

Michael moved toward Gabriel as if to carry him back to Heaven. "You can return to us. Come with me." He swallowed, thinking, *Isn't it better than waking up in the middle of the night talking to _him_?*

"You keep saying that." Gabriel looked at the flock as they picked over the field. "I'll feel the same no matter what the locale. Here I might end up being useful."

Michael touched Gabriel's arm. "Make me useful too. Tell me what you need. I can't reverse God's judgment, but if you had to choose, what one thing can I give you to help?"

Gabriel didn't say anything at first, but Michael could feel him pondering. Of course: ask a Cherub a complicated question, even a Cherub living in a human body, and you weren't going to get an unconsidered response. More than any answer Gabriel could give, this meant Gabriel himself didn't know what would help. So Michael shadowed Gabriel while he did his morning's work, neither of them speaking but at the same time sharing a togetherness more important than speech.

Finally, as if no time at all had passed between question and response, Gabriel answered. "Memory," he said. "Ask God for me to remember before I wake up, that way every day doesn't begin with a shock."

Adar 27

I'm not doing enough with this year. I've given Him permission to remake me or even destroy me, but since He hasn't taken me up on the offer, I assume He plans another course of action. After all, the one who bears the blame in this situation is me, so it's not fitting that God shoulder the work to fix it. The severity of the sentence indicates that I can discount it as completely a punishment for disobedience. I don't doubt that's the occasion of the chastisement, but God frequently works with a two-fold agenda. It's not unreasonable to assume He has a secondary goal besides merely cramming it into my mind that orders get fulfilled to the letter.

In the past we've seen a severe punishment meted out for a small offense when God wants to work down the damage from other offenses, such as how God punished Moses for striking the rock twice at Meribah. Usually the secondary offenses take the form of illicit services performed in His name which He wouldn't reprove at the time, but which required justice nevertheless. The wrongful action itself was not intended to be hurtful.

If that's the case with me, then I should hypothesize potential secondary offenses: based on the isolation part of the punishment, I'll assume it's either my blaming Michael for the attack at Sodom, or else my distance from Raphael when he became Azariah.

I didn't consider my actions harmful either time, and I still don't, but were they hurtful? I never sinned, so direct punishment would have been inappropriate. I stand by my actions, though, because I wasn't wrong either time. Once I recovered from the attack at Sodom I made it clear that I didn't hold Michael at fault. So it must be the Azariah business.

At any rate, what should I learn by living here?

Whatever it is, it ought to contribute to my ultimate purpose, whatever task it is God created me specifically to do. Which, if I knew what it was, would tell me what I needed to add to myself or remove in order to achieve it better. But lacking a destination, it's hard to nail down how exactly to arrive.

I suppose I have to discern that part. God will provide the stimulus, but He holds me responsible for maximizing my response.

Nissan 2

During his watch, Gabriel turned to find an Angel inches from his face.

Jumping backward, he gasped.

The Angel glowed softly but shed no light on the field. An apology; the Angel hadn't meant to surprise him.

Surprised. Sometimes Gabriel hated these limited senses.

The Angel moved close enough that Gabriel's breath would have touched him had the angel been in a body. He fought the urge to back away, wondering when he'd acquired the sense of a personal sphere, but at the same time reading the angel's unspoken words. Distress, introduction, Saul's image in Gabriel's mind, death, and then a question.

Sorting the impulses, Gabriel took a deep breath. In human terms—an angel wouldn't have needed to translate, but here it was: Saul's guardian angel, distressed because Saul was dying, nervous about what would happen next, wanting help.

Gabriel put forward a query, a sense of his own rootedness, another query.

The Angel replied only by repeating the sense of distress—an unformed, urgent need.

Gabriel looked at the sheep. The Angel reached for his hand.

He pulled away and went to Zachary. "Get up. It's your turn."

As the shepherd got to his feet, Gabriel took the Angel's hand, and he shifted into his angelic body.

His senses exploded, a gush like the blast at the bottom of a waterfall. The Angel carried him with a thought back to Saul while Gabriel tried to recover his bearings.

As the guardian crouched over a bed, Gabriel realized he was in Saul's house, surrounded by Saul's servants and family. The guardian touched his charge, then looked up, eyes hollow.

Gabriel moved near them, still uncertain what the Angel thought he could do, why he was here at all. In fact, he realized, every angel in the household was waiting on him.

This wasn't his specialty. If Saul had needed truth revealed, Gabriel would have done it without hesitation, but there was no truth to be absorbed now. He rested his hands on the man's soul to feel for any pervasive sin, but he couldn't detect anything blocking the flow of grace. Little faults, nothing extraordinary.

Demons tried to enter the room. The household guardians kept them at bay. Saul's guardian cuddled around Saul. A moment after, Gabriel felt a sweet vibration passing between the two of them, two souls harmonized to one another, the guardian woven around and through the human's soul, the two in tandem stronger than the one alone.

The guardian touched Saul's soul, stroking it, and a moment later Gabriel realized the guardian was speaking so subtly that no one other than the man and God could understand it all.

A bond. Gabriel tried not to think it, but now that he'd noticed it, he kept noticing it: an angel/human bond, a oneness that shouldn't be separated, and here he was alone and separated

Tishri

Cheshvan

Kislev

Tevet

Schevat

Adar

Nissan

Iyar

Sivan

Tammuz

Av

Elul

from Raphael.

He turned away, saw the other guardians watching him, became overly-conscious of himself: dimmer, weaker. Trembling. Alone.

The guardian touched a wingtip to his: he wanted to know what to do.

It wasn't a matter of doing, Gabriel realized. The man needed nothing: there was nothing any of them could do for him, no healing (plainly it was time; the hand of God was on the man's heart) and no conversion. The man's soul would enter Sheol and there await the Redeemer in sleep for as long as it took.

About to say that, Gabriel halted. There was a need here. But it wasn't Saul.

"Come here," he said, and the guardian pulled up beside him. "Feel this." He ran his hands along the man's soul, guiding the guardian's perception so the angel could feel the places the man's soul was anchored into the body, five primary points and countless tinier fastenings. "Observe how that's pulling away. Normally you wouldn't be able to work your fingers around there." The guardian assented. "That's going to continue. It's like a nut pulling away from the side of the shell. Think of a deciduous tree turning colors for autumn. His soul is ready."

The guardian pushed an urgent question.

"When it's time, you'll take him like this," and Gabriel showed the guardian how he'd position himself. "You won't think about it then. It will feel right. You'll find his soul in your hands, and you'll carry him before God for judgment."

The Angel's soul trilled, but his gaze remained steady.

Gabriel said, "After a certain point, you won't be able to follow."

The Angel started.

"It will be just him and God. But afterward, he'll be released to you again, and you'll escort him to Sheol."

The angel waited. Gabriel looked back at Saul, then at the Angel. He wanted to say, "And that's it. What more do you want?" but a moment later he realized the difference: the guardian was tense, but no longer frightened. There was still an expectancy, but minus the urgency.

"Until then, we'll pray." Gabriel backed off, and the guardian again melted again around the man.

The hour of death, not a clock-hour so much as a time surrounding death, the time for the soul to firm up into its eternal proportions and make its vector toward God or toward itself; a time for demons to try to change that direction and a time for the angels to hold territory so that moment could stand unbreached between God and His creation.

At some point Archangels arrived, defenders. The guardian and the man stayed at the eye of this spiritual hurricane while Satan's forces acted. Close to the center, Gabriel waited, praying with the other household guardians. Watching.

Abruptly the guardian flushed with power. Driven, he surrounded the man's soul like a sea-star surrounding a mussel. With tendrils of light streaming from his form, the guardian gripped the man, faced him straight in the eyes, and then the man's soul birthed itself out of his body and into the guardian's heart. Gabriel felt the relief of the moment, the thrill as the guardian clamped down on what was dearest, and next the quiet as the Angel flashed away, to God.

The Archangels departed. The demons vanished. The household guardians continued praying. Gabriel found himself in silence. Alone again.

He returned to the sheep field, still in angelic form, to find Zachary shepherding while half-asleep. He called the sheep together but didn't revert back to human. The exhaustion, the aches, the hunger – he could stay like this a few minutes longer.

I think that was all I could do for Saul, he prayed. *It wasn't anything in the long run. It all would have happened the same way without me.*

Silence. He thought toward God, *He was so nervous, though. Maybe it helped him, just knowing what was about to happen.*

That look on the guardian's face, when instinct took over and he could finally act. The moment to release his strength and midwife that soul out, grasp it close, and then carry it home. The

183

easing of the tension: would Gabriel ever feel that? How long had it been since he'd last seen God's face?

With a couple of hours until sunrise, Gabriel settled on the ground. *Father, if I'm done with that work, and I think I am, I guess I'll go back into a body now.*

The next moment, he found himself still seated, but on a road and not in a field, the air hotter and dryer, and the sun just rising.

His clothing was different: a knee-length tunic, short sleeves, a shawl with long fringes. A belt—at least he was still wearing a belt. But this was cotton, not wool. What was going on?

He scrambled to his knees, pressed his palm to the ground. *Where? Where?*

His eyes flew open. "Michael?"

Perhaps in response to his shrill tone, it wasn't even a second before the Archangel appeared holding Gabriel's pack.

Gabriel was shaking. "I'm in Elam?"

"About a mile north of the port-city of Susa." Michael handed him the pack, unconcerned by the change in clothes, the change in appearance, the change in location. But then again, would Gabriel even have registered the importance of those details before this year?

His head felt numb. "But that's hundreds of miles—"

"You aren't needed in Lebonah."

Gabriel scrambled to his feet. "But it's my turn to cook breakfast."

That wasn't what he wanted to say. It was just the thing that made most sense, the only practical thing he could grasp.

Michael shrugged. "They won't starve. I'll stop by later and tell them you were called away. That man Jacob, I think he'll make a good overseer until Saul's son takes over."

So much for predictability.

After a pause, Gabriel realized Michael wasn't going to add anything. This was ridiculous—he shouldn't have to beg for information, not when God had upended his existence. But instead Michael stood, an air of expectancy sparking around him, and Gabriel felt only flustered and abandoned. He'd worked for months to carve himself a niche in the Holy Land where he'd be useful, and his reward was God kicking him out of Israel.

His eyes stung, but he only picked up his pack.

Michael put out his hand. "Where will you go?"

Gabriel stared at the road curling before him. What did it matter where he went? God wouldn't be there.

"I'm facing north," he said, so north he went.

Farmer

Nissan 5

Camped for the night, Gabriel was preparing dinner when another traveler hailed him in Aramaic with a strong Assyrian influence. Gabriel discerned the language and returned the greeting, but his voice cracked: he hadn't spoken to anyone in two days.

The traveler stopped. With bright eyes and smooth cheeks he looked to be in late adolescence.

"Would you like to join me?" Gabriel said. His dinner consisted of some dried fish and roasted round cakes with dates, but he had enough for two.

The young man dropped his bag on the ground. "I would, thanks! I'm Raguel, son of Gabelus. What's your name?"

"Gabriel." He said it with an Assyrian accent, but it was his name nonetheless. "Where are you heading?"

"Ecbatana. Yourself?"

"North as well, but at the moment I have no destination."

Watching the boy Raguel unload his belongings from his donkey, Gabriel thought about the angel of the same name, and he shifted a little into the angelic realm to test; the boy's spirit didn't flicker with a preternatural glow, and he had his own guardian angel. His frame, while muscular, still lacked a man's shoulders. His legs had gotten covered with road dust, and his face was smudged where dirt mingled with sweat. Like Gabriel, he wore a knee-length tunic with the ubiquitous fringes and embroidery on the sleeves, but it looked to be finer than Gabriel's.

Taking a seat at the campfire, Raguel ran his hands over his shoulders where he'd carried his pack. "So, traveler Gabriel, with a name like that, I assume you're an Israelite exile just like my family. Were you named after the angel?"

"We were named at the same time," he said dryly.

Raguel chuckled. "Yeah, yeah, from all eternity, by God's mouth, but your parents named you after an archangel. What an honor!"

"For him or for me?" asked Gabriel, at which Raguel laughed out loud. "You're named after an angel, too, you know. Raguel is the name of one of the Seven."

"My grandfather tells me that's what the Patriarch Enoch said." Raguel chuckled. "Gabriel's also one of the Seven."

Gabriel murmured, "That's what they say."

"So, two people with angel names meet on a road. It sounds like it should be a book in the scriptures." The young man's eyes crinkled with a laugh. "Actually I'm named after my great-grandfather."

While Gabriel finished preparing the meal, the young man asked, "How come you don't have a destination? No home or a family?"

Gabriel didn't look up. "I want to find work somewhere."

The young man said, "Oh! My family can hire you."

"If you have need of me, by all means," said Gabriel. "Otherwise, I'll keep going."

Raguel said, "Come with me as far as Ecbatana and see how it turns out. As long as you have no other place to go, how could it hurt?"

"It can't." Gabriel hesitated. "What exactly does your family do?"

"We devour random travelers." Raguel laughed out loud. "You don't need to be so cautious. We farm."

Amused, Gabriel said, "Lucky me."

"Harvest time gets crazy, you know? I have six uncles and a lot of aunts, and about thirty myriad cousins, and we're out in the field all day every day."

Gabriel passed some fish and a date cake to Raguel, who began eating but then stopped long enough to squeeze in a few whispered prayers.

Gabriel said, "It sounds like you don't need help."

"Oh, no," the young man swallowed to say. "My father and uncles always bring in servants for the planting and harvesting. They sent me out on business because no one else could be spared. I'm supposed to be back right away for the start of the barley harvest and the sheep shearing. But I got delayed, and that's why I was walking at almost dark. Trust me, they'll take you on."

While Gabriel took some food for himself, Raguel added, "My family has a policy of always being kind to travelers."

Gabriel shrugged. "That's doubly lucky."

"It's my grandfather's special idea, passed on to him by *his* father, but I don't know if it goes back any more."

Gabriel stopped eating as though choked. He considered the area, the time, and the names he had heard so far, and he reached a dreadful conclusion.

Is it wrong to stay with him? he prayed, but he heard no answer.

Gabriel and Raguel prayed together that night and rose before dawn. Raguel talked constantly, but it wasn't invasive. He had a knack for conversation that Gabriel had never mastered, letting one topic flow into the next into the next as one thing reminded him of something else. Although superficial, conversation was easy to follow, and Gabriel resisted his impulse to grab a topic in a stranglehold and wring every bit of information from it. The only downside was that eventually Raguel asked how Gabriel had ended up homeless.

Gabriel experimented with Raguel's technique for redirecting the conversation (and succeeded!) twice before Raguel finally pressed for an answer. So Gabriel told him he was a prince, but he'd displeased his father the king and gotten sent away.

Raguel whistled. "Will you ever be able to return?"

"I have to wait a while. Maybe after the harvest I can try again."

"I hope he takes you back," said Raguel. "What kingdom is it?" Gabriel replied with the holy name of Heaven, which Raguel didn't recognize. "Is it one of those little city-states no one's ever heard of?"

Gabriel sighed. "Sometimes it feels that way."

"My dad says that since Nineveh fell there's a new kingdom popping up every month. But your home sounds Hebrew."

Gabriel said, "Oh, you speak Hebrew? I do too."

Raguel's eyes popped. "You're kidding! Could you speak to me in Hebrew so I'll know it really well by the time we get home? My grandfather will be so surprised. I can barely understand it, but my grandfather says we have to keep praying in it because that's what the scriptures are written in, just in case we ever return to Samaria. That's where my great-grandparents come from."

"How well can you understand me?" Gabriel asked in Hebrew.

Raguel's eyes got big, and after some work, he said, "Um, okay?"

It was a gift, Raguel's presence: a pupil. A Cherub. A subject in need of learning and a long road on which to learn it, a road that suddenly seemed a lot shorter than it had before.

Nissan 9

Raguel had a better Hebrew background than he had admitted, and fluency came with constant exposure. One night Gabriel prayed for an hour after the young man went to bed, and the next day Raguel found himself thinking in Hebrew when he wanted to.

Meanwhile, Gabriel wrestled with the ethics of the situation, and whether staying with a traveler he'd met by coincidence was breaking the spirit of the law to avoid Raphael—or had it really been coincidence? Was he being tempted?

He considered asking Michael, but he was a Cherub—he ought to be able to figure this out himself.

Raguel didn't have to tell Gabriel when they drew close to his home about four hours after noon. Gabriel recognized the land, the fences on the border of the property, and the layout of the trees. His mouth went dry, and he drank the last of the water from his supply. Raguel recited psalms in Hebrew right through Gabriel's silence, upping the pace as they approached the gates of the house.

The house sat among fields, two stories tall, mudbrick and wood construction with a tiled roof. It sprawled in the multigenerational manner of farm houses everywhere, rooms added as necessary. Nearby stood a barn, and beside them a stand of trees with their crowns just tall enough to block the setting sun. Gabriel knew there would be a spring feeding the trees, and beyond them a row of grain silos. Further out lay crops absorbing the light, readying for harvest. Approaching the property from ground-level was a new perspective; every other time Gabriel had been here, he'd waited in a tree or on the roof.

Raguel let out a shout at the gates, and instantly family members poured from the doors, from the barn, and from behind the house. Gabriel halted as Raguel let go of his donkey's lead to run toward the crowd, talking in rapid bursts as boys and girls his age came to welcome him back, little children, then women dusting their hands on their aprons. And finally an older man who gave Raguel a firm hug, then held him at arms' length to inspect.

Gabriel turned away quickly, grabbing the donkey's tether and bringing it to stand near his shoulder.

Raguel called him, then ran toward Gabriel, who tried to look impassive as he approached the family. "This is Gabriel!" Raguel said, and the family welcomed him as well, thanking him for "looking after" Raguel on his trip, inviting him to come inside. Someone took the donkey from him, and a moment later Gabriel found a four-year-old girl clinging to his leg asking to be carried. He lifted her as everyone went into the house. More chaos: the scents of meat, bread, garlic. Onions and herbs were strung across the ceiling. The women brought him and Raguel water, barley cakes and wine and promised a proper meal in a couple of hours.

At some point, Raguel took off to go talk to his grandfather, and Gabriel found himself alone—alone except for ten family members whose names he all knew even though he hadn't been introduced.

"Would you like anything else?" said a woman who looked enough like Raguel to be his mother. Which Gabriel knew she was.

"If you don't mind," Gabriel said, "I'd like to clean up."

They led him to the well, gave him a water basin and a towel, and then left him alone.

I hope it's all right to be here, Gabriel prayed in the blessed silence. *Please stop me if it isn't.*

Ten minutes later, Gabriel returned to kitchen. The little girl scampered over to him, took the basin and the towel, then darted away again, leaving him at the threshold alone.

Gabriel's heart hammered. He wanted to run.

The girl returned. Taking his hand, she led him through a series of rooms to the front entrance where her father—Raguel's father—was standing.

"That's good, Rafaela," said the man. "Now run along."

The girl beamed at Gabriel before darting off.

The man turned his full attention to Gabriel. "So," he said in Assyrian Aramaic, "you accompanied Raguel from Susa?"

Gabriel nodded.

Raguel's father squinted at him. "My name is Gabelus, by the way. You're Gabriel?"

With that Akkadian influence, the name sounded more like "Zhavreel." Gabriel nodded again.

Gabelus regarded him. "You don't speak very much, although apparently you speak Hebrew well enough. My son hasn't stopped chattering since he arrived, and I'm afraid he's going to wear out his grandfather's ears before he gets used to the idea that yes, we can say the same thing two ways." Gabriel smiled. "You've had to put up with him for days, I know," Gabelus said, "but it's a new experience for me not to be able to shut him up. You taught him quickly."

Gabriel said, "We had a lot of time."

Gabelus grimaced. "He says you're a prince, but you're at odds with your king. Is this true?"

Gabriel tensed as he agreed. He could predict the man's next question.

"What have you done?"

"I disobeyed my father in a small matter."

Gabelus was examining him more minutely than even Saul had: his character, whether he was lying, and whether he was a danger to the children.

Gabelus said, "Why weren't you thrown in prison?"

"Arguably I should have been." Gabriel bit his lip. "But he is my Father. And my sisters pleaded for me."

Gabelus said, "Is he a harsh king?"

"Not usually." Gabriel looked down. "I'm not good for much, but Raguel mentioned I might work for your family."

"In Hebrew, no doubt." Gabelus had not stopped openly studying him, and Gabriel became very conscious of how Gabelus was taller, broader, his hair thicker. How odd, to feel smaller than a man. More than that: he was trembling.

Around the back of the house, a number of children played, and for a moment both men in the courtyard could hear them daring one another. Half an hour ago, they'd all run outside to welcome home their brother, their cousin. And Gabriel realized, when he returned home, it would be through the back door, an embarrassment no one would call attention to, although maybe some would be relieved it was all over.

His gaze dropped. He couldn't help it.

Gabelus rested a hand on his shoulder. "We do hire workers for the harvest. But first my father wants to meet you."

Gabelus led him down the hall, and Gabriel followed with his mouth dry and his fingers clenching his belt.

Raguel nearly crashed into them in the hallway. "Oh, you're coming. Grandfather wanted you now."

They entered a courtyard in the center of the house, open to the warm air and the waning sunlight. A gentleman sixty years old, white-haired and leathery, sat in a chair beside a potted tree. Raguel held Gabriel back by the door while Gabelus approached.

Gabriel kept an eye on the two men's exchange while Raguel said, "I think you can stay! He just wants to speak to you first."

Gabriel wished he had his angelic hearing to get a jump on what the men were saying. Gabelus had his back to him, blocking Gabriel's view of the older man. When Gabelus waved them over, Raguel trotted to his grandfather while Gabriel trailed.

"Grandfather, this is Gabriel." Raguel looked at Gabriel. "Gabriel, this is my grandfather, Tobias son of Tobit."

Gabriel tried very hard not to look the way he felt.

Tobias looked over Gabriel as if appraising him. "For some reason I thought you would be taller. Sit, please." The old man gestured to the chair near his own. "You may leave, Raguel."

All was spoken in fluent Hebrew. Gabelus and his son left the courtyard, and the head of the household smiled at Gabriel. "Has my family welcomed you?"

Gabriel gripped the armrests until the tendons hurt, but at least his hands weren't trembling. "They've been very hospitable, thank you."

"I only wish my wife Sarah were still with us, so she could greet you too. She was so beautiful, so charming." Tobias had a wistful smile, then he looked over Gabriel and chuckled. "You can relax, you know."

Gabriel unclenched his hands from the chair. "I'm sorry."

Tobias nodded. "I'm curious as to what sort of guide my grandson found on the road. Raguel says you're a prince and that you want work. You can see where that would leave an old man with questions."

Gabriel looked him over and remembered a boy Raguel's age, walking beside a Seraph without knowing it, Raphael's gold-toned eyes and easy smile and his way of making just the right quip — and Gabriel clenched the armrests again. His voice didn't want to work, but he forced it. "I've worked as a shepherd for the past five months, but Raguel says you need help for the harvest. I can learn to do that."

"We're in the middle of shearing," Tobias said.

Gabriel bit his lip. "I don't shear."

For the first time harshness had came into Tobias's tone. "It's beneath you?"

Gabriel stared at the ground. "You don't want me coming near your sheep with a blade, not if you love your sheep. I was much better at driving them in and out of a stream to get them rinsed off prior to shearing. And sorting the fleeces afterward."

Tobias said, "Let me see your hands."

Puzzled, Gabriel let Tobias examine his palms, his fingers, and nails. Tobias nodded. "You've done hard work. You've been a shepherd for five months?" When Gabriel agreed, Tobias added, "You look like you're about twenty?"

Gabriel nodded.

"How comes a prince to be wandering Media?"

Gabriel began with, "I've—" and then stopped as if struck.

For the past twenty-four hours Gabriel had worked on how to present his story, always staring with, "I've fallen from favor." But here in the moment, he couldn't do it, couldn't say *fallen*, not before this man, not before God.

He averted his eyes. "My Father...forced me out." That hadn't been easy to say either, but Gabriel tried to forge his way back into the rest of the script. "My Father had a disobedient servant. He wanted me to destroy the servant and the servant's house together, but I let him escape. Eventually I'll be able to return to my Father and beg His mercy, but I won't try until at least after the harvest."

"Your father gave you a timetable?" Tobias looked cautious. "Does this happen often?"

Gabriel avoided his eyes. "It's never happened before."

Tobias said, "Do you want to return home?"

He couldn't manage more than a whisper. "More than anything."

A pair of birds passed overhead, and Gabriel followed them with his eyes until they disappeared. He wasn't going to be allowed to stay. Tobias's guardian didn't like him—he knew that. Ezdrael must be shouting at Tobias not to trust him, and why should he? There were too many unanswered questions. He wasn't even handling this interview well.

Tobias said, "You have the name of an angel."

Gabriel stared at the ground. "I hear you journeyed with one."

"Azariah." Tobias said the name as if tasting wine, and Gabriel winced. "He called himself Azariah, but later he told me his real name was Raphael. I named my first two sons after him."

Frozen, Gabriel couldn't think of how to react. What he wanted to do was beg for a full recounting of the story, every moment, every look on Raphael's face, every thought that had flitted through the boy's mind as they walked, the awe of the moment Raphael revealed his true nature. Everything, everything.

And at the same time, he couldn't: every angel in the house knew why he didn't know those things, what he'd done, what he'd failed to do.

Still, a normal person would respond, should respond, so Gabriel said, "I'd like to hear about it." What was a guest supposed to say in a situation like this? "Have you ever written it down? I'd love to read it."

The man laughed. "And here I thought I'd never get you interested in anything." As Gabriel's cheeks grew hot, Tobias said, "Will you accept an invitation to dinner?"

Gabriel nodded.

"Good." The old man rose from his chair and kissed Gabriel on the cheek. "Because you're hired."

By now the family had gathered for supper: five brothers (the other two had gone to live in Nineveh before its destruction); their wives and children; Tobias's daughters and their families; and Tobias.

Gabriel expected to be dismissed to the barn to eat, so it surprised him to be introduced and then given a place in the common room. He had Raguel on one side and Rafaela glued to the other, although at some point she ended up on his lap while he cut her food. He took only a minimum of the lamb and lentil stew, knowing the best part ought to go to the family. Rafaela filched his barley cake and slipped him her lentils.

During supper, Gabriel had to repeat his story. They were, it chagrined him to discover, interested. Zachary and Jacob hadn't seemed to care when he'd implied everyone he knew had been slaughtered. Still, he managed to come up with answers for every question except one.

Tobias's daughter Angela said, "Why didn't your mother intervene?"

He blinked at her.

"Didn't she say something?"

Gabriel abruptly felt orphaned. He had only one Parent. While adept at linguistic sleight of hand, he couldn't come up with any way to make it sound as if he had a mother at all. "My siblings begged for mercy."

"But your mother," Angela said, "how could a mother stand by and watch her son get thrown out of the household? She should have followed you out onto the road and stayed with you."

Raguel's mother put her hand on Gabriel's shoulder as she passed, taking Gabriel's empty plate. "Is your mother living?"

Relief dawned. "No."

"Oh," gasped Angela. "I didn't realize! How did it happen? How old were you?"

Gabelus said, "Angela, give the man room to breathe."

A moment later, Raguel's mother returned Gabriel's plate, reloaded. He looked up in surprise. It was the first time all year that anyone cared if he had enough to eat.

After dinner and evening prayers, Tobias said, "I have need of my hired man."

Gabelus laughed out loud. "You're going to tell him your story?"

Tobias intoned, "Would you rather I told it again to you?"

"Nope!" Gabelus roared with laughter. "Why do you think I recommended you hire him?"

Gabriel just kept his head down and his gaze lowered. Tobias took him by the arm, and he brought him out to the courtyard.

Two hours later, Tobias brought him back to Angela. Gabriel asked for a space to sleep in the hay loft. Instead Raguel showed him a room they would share, with Gabriel's bed-roll already spread on the floor and his belongings stashed in a corner.

Raguel's mother poked her head into the room. "Oh, good, you're still awake." She handed him a pillow. "I couldn't start this until after dinner, and I was afraid I wouldn't get it done in time."

Gabriel clutched it, feeling the feathers through the fabric. "Thank you. I could have just folded up my overtunic."

"It's no trouble at all," she said. "Everyone needs something soft." Then she kissed Raguel on the cheek and left them.

Gabriel prayed with Raguel and then in the dark prayed himself to sleep.

Gabriel awoke in the silent house, moonlight shining through the window. With his eyes clenched and his breath uneven, he pressed his palms against his eyes.

Another midnight awakening in a city filled with horrible men... a false name, a separation, a journey... "I'm very, very, very angry at you."

He thought about the boy Raguel surrounded by a family that rejoiced in his return. About Gabelus hugging his son and then looking him over to make sure he was all right. When Gabriel went home, he could only picture the inverse: his Father would look him over, and if he passed inspection, God would hug him; and only then would the other angels greet him.

He fell against the pillow Raguel's mother had made for him, and he sobbed.

I want you to have empathy for them. I want you to feel why I love them.

He tried to keep as quiet as possible, mindful that he didn't awaken Raguel, too keenly aware that there were guardians in the house, at least one of whom disliked him, and that they'd see him no matter what he did to hide. He couldn't help it. He kept his face on the pillow.

You aren't the first to try to stare me down, Gebher'el.

He struggled to remember the Vision, the way God used to look at him when He still loved him, and instead there was emptiness, only that final look with that expression he didn't want to name, and nowadays nothing at all, just a dryness inside and now this family outside, stitching together a pillow because they thought everyone deserved something soft.

You have to draw closer to humankind, to feel their fears and pressures.

Gabriel had tried to stay quiet, but a subtle pressure like hands touched his shoulders. He only gripped his pillow tighter and turned his head away.

You left and you stayed away.

He curled around himself, but in the next moment he could feel Uriel draped over and behind him in a hug. His cheeks burning, Gabriel tried to avoid Uriel's embrace but then gave up and huddled beneath the Throne's wings. The feelings flooded him, and he stopped fighting.

Uriel's black-curled head touched Gabriel's. The hold didn't slacken or tighten, only stayed, but Gabriel ached with tension. He'd be all right—he'd have to be all right. He tried not to think any more, tried not to think about what happened, that—

—he'd displeased God. He'd failed his Father.

It overwhelmed Gabriel like a tsunami, that horrified sense of failure, and then even Uriel's calm couldn't keep him together. He'd displeased God, and there was no remedy for that. Nothing at all, not even time.

Uriel rode it out with him until finally Gabriel lay scared and sick, waiting for the dam to break again—that trembling thought, he'd angered God, don't think it again. He didn't sleep again for hours, but Uriel didn't leave.

Nissan 10

The next morning, Gabelus sent Gabriel, who couldn't meet anyone's eyes, out with the workers to harvest the barley. Gabriel

198

took an ox, hitched it to a cart, and went into the field. The other men were working within shouting distance but not close enough to hear a speaking voice.

Uriel sat on the back of the ox and hummed, calling to the butterflies and birds.

"Uriel," said Gabriel, and the Throne fixed round eyes on the Cherub, "are things all right in Heaven?"

The Throne's head tilted, eyes rounding.

Gabriel swallowed. "Is it a problem that you're here? Am I a bother?"

Uriel shrugged with a smile.

Gabriel continued swinging his sickle and gathering the severed stalks. "But what I want to know... are you better off without me?"

Uriel sat straight-spined and frowning.

"Does Raphael miss me?" he blurted out.

Uriel turned away those round eyes and almost disappeared because what Uriel projected couldn't always be controlled.

Gabriel withdrew his attention as much as possible from the Throne.

"Could you give him a message from me?" Gabriel kept his head down. "If it doesn't cross the Divine Will, could you please tell him I miss him?"

He lifted his eyes to Uriel, who observed Gabriel with grace-induced blankness. Gabriel flinched and kept harvesting grain.

Rules. He'd broken the smallest fragment of a rule, and now he had to abide by them all. Fully. Asking someone else to break the rule was itself breaking the rule. Giving him relief now wasn't mercy. That was chaos.

He knew that. Still, it was hard to talk, hard to form the words and tell Uriel he deserved all this. He deserved the loneliness, the heat, the pain. The only thing he could manage was, "I'm sorry."

A finger touched his chin, and Gabriel looked up to see Uriel lying across the back of the ox, nose to nose with him. The Throne winked.

"If you decide you prefer not to stay," and Gabriel had no trace of emotion in his voice, "you shouldn't."

Uriel shrugged, sitting upright, but then stretched and leaped down to walk for a while.

"It is a nice world," replied Gabriel. "It's just a shame I'm in it."

Uriel's sandals vanished, leaving nothing between the soil and angelic feet. Gabriel forced a smile. The ox walked steadily, but the day passed more quickly than Gabriel might have predicted. He slept through the next night, again with Uriel nearby.

Uriel stayed two more days, meandering while Gabriel worked but always at the edge of his senses. Uriel told him what the other angels had been up to. Uriel sang. Uriel prayed with him and over him.

Uriel left one day from the field while Gabriel continued harvesting. The Throne gave a good-bye with midnight eyes, then walked off on bare feet. Gabriel watched the lavender wings until Uriel stepped over the edge of a hill, and even afterward he kept checking back. Then, when they called for dinner, Gabriel broke off work and returned to the house.

After dinner, Gabriel walked outside to pray and found Michael under a tree.

Seeing him, Gabriel cringed, then leaned on the fence and stared at his hands. "So you're taking shifts again?"

Michael said, "Yes," and hugged him.

Gabriel closed his eyes. "You don't have to do this. I'm not helpless."

Michael said, "Neither are we. Uriel called a meeting. We've let you down."

Gabriel said, "I told you not to bother yourself about me."

Michael said, "And we respected that, but I need you to think about this, and think about it hard."

Gabriel's gaze dropped. "I'm a Cherub. That's what I do."

"Then answer this: why is it worse for you when people treat you well?"

Gabriel shivered. "I don't deserve any better."

Michael sounded less like a friend now than a commanding officer, and Gabriel closed his eyes. Michael said, "You're going to let us decide what we're willing to give you. I'm asking if you're willing to accept what we can give. Remiel doesn't even want me to allow you that option, by the way," Michael added, suddenly softer. "She's furious at all of us, herself most of all. On behalf of all of us, I'm asking your forgiveness."

Gabriel tried to seek out Michael's gaze, but he couldn't maintain the contact. "There's nothing to forgive, but if you insist."

Michael said, "And you'll accept our help? Can we drop in uninvited, since you never invite us?"

That military tone again. Gabriel shivered. *Why is it worse for you when people treat you well?* Because... A question he couldn't answer, at least not now. He couldn't even ascertain the truth of the assumption. Gabriel said, "Why are you doing this?"

Michael said, "Because I'm your friend. And I want you to let me be your friend."

A breeze picked up, and Gabriel wrapped his arms around himself.

Michael said, "Well?"

Gabriel said, "Since you insist, I offer you a standing invitation. Please feel free to join me whenever you wish."

"Thank you." Michael's wings relaxed, and he sounded cheerful again. "Satan's issued an all-points bulletin, by the way. He's not certain where you went."

"I'd like to keep it that way," Gabriel said. "The first thing Satan's going to do is demand a worldwide census of newcomers and anyone named Gabriel, and then some demon will remember that Uriel stayed for three days. It'll take Satan less than two weeks."

"Do you like it here?" asked Michael.

"Have I been asked to leave?" Gabriel's detached tone broke into a higher pitch as he faced Michael. He stepped closer, speaking urgently. "When I first met him, I didn't realize Raguel belonged to Tobias' family. I didn't plan this—"

"You're all right." Michael raised his hands. "We won this grace for you by prayer."

Gabriel laughed, something he hadn't expected to do. "Oh. Really? Thank you."

Michael nodded. "See? That wasn't so hard."

Gabriel bit his lip. "Are you sure you thought this through? Raphael visits Tobias often. It's going to be hard for him."

"I'm not certain God will permit him to notice you," Michael said. "This separation is as much for him as for you."

Gabriel stopped what he would have said and cocked his head. "Raphael needed time away from me? I was hurting him too?"

Michael huffed. "I think it's straight-out punishment, to be honest. I wasn't prepared for how violently Raphael protested your sentencing."

Gabriel focused on nothing, envisioning chaos around the throne of God: himself rocketing out one side of Heaven and Raphael rushing forward, engulfed in flame, protesting. But— There had been a time between, before he'd left. Nearly a minute. Surely Raphael hadn't been silent all that time?

Michael was saying, "The way he exploded—when Raphael was standing over you, I was afraid he was going to cinder you both."

"You nearly lost both of us? No, wait, stop talking. You're not supposed to tell me about him." Gabriel leaned his head on the fence post and gripped the wood hard enough to hurt. "I don't want to get you in trouble. Uriel already reprimanded me for asking."

Pain shot up his arms, and he forced his fists to unclench. He rubbed his forearm hard, then tried to work out a sentence, only nothing would come. Just the image of Raphael doing everything in his power to keep God from acting as justice demanded; Raphael reacting to helplessness with fury; Raphael at all.

Michael put an arm over his shoulder. Gabriel still couldn't find any words, any coherent thoughts, nothing.

A figure appeared in the house entrance. "Gabriel," called Raguel, "evening prayer!"

Of course—silence and humanity never meshed, not fully. Gabriel swallowed. "I'm coming." He lowered his voice. "Can you join us?"

Michael said, "I have your permission?"

Gabriel shot him a nasty look, and Michael said, "Fine, I'll drop it."

At the door, Raguel peered at Gabriel. "Who were you talking to?"

Gabriel's voice was flat. "Angels."

"You believe in that?" Raguel put adolescent emphasis on the word 'believe'.

Gabriel looked at him sideways. "Don't you?"

"I thought only my family did." Raguel laughed shortly. "When you talk to angels, do they answer you?"

Gabriel said, "Angels always answer."

Raguel shook his head.

"Well, they answer," Gabriel said, "but when they speak, people can't understand them."

Michael laughed, but Raguel couldn't understand him.

The trio entered the courtyard. Raguel sat with the grandsons, and Gabriel joined him. Michael put his hands on Gabriel's shoulders.

When Michael's touch pumped him full of electricity, Gabriel suddenly saw the courtyard crowded with angels. He could see the guardians of the family, angelic hands on human shoulders. Some left their charges to report to Michael, but they returned immediately. Michael's own glow cast shadows over the area.

A bright spot appeared: the golden glow of Remiel. She sat cross-legged at the front, soon joined by Saraquael. Next came Raguel-senior with Dobiel. Uriel arrived and took a place beside Remiel.

Maybe Raphael had come too, but Gabriel could neither feel nor see the Seraph, and he hoped it was as Michael said, that Raphael couldn't sense him either. Michael bi-located, simultaneously with Gabriel and with the Seven. An incredible honor, and yet the family would never know.

The evening prayer, so splendid in Hebrew and touching when translated, flowed back and forth: from Tobias to the family, from Tobias to the men, from Tobias to the women, from the women to the men. Praises, lamentations, requests, and more praises.

Gabriel felt his heart rise to an angelic prayer-level and his thought-processes alter to the state that used to be normal. When the prayers ended, he still felt buoyant. He had chores to do in the barn, and he kept meditating while he worked.

Nissan 22

Passover ended yesterday. I'd never experienced a Passover from this side, and I kept comparing what we were doing here to what Michael and Raphael would be doing now in Heaven, in our real celebration. It isn't the same. It isn't even close, but here I am, and I might as well document my observations.

Tobias counted all the servants as part of the household, which was a relief as I had no idea what I would do regarding a lamb. The whole eight days possessed an awkward duality because on the outside, it didn't look any different. It felt different to me, but even at that, I wasn't sure if I was seeking that difference and perhaps it isn't really there to human senses.

The Passover Seders united everyone. There were two on the first two days and one last night. I forgot about that extra Seder—in the Holy Land, there are only the ends. The youngest of Tobias's grandchildren asked the questions, and we ate the lamb and the unleavened bread together. Today, thank heaven, we got to eat leavened bread again—I had no idea what a sacrifice that would be. Bread never tasted breadier, and that's after only six months in this world. The unleavened stuff is like chewing parchment and harder to digest. After five days, I didn't want to eat any more of it, and it didn't seem I was alone. I tried to rejoice that God had delivered His people from Egypt, but the sad truth is that I'd done that many times before, so the majority of my rejoicing had to do with yeasted bread. How humiliating. I should have handled that better.

For a little while, during the Seders, I felt at home. Not that I belong here—I don't—but that suddenly I was a son of Abraham, that I was one of the people delivered from Egypt and there's a star scattered in the sky for me. That I had been delivered from slavery by miracles and human stubbornness, and that I'd been spared the passage of the Angel of Death, and here I was, saved and remembering. Remembering.

I do remember it, of course. But for once, I seemed to remember from the other side. Very strange, this common fiction, and yet we all partook of the same story, the same pretending.

Today, we returned to the fields. I turned at one point to find a widow and her sons gleaning behind me. She looked exhausted. The boys' clothes needed patching, if not replacing. I'm hardly the most thorough harvester, but there wasn't much left behind me. I felt bad for her—she's hungry, I'm hungry, but at least her need can be met—and I thought for an instant to toss my entire sheaf on the ground and begin a new one.

But that would have been stealing from Tobias. I didn't know what to do, whether to work inefficiently and let fall more than I would have, or to give her what I had, or to continue as if she weren't there. Every choice seemed wrong. It was hot; I was tired; I felt sick from the last meal of unleavened bread. I couldn't balance one precept against the next—because just yesterday, wasn't I feeling like kin to them, that we'd been rescued from Egypt together? Could compassion be wrong? But what about when compassion dictates you break the law? For a minute, I felt blinded. I felt human.

Tobias saw her, and he crossed the field to harvest alongside me in silence. At one point, he did toss his entire sheaf to the ground and keep walking. The widow thanked him. He demurred. After she left, he murmured, "I'm clumsy that way sometimes. And if you are similarly clumsy, God will make up the lack. I've learned that much in this life. God will never be outdone in generosity."

There's a lot to balance in this world. I'm never certain I'm accounting for the right factors. He left me to continue

205

*harvesting in the sun and the silence, thinking about leavened
bread after sundown and a widow with barley grain to make
her own.*

Nissan 27

He'd been on the farm a month. Alone after evening prayers,
Gabriel was raking out a stall in the barn, and as he worked, he
sang.

*Light in my darkness, strength in my weakness,
I know you're there, I know you're there
At the core of something so vast.
Hold me close, keep me safe,
Scatter the night, lead me home
From the midst of something so vast.*

It wasn't exactly art, but then again, it had a rhythm and a
tune, and he was at the very end of the day.

A baritone joined his tenor to repeat the verse.

Gabriel whirled with the pitchfork brandished at waist level.
"No!"

Sitting on the side of a stall, Satan raised his hands, palms
outward. "We haven't even had time to talk!"

"Michael!"

Both the Archangel and Raguel-senior appeared instantly,
each with his sword unsheathed.

"Yeah, you'd better call your little friends." Satan smirked,
arms folded. "It helps to have them reinforce your brainwashing."

"In the name of God, get out of here!" Gabriel shouted.

Satan flashed away, and with him the sense of three or four
watchers.

Gasping, Gabriel dropped the pitchfork, then sagged against
the wall.

Raguel laughed, and the sound rumbled all the way into Hell.
Michael scanned the barn, searching out any other demons.

"Thanks." Gabriel groped for his pitchfork with shaking
hands. "I'm glad you came."

Michael shrugged. "We said we would."

"It's no trouble at all, little man," said Raguel the Principality, his booming voice unusually so. "We look out for your safety. No one who upsets you goes unpunished."

"You drove him off yourself, you know." Michael murmured low enough that he wouldn't be overheard. "You didn't need us at all."

"I think I did," whispered Gabriel. "You frightened him; I didn't."

Michael's eyes crinkled. "We only showed up." He turned to Raguel "Everything's under control here. Would you mind if I went back?" He turned to Gabriel as if to say goodbye, hesitated, then crushed him in a hug. "Thank you." His whisper broke in the middle. "I thank God you called for us."

Before Gabriel could react, Michael vanished.

Gabriel stared as if he'd just witnessed a murder.

Raguel was leaning on the edge of the stall. "Say, could I help?" After a moment, he said, "Gabriel? Are you all right?"

Gabriel turned to him, blinking. "I'm sorry?"

"Satan didn't hurt you, did he?"

Michael's hug... Michael's words... No, don't think about that. Michael had to know he wasn't to blame for Satan's early visits. Shouldn't he?

Raguel looked concerned, and Gabriel replayed the conversation again. "No, I'm unhurt."

And then Raguel did the impossible: Gabriel saw the moment Raguel asked something of God. It could have been anything: reassurance that Gabriel wanted him there, or permission to stay, or double-checking that Satan was really gone. It didn't matter what the content of the question. What mattered was, Raguel got an answer.

Reeling from the light in Raguel's eyes, Gabriel turned away, then found himself blinking hard and having to let the pitchfork take his weight. "I— Did I summon Michael away from something important?"

Raguel leaned against the wall with a smile. "Nothing more important than you."

Still thinking about that light in Raguel's eyes, the relief on Michael's face, Gabriel couldn't find it in himself to agree.

Iyar 2

Gabriel had a dream of the Vision and a human touch. He awoke abruptly in the middle, both lonely and uncomfortable.

Even as he tried to settle back to sleep, a fire rose in the air, spiritual energy crackling around him until it suffused the room. His soul reacted, uncoiling as it attempted to connect with Seraphic fire.

He looked up to find Asmodeus staring into his eyes, pouring out Seraphic energy Gabriel had been deprived for seven months.

No!

Even as his soul tried to respond, Gabriel's hands knotted in the blanket, and he clenched his teeth, breathing hard. *God, I can't—I shouldn't—I don't—*

His throat tightened, and tension spread through his body until he couldn't do more than hang onto himself. *No.* He'd run out of water once, but even then he hadn't wanted a drink as badly as he craved this fire, just a little bit, just once. He curled tight and closed his eyes.

The door opened, and an acrid stench filled the room, surrounding Asmodeus and Gabriel. The fallen Seraph fled; something swallowed the dark fire. Gabriel curled up, knees under his stomach, arms covering his face.

A hand rested on his shoulder. "Did it hurt you?"

Gabriel raised his face to see Tobias. He couldn't stop gasping, like a man come up from under water. "He didn't. Thank you. I didn't know what to do."

Tobias gestured to a censer he held in his other hand. "This was a trick Azariah showed me."

Gabriel sat up. Conscious of Raguel still asleep, he whispered, "You knew? How?"

"I woke up feeling it. It's the demon that haunted Sarah, but it's come back a few times since then. I awaken with the sense that the house is on fire, and every time I've been able to drive it away."

Raguel stirred. Tobias said, "Come with me."

Gabriel followed him in the dark, picking his steps with care. His nerves still felt hyper-sensitive, and he could hear the breathing of the sleeping family members as well as insects outside, smell the burnt fish liver, feel the night's chill alive against his skin like a dozen ants crawling. Tobias led him down the staircase and into the kitchen, where he lit a lamp. Gabriel sat by the table, eyes closed, and he shivered.

"Are you cold?"

Those dark eyes. That welcome fire.

"Not really. I had a dream." Now there was just a dark night and this little fire. Gabriel felt his cheeks flush. "I'll be all right."

Tobias settled at the table as well, and he touched Gabriel's hand. "You don't need to be embarrassed about dreams. If it was there, it probably made the dream in the first place."

Gabriel looked up. "I was back in my father's house, but when I woke up, it was just so...lonely. I wanted to be home."

"You didn't need it to give you that dream," Tobias admitted.

Gabriel averted his eyes as Tobias arose from the table. Leaning forward, Gabriel rubbed his temples, then the ridge of bone over his eyes, then pushed his fingers beneath his hair. In the past months he'd learned the difference between "This stimulates the pressure points and increases blood-flow to the craniofacial muscles" and "Oh, yeah, keep doing that." He tried to rub out the tension, but it wouldn't go.

Tobias poured two cups of wine, then set one in front of each of them. "You'll need this."

Gabriel looked up from his hands. "I'll pass out in front of you."

"Do all your people react that way?"

He shook his head. "I think I'm the only one."

Tobias let him sip it silently for a minute, then said, "Are we good enough to you?"

Gabriel's eyes gleamed. "You're better to me than I deserve."

Tobias waved off the comment. "We can't replace your home, though."

Gabriel looked aside.

"Maybe you could go back early," Tobias said.

Gabriel shook his head. Tobias waited for him to speak, but nothing emerged.

"I'll travel with you," Tobias said. "If your father won't see you, maybe he'll speak to me."

"If I thought it would work," Gabriel whispered, still staring at the wall, "I would beg you to do it."

"Why are you so sure it won't?"

"What would you say to him?"

Tobias lowered his voice. "Your highness, I would approach you about the matter of my hired man."

Gabriel focused on the cup, but he imitated God's intonation. "What is your servant to me?"

"Sir, he belongs in your kingdom, but his father has disowned him for a slight infraction."

"Are you questioning his father's authority?"

Tobias smiled. "My hired man is hard-working and impresses me with his quiet demeanor. His father disowned him in haste for a mistake in judgment. Perhaps his father would see his son and be merciful."

Gabriel sounded dark. "Perhaps your hired man has more value as your slave than he ever did as someone's son."

"Take it easy on yourself." Tobias frowned. "That was uncalled for."

Gabriel's voice went dreamy, a pitch between tenor and soprano. "Perhaps he resisted all the lessons his father tried to teach him gently, and perhaps harshness is fit repayment for arrogance, and isolation for inaccessibility. Could it be he drove his own father to desperate measures? If his father saw no other means to soften his son's heart, what man should question it? Would you prevent the son from becoming an heir to be proud of?"

Tobias said, "Stop, Gabriel."

Gabriel's eyes focused on nothing at all. "You have to strike even your best arrow from the sky to change its course."

Tobias flinched.

Gabriel blinked. "Did I just—?"

His speech had reverted to normal.

Tobias said, "You've internalized his voice."

Gabriel knotted his hands around the cup. "I didn't think that could happen any longer." He shuddered. "He said I won't see his face until the year is up. You heard it. He was disgusted with me. Ashamed of me." He leaned forward so his elbows pressed into his ribs. "He doesn't even miss me."

"Hold it there," Tobias said. "You have no children, so listen to what a father has to say. Even with all these children and grandchildren around me, I miss them when one of them travels. I miss my sons who've moved to other cities and my daughter who married into another household." He smiled. "Now, that doesn't mean I don't get fed up with them," Tobias added, and Gabriel chuckled. "I've gotten to the point of thinking I never wanted to see one or another of them again. But given time, I repent of my anger, and I take them back into my heart again."

Gabriel closed his eyes. "His anger was right."

"You're insistent about that," Tobias said.

"Raphael asked you to grab the fish by the gills. What if you'd just kicked it off and let it swim away? How would you have had the means to drive off the demon? How could you have healed your father?" He shook his head. "Sometimes you get only one chance to do it right. After that, anything else is second best."

"Some fathers are too harsh."

"He should have killed me on the spot," Gabriel said. "My family pleaded for mercy."

Tobias's brow furrowed. "Didn't you ask him for mercy?"

Gabriel looked up slowly. "It never even occurred to me."

Tobias said, "Maybe you could try now."

Gabriel leaned against the table, and he rubbed his temples again. *Keep doing that.* His whole body felt looser, his eyes heavier, his senses disconnected.

"You're not the youngest, right?" Tobias said. "The little ones are probably pestering your father all the time. 'Where's Gabriel?' 'When is Gabriel coming back?'" Gabriel smiled weakly. "He might take you back just to keep them quiet."

Gabriel struggled to say, "I can imagine it."

211

"You could return to us if he refuses to let you see him," Tobias said.

When Gabriel didn't say anything, Tobias poured him some more wine. "Finish that and then go upstairs. I'm sure the demon won't come back tonight."

Gabriel didn't move. Tobias settled back at the table. "You might send word where you are. Then if your father relented, he could send for you." Tobias drank some of his own wine. "At least they wouldn't be worried."

Gabriel's face was tight. Tobias could probably see even in the light of the lamp that his shoulders were as rigid as iron bands.

"Let me tell you one more thing," Tobias said. "Before Gabelus, Sarah had another baby. He was born the last day of the rainy season, and the next morning dawned clear, but the baby had died." Tobias shook his head. "He was perfectly formed. Little wrinkled feet, tiny fingers, his face still pushed in, his ears flat as a sheet of parchment. Thick black hair." Tobias sighed. "We laid him in the ground and planted a tree on the spot come spring."

Gabriel bit his lip. Raphael had approached him that day, vibrating but dim. *"Tobias and Sarah named their baby after you, but the baby's going to die before morning."* Gabriel had been working out a calculus problem with three other Cherubim, and he'd said, *"Was there demonic activity? Are you allowed to heal him? Then it's God's will that the child die."* Raphael had protested that Tobias would grieve. *"Probably, but soon he'll realize the child is in a safe place. He'll never sin. He'll rest in Sheol until the Redeemer arrives to set him free. Just explain that to him."* And he'd turned back to the other Cherubim to argue about the range of an integral.

About to speak, Gabriel cut himself off.

"You were going to say it was God's will," Tobias said dryly.

"No." Gabriel choked on the word. "I was going to say, I'm sorry." His head dropped. "I'm truly sorry."

"We had Gabelus the next year," Tobias said, "but I think about that baby sometimes, especially at the close of the rains. I remember another daughter we lost to a fever when she was four. People say how proud I must be of my children, and I am—but when they say this, I always think of *all* my children. Even with this many, I remember the little lost ones, and I can see the hole they've left in my family by their departure."

Gabriel shivered.

"You need to get back to sleep," Tobias said, standing. "Come on. Back to bed with you."

Gabriel drained the cup, then followed him up the stairs. "So you're saying that just the way you still love your Gabriel, my father still loves his?"

Tobias turned. "I thought I didn't tell you the baby's name."

Gabriel tried to focus on the man's face. "I thought you did."

"Then yes, that's what I'm saying." Tobias continued climbing the staircase, then guided Gabriel through the dark to his room. "I'll leave the censer in your room for the rest of the night."

Gabriel said, "It wasn't the fish that expelled the demon."

Tobias said, "Maybe you're right. Maybe it was just something Azariah made me do while he drove it off."

Gabriel said, "I was thinking it was your faith."

"Then I'll have faith enough for both of us." Tobias kissed his cheek. "Trust that your father still loves you, even after all this."

Sivan 6

The wheat harvest over, all the workers turned their attention to the oats. After the oat harvest would come the lentils, the dates, the flax, the figs, the grapes, and finally the olives.

The attacks by Satan grew fierce, although now Gabriel called for assistance whenever demons confronted him. Sometimes they didn't focus on him: the demons might attack his work. Animals might become belligerent, accidents might happen with materials or equipment, or the weather might become too brutal to permit work. They attacked Gabriel's prayer life. At times he couldn't concentrate, and the whole effort seemed redundant. *Why pray when in time you'll return to God? Why struggle now, when it'll be so much easier later on?* They caught Gabriel in questions: did he pray correctly? Did he work toward the correct ends for the correct reasons? Should he devote his prayers to other things?

Tishri

Cheshvan

Kislev

Tevet

Schevat

Adar

Nissan

Iyar

Sivan

Tammuz

Av

Elul

The fallen Seraphim tried multiple times to do what Asmodeus had, leaving sparks like a trail of bread crumbs wherever Gabriel went, until he wondered some days why the Earth itself wasn't on fire. It raked him with longing until he found himself queasy and shivering, yearning for the interior contact that would enliven him and how he'd return his own Cherubic calm to the Seraph. He never gave in; he didn't want a demon in his heart.

After a couple of weeks of this, he learned by accident that if he got excited about something else, he could mimic a Seraph's enthusiasm and kindle a small fire within himself. Although weak, it removed the urgency. Intense sadness sometimes accomplished the same. It took work, but eventually he learned the shortcuts: he could meditate on returning home; he could get Raguel to talk about something the boy found exciting; he could coax the family to trade funny stories.

The demons found Gabriel's most vulnerable area: sleep. If they woke him in the night, he usually returned to sleep without remembering. Striking from miles away, sometimes even from Hell to avoid detection by Raguel-junior's guardian, they could wake him forty or fifty times a night. Gabriel showed signs of fatigue, but Saraquael discovered the attacks, and afterward Gabriel slept with a guardian.

The enemy responded by attacking through his dreams. A crippled Vision came to him during dreaming, once every few nights, never enough to predict, never enough to satisfy. The effect was that of allowing a starving man to smell food without eating, and Gabriel awakened from these dreams longing for company, longing for God.

Sivan 8

After working through the morning, Gabriel broke for lunch with the other men. The sun was hot enough to soften metal, but he shivered.

Raguel spoke to his father, who sent Gabriel back to the house. The women got one look at him and told him to go to bed. He protested, but Raguel's mother ushered him upstairs. "Two of the children are sick too," she said. "Joshua has a high fever, and Rafaela is vomiting."

She promised to bring him something to drink, but Gabriel found himself unnerved by the notion of vomiting. He knew the physical process and could have described exactly which muscles would tense, which would relax, and to what effect. He understood the reason it could happen. But until that minute, when faced with the idea that it might happen to him, his body had seemed tame. Now it transformed into a wild thing, able to do whatever it wanted without permission.

Raguel's mother returned with a cup of broth. He sipped, concerned he'd see it again. He wasn't even queasy.

It shocked him how little of a human body was under control of its owner. The body breathed without permission, digested food without guidance, and transmitted pain the human would rather not feel. Living this way was like clinging to an enraged bull. The actions a human chose to do with the body were so minimal in comparison to the actions a human didn't choose, such as growing hair. Such as getting sick.

Gabriel dozed through the afternoon, alternating praying with sleeping with writing a nerve-wracked journal entry with sleeping again. At the dinner hour, he awakened to find Rafaela curled at his back, so he slept again until Rafaela's mother lifted her away from him. He didn't eat anything.

The next morning he avoided breakfast and gathered with the other men to go back to the fields to tend the grapes. Gabelus sent him back to the kitchen.

"You really don't look good," Angela said. Gabriel insisted he could work, so she sent him into the cellar to make room for the harvest that would be coming in through the rest of the summer.

215

Sliding around crates and baskets sounded like an easy job, except that after half an hour Gabriel had barely started, and his head felt full of cotton. He was shivering again.

He sensed someone arrive, and he looked up to find a golden angel: Remiel. She smiled at him, and then an abrupt concern came to her pale eyes. "You look like death warmed over."

Gabriel sat on one of the crates. "Maybe just death left out in the sun."

"What do you need to do?" He told her, and Remiel moved things around while he watched, dazed. The household guardians came down to give her pointers. There was a vague sense that she shouldn't be doing this, but he couldn't put it into words, and after a while she sat beside him. "I think everything is where they needed it."

Gabriel felt cold, which was odd because he knew his body was actually too hot, but right now he wanted to stop trying to think. He needed to lie down.

Remiel helped him stand, and when he faced the staircase, she said, "You can't climb that," and made him hold onto her while she flashed him to the top. From there he got to the kitchen. He sat at the table, stunned.

Raguel's mother brought him broth heavy with herbs.

He thought about stomach spasms and relaxation of the esophageal ring. "I really don't want this."

"It was Sarah's remedy," Raguel's mother said. "She insisted on making it for any kind of illness. It doesn't smell good, but it's something of a staple in this home."

"In my home," Gabriel said, "they'd just let you be sick," and she laughed.

Angela came back upstairs, openly surprised Gabriel had managed to do as much as had been done. She told him to sleep again.

He awoke hearing clean-up sounds after the midday meal, but he still didn't feel hungry. He also didn't feel exhausted, so he retrieved his journal, got out Saraquael's feather quill, and inked it up.

Gabriel liked looking at the ink and thinking it was all his thoughts not yet stretched out. Ideas waiting to be thought: just add water. He wasn't particularly coherent, but then again, no one was going to read this but himself, and it was nice to hear an angelic voice in this world even if it was slightly delirious.

Of course that was when Tobias entered the room.

Gabriel snatched back the parchment. *God! Saraquael said I wouldn't get caught!* He sat up and started shoving the parchment into his pack.

Tobias squinted. "You're writing to your father?"

Gabriel shook his head.

Tobias said, "Poetry? Scripture?"

"Nothing that profound. One of my brothers asked me to keep a record."

Tobias came closer, but Gabriel pushed the pack into the corner.

"Is that yours?" Tobias said, picking up the quill.

Gabriel capped the ink with shaking hands. "It came from home with me."

"Amazing." Tobias touched the white and teal feather, let it balance in its hand. "One of the benefits of being raised a prince. Do you know what kind of bird grew this?"

How could he answer this without lying? "Just one that's native to our area." Maybe if he changed the subject—? "When the tip wears down, I can re-cut it, and it takes the punishment pretty well."

Tobias handed it back, and Gabriel cleaned the end with a soft cloth.

"Actually," Tobias said, "bring that with you, and come downstairs."

Saraquael, please, he sent, *as soon as I'm out of the room, get that journal and hide it.*

He felt an affirmative as he stood.

In the kitchen, Gabriel waited at the table, wondering the whole time if Tobias were hunting for the journal. Instead the man returned with a sheet of parchment.

The cooking fire usually made it warm in here, and especially in this season, it ought to have been uncomfortable, but for once Gabriel felt it just right. Angela and Raguel's mother were cooking, but the rest of the women were doing laundry or mending, spinning, or weaving.

Tobias said, "Gabelus is heading into the city. I want you to write to your father."

Gabriel sat back from the table. "But—"

"I'll have him find someone heading back toward Canaan to carry your letter for you."

Gabriel tried to focus. "I don't have any money to pay a messenger."

Tobias said, "You've worked here two months. That's twenty-six drachmae."

Gabriel furrowed his brow.

Tobias said, "You thought I wasn't going to pay you?"

"You're giving me a room and food," Gabriel said.

"You're incredibly naïve," Angela said with a laugh, and Raguel's mother interjected, "Perhaps his last employer was unscrupulous."

Tobias said, "Write to him."

Gabriel inked up the quill and sat before the blank parchment wondering what to do. In retrospect, it was inadvisable to have changed his story. He wouldn't have had to write to an entire family slaughtered by marauders.

He wrote in his native tongue, in the higher script. "Gabriel, a servant in abeyance to the Lord Most High, Cherub and one of the Seven, to my God and Father the King, my source and destination, my Creator and Judge. Praise and honor to you."

He looked up. "What should I tell him?"

Tobias sat beside him to look over the parchment. "That's a beautiful alphabet."

Gabriel opened his hands. "It's a beautiful quill and a beautiful script, but that doesn't make the words beautiful. What do you want me to say?"

Tobias sounded amused. "You're doing this solely to obey your employer, aren't you?"

Gabriel looked at his hands. It was hard to string thoughts together.

Raguel's mother looked over his shoulder. "It is very pretty. Tell him where you are and that you're safe. That's the first thing I would want to know."

Angela added, "Assure him that you're being treated well. We don't want soldiers showing up at our gates."

Gabriel sighed. "I would hardly worry about that."

He returned to the page. "I am writing to you from a farm outside Ecbatana, in the employment of Tobias son of Tobit son of Raguel, exiles from Naphtali. I have worked here two months, aiding in their harvest as well as learning the care of livestock and the proper management of a household. I am well-paid and well-fed, and the patriarch of the family treats me fairly. If you or any of my family have been concerned as to my safety, you may rest easily. Such a household is an answer to prayer, and I am blessed to live here."

He stopped and looked up at Tobias. "Now what?" and Tobias asked him to translate what he'd written, so he did.

"Just how many languages do you know?" Tobias asked.

"About as many as I'll ever need to," Gabriel said.

Tobias said, "Now ask him if you can return."

Raguel's mother said, "Not yet. First you apologize."

Gabriel said, "Is there a formula for this kind of letter?"

"It just makes sense," she said. "Before you ask to come home, you soften him up."

Gabriel turned back to the parchment. "I beg your forgiveness for my disobedience. You deserve my allegiance and loyalty, and I should not have assumed I could operate on my own authority. I'm sorry I failed you and for the disgrace I brought on your house."

He stopped, staring at the page.

"Now," Tobias said softly, one hand on his shoulder, "ask for mercy."

Gabriel blinked hard, then took a deep breath. "I would ask for your mercy. Please reconsider your just judgment and have pity on me, and bring me home again. Let me see your face. I'm sorry. I miss you. I want to go back."

Gabriel realized there were tears in his eyes only when the ink smudged. He sat back from the table.

He felt hands resting on his shoulders, and a moment later he realized it wasn't Raguel's mother, but rather her guardian embracing him, head beside his head, wings wrapped around him. Gabriel leaned into the presence, and the guardian remained intangibly near, whispering to the human part of his being in the way only angels of the ninth choir can.

Tobias said, "Is that all?"

Gabriel whispered, "I don't know what else to say."

Raguel's mother hugged him, and Gabriel startled to realize how similar the feeling of her was to the feeling of her guardian.

"Read it back to me," Tobias said.

Gabriel skipped the introduction, clumsily adjusting the wording as he translated to make it less obvious to whom he was writing. Tobias nodded. "Then sign it and seal it, and we'll get it delivered."

Gabriel finished the letter with, "All praise to you and your servants. I am always yours," and he signed with his sigil. He folded the letter, and with Tobias's sealing wax, Gabriel made pools in two places, sealing one with Tobias's seal and the other with his thumbprint, then writing an X over the folded part of the letter.

"That's an interesting way to seal it," Tobias said.

It was just the way Gabriel had seen it done before. "You can replace a seal," Gabriel said, "but if the X isn't matched properly, you know it's been opened."

Angela passed the letter to Tobias, then rested her wrist against Gabriel's forehead. "You're feverish again. Back upstairs. You shouldn't have been down here to begin with."

Gabriel went back up the steps, leaving the letter with the family.

Raguel's mother murmured, "Poor kid."

Angela huffed. "He's not poor. And he's not a kid."

Raguel's mother smiled at her. "He's so close in age to Raguel."

Angela stopped whatever she was about to say as Gabelus came into the kitchen. Tobias handed him the letter, and Gabelus slipped it into his bag.

"Do you think it will work?" Gabelus said.

Tobias said, "It depends on whatever it is Gabriel isn't telling us."

Raguel's mother paused in her cooking. "You don't think he's lying, do you?"

Tobias shook his head. "It doesn't feel as if whatever he's holding back would fundamentally change things, but there's something."

Gabelus leaned against the wall. "What do you think it might be?"

Tobias opened his hands "Well, let's break open his story. He claims he's a prince whose father threw him out. Why would a king do that?"

"He's a harsh king?" Angela said.

Raguel's mother said, "Given how all-consuming Nineveh was until its fall, he'd have to be strong to hang on this long."

"Not necessarily," Gabelus said. "Consider the timing. Nineveh fell three years ago, and all the little city-states in Canaan suddenly find themselves without an overlord. His father may have been under Ninevite control until then. The city-states are scrambling for any vestige of control they can get before Babylon tightens its hold. That means alliances between them. That means a lot of politicking."

Angela and Raguel's mother watched. "And?"

Gabelus said, "And amid all that political maneuvering, one of the kings throws his son out of his kingdom because of a small infraction. How does that make him look to the other kings?"

Tobias nodded. "If a king threw his son in prison, no one would think twice. But if he forced his son out bodily and made him find a home in another one of the city-states, a living reminder of his intolerance, that makes him look especially harsh and unmotivated by sentiment, and less likely to be backstabbed."

Angela said, "That's obnoxious!"

"Of course it is," Tobias said. "But let's broaden the picture. Gabriel says he has a lot of brothers and sisters. Who do kings' daughters ordinarily marry? They marry the children of other powerful people. Why wouldn't Gabriel stay with one of them?"

"He could be afraid he'd be killed by his father's enemies," Gabelus said.

"Or maybe," said Angela, "he resented being on display as evidence of his father's power."

Tobias pointed at her. "Now *that* would explain why he's all the way in Ecbatana rather than somewhere closer to home."

Raguel's mother said, "That doesn't fit. He doesn't resent his father. He worships him."

Tobias squinted at her. "It's funny you should say it that way. I noticed that too."

Gabelus said, "More likely he's trying to save his reputation in case he assumes the kingship later."

Raguel's mother said, "But he's one of the youngest."

They turned to her. "He is?"

She nodded as she stirred the beans in the pot. "If his father managed to hang onto power under Ninevite rule, then his father was probably king before then, meaning he's old. His likely heirs would be our age."

Tobias said, "His father might suspect he's dying, and he might have sent Gabriel away to keep him safe from the backstabbing and relay seizures of power among the older brothers."

Angela said, "Have we nailed down how many consanguine brothers he has?"

"But that doesn't matter. He acts like a youngest," Raguel's mother said. "You just saw he has no idea how wages accumulate. Ordinary interactions are a revelation to him. He's uncomfortable around more than three people. He's clearly educated, but he's not wise about the way the world works."

"He doesn't act like a prince." Angela turned to Gabelus. "Has he ever objected to anything you asked him to do?"

"No, and I've asked him to do pretty much everything," Gabelus said. "At the most he'll ask for someone to get him started until he learns, but then he finishes without a protest."

Tobias was frowning. "I'm not sure how this makes him not like a prince."

Raguel's mother said, "He didn't grow up with servants. He leaves a place exactly the way it was when he arrived. If you check his room after he's left for the morning, everything is folded and stored. I've noticed Raguel's side of the room gets straightened as well, and I assume it's Gabriel's work because that never was Raguel's way. It's a matter of straightening the blankets and the pillows, no more, but he does it."

Angela said, "And he's not arrogant."

Tobias chuckled. "But you can see he's got it in him. Ask him sometime about the Law and he'll start a lecture that has no end in sight."

Raguel's mother laughed out loud. "Any Levite could do as much."

"But he *knows* the answer to whatever you're asking, and if you contradict him, he knows you're wrong." Tobias had a sparkle in his eyes. "He said his father called him arrogant, and I went digging around until I found it."

Gabelus said, "Sometimes when I tell him how to do something, he'll have an odd reluctance, and if I ask about it, he'll tell me that isn't the best way to do the work—work which arguably he's never done before. But he'll be insistent until either I let him do it his way or order him to do it mine." He shrugged. "I guess I'd call that arrogance."

Raguel's mother said, "But if you don't ask him, will he volunteer the information?"

Gabelus shook his head.

"And is his way more efficient?"

Gabelus admitted sometimes it was.

"I have a bigger issue," Tobias said, "What are the two things you would expect a prince to talk about? And what two things does he never talk about?"

Raguel's mother said, "Politics."

Angela said, "War."

"We did ask about politics the first day he showed up," Gabelus said. "We asked what the little city-states were doing about Babylon, and he answered about a couple of them, and then said whatever happened, he was sure his father would be involved in it. But no details."

Raguel's mother said, "You always tell us a king's secret is prudent to keep."

"Which might be another reason he's this far from home," Angela said. "His father's enemies would pump him for information."

"He's very circumspect," Raguel's mother said. "And maybe he never talks about war because he's been sheltered."

"But he should have been trained to fight," Gabelus said.

Tobias winked. "When he's feeling better, why don't you try him out with that?"

"I'm not that good with a sword," Gabelus said. "But Azariah trained soldiers, and he loves to show off."

Tobias chuckled. "When you get to Ecbatana, send word to him." Then he took a deep breath. "I still suspect there's more to the story."

"Add it up," Angela said. "A prince younger than the others, not trained to take over the kingdom, raised in the king's household but not with servants, a mother with no political power, educated thoroughly in useless skills, and not imprisoned when he disobeyed. Clearly he was born on the wrong side of the bed."

Tobias's eyes widened. "That's a twist I hadn't thought of. He did refer to himself as an embarrassment to his father."

Raguel's mother said, "What were you thinking?"

He shrugged. "Just looking for another explanation, but Angela's will do." He looked at Raguel's mother. "Will the letter work? I don't think so. But I wanted to see what he would do if we forced the issue, and at the very least, his family ought to know he's safe."

In his room, Gabriel made sure the journal scroll was gone, put away the quill and the ink, and then lay down with the blanket tight to his shoulders. He was shivering again, but the next thing he did was call for Michael. Saraquael came instead. Michael was involved with an issue in Rome.

"There's a letter I need you to intercept," Gabriel said. Saraquael promised he'd take care of it, then laid a hand on his head.

Gabriel felt himself coming back to the surface of his consciousness, hearing small movements in the room, but his brain was churning over the contents of the letter, wishing he could change printed words after they'd vanished, wondering if Tobias still had the letter in the house, then going back over the whole letter again, from the greeting right down to the—

"Oh, no!" He bolted up in bed.

"Gabriel?" It was Raguel in the room with him. "Are you all right?"

Gabriel blinked—he was so careless—why had he done that?—

Raguel moved over next to him. "What's wrong?"

"I'm okay." His heart was hammering. "I just remembered something."

The light had changed in the room, so while it wasn't dark, Gabriel assumed it was after dinner. He still didn't feel hungry. In fact, he wanted to lie back down again, and that's what he did. The room wobbled.

"Would you like something to eat?" Raguel said.

The thought of food wasn't a happy one. "I just want to sleep."

Raguel nodded. "I'll be in the barn repairing some equipment, but there are folks downstairs if you need anything." And he left.

Gabriel closed his eyes and berated himself, because when he'd finished the letter, he hadn't signed his name. He'd drawn his insignia.

Careless, careless, careless.

If Tobias hadn't noticed, Gabriel had no one to thank but God. Tobias had read widely enough that he must have seen angelic insignias, and each was distinctive. If he'd noticed what Gabriel had drawn, it wouldn't take him any longer than the time to walk to his study, pull out the right scroll, and unroll it to "Gabriel," and there would be the same sigil.

Do not—do *not*—do things that close to home when battling a fever.

God, he prayed, *please don't let that lapse have revealed who I am. Please. I'm so sorry. I wasn't even thinking when I did it.*

The problem was, you didn't have to be thinking in order to make a life-changing mistake. Wasn't this whole year a monument to that?

A moment later, he felt a presence in the room. Remiel.

She sat with her feet tucked beneath her and her earrings sparkling in the sunset. She opened her hands to reveal his letter. "Look what I've been paid to deliver."

Gabriel sighed. "Thank you."

"This is the kind of thing angels were made for." She grinned. "Also, I have a message for you. Tobias didn't make the connection, whatever that means."

Gabriel let out a long breath.

She sat back. "So I'll deliver this, then." She paused. "You're still not feeling well, are you?" Without waiting for an answer, she laid her hand on Gabriel's shoulder, and she frowned. "This isn't any good—it's still rising."

Remiel guided him back to lying-down, leaving Gabriel feeling unsettled, as if he needed to say something he hadn't even thought of yet. But her hands rested on his head, and her electricity hummed through him from his head downward, and as she worked everything turned liquid to his mind, ungraspable, comfortable. He breathed deeply, his body safe, less unpredictable with an angel at his side striking out all the bad things. She had reached his upper chest when the static overwhelmed him, and when he awoke again, she had made it down to his knees, and she told him to go back to sleep, all was well. Lacking the strength to do more than obey, he faded out again, and the next thing he knew, there was daylight.

He sat up, knowing the temperature was just right, there was no cotton in his head, and his body felt tame.

Tell her thank you, he prayed.

At breakfast, food had never tasted that good before. The bread was filling, the fruit juicy. He insisted he could work a full day in the fields, and he did.

That night, the family had a surprise visit from Tobias's son Azariah. The women brought out the special wine and fruit to make the meal more festive. Gabriel watched from the sidelines as Azariah regaled the family with humorous stories about his service in the Ninevite army. Raguel sat right next to him during the meal, and he hung onto every word the way he had when traveling with Gabriel.

After dinner, Azariah offered to show Raguel some moves with a sword, and Raguel all but jumped in place.

Gabriel headed toward the barn for his after-dinner work, but Tobias pressed him to stay. "Raguel wants you to watch."

Gabriel laughed. "Raguel doesn't care." But Tobias insisted, and it was better than muck-raking, so Gabriel sat on the fence. Azariah pulled out two training swords, wooden and blunt-edged.

Gabelus stood near Gabriel. "What do you think?" When Gabriel looked at him in puzzlement, he said, "About Raguel learning to fight."

He shrugged. "I would hope he never needs to."

Azariah gave Raguel a few pointers, and they knocked swords together, but nothing intensive. Then Azariah turned to Gabriel.

In a loud voice, he called, "Hey, why don't you give it a go?"

Gabriel looked around for someone else he might be talking to, but no, Gabelus, Angela, Tobias, and Raguel's mother were all watching him.

Oh, for crying out loud. He'd been set up.

"I'd rather not." What could they hope to accomplish? He could come up with ten possible outcomes without thinking too hard, but none that made any sense.

Raguel ran over to him with the training sword. "Please? Let's see!"

Climbing off the fence as slowly as he could, Gabriel recreated Azariah in his mind: taller and stockier, and based on that lesson with Raguel, a fluid familiarity with the sword. Of course Gabriel had used a sword before, but that was in his angelic body, using a sword forged by God from Gabriel's own angelic will. And angels didn't use swords to kill. When they fought demons, they fought to restrain. Half of what he knew in Heaven would be useless on Earth, and half of what remained would be laughable with a sword not part of his makeup.

Raguel pushed him forward, and Gabriel found himself before a man who had killed in the service of Nineveh.

"Let's go," Azariah said.

Gabriel did know how to defend with a sword, and he managed through the first few volleys. Azariah never landed a direct hit, not even when he stopped treating Gabriel as a student. Gabriel's human body wasn't conditioned for this kind of fight, all the more reason to escape being struck. Although the swords were blunt, he'd parried several blows forceful enough to break bones.

From the fence, Tobias called, "Gabriel, your continued employment is not contingent on letting my son win."

Azariah charged, and Gabriel defended against a full onslaught, each strike traveling up his arms all the way to his shoulder until even his teeth hurt with the repeated blows.

"Now we've got something," Gabelus said behind him.

With a shock, Gabriel realized—Azariah wanted to test himself against a warrior prince.

In that distracted moment, Azariah attacked, and Gabriel blocked, blocked, blocked a third time, and at the fourth blow he panicked, took a step backward to brace himself while he slid his left hand to the tip of the sword. He grasped it lengthwise in front of him as a focus for his angelic power—which he couldn't access.

Azariah's sword cracked onto the center of the blade, ripping it from his hands. Gabriel darted back, knocked to the ground.

His sword tip in front of Gabriel's chest, Azariah laughed. "What kind of move was that?"

228

"Sheer desperation?" offered Gabriel.

"I could have taken your head off." Azariah extended Gabriel a hand. "Not to mention you'd have sliced your palm down the middle."

"That's why I'll never march off to war." Gabriel let Azariah pull him to his feet.

Brilliant—first he signed a letter with his real name, and then he tried to use a wooden sword as a power-focus. He should just glow like the sun and ascend into Heaven to save them the trouble of figuring it out for themselves.

But when he looked up, Tobias and Gabelus were only murmuring to each other, and Raguel's mother wanted to see his hands. She offered to help him bandage his right one, red and tingling.

As he passed Tobias, Gabriel heard him murmur, "Clearly some training" and Gabelus replied, "His father must have ordered him to strike an unarmed man."

Gabriel chilled. Was that what they'd been after?

Inside the house, he said to Raguel's mother, "I wasn't a soldier."

She patted his arm. "Don't let the men get to you. They think they know what princes should be able to do."

"I'd think that would be obvious." Gabriel stared at the table. "Princes should be able to speak ten languages and not disobey their fathers."

He returned with his hand dabbed in ointment and wrapped in a loose bandage, wondering whether he'd be able to write in the journal or if he'd better leave well enough alone. He could compose this entry in his head without writing it: "Dear God: In the past day and a half, I made a fool of myself twice." Perhaps he'd just leave this one out of the permanent record.

Outside, Tobias was standing at the fence. "You're a good sport. Thank you for letting my son hack into you." He reached into his pocket. "Here."

He handed Gabriel a heavy fruit, red but with a crown. Gabriel beamed. "Really? A pomegranate?"

Tobias chuckled. "Have you ever tried one? Here, they're tricky to open." With his knife, Tobias cut a line into the rind, then popped off the top. Gabriel watched as the man cored out the heart (a feeling all too familiar) and then found the intersection of each membrane and slit the rind toward the base. A little pressure in the center, and he'd opened it into six chambers.

Tobias handed it over, but Gabriel gave back half. He picked up one of the chambers and took a bite.

Sweetness burst from the fruit, and then—*a wall, a temple, cedar*—then came the tears.

Sweet. *It's sweet and bitter together.*

"Gabriel?" Tobias put his hands on Gabriel's arm. "Are you okay? Is the fruit bad?"

"No, I—" Human senses linked to memories, nothing like he'd expected. "My Father... I was so much younger. I was out at one of his building sites." He closed his eyes, but he couldn't block the tears. The flavor. Raphael and Michael, talking about antioxidants. "Sitting on a wall, watching the men work." He pulled another pip from the white membrane and re-lived the contradictory flavors. "I was with my friends. My Father gave me a pomegranate." Sweet. Bitter and sweet at the same time. "He wanted me to taste it. I'd never tasted one."

A man in danger. An idol. A fruit he'd known everything about except why it was important.

Tobias hugged him. "I'm sorry. I didn't mean to make you miss your father more. That's a wonderful memory."

"You didn't know," Gabriel whispered. "I didn't realize either. Thank you."

Gabriel ate some more. Sweet juice. Bitter seeds. His stomach clenched.

"You didn't ask about your letter," Tobias said. "Gabelus found a family traveling near where the letter needed to go, and for four drachmae they took it. It should take them a couple of weeks to make the trip, then your father a couple of weeks to get word back."

Gabriel nudged a rock with his sandal. "He's not going to send for me. You and I both know that. Please don't pretend, and I won't pretend."

Tobias said, "There's always hope."

"Not always." Gabriel ran his fingertip over the pomegranate pips. "For me there's only time."

Sivan 19

Sabbath. Private prayer time after the family's morning prayers. Kneeling by the creek out behind the barn, Gabriel closed his eyes.

In his native tongue, Gabriel sang. He didn't have the range of his angelic voice, and he didn't have an orchestra, but he had a hymn. Raphael had written this one, and in some crippled fashion it was a way they could be together right now.

He tingled as he sang, acutely aware of the world around him, and realized another angel sang with him. As he moved through the words, the voice became Michael's, and then afterward he felt what might be Remiel.

Before Gabriel could identify any of the other voices, someone crashed through the brush toward him. "Gabriel! That's awesome!"

Gabriel scrambled to a stand, a little dazed and a lot homesick for the song and the peace of being with God however he was able. Raguel scrambled over the rocks toward him. "I didn't know you could sing like that!"

"Careful, it's easy to slip." Gabriel gestured to the rocks at the creek edge. "I'm not really that great—"

"You sang on the road, but it wasn't like that. Those were just road songs. This was a hymn. What language was it?"

Gabriel said, "Did anyone ever tell you that you ask too many questions?"

Raguel paused a moment. "I think you did."

"Smart man," Gabriel said, and Raguel laughed out loud.

"Well, go on!" Raguel sat on one of the larger rocks. "It's not like we forbid singing on the Sabbath. Heaven knows we forbid everything else."

Gabriel said, "There's a purpose to resting."

Raguel raised his hands. "I get that. I like resting. It's everyone fussing over whether you're resting *enough* or if you've taken more steps than a Sabbath's journey. I don't even see why we need one."

Gabriel said, "It's a clever thing, setting aside time. When people set up idols, they make a sacred place for them, a location. God set apart a sacred *time* for himself, and that made history and time sacred."

Raguel pointed at him. "Did anyone ever tell you that you answer too many questions?"

Gabriel said, "Everyone."

"Smart people," said Raguel. "But yeah, if God asks us to quit working one day a week, that's fine by me. It just shows us the work we do the rest of the week is useless."

Gabriel frowned. "I wouldn't say that. I like working. And if you think about it, God rested on that first Sabbath, but He's worked every Sabbath since then."

Raguel shook his head. "You're making me confused." He hesitated. "You like working?"

Gabriel nodded. "Sabbaths are hard because it feels as if we're just waiting for the work to begin again, and even though working for your family is harder than what I was doing before, it feels right. I like pulling my own weight."

"That's good," Raguel said as they headed back to the house. "Because I really like having you here, and I know my Dad thinks you work well. If you decide not to go home, I bet Grandpa would adopt you so you'd always be a part of our family."

Back at the house they found a crowd of the family beneath a cedar tree.

Raguel's mother met them at the edge. "Rafaela's kitten is caught in the top branches."

Rafaela cried at the base of the trunk. "Pearl!" she screamed. "Please come down!"

Gabriel shielded his eyes and scanned the height of the tree. No, that was too far up for the kitten to come down on her own. She'd fall.

Gabriel grasped the trunk.

Gabelus said, "Climbing is work."

Gabriel knew the rules. "Sabbath or not, you save a life."

With a scramble, Gabriel made his way onto the lowest limb and ascended. A rustling informed him that Raguel followed not far below.

Angels fly. Vertigo had never troubled Gabriel; it didn't enter his mind that perhaps people didn't live in trees for a good reason. He advanced through the branch-maze, pushing himself with his legs as often as grasping with his arms, and eventually the foliage that looked so thick from the outside dissolved into bare-boned branches.

The tree swayed, and the leaves whispered against one another like conspirators. It wasn't apparent where to put his hands next, and he craned back his neck to get a dizzying view of the kitten, still four cubits above.

Last summer, Gabriel had rested his ear against this trunk and talked to the tree, finding out how old it was, learning which had been the good years. He'd rejoiced with the leaves as they basked in the sunlight, each one contributing little to the whole but all together powering a life towering above the plains. Legs swinging, wings relaxed, he'd watched the flax harvest and talked to God and waited for Raphael. It might have been on this branch. Was this the tree with the dead Gabriel beneath?

Gabriel gripped the trunk, wishing he could grab himself from back then and give himself a shake. *Look at yourself!* he shouted at himself a year ago, a Gabriel adoring mysteries in a tree rather than visiting a human household with his friend. *Go down there— be with Raphael! Don't throw away the gift of time together! Trust in God! You've got to change something or you'll fall— you'll fall—*

"You okay?" Raguel called.

Gabriel got a grip on himself and continued climbing.

On branches at right angles to one another, the pair stood at a dizzying height. Gabriel's fingers could finally stroke the tiny head. He shifted a bit into his angelic abilities so he could talk to the animal as he gathered her into his hand. "Easy, Pearl, you kitten of great value."

Raguel, a little lower than himself, said, "Hand her to me and you go down, then I'll hand her back to you."

As Raguel secured the kitten, Gabriel shifted his weight to descend, and his foot slipped.

He reacted instinctively by flexing his spine and trying to flare wings he didn't have.

Raguel lunged for him, but his fingers did no more than brush Gabriel's arm, and Gabriel's grasp met only air.

A blurred world met Gabriel's mind. As he sought a landmark in the haze, he tried to turn away from a peculiar pressure in his head, but pain stabbed through his left side. A grassy smell surrounded him, and something firm but warm pressed into the back of his neck. He reached for the Vision, but it wasn't there, and that scared him, so he tried again, only he couldn't find God. There was a rapid rasping, high-pitched and scary-sounding. He wanted the sound to stop until he realized it came with his every breath. Why was he breathing? Why wasn't God here?

Someone stroked his hand. He clutched for them, and then his heart flailed trying to find God until he plummeted into another unwilling sleep.

"Can you hear me?" said a familiar voice after a dark time. "Talk to me."

He reached for God. Nothing. *God*? Nothing. *Father*? Nothing. *Where are you? Why aren't you with me? Why can't I see you?*

"Gabriel?" the voice said.

Stay here, Gabriel tried to say. He wasn't sure the words ever emerged. *Don't leave me alone!*

Existence faded into another whirlpool, and then he became aware of stroking on his arm, coolness and a bitter smell. Some kind of salve. His arm felt clumsy and far away. Lots of murmured speech. Someone held a warm cloth that smelled of barley and herbs to the back of his skull.

He reached for God. Nothing.

"Where are you?" he asked with urgency. He slurred his words.

"Easy." A smooth voice. "Drink this."

Hands on his body, and Gabriel flexed, struggled – they were touching him, hurting him, going to push him down and violate him – Sodom. "Leave me alone!" he shouted, but pain stabbed through his head, and he crumpled.

"Gabriel!" came a stern voice. It sounded...like authority. He knew it. Not sure who it was, but he knew it. "Stop it! You're safe, but you have to drink this."

Someone touched him, but he struck out again. "Don't touch him," said the authoritative voice. "Just help him drink."

There was a cup in his hands. It stank of herbs and myrrh and something else. *Drink it*, repeated the voice. Gabriel gagged it down, then closed his eyes.

"Try to stay awake," said Tobias. That was Tobias. Gabriel was supposed to do what Tobias said.

"Stay with us." Tobias again, urgent.

Gabriel couldn't do more than murmur. "I want my Father. I want Raphael."

He was speaking in his native tongue. It wasn't the language the others were using, but even though he understood them fine, he couldn't produce their words. Whatever was in the cup left his tongue leaden and language at a distance. He pushed, because maybe they'd understand and help, but their word for "Father" wouldn't come.

He tried to lie down again, but someone held him upright. He struck out, unable to see who it was, and he heard a crash and smelled wine. "Why are you fighting us?" someone shouted at him. "We're trying to keep you from dying! Do you want to die?"

Tumult around him, so many voices, too much motion. Gabriel felt another cup pressed into his hands, warm. "Drink," said a voice, a woman's. "I'm not touching you. Just drink. You need to get better. I'm going to stay here, but I'm not going to touch you."

Gabriel took the cup. But the world was so unsteady, so frightening. He only wanted his Father.

Gabriel awoke restless, and in the next moment he realized how uncomfortable he was, how he was in a cold sweat, and how his stomach was spasming. Garlic, wine, grease—he could taste everything they'd put into him in the last hours, and he wanted it out. He tried to turn onto his left side, but fire flashed up his body, and his head throbbed. He rolled to the other side and drew up his knees, but he couldn't get all the way over. Someone had bound his arm to his chest.

"Easy," someone said, and in the next moment another angel was all around him, breathing with him and quelling the nausea. "They may be misguided, but they worked hard feeding you even that little bit. You'd be ungrateful to get rid of it now."

Gabriel curled around himself and shivered.

Silence for a moment, silence and peace, stillness inside. Relief. He could relax again.

Then, gathering himself, Gabriel noted the sarcasm and the spiked hair and groped in his mind until names and places tumbled into their rightful boxes. Remiel.

Gabriel whispered, "What happened?"

"Do you remember climbing an insanely tall tree?" She stayed behind him, her wings over his left side, warming the air around him. "Our adversary got his wish: you're finally a fallen angel."

Gabriel probed inside himself, then fought renewed dread: the damage went deep.

Remiel geared up her glow slowly, mindful not to hurt his dilated pupils. "You broke your upper left humerus and dislocated your left shoulder, as well as getting yourself a scary concussion."

Keeping his voice low only made him sound stunned. "No half measures."

"As anyone would expect from you. When you do a job, you do it thoroughly." Remiel brushed a few strands of hair from his eyes, but she stopped when Gabriel flinched. "Gabelus's guardian protected your spine when you hit the ground, and Rafaela's guardian shielded your head. Even so, when I arrived, you were minutes away from a grand mal seizure."

Her subdued light revealed a blue kimono, and the silk slipped over him whenever she moved. Gabriel tried to concentrate on the softness of silk rather than the sharpness of pain. "There was a kitten, right? What happened to it?"

"She's none the worse for wear."

"Did I actually get to the top of the tree?" When Remiel assented, he said, "I hate this. I've never forgotten anything before. It's like a pit in my brain." Gabriel sighed, then gasped. "Raphael doesn't know, does he?"

She squeezed his hand. "He doesn't. They did pray to God to send Raphael, but I intercepted the prayer."

Gabriel let out a long sigh. "Good. I was afraid—"

"It would have been rough for him to stay away," Remiel said.

The world felt like a whirlpool. Gabriel closed his eyes. "Don't let him fall."

"You should have worried about falls twelve hours ago." Remiel hugged him. "I now know what an acute subdural hematoma is, by the way, and now I also know how to get rid of one."

Gabriel touched the splint, and even that light contact made him gasp. "I don't suppose you could mend this?"

"Not without the family realizing." She sat up and away from him, but her warmth remained. "Everyone heard it snap."

"That's a disquieting thought." Gabriel tried to sit up, but it didn't work very well, so he lay back down. "If you fix it, I won't tell anyone."

Remiel stuck out her tongue at him.

Gabriel wanted to shrug but suspected that would be a painful move. "I could get back to work sooner."

"You're not going to go back to work."

"But I have to!" Gabriel kept his voice low so as not to awaken Raguel, unintentionally sounding infuriated. "Tobias won't keep someone who's useless."

She didn't answer because he knew—he could feel it, could feel the futility of protesting. Why should God break the laws of Creation to keep Gabriel in a home where he shouldn't have been in the first place?

Gabriel closed his eyes against a bout of dizziness and nausea. Remiel touched his throat, and the churning stopped again.

"They've been giving me wine for the pain, haven't they?"

"Laced with myrrh at a strength that would drop a camel." Remiel chuckled. "I wasn't sure if you'd awaken from the first dose, but you looked ecstatic."

Gabriel smiled ruefully. "I'll sleep through the next two weeks."

"Future generations will also have scathing things to say about using alcohol to treat a head injury." Remiel stroked his cheek.

He closed his eyes. "I want Raphael."

Remiel yanked back, eyes glinting. "I did my best! I told you, there was an audible snap. I could also have hung a big sign around your neck that said 'Hey, look, I'm an archangel.'"

Remiel's glow suddenly hurt, and Gabriel covered his eyes. Nothing made sense. Raphael could have fixed this. God could fix this. His inner eyes reflexively reached for God. Nothing, a lightning bolt of nothing. "It just hurts," he whispered. "It doesn't stop."

Remiel's wings flared. "I shield you from your enemies and your friends and your wounds. And if you'd rather I go, I ask your forgiveness, and I'll leave."

Gabriel curled around himself, screwed his eyes as tight as he could. The world wouldn't stay on one axis. "I'm sorry," he managed. "I'm not judging you."

His soul reached for hers, and she didn't clamp shut. He let her see the emptiness, the unfilled space God should inhabit, and she recoiled further. Recoiled not as much in disgust as in horror, but then she moved in closer. He sent, *It's not you. It's not Raphael. I miss Him. He's not here.*

Remiel folded back around him, but it didn't ease the pain. And then she did something he never expected: she opened the same way and revealed a kindred emptiness, the spots of her soul scooped-out and brittle after the loss of her brother, and she'd never get him back.

Gabriel curled up in her emptiness, and she curled up in his, and for a moment he felt understood, and he understood her. All of her.

She murmured, "I shouldn't have gotten mad. Please forgive me. You're post-concussive or whatever they call it."

"You healed the concussion." Gabriel drew up his knees and closed his eyes. "I'm just difficult to be around."

"You still have a concussion. I only made sure it wouldn't kill you." At her touch, the world grew fuzzier. "You're looking in worse shape every minute. Get some sleep."

Gabriel reached up to touch her shoulder, ignoring the nausea resulting from the untoward movement. "I'm sorry."

"Don't be sorry. I love you." Remiel tucked the blankets around him and cupped her palm around his shoulder, then laid her hand over his eyes. "Just try to get some sleep so you can heal."

Sivan 20

When Gabriel awoke, daylight streamed through the window, and Raguel had already gone to work. He couldn't see Remiel. Tentatively, he used his right arm to help himself stand.

A warning flashed at the peripheries of his consciousness, one of the household guardians, and then it departed.

Dizzy at first, Gabriel had to lean on the wall, shielding his eyes because of the blinding daylight. When the room returned to a constant axis, he made his way into the hall. He tried to head downstairs to the kitchen, but he stumbled and had to rest against the wall again before he could continue.

Angela came up the steps at the same time he started down, and she let out a shriek. "What are you doing? Get back to bed!"

He squinted uneasily.

"Go back to your room. I'll bring you something to eat."

"There's no need." He swayed on the top step. "I'll come down."

Angela stalked up the stairs, forced Gabriel around and back to his room. "You get yourself into bed before you collapse. Someone will bring you a meal."

Gabriel sat to wait, but then it felt better to be lying prone, and then it felt even better to have his eyes shut, and when he felt himself becoming aware again, he found Tobias sitting on Raguel's bed in prayer. At his side were a cup and a bowl. The room smelled of bread.

Gabriel said nothing, only thought about what he might be praying for.

Tobias opened his eyes to find Gabriel watching him, and he smiled. "You're awake. I was wondering if Angela hadn't imagined the whole scenario."

Gabriel shook his head.

"I hoped you might feel hungry," said the old man, moving to sit closer to Gabriel, "so I took some of the new bread and a couple of fruits. Angela got miffed about the new bread, but I think she understands our honorable cause."

"I don't mean to cause trouble." Gabriel yawned, but that made his head ache. He tried to prop himself on his right arm. He'd had no idea the room got so bright in the middle of the day, and he felt every shift in the floor boards like a boat on the ocean. "I could have gone down myself."

"Yes, by falling, and we'll have no more of that."

Gabriel positioned himself cross-legged, and Tobias handed him the cup. The smell of juice made him flinch, but Tobias wanted him to drink, so Gabriel sipped it, then paused heavily.

"Oh, you can stay with us," Tobias said. "That was never a question. This happened while you helped my granddaughter, after all, and where else could you go?"

Gabriel could already tell the juice and his stomach weren't going to get along, so he set the cup to the side. "I should go home." He tried to sound neutral. "My Father wouldn't forbid my family to take me in; He just wouldn't treat me like a son."

"You're my son until your real father receives you," Tobias said, "and my sons don't say ridiculous things. You'll stay here."

"You took me in as a kindness to a traveler," said Gabriel. "I've outstayed my welcome."

"It's a kindness to a traveler not to let him become one if I can help it. Especially a man with a broken arm."

"What value could I possibly have?" Gabriel asked.

Tobias said, "You don't need your arm to teach."

Teacher

Sivan 22

Hi, God. It's good to be coherent again.

Tobias decided to keep me. He's a wonderful man, and I can understand why You chose him to be visited by Raphael with hundreds of other families in grave predicaments all over the world. By the way, it's fortunate that I can write with my right hand, otherwise this journal would stop for a few weeks. Although it galls me, I've become attached to writing. Father, chalk one up for Saraquael.

How do I feel? That's what I'm supposed to write about, and for the first time I have an answer: I'm in pain. My eyes bother me if I focus on close objects for too long, a category into which written characters neatly fit, so I take this slowly. My arm aches until I touch it, when it scales up to hurting. When they tightened the bandage this morning, I learned that some things can hurt so much you can't even breathe. I actually saw sparks.

This pain system is remarkably inefficient. If its purpose is to let me know something is wrong, it can stop now. I know: the bone broke. What's the point of the arm and the shoulder and the head whining at me, "We're still damaged. We're still damaged. We're still damaged"? It's like being surrounded by thirsty toddlers asking for water. Although maybe if it went away, I'd stop paying attention and injure it again, the way a man's conscience stops bothering him about habitual sin. Maybe a thousand years ago, my own conscience told me something once. Maybe I buried it, and maybe it should have kept singing, pestering me, reminding me. But I've lost track of the point.

So odd, this idea that the family intends to keep me around. There's ample reason to throw me out of the household: I'm as useless to them as I am to the other angels.

What an amazing family. They have the most lively trust in You that I've encountered so far. Tobias founded the whole family on You, and that makes it a true community.

Community. I guess I never really considered it vital to the soul. All the community I need is God: that was my working hypothesis. But there's more than one of us, so does that mean that interaction on a level is as necessary as vertical interaction to the Almighty?

It's a thought.

I never relied on my friends. We coexisted. I think they loved me, but it never occurred to me to wonder if I loved them. I do love them. I never needed them, never asked for help from anyone but Raphael, but now he's gone and the rest do more for me that I would have imagined. I didn't ask for any of it. It's not even necessary, but they've remained constantly—watching, if not visible.

How does that make me feel?

I'm not good at this, even after so long. Raphael always did the feeling for me. In a difficult situation, I took my cue from him. I can't do that now. But I guess it hindered me even then. I tried to be a team by giving him what I considered the 'dirty work' but what he loved to do. So I wasn't whole then, either, just leaning. Maybe I became more entire when You cut me off.

How does that make me feel?

Make me—feelings are compulsions: we don't have a choice. No one ever said, "I'll feel excited today." How does this make me feel?

Well, it feels good to ask that. I've never not had an answer before. A right answer. One I could debate, define, deduce. A premier experience, and I feel excited.

243

It denies my nature, though, or do I simply misunderstand myself? Even so, I'm not angelic any longer. I've become a man. Angels don't write journals. Angels don't get headaches.

Angels see God. Sometimes. Most of us.

But I've mislaid the point I wanted to make, that being my new-found community. Tobias and Raguel-junior and the whole family genuinely care about me, and it's all built on their service to You. It's a family that Raphael founded. He sowed; I reap.

Father God, I wish I hadn't left him then. I wish I hadn't acted so stand-offish. I think I was wrong then. I had no idea what it would be like being alone.

It's an exercise in lateral outreach. How does that make me feel?

Too much, too fast. You gave me a full year for this. I have time.

Sivan 23

Remiel sat on a writing desk in Tobias's study while Gabriel prowled the scrolls. "I have to admit," she said, "it does my heart good to watch you sort through this stuff. That way I don't have to."

Gabriel smiled. "There's so much here! But much as I'd like to spend the next months reading, what I really need is a guidebook on how to teach Hebrew to human children." What if someone had already written one? Would it be breaking the rules to have Remiel scour up one and deliver it overnight? "Teaching angels is easy: you explain, and they get it. Human brains require trickery, mnemonics, repetition, and all these other techniques I never really utilized before. You teach a child to spin by making him spin and eventually the muscles take over without conscious thought. But teaching a language?"

Remiel chuckled. "Better you than me."

Gabriel studied her until she arched her eyebrows. He said, "I agree."

"Hey!" Laughing, she fired an arrow of light right through him. It tingled where it passed. "You're mean. Michael! Gabriel's being mean to me!"

Michael appeared. "I'm sorry, what?"

Remiel dissolved in giggles, and Gabriel grinned. "She requires your defense."

Michael shook his head. "I'm on break now. You'll have to call a legion of Principalities instead." He looked at the scroll on the writing desk. "Should you be working your arm that much?"

Remiel said, "It's knitting a bit crooked, but otherwise fine. I bet Gabriel had no idea how resilient the human body was."

Gabriel huffed. "I could have lived forever without that knowledge, too."

Remiel made a face at him. "You need a sense of humor about it."

"You can afford to have a sense of humor about it because you're not living it." Then Gabriel paused. "I'm sorry. I shouldn't be bitter. I'm convalescing, and that's a new experience. That and living completely off the charity of others."

Michael said, "You're going to teach."

"They don't really need a teacher." Gabriel rolled through the scroll looking for a specific passage. "Although housing me in return for questionable services is of great merit to Tobias's soul, it's very frustrating to me. I shouldn't have snapped. Please forgive me."

She winked. "It's okay, Sport. I've been there."

Gabriel forced his gaze to Michael. "It's like that with you, too. You're always on call, and you're being a better friend to me than I would have been to you if positions were reversed. Thank you."

Michael's eyes widened. "You're welcome. I told you it's not a problem."

"Michael's great." Remiel turned to Michael. "I'm not just saying that to embarrass you."

Gabriel looked at her. "He's very non-assuming."

She said, "Whatever that means."

Gabriel frowned. "Does that make me *assuming?*"

She leaned forward. "And I really don't know what that means."

Gabriel leaned on the desk, but then his arm shot fire through the rest of him, and he jerked back. So easy to forget, but not easy

245

to forget for a long time. "I'm always assuming something—usually right, always defendable. But Michael, you don't do that. You're sometimes wrong, sometimes right, always graced, and always God's. You make other people strong. I wish I could do that."

Michael shook his head. "Should I call Saraquael and host a little admiration party in my honor?"

Gabriel rubbed his arm. It still ached. "Well as long as I'm wishing, I'll also ask for Saraquael's knack for making people feel special and Uriel's utter acceptance of every soul."

Michael said, "But you bring people to know God. That's important too."

Gabriel had stopped moving through the scroll, just staring at a passage too complicated for teaching children. "But maybe... maybe whenever someone asked me to listen, I gave an analysis while you gave understanding and Saraquael gave undivided attention."

He took a seat. Why should it be so hard to stand nowadays? His legs weren't hurt. "The thing is, that's what Cherubim do. We stay detached from our arguments and dismantle others' theories, and that's how we derive truth. It's not bad, except maybe I've done that at times that weren't appropriate, or made people re-define views they didn't want to re-define."

He looked up at Remiel. "You can't tell me that's not true."

She grimaced. "It's true."

He looked at Michael, who also said, "Well, yes."

He traced his fingers over the parchment. "You guys put up for centuries with someone who wouldn't back off from sensitive subjects and reacted to a confession by dissecting the speaker. That's not right. You have to knock the arrow out of the air."

Michael said, "Maybe you weren't quite that bad."

Gabriel said, "Maybe I can improve."

Remiel said, "You're a Cherub – define improvement. Goodness comes in so many styles that you'd go mad trying to combine them all."

Gabriel went back to scanning the text. "Cherubim have to detach ourselves from our arguments or else we'd get entangled in our own opinions and have a harder time finding truth. But what did it get me, except detached from God?" He rubbed his temples. "For a Cherub, I'm so stupid sometimes."

Michael knelt on the floor in front of Gabriel and rested his hands on top of Gabriel's. "No, you're being too hard on yourself. You grew in the wrong direction. You're making corrections now, and God's guiding them. You're going to be all right."

Gabriel leaned forward. "What if I forget what it's like seeing God?"

Remiel said, "You can't forget that. It's like existing. The Vision has nothing to do with you handling it correctly. It's not as though you'd blink and miss out on God Almighty."

Gabriel laughed out loud, and then he realized he was laughing and laughed even harder. "What if the Vision comes back and I miss it because I'm facing the wrong way?"

Remiel laughed too then. "Whoops! Too bad."

Michael squeezed his hands. "You're doing much better than you were. Now that you're making lesson plans for the children, you actually smile in your sleep. You always slept frowning before. And you've stopped referring to yourself as fallen."

Gabriel hesitated. "That's not a good thing. The demons don't refer to themselves as fallen either." He rubbed his chin. "So what am I if not semi-fallen?"

Remiel said to Michael, "Now you've done it."

"Buried?" Gabriel frowned. "Blinded?" He shook his head and said, "Hey, Raphael, I need an opinion."

And froze, with ice right through his heart.

That hurt. That hadn't happened for months.

He closed his eyes, but Remiel rushed to him. "Oh, I hated when I did that. I'm sorry. It just springs up on you."

Gabriel swallowed hard and tried to make the unshed tears stay unshed. "Raphael said Tobias did that right before burying Sarah, tried to ask her a question about her burial." He rubbed his eyes. "I'm sorry."

Remiel pressed her forehead against his. "It's okay. No, actually, it's not okay. It stinks. It truly does."

What are you doing now, Raphael? What kind of angel am I? Do you ever try to ask me something, or are you used to reaching for your other bonded Cherubim? Do you still pray for me? Did you see the sunset the other night, when all the sky turned pink except for some clouds that were utterly black on the tops and the sides but lifted blue along their bottoms? Have you written any music lately? Did you ever notice the way bees clean their faces when they sit, rubbing their front feet over the flat parts? I bet you never knew that just touching a tomato plant will leave your hands smelling like tomatoes for a few minutes. I wanted to show you that rock I hit with my shovel last month only to have it splinter into lots of flat sheets. I wanted to tell you that even after all these months I miss you like blazes, and I'm sorry I abandoned you.

But maybe you know that. I wanted to tell you all those things before I forgot them, only I can't save up all those moments to bring them to you any longer, and now when my first reaction to something is "Raphael would have loved to know that," I don't try to keep it in my mind. I'm sorry. Because somewhere in Heaven, I'm sure you're doing the same. And I hate that.

Sivan 27

With the side-effects of the concussion fading and Gabriel's eyes able to withstand brightly-lit places, he started teaching Tobias's grandchildren and the servants' children.

Every day, Gabriel awakened before sunrise and spent an hour with the Torah. One at a time, the children came to him after breakfast, and Gabriel taught them new words, new tenses, and old variants on new words. He threw in a few close-reading tips when they stumbled through a section of the Torah. With the older children, who already knew the Torah well, he had some difficulty convincing them not to recite from memory, so he tried to make it fun. He gave them scavenger hunts and pop quizzes and word puzzles.

Children were loud. Their high-pitched voices were perfectly designed to pierce right through his skull (*Another design flaw,*

Father?) and he tired out quickly. On the other hand, repeated and constant exposure to a language they were already familiar with helped them pick it up a lot faster than he thought they would.

Teaching the children to read was a lot more fun. Gabriel used the Torah to demonstrate letters and words. He drew the characters with a brush on broken pottery shards or had them trace letters in the ground.

Satan appeared one morning as Gabriel listened to one of the children reciting in Hebrew, tapping his foot and smiling sharply. Gabriel's shifted his eyes without turning his head. A Seraphic warmth permeated the room, but this he ignored. The child continued without knowing about the new visitor.

"You're barred from direct contact with Raphael," said Satan in flawless Hebrew, "and none of the angels who call themselves your friends consent to shuttling messages. I alone know how you think at the moment, and I will ease your mind. I'll transport those messages for you and provide you and Raphael the consolation you require during your disgrace."

Gabriel's eyes narrowed, but he said nothing. The student continued reciting.

"I'm going now as a favor," said Satan. "I'll tell Raphael you pray for him and think of him often."

Gabriel had no time to object. Satan vanished.

Gabriel turned back to the student.

The message was true, no matter its origin. In all likelihood, Raphael wouldn't even consider responding. But the fact that Satan was trying this now when he'd never tried to approach Raphael before – did that mean he thought he had a chance? Could he really use Gabriel to nab Raphael?

Fallen bonded pairs always changed, manacled to one another's souls, hating each other the way they hated God, each blaming the other, each trying his best to deprive the other of every privacy. They'd work together because they had to, but they knew each other well enough to wound each other right down to the core. Insults. Resentment. Disgust.

Raphael. Hating him.

Gabriel shuddered, and he leaned against the table. The student stopped. "Are you all right?"

"Say it in Hebrew," Gabriel said.

Raphael wouldn't listen. He'd laugh Satan out of the choirs. The other angels would intervene.

Although they hadn't helped him when Satan came.

Satan was a Seraph too. What if he played up Raphael's Seraphic fervor and worked on the loneliness, on the separation—what if he did, and Raphael listened?

Gabriel shivered, at which the young student asked again (in Hebrew) if Gabriel felt all right.

Raphael, *his* Raphael, evil. That Gabriel from the dream had never left him, that vision of himself with a dark twist. Raphael should never have a dark twist, fiery with hatred and his eyes wild rather than Gabriel's would-be cold.

Gabriel said, "Look over the passage again. I'll be right back."

He walked from the room, from the house. No one stood outside, and no one watched. Raphael. A cold-eyed Cherub with black armor, and a disgusted Seraph filled with loathing.

Gabriel ran without thinking.

God, he prayed, *grab me!*

He leaped into the air and transformed into an angel.

One panicked thought brought him to the ring of the Seven. His drawn sword blazed so brightly it blinded him.

Satan stood at the periphery of the ring by an empty space.

"Lucifer!" Gabriel used his momentum behind his descending sword. "No!"

Satan laughed and met Gabriel's sword with his own. The block jarred Gabriel's arm all the way to the shoulder as though he remained human.

"And you think you can stop me?"

Still airborne, Gabriel swung again. "Leave us alone!"

Satan might have done more than block Gabriel's strike, but suddenly a half-dozen angels clustered near. Michael and Raguel with their flashing swords, short-haired and golden-armored Remiel, Uriel with a stronger core than any of the Seven understood, Saraquael glowing white, and Dobiel who regarded Satan with disgust.

Satan's eyes had gone wide, but it was at Gabriel he stared. "You can't even see each other?"

"Go!" Flush with energy, Gabriel raised his sword. "In the name of God, leave!"

With a glimmer, Satan turned to the left. "He's living with—"

"No!" Gabriel unfurled all six wings and emitted a concussion forceful enough to silence the final words. The power knocked everyone backward, even Raguel. Satan vanished.

Gabriel's sword clattered to the ground, and he dropped to hands and knees, shaking. His weapon flickered where it lay.

Saraquael and Michael exchanged looks, glanced at the same point to Gabriel's left, and flashed away.

Gabriel's head dropped. "Please watch Raphael. Don't let him get fired up."

Raguel crouched near the Cherub. "We won't let that happen."

Gabriel visage had glowed when he'd arrived, but that energy dropped off. He turned his head by reflex to look at the Throne of God, just inside the circle of Seven...and saw nothing.

He crumpled to his knees, shivering with the memory of a smile and the glory he should have been able to see.

Uriel helped Gabriel to a stand. "Would we let Raphael leave? No. And you watch your own flame. You burn brightly yourself when you're needed."

Gabriel looked back again at the empty spot, but Uriel raised a hand to his cheek and guided his gaze away.

Uriel brought Gabriel back home, restoring Gabriel to human form with a blessing. The children had finished up the work he'd left, so he dismissed them to their chores, then wandered into the kitchen. Angela and some of the young women were working.

Gabriel looked in the cooking pot where one of the girls had just dumped a chicken carcass.

"What's that for?" he asked.

The girl, a year older than Raguel, looked at Gabriel uncertainly. "Making broth."

Gabriel looked back into the pot. Water and chicken bones. It made sense that broth came from somewhere, but he never considered how the remains of one meal could make the base of the next.

The girl said, "I have to chop up the vegetables, and then I'll be finished."

Gabriel followed her to the table and took another knife.

"What are you doing?" asked the girl.

"I can help," said Gabriel.

She hesitated and then got a glint in her eye. "Sure. Why don't you help?" She patted the table top. "You can sit right next to me."

Vegetables got chopped and herbs got chopped. Dirty looks got exchanged between the young women. Tobias's granddaughter who'd invited Gabriel to sit chatted with him about the things he'd done since arriving at the farm, although there wasn't really a lot of room because she kept being close enough to brush his arm. Frequently he didn't need to answer her questions because the other women would talk over her.

This year had given Gabriel a different perspective on eating. Food and meals and hunger had all been new with a tremulous uncertainty at the beginning of the year, but within days they became the most predictable. He had never experienced hunger, and so he'd understood the manna in the desert as something of a staple without recognizing the neediness of a person being fed. He had encouraged Hagar to eat because her body needed it, not comprehending that someone's concern for whether you eat equates to someone's care that you're alive at all.

It hadn't been until his arrival here that he understood a "meal" as a concept rather than a set time with a single purpose. The shepherds had prepared and consumed food, but it was just business. Here he would work from sunup until mid-day, break for food with the other men in the fields, and then continue until nightfall. Then they'd return spent to the house, muscles aching. At the door they'd be greeted by scents that instantly reminded the body of how much work it had done, the motion and the standing and the walking, and how much it longed for something. Hunger meant lacking, and Gabriel had never lacked anything, so every night it was a revelation to feel the reminder that he could be filled, that others shared the same emptiness, and that they all would meet that need together.

More than the food, there would be laughter, stories, company, Rafaela's touch as she slipped her hateful mushrooms onto his plate or sneaked away one of his barley cakes (and then Angela would see Gabriel's plate empty and give him another— Rafaela profited immensely from sitting beside him). The family would share a sense of purpose along with sharing a victory against the cold, against hunger, against interior emptiness.

The whole day revolved around food: Gabriel fed animals that would become food, harvested or tended plants that would become food, and then returned to the house and was given food so he could do it again the next day.

He'd cooked with the other shepherds, a task Gabriel had understood at its most pragmatic as heating comestibles until a respectable portion of the bacteria perished, making some adjustments for flavor. What took place in Tobias's kitchen involved talk, connection, transformation, beauty, and teamwork. Gabriel did his portion while absorbing the sense of togetherness. *Community.* Was this how it felt to an outsider watching the angels, or at least, should it feel that way? Everyone with his own job, the fire of God alight in the background, and in the end something that fed them all? And would he ever partake of that again?

When the cutting and chopping ended, Gabriel looked into the pot. Wonder of wonders, the water had a familiar scent, and it was tinged with a brothy color.

"You never made broth before?" Angela said, coming in behind him.

"It's like a miracle," Gabriel said.

"It's the miracle of hot water," Angela said. "It draws all the good stuff out of what you'd otherwise have to throw away. Now get out of the kitchen before you distract the girls."

Rafaela had followed Angela holding onto her tunic. Gabriel said, "One of my jobs is to distract the children."

Angela sighed, and over the protests of the older girls she said, "Yes, that's a good idea. Take Rafaela outside, and distract her."

Tammuz 4

Gabriel's arm came out of the splint, and yes, it was crooked. Crooked and weak.

Unable to work in the field, Gabriel clocked long hours with the children. He toured the house and taught them the names of every object. Their Hebrew chattering grew in speed and fluency.

Because Angela insisted less work got done with him than without him, Gabriel avoided the meal preparation. Instead he ended up outside most afternoons processing fleeces with the younger boys and some of the girls. In the courtyard the children spun while Gabriel combed wool (and, coincidentally, continued language lessons). The family had a table with a comb fixed to the far end. Gabriel would force the wool through to make it smooth and strain out bits of straw. This also aligned the fibers for spinning.

He found it peaceful, mindless work during which he could set his thoughts or prayers free while the sun warmed him and while the family members spoke among themselves. He forgot himself once and started singing, much to the others' amusement. He wasn't sure how seriously to take their requests afterward that he sing while they worked.

He couldn't spin because he couldn't raise his left arm for that long, but it looked soothing. Combing didn't hurt because his right arm did all the work, with the left hand only resting on the wool to guide it. These were long afternoons made shorter with the labor, with the scent of the wool both sheepish and linty, the prayers in his heart and the songs in his soul.

Watching one of the girls spin one afternoon while he combed, Gabriel internalized the action in his mind. The girl had a suspended spindle with a whorl at the top and a groove for casting on the yarn. She used her hands to twirl the spindle, to make sure it had the correct twist, and to feed the fleece into it. The spinning motion twisted the fibers into a thin, strong yarn.

Gabriel let the different parts fall together in his mind, and he felt through the rotation, felt the fibers joining, stretching, twisting. He watched the spindle, wondered how else she could keep it spinning, if maybe she could use the yarn itself to keep the rotation going, if maybe she could suspend the spindle from something else in order to free her hands, wondered if there was a way to use her unoccupied feet to provide power for the spindle, if maybe there could be another way of keeping tension on the yarn.

Gabriel said, "I wonder if you could use a—"

Don't!

The girl looked up at Gabriel even as he reeled from the force of God's warning. "Use what?" she said.

For a moment, Gabriel considered finishing the sentence just to hear God's voice again, but no matter how badly he wanted to hear Him, he also wasn't stupid. "Never mind. I was just thinking out loud."

In his head, to God: *They could use a wheel for this!* Then, *Why can't I tell them my idea? It wouldn't take much to put it together.* More silence. *It would help them beyond measure to have an easier method of spinning. I could repay them.*

Gabriel felt it in his heart: this wasn't about repayment.

I know they didn't take me in for material gain, Gabriel replied, *but what else do I have to offer?*

God didn't reply again.

Why were you even talking to me in the first place? Gabriel thought darkly. *I thought that was forbidden.*

The girl said, "Are you mad?" and one of the boys said, "You look upset."

"I'm frustrated," Gabriel said, a little startled that they'd identified a feeling of which he was barely aware, "but it's nothing to do with you."

Because by now he could visualize a spinning wheel in his mind—the wheel to turn the spindle, powered by treadles, the ratio of the wheel to the spindle determining the number of twists per inch, the tension on the yarn determined by a drive band between the two—and he knew how much faster it would be than what they were stuck doing now. He could feel the proportions, the power in this simple design, and only by adding into the equation one thing: a wheel.

He could give back everything to them, everything they'd given him and incalculably more, and it wouldn't take much time. He could work on it at night after the rest of his work was done. He could predict without calculating the savings in the effort, in time, and the way he wouldn't have to feel as if he were living off their good nature and taking advantage of everyone's prayers, everyone's generosity, and everyone else's hard work.

This isn't about repayment, God had told his heart, and Gabriel thought back to him now, *Then what can it be about? Aren't I here to repay you for disobeying? Why mustn't I repay them for* <u>obeying</u> *you?*

No answer. Gabriel watched the girl twirling the drop spindle, and in his mind he let the wheels turn.

Tammuz 18

When Angela asked one of the girls to fetch water, Gabriel volunteered instead. In the noon heat, he hefted the jug and headed out to the well.

Sitting on the well was Raphael.

Gabriel dropped the jug, wide-eyed. Raphael leaped to a stand with a compulsive smile. "Gabriel! You're here! You've been here all along!"

Thoughts raced through his head: confusion, sadness, tentative happiness, loneliness—and then deception.

"Damn you further." He picked up the jug and continued toward the well.

The figure moved closer. Those were Raphael's fluid movements, but no way was it the same soul. "But—Gabriel?"

The charge of Seraph fire flurried through the air like snow. That wasn't Raphael's fire. Gabriel would know Raphael's anywhere. This was just...fire. Thrilling to have, but not the one he missed.

Gabriel said, "No."

"It's been such a long time."

He started hauling up water. "Leave."

"Satan told me where you were. I had to come."

The spiritual fire dissipated in the air when it should be flickering in his heart. Gabriel stared at the rope. "Go away."

"You're being unfair." Oh, the light in his eyes—it was a perfect imitation. "Why won't you believe God could be merciful to us?"

Gabriel poured the water into the jug but he could only think of pouring fire into himself. He felt like a candle with no wick.

The Seraph leaned closer. "Gabriel—"

"No. In God's holy name, leave me alone."

Gabriel took the filled jug and returned to the kitchen. Walked away from the fire. Somehow. As he set down the jug in the kitchen, he sighed.

"Are you all right?" asked Angela. "You're pale. I shouldn't have sent you out for the water."

"I'm fine," said Gabriel. "My convalescence doesn't preclude light housework."

"You only speak formally when you know I'm right," Angela said.

Gabriel looked down. "My speech pattern bears no relation to my physical condition."

Angela leaned forward. "If you don't go inside and rest until dinner, I'll send Rafaela in for Tobias, and then *he'll* make you rest. What do you say?"

Gabriel met her eyes with some relief—after walking away from the fire outside, his heart connected with the Seraphic soul in this woman. She felt nothing like Raphael, far too rough, but she still carried that charge. "I'll go back to combing wool," Gabriel said. "Surely you agree that isn't too taxing."

Angela walked away, leaving Gabriel feeling again like a smothered candle.

At the wool comb, Gabriel managed to kindle up a little fire in himself, but although it eased some of the craving, it didn't remove the loneliness. From where he worked, he saw Rafaela trot through the corridor away from the kitchen. Moments later, Rafaela trotted back, and Tobias entered the courtyard.

"Gabriel," said the head of the house with an amused smile, "you're paler than the wool."

Gabriel avoided Tobias's eyes.

Tobias said, "And you're shaking. You do realize the wool comb can rip the skin off your hands if you're not paying attention, don't you?"

Gabriel squinted. "Is it hard to wash blood out of a fleece?"

"I'd rather not find out." Tobias shook his head. "You're in a cold sweat, too. You're rather intelligent, so I'd think you could figure out you aren't expected to work when you're feeling this bad. Come with me please."

Inside the house, Gabriel said, "I'm not sick." He took a deep breath. "After Sarah died, did you ever grieve so much it physically hurt?"

Tobias nodded. "I told myself I'd see her again," and then when Gabriel asked if that helped, Tobias said, "Not really. I wanted to see her now." And Gabriel only walked with his eyes downcast.

Tobias led him into his library and invited him to take a seat.

"I'm glad you've been using the library to teach the children. My father-in-law collected scrolls," said Tobias, "and I inherited all these. Most are religious texts and some are myth, but sometimes the myth is hard to tease out from the real stories. Have you read much myth?"

"My Father has scrolls from many places," Gabriel said. "I read as many as I can," he added, meaning in his Cherubic way, "All of them. Twice."

"Have you ever seen this one?" Tobias pulled a scroll from a cubby. "It has mention of the demon who tormented Sarah."

Gabriel looked closer. "Asmodeus gets around a lot even though you expelled him."

"Azariah chased it all the way into upper Egypt and then bound it hand and foot, but I guess it worked itself loose." Tobias laughed. "Do you know, Azariah never interfered. He gave me instructions, and I followed them. Even with the fish, he only told me how to catch it and didn't leap in and grab it himself."

Gabriel chuckled. "Maybe he didn't want to get wet."

Tobias's eyes crinkled. "That's very funny."

Gabriel looked down, but he smiled.

"When the grape harvest begins," Tobias ventured, "we'll be celebrating Tu B'av. There's a bonfire and a feast, and we sing, and the girls dance."

Gabriel nodded.

"I'd like you to teach the children to sing in Hebrew," said Tobias. "One or two songs."

Gabriel nodded again. "Is there anything else?"

"No, but you might want to begin right away. I'm not certain, but I think my grandchildren aren't a Heavenly choir."

Both men laughed. "I'll do my best," said Gabriel.

Gabriel began work that night. The children were not the heavenly chorus, and his perfect pitch took a beating.

Tammuz 27

Satan hasn't come again as Raphael, if it was Satan in the first place. I've begun wondering if I made a mistake, if Raphael really did come for me... and I turned him away.

More than that, though, a new worry crept in today: because none of my friends mentioned the incident, if Raphael showed up, it means Raphael deliberately disobeyed God. Bluntly, that would mean damnation. That terrifies me. What will I do if I can't ever see Raphael again? How would I forgive God for taking me away when He knew how it would affect him?

That's what damnation would mean. No matter what the pain, total separation would have to be the consequence. That's my worst fear, and it's not unjustified, although I ought to think logically: if Raphael fell, Michael or Remiel would say something, if only to protect me.

They would, but can they? God won't permit me to know anything about Raphael, maybe up to and including rebellion, so I can't even ask about Raphael's state of soul because no one should answer.

How does that make me feel? It scares the life out of me.

In the grand scheme that divides the world into Fact and Lie, I don't lie to myself. But I don't know how much of this scenario I've imagined. Without debate partners, I come too close to believing every strange idea I conceive. And during this, Satan (if it's him) or Raphael (likewise) leaves me on my own to thrash over the question. Raphael would stay away if I asked him to. Satan would stay away just to leave me wondering what happened.

Another thing. Michael came to me yesterday. He looked so inordinately happy. "You've got less than two months to go!"

I cringed and said, "Please don't tell me that."

"You aren't keeping track?" asked Michael.

Michael doesn't understand this apparent laxity. After all, the punishment will end in exactly one year. Anyone should mark off the days and grow excited when the days remaining hit the two-digits and then wait with a rapidly-beating heart through all the last month, like a woman anticipating the birth of a baby.

I say this: this is not a pregnancy with a baby at the end of the term. Even one day out of the Lord's love passes with wretched slowness, and every sight becomes a torture. Flowers, sunsets, people, rocks, houses, mud, grass, stars: they all make me flinch because once I saw the hand of God in all these, and now I can't. The knot of emptiness rings in the silence of my ears, speaks to me in the tastes of everything I eat, and reeks whenever I inhale because that other, that flicker of God in all, doesn't saturate me. No matter how I distract myself or how hard I work or how much I study or teach, my heart knows that absence. Every time I encounter a new object, I feel the pluck as another way I might have discovered God hurls itself into the twisting of time.

I'm getting emotional, I know, but this is my journal, and I'm allowed to now. I have to. If never again, if never for anything else, now is the time.

To do what Michael expected, to say "Only fifty-nine days left!" would hurt as much as saying "Only fifty-nine million years left!" or even "Only 5.9 seconds left!" A moment without God has no value.

God will take me back when the time expires. Until then, why count days or label hours? God keeps His promises without outside countdowns.

Michael insists I could see my progress and take encouragement. I respond: my "progress" consists of survival, which cannot (for an angel) be considered improvement. Time carries me like any other creature. My supposed "progress" doesn't encourage me because I've made none. I'm still just me, Gabriel.

Av 15

Raguel tossed more wood on the bonfire, then turned to Gabriel. "Isn't this fun? Did you ever do things like this at home?"

In the early darkness, the family festival grew louder. The women brought out food for the feast, and Gabelus called one of the servants to bring out more wine.

Rather than say, "Parties are merely a series of steps to be endured to get to the other side," Gabriel nodded. The general level of noise gave him an excuse not to try talking, plus the number of people laughing, moving, crowding – Raguel had plenty to do rather than have a conversation.

Tobias found Gabriel in the tumult. "Are the children ready to sing?"

Gabriel had to speak loudly to be heard. "I hope so."

Tobias laughed, and they started gathering children, then re-gathering them as inevitably some wandered away. *Like shepherding, in a*

Tishri

Cheshvan

Kislev

Tevet

Schevat

Adar

Nissan

Iyar

Sivan

Tammuz

Av

Elul

way, Gabriel thought to God, *except the sheep had the good sense to stay where I put them.*

Eventually, though, the children were mostly in one place, and Tobias quieted down the adults enough that Gabriel could start playing the family's ten-stringed lyre. There were children off-key, two who stood with the others but refused to sing, and one who started sobbing and ran for his mother. Overall, about what Gabriel had expected.

The family cheered for the children, and Tobias called, "Do you have another?"

The children shouted their responses – they'd worked hard, and Gabriel braced himself. Either this would work, or else he'd be packing his lone bag for more traveling before that bonfire had burnt out.

The children giggled and began to sing:

"Children are a heritage from the Lord,

And young ones are His reward.

Like arrows in the hand of a hero,

So are the children of one's youth.

Happy is the man who has his quiver full of children,

His sons in his arms,

And his daughters carried on his shoulders."

Tobias was roaring with laughter, and the children broke from their group to run to their parents. Tobias slapped Gabriel on the back. "My clever, clever hired man, spoiling my grandchildren by making them think they're so important."

Relieved that he wouldn't see sunrise on the roadside, Gabriel laughed. "Well, Solomon said it first."

"And we cannot argue with the wisdom of Solomon!" Tobias kissed Gabriel on both cheeks. "Thank you. You've done wonders with them."

The eating and drinking continued, the dancing, and the music. Children went off to bed one at a time, Rafaela rubbing her eyes and mumbling protests while Gabelus carried her indoors.

Tobias pointed to where the unmarried girls danced in white. "You don't have a wife. Are you promised to anyone?"

Gabriel swallowed hard. "Not to the best of my knowledge, no."

Tobias put his hand on Gabriel's shoulder. "Would you like to contract with one of my granddaughters?"

Gabriel said, "I mean no offense, but consider what you're offering. I'm a foreigner and an exile."

Tobias looked him in the eyes. "And I made the offer anyhow. I would be honored to have you in my family."

Gabriel kissed Tobias on the cheek. "I would be honored too. But I'll decline to ask for any of your granddaughters in marriage."

Tobias smiled at him. "I expected as much, but I won't find a better husband."

Gabriel said, "Didn't Raphael say God set Sarah aside for you from before the world began? Surely He's set aside someone for them, too."

Tobias said, "Are you sure your Father hasn't set someone aside for you?"

Gabriel's stomach clenched, and he looked right at Tobias, because the way he'd just said *father*, the way he'd drawn that parallel – did he know?

"Hey!" Raguel rushed up to Gabriel and grabbed his hand. "You need to keep playing music. That's another prince-thing, right? Playing music in palaces?" He turned to Tobias. "You heard him! Isn't he amazing? You have to make him do it again!"

Thank you, God, for distractions. Gabriel said to Raguel, "If I play, will you sing?"

Tobias said, "Yes, do it."

Raguel said, "If I sing, no one's going to appreciate your music."

Gabriel said, "Name a song. If I know it, I'll accompany you."

So they started. Raguel picked a song, and Gabriel thought he remembered it, and they struggled until they were both in the same key. Gabelus joined, and then Tobias, and soon it felt as if most of the family was either pounding out the song or else dancing to the rhythms. Raguel was right: no one could possibly hear Gabriel's lyre, but that was good and right. Get the family started and let them enjoy each other. He didn't really belong anyhow.

At the end of the song, someone shouted out for another, and they did a few boisterous verses. Angela made a request, and Gabriel started playing a slower song, a sadder song from just after the exile. She mixed up some of the words, then stopped, and Gabriel took over, singing and playing until she could join back in, only she never did.

He looked up. The family was watching. "I'm sorry." His cheeks flushed. "Any other requests?"

"Sing the one you sang by the river," said Raguel.

Gabriel hesitated. "I can't. That's not – none of you would know that. It's from home. It's not even a language you know."

Tobias said, "I would very much like to hear a song from your home."

Did Tobias know? And if so...didn't Gabriel owe him at least this much?

He thought about the strings on this instrument, matching them to the notes he remembered, and after a false start, he began.

This was Raphael's song, and it was poetic and lively and brilliant, but when Gabriel sang, it turned wrenching. The chorus repeated a simple praise with only minor changes, an homage to the holy-holy-holy of the Seraphim, but instead of awed, Gabriel sounded sad. He pushed on the melody, trying to remember Raphael playing the tune while Gabriel sang for God, and back then in those days they'd all been together rather than split in thirds. But no, Raphael was with God. Raphael would never leave God.

Raguel joined the repetitions on the chorus, and Gabriel missed the next three notes, then halted. Raguel was only imitating the sounds, but what if Raphael heard? Raphael probably couldn't hear Gabriel, but he'd be able to hear someone singing *with* Gabriel, and what if—?

Raguel said, "I'm sorry! I didn't mean to throw you off! You were amazing!"

Unable to speak, Gabriel just started playing a different song, a song he'd heard from the men in the fields, and a chorus started. He got them going loudly, then handed off the lyre and walked into the darkness away from the crowd.

Over at the fence he saw Michael. The Archangel's eyes shone with moonlight and didn't reflect the fire. He reached forward with his wings, as though to touch Gabriel's wingtips with his own. Gabriel extended his hands.

The music and dancing continued. Gabriel leaned on the fence and looked into the stars. "It's quiet out there. Somewhere."

Michael said, "Do you need to get away?"

"It's not as if they could hear us talking. I'm surprised they can hear each other." Gabriel chuckled dryly. "It's exhausting. I should have gone to bed with the children."

Michael said, "Let's walk, then."

Gabriel made his way toward the now-harvested barley field, putting the celebration at his back. They crested a small hill, and on the other side the sounds faded. Trying to relax, Gabriel started to say, "That's better—" when a glow formed off to his right, and with it the sensation of Raphael's presence.

Gabriel jumped, grabbing Michael's hand. He turned toward the light and saw Satan—and at his side, Raphael.

Gabriel screamed, "No!"

Satan put an arm over Raphael's shoulder. "Look who I have! Being apart from you was too much for the poor soul, so I'm facilitating a reunion."

Seraph fire poured from Raphael, and Gabriel shoved himself backward into Michael. Raphael's power, so familiar, so individual—this was his. It sparkled with his distinct signature.

Him.

Here.

Defying God.

Gabriel blinked tear-filled eyes. "No! Go back!"

Satan turned to Raphael. "Go to him. Tell him."

"You were playing my song." Raphael approached, hands out. "I heard you, and I couldn't stand it anymore. You were calling me. I had to come tonight."

"Go away," Gabriel pleaded. "I didn't want that. Please don't come near me."

"You say you love me, but you're fighting me off. You're always denying what you feel." Raphael looked hurt. "That's lying, and isn't a lie also a sin?"

The Seraph fire swirled around him, and Gabriel's mouth watered. His head pounded, and his hands shook.

"I don't have a home any longer, only you." Raphael extended his wings. "Please, Gabriel. Just touch me again. I've wanted to be with you every day since you left, and I couldn't stand it anymore. Lucifer's going to help us. I need you."

Gabriel gripped Michael's hand with all his human-angelic strength. The fire, so delicious when it got inside, so welcome—he knew exactly how it would feel. *God—* He tried to back into Michael further, but there was nowhere else to go. He wanted it. No, he craved it. He couldn't think about anything else right now. Fire. The hunger flared so urgently inside. Raphael's fire. Raphael.

"Just relax and let it happen. Be the other half of me." Standing within two cubits of him, Raphael extended a hand. "I love you."

Gabriel kept his jaw tight against his skull, kept his fingers wound into Michael's, tried to twist sideways or somehow find a way it didn't tantalize so much, but there was no relief from the ever-present sparks. Michael held his hands and kept one wing wrapped about Gabriel. He tried to concentrate on Michael, but he couldn't drag his entire attention away from the Seraph and that beautiful fire. *Just once. Just a little bit. Oh, God, this hurts. Please don't condemn him. Maybe he didn't realize. Please have mercy on him. Please don't let me respond. Stop me!*

Raphael reached forward, tears streaming down his face as he tried to get into Gabriel's heart; that niche never could be erased, not even by hellfire.

Satan huffed. "You're being ungrateful. You're everything to him, and you're stringing him along."

The breeze picked up, and Gabriel's teeth chattered; he was doused in sweat. Nausea broke over him as he tried to look away, but he couldn't. *Fire.*

Michael pressed closer to him. "Don't talk any more," he murmured. "Send him away. You have the authority."

Gabriel tilted back his head, his eyes still closed. His throat ached, and his entire body tingled. "In the name of God," he said, "in the name of our Father, go home!"

Satan and Raphael vanished together.

Gabriel felt him go, felt his heart's signature vanish to leave the world a thousand times emptier than before. His heart beat so quickly he wondered if he were about to have a seizure. He staggered to a rock and put his head between his knees.

Raphael. Mercy. Justice. Forever. He extended his senses, tentative, and felt a big echoing empty.

"He's gone."

His own whisper made it real, and the tears came.

Gabriel sobbed into Michael's wings until his face was a mess and his ribs ached and he couldn't breathe. His soul had been peeled and cored, and it was all over. Michael solidified around him, but Gabriel couldn't look up, didn't want comfort and didn't want to be alone.

"You made it." Michael's whisper sounded frightened. "I know that was scary, but you made it."

I destroy everything. Everything he loved, every*one* he loved, just gone, better off without him. Wouldn't it have been better for Raphael if Gabriel never existed, better alone than in fire? And would God let him out? He'd never let anyone out before, but what if they prayed, if they pleaded—could it make a difference?

Gabriel quieted, but when Michael stroked his hair, the tears started again.

In the distance, light and sound from the bonfire.

Michael murmured, "You're so strong. It's okay."

It's not okay. I'm weak. I did this. I ruined everything.

He couldn't even run. God was the only one he'd have run to, and he couldn't go there. So instead he pressed closer to Michael because Michael still had God, and that was as near as he could get.

"I'm sorry," Gabriel choked. "I'm just so sorry."

"You did fine." Michael gripped him. "You're scaring me. Is this a shock reaction?"

Shock reaction? "I'm not heartless!" Gabriel tightened up, and the tears returned. Didn't they ever dry up? "I as good as murdered him! I wish I'd never met him."

"You didn't murder him." Michael sounded mystified. "You sent him away."

The fabric of Michael's clothes was wet against his cheeks. "He's in Hell because of me."

"He's in Hell because of his own choices."

"He chose it because of me!" Gabriel pushed back even though he could barely see Michael. "Don't try to make it better! What the hell do you know about bonding? He wouldn't have left God except to be with me, and I'm *here* and I should have been *there,* and—"

"Whoa, wait!" Michael grabbed his shoulders. "What are you talking about? Satan never bonded anyone."

"I'm not talking about Satan! I just want Raphael back! Why didn't you stop him? Can't you do something now? Go ask God, plead with him, do *something* rather than sitting here telling me to get over it!"

Michael clutched Gabriel tighter. "Raphael's fine—what are you talking about? He's fine!"

Gabriel's vision went white. "Fine in Hell?"

"Fine about an arrow-flight away from you fine!" Michael's eyes were wide. "Fine like close-enough-that-if-I-called-he'd-turn-his-head fine. Why would he be in Hell?"

Gabriel shook his head. Then, "But—Raphael ...Raphael was with Satan!" He choked. "His energy. I'd recognize it anywhere."

Michael turned his head, then looked back at Gabriel. Back again. Back to Gabriel "I promise you, whatever you saw—the one who approached you was Satan. There wasn't anyone else." Michael sounded urgent. "I don't know the first thing about Cherub-Seraph bonds, but that was Satan."

Gabriel blinked. "You mean—" His legs trembled, and he dropped to the ground before he had chance to fall. "Satan just tried to bond with me?"

Michael went bloodless. "Bond with you?" He started to stand. "I'll chain him at the bottom of the lake of fire!"

"No, stay!" Gabriel yanked Michael back. His hands weren't working right, and he couldn't stop the shaking. "It felt just like Raphael. That energy. He'd have chained me to him."

Michael hugged him. "You're safe. It didn't work."

"Are you sure?" Gabriel bit his lip. "Really sure—?"

"I promise. Raphael's fine."

Gabriel put his face in his hands. He tried to kindle up his own fire, just to take the edge off the longing, but he couldn't.

Michael held him. "I'm so sorry. I didn't realize."

Gabriel closed his eyes.

Raphael. Safe.

Safe, somewhere. Well, safe in whatever direction Michael had been looking before. It was okay. Gabriel could starve through a year as long as Raphael was safe.

"You're freezing." Michael dropped his wings and wrapped them tight around Gabriel. "Do you want to go back toward the bonfire?"

"No, it's—" Gabriel shuddered, and he rubbed his arms. "Not real heat. He was baiting me with Seraph fire." He rubbed his eyes, but still he shivered all over, his nerves livid as they hungered for the energy. "I'm in a human body, but it's Cherub instinct, or reflex, or something."

Michael's eyes widened. "You're in withdrawal?"

It sounded so disgusting that way. "Can you pray over me?"

"That makes what he did twice as lousy," Michael muttered. He rested his hands on Gabriel, and momentarily the tremors eased, then the nausea faded, and he breathed without pain.

Watching the reflected beauty fading from Michael's eyes, Gabriel tried to get used to feeling normal again rather than one knot of anticipation. He shivered. What if...? "Are you sure Raphael's safe?"

"I promise," Michael said.

Gabriel sagged against Michael's arm without any strength of his own.

Then in the next moment, he realized—*without any strength of his own.*

Gebher'el. "God's Strength."

Oh, God, have mercy on me. It broke over him then just how small he was, how capable of falling, how he was in some sense a sinner because without God supporting him, he was capable of every kind of sin. He'd been holding onto himself so tightly this entire year, for thousands before this, so glad he was the way God had made him that he never needed to change any of it. Only wasn't that denying God the glory for the graces he was giving Gabriel every minute? Because without that grace, Gabriel would have fallen just now—would have fallen at the winnowing, would have fallen a hundred times in between.

Gabriel looked up at Michael and realized Michael embodied without even realizing it what Gabriel was just now taking to heart: they were empty vessels on their own, valuable only because God had arrived to fill them, and beyond that—

He shuddered. *God, have mercy on me.* How many times had he resisted realizing? Being strong and knowing you were doing the right thing was a very comfortable place to be. Being without strength of your own, knowing God guided you and protected you—it was undiluted helplessness. But ultimately, that was what God had wanted him to learn.

Because now, how could he look down on the people with him? How could he think he was better than they were, when he was only what God decided to give him and nothing more? How could he say, "Thank you God for making me like me and not like them," when he'd had nothing to do with it in the first place? *Have mercy.*

Inside the Spirit warmed him—he was right, and this was good.

Michael looked anguished. "I'm sorry I didn't tell you while it was happening. I thought Satan was shedding power to look good."

Gabriel blinked—oh, right, Satan as Raphael. He shook his head. "It was a test. I needed to learn—" *Have mercy on me...* "

Michael reached for his hand.

"I need you to pray with me." Gabriel took a deep breath and was surprised when it caught. "Like a guardian would—counterprayer."

He reached for Michael's heart, and Michael wrapped around him.

Father, Gabriel prayed, and he felt Michael moving through the contact, *Father, I don't know how to do this—* And then he lost the words, and he couldn't do anything more than just hold himself out toward his Father and show him the broken pieces, the sorrow over what he hadn't realized sooner, the ways he'd denied God His glory by acting as if he were responsible for his own goodness. And then he couldn't go on.

Michael hadn't pulled back in disgust; instead he radiated surprise.

God beckoned him to continue.

Please have mercy on me, Gabriel prayed. *I'm sorry. I'm sorry for resisting you so long. Thank you for loving me despite myself. Thank you for teaching me.* He quivered, but finally he said, *Thank you for this year.*

If Michael was surprised before, now he was openly shocked.

Gabriel closed his eyes. *Thank you.* His heart brimmed over, and then it was his eyes, and he wanted so much to hide himself, but Michael stayed.

The family's laughter and talk still formed the night's background, and the bonfire's glow reflected off the clouds.

And then, for a bare second, God shimmered inside, and Gabriel realized God was thanking him too.

Elul

The grape pressing began, and Gabriel worked full time amidst the smell of young wine. In the mornings he'd leave a house full of Hebrew-chattering children and work in the barn with Raguel. The boy had begun asking a lot of questions about

Tishri

Cheshvan

Kislev

Tevet

Schevat

Adar

Nissan

Iyar

Sivan

Tammuz

Av

Elul

God, and Gabriel used every minute as a teaching tool. They both knew he would leave soon.

Satan returned, but Gabriel retreated into the knowledge of his own smallness and in that way found himself shielded. Satan could look like Raphael; he could feel like Raphael; he could stream fire into the air. It held no attraction for him, and for what it was worth, Satan looked shocked. Gabriel focused only on the grace of God, not on his own ability to defend himself, and Satan's words passed through leaving no wake.

Tobias didn't want to risk Gabriel re-injuring his arm by sending him out into the fields again for harvesting. Instead he sent Gabriel to care for the sheep. The work was as before, but Gabriel found it new. There was less physical exertion than cutting barley, but more movement, more elements to keep track of. He prayed during the long hours, shared observations with the shepherds without trying to teach them. They played their home-grown music on home-grown instruments with home-grown voices, and he didn't object any longer. He sang with them and worked with them as a team, trying to anticipate what they wanted. It was the same work, but even so, it wasn't the same.

Elul 26

Even now, Gabriel refused to figure out the day and the hour. God knew when it would come and would fulfill everything in the right time. If Gabriel still had lessons to learn, then he needed to learn them and not watch the calendar.

Gabriel wondered how it would happen, if there would be a warning, if his vision would suddenly shift long-distance and he'd see God's face or if it would break over him like a wave, if he'd cry out, if he'd collapse, if his heart would stop (for the sake of the family, he hoped he wouldn't return to Heaven by dying). He wondered if the other angels would be there, if Satan would give him one last challenge, if Raphael would come (and if so, if he'd accept it was him). Would God test him before readmitting him? Would he pass?

What he would say to God? What things might God say to him? Wonderful things. Terrifying things.

He had numerous theories, but at the beginning of the end, it was the boy Raguel who burst into the stable where Gabriel cleaned out stalls after evening prayers. "Gabriel, you've got to come right now! Don't even finish your work!"

Raguel dragged Gabriel to the basin and made him wash his hands and face.

Gabriel watched from the corners of his eyes while he followed instructions. "Could you explain—?"

"Yes—oh, I hadn't said—your brother's here!"

Gabriel dropped the soap. "What?"

"Come on!" Raguel brought him to the house at a run.

The instant he entered the courtyard, Gabriel recognized Saraquael in human form. Stunned, he stared.

Tobias turned from Saraquael's side. "He says he's your brother Saraquah."

Saraquael – Saraquah – rushed at Gabriel and embraced him, and Gabriel laughed out loud. Saraquah kissed him on both cheeks and then held him close.

Gabriel had gone numb. "I never expected to see you."

"I'm truly thankful I found you," said Saraquah. He felt large to Gabriel, strong, and he smelled like tea leaves. "We had almost given up hope at home, and most of the family are grieving."

Raguel gaped at Saraquah—the high language, the clothes, the bearing.

Saraquah took a step back. "Father received your letter. I've come for you."

Gabriel fumbled for Saraquah's hand. He was trembling.

Saraquael said, "Our Father has repented of His anger, and He wants you with him. He sent me to bring you home."

Gabriel's eyes watered. He couldn't see.

"That's terrific!" Raguel gave Gabriel a push. "You can go back to your family now!"

Gabriel turned to the boy, realizing Raguel had thought of his friend's happiness before becoming conscious that he would lose him forever in a way as certain as death, and possibly separation is worse than that.

"I am continuing on to Rages on a family matter," said Saraquah, "but you have to return with our people."

"Shouldn't I accompany you?" asked Gabriel, his eyes asking more.

"It would be better if you joined Father quickly."

Gabriel's eyes met Saraquah's, as though no other creature inhabited the courtyard.

"He's missed you," Saraquael said. "We all have."

"You must stay the night," said Tobias.

The prince removed his wallet from his belt-pouch. "How much will you accept in compensation?"

Tobias laughed. "Please don't insult me with money. An angel once befriended me and took nothing in return. It's a debt I repay with kindness to strangers."

"Have you eaten yet, Saraquah?" asked Gabelus.

"Yes, I have, but thank you. All I shall ask of you is a place to spend the night."

"Stay in my room," Raguel volunteered. "Please, Gabriel and I have enough space to spare."

"Saraquah is a prince," Gabelus reminded the boy.

"So is Gabriel," the son said.

Gabelus looked from one to the other. One wore a bright green tunic with a long cloak, mahogany-finished walking staff, leather travel-pack, and new sandals. The other wore a dirt-dusted tunic and had just come in from shoveling manure.

"I would appreciate the chance to stay with my brother, if you wouldn't mind," said Saraquah. "I haven't seen him in quite a while."

Raguel beamed when his father agreed.

Late that night, after a talked-out Raguel finally succumbed to sleep, Saraquael sat closer to Gabriel and murmured in their native tongue.

"God wants you to leave here tomorrow for one final task."

"Must I?"

Saraquael smiled. "They're well-staffed for the planting. He wants you to take the eastern road."

Gabriel looked aside. "Do you know where I'm going?"

"I'm sorry, but I don't. You may receive further instructions tomorrow."

Gabriel shuddered.

"It *is* getting close." Saraquael touched Gabriel's hand. "Have you kept track of the days?"

Gabriel shook his head. "I— No, I couldn't."

Saraquael squeezed. "Be strong. You've stayed strong for so long, and it won't last too much longer. We're with you now— especially now," he added.

Gabriel leaned closer to him. "I have to know, now, before I see Him again: does He still— Does He really want me back?"

Saraquael's fingers tightened on him. "I can't say yes strongly enough."

Gabriel bit his lip. "But does He still love me? Can He forgive me?"

"He can," Saraquael said. "He has. And He does."

When Gabriel still didn't look up, Saraquael said, "I have a message for you."

Gabriel raised his eyes.

Saraquael gleamed with God's light, and Gabriel leaned forward to catch it all even as Saraquael's voice flowed into the dreaming speech: "You've done well with this year. The arrow is going to strike the center of the target. And it's good. It's very good."

Gabriel ducked his head to hide his wet eyes.

Saraquael shook his head briefly to clear his mind. "The rest of the message He wants to give you himself." Saraquael touched Gabriel's shoulder. "Hey, don't make me cry too."

Gabriel hugged Saraquael. "It's hard to believe."

"But I believe it." Saraquael put a hand on Gabriel's hair. "And you have to see the party we've planned for you."

Gabriel laughed against his shoulder. "I was thinking of hiding away and staring into the face of God for about five hundred years."

Saraquael sat back as Gabriel dried his eyes. "You can do that—but when you're ready, we've got the band lined up, because you're coming home."

Elul 27

Gabriel awoke before Saraquael, and he prayed. He prayed his uncertainty, his baffling reluctance to leave, his fear of what he didn't know. He prayed his sadness at still being separated from God, and he tried to pray up some excitement that he'd return, but excitement wouldn't come. Not when he was still in the middle of loss.

Listening to the night becoming morning, Gabriel reviewed the year he'd endured and found himself yielding to curiosity. He counted days. He had to shift into the angelic realm—only his mind—but once he did, he could recall every day. He noted the halfway mark, used other indicators for the time of the concussion (which in this state he could remember perfectly, and wished he couldn't) and decided that if he were working on the calendar year, then he had approximately thirty-four hours remaining.

Which felt exactly as he'd thought it would—insurmountable. He curled on his side, trying in futility to think other things.

Thirty-three hours remained when Saraquael and Raguel awoke, and Gabriel joined them in readying for the day. He realized he looked as bleak as he felt when Raguel avoided his eyes and Saraquael touched his arm for the third time. Thirty-two and three-quarter hours. He hadn't said a word aloud all morning.

The time came. Gabriel didn't leave with much: he took only his pack and his crooked arm.

"I owe you your wages," Tobias said. Gabriel insisted he didn't need them. Tobias forced them on him anyhow. "The only hired man I never paid got out of it by ascending into heaven. Unless you plan to do that, you're taking the money." So Gabriel took the money.

He pulled Raguel aside before the boy went into the fields. "I wanted to say goodbye."

Raguel swallowed hard. "We had you for almost half a year." He stared at the ground. "And I'll pray for you. That's good, right?"

Gabriel hugged him, and Raguel tucked his face against his shoulder. "No, it's not really enough. But I'll send word." Gabriel tightened his grip. "I'm not sure how, but I'll get word to you after I'm home."

Rafaela cried shamelessly. "I love you," she kept saying in Hebrew. "Don't go. I love you."

Gabriel gave her one last barley cake before he left. Then he and Saraquael parted company at the gates.

As he traveled, Gabriel recalculated the hours—twenty-nine. He re-added the days and double-checked by correlating the Sabbaths. Twenty-eight and a half hours.

May God have mercy, he thought in time with his own steps. He wanted home. He didn't want another day of this dryness—of being alone in his own heart. And what if the calendar year wasn't the guidepost? What if God intended a solar year?

I still have so much to learn. He swallowed hard. *There are so many ways I've fallen short and I have so much ground to make up that it only makes sense if you want me away longer than a year. If you want me to keep growing, if it's better that way.* He blinked hard to keep back the tears. *I want to come home, you know I do, but I spent hours every day sleeping. I could have spent them learning. If you want me to make up the time, then do it.*

Twenty-seven hours. He passed a family traveling on the road and handed off the money to them.

He could call for Michael or Remiel to walk with him, but it wouldn't help. Inside, his heart burned. He recited psalms in the hollow of his mind, the places God ought to be filling.

Between one step and the next, he looked up to find Michael.

"Now." Michael extended a hand. "It's time."

Gabriel jerked back.

A dozen angels crowded him, and Gabriel's human senses overwhelmed him: the air broiled around him, his stomach protested, and an aura glowed around everything. Even the air smelled nauseous.

The veneer of Michael's features took on the glint of Satan's green eyes. "Come on—I'm taking you home!"

"Leave me alone!" Gabriel shouted. "Michael! Help!"

Laughter all around. The real Michael appeared, bringing more angels, more confusion. Satan's eyes narrowed. "Don't fight me. You've got to come now!"

He grabbed Gabriel's hands, and with a wrenching squeeze, Gabriel felt himself strong-armed into his angelic form. He knifed open his wings and discharged all his energy to get some distance, then turned toward the Michael with Satan's eyes. "It's not time, you liar! I have one more day."

Satan said to one of the demons, "You told me he didn't know."

Then both Satan and Michael turned, and Gabriel looked where they did only to see Satan again in a new place. Even in angelic form, turning so rapidly left him as dizzy as when he'd had a concussion.

Michael was saying "What is he doing here?" and Satan said, "Well this is a whole new level of chaos."

Trying to back away from Satan, Gabriel reached for God reflexively.

Inside he heard the unmistakable sound of God's voice: *Grab him and don't let go.*

He had no idea why to grab Satan, but he didn't analyze. Michael tried to snatch him from behind, but Gabriel flung himself at Satan and clutched him around the waist.

Even as Satan let out a surprised cry, another demon shouted, "Bring him home! Carry him home now!"

"Let go of him, Gabriel!" Michael bellowed. "Do you want to be damned?"

Satan's fire swirled around them both, and Gabriel closed his eyes against the longing it evoked, tried not to hear the hurt behind Michael's rage. Someone was trying to pull him off, and he grabbed tighter as one force dragged him toward Heaven and the other to Hell, and all the while the fabric of Creation groaned in protest.

It made sense—Satan's subordinates wouldn't discharge their energy at him and risk hitting their master. Maybe. Maybe Satan wanted to force him into the Abyss, only he couldn't if Gabriel held him so tightly that he'd be dragged in too— But oh, the fire. His head pounded, and his mouth watered, and his arms ached from the strain.

Michael shouted, "By the authority of God invested in me, you have to let him go!"

In the next moment, Gabriel's hold slipped.

As he snatched to make sure Satan didn't escape him, he loosened the control over his own hungry soul. The Cherub part of him reacted to the flames, swallowing them the way only a Cherub can.

With a cry midway between a gasp and a shout, Gabriel sucked all Satan's fire into himself, igniting all the parts that had so long craved to touch flame. His neck snapped back, and his wings flared. It felt delicious and right and perfect for the first instant, and then as the fire swirled back up through him— horrifying.

Satan hollered, "No! I wasn't trying to do that!"

I'm sorry! God, I'm sorry!

Gabriel nearly let go, but God had said, had told him—

Maybe it was just to keep Michael protected. Maybe God had intended all along to winnow him. It would look more like Gabriel's choice this way, if he was going to fail anyhow.

"That shouldn't have been allowed to happen!" Michael was shouting at someone. "You swore to me it was impossible!"

New fire surged, not inside like a Seraph's but all over the outside of him, like being plunged into a lake of lava. Gabriel screamed. His neck arched, and his body spasmed.

Satan twisted in his arms, trying to push him off. Gabriel clung to him anyhow, trying to focus past the pain.

Behind him, a presence. "Carry him back!"

"But he's hurting—"

"You've got him—bring him back."

Reality twisted as Gabriel felt himself torn off the plane of Creation.

I'm sorry, he kept praying, tears streaming from clenched eyes. It might be the last time he could ever pray—it started with a year and would end with eternity. *Tell Raphael I'm sorry. Forgive me. I love you, and I'm sorry.*

Then Gabriel's inner eyes opened, and he saw his Father.

Time stopped.

There was nothing, nothing else, just him and his Creator, face to Face, all of him and all of God, moment to moment. No pain, no longing, no fire, no sorrow. Only the pair of them together as if never parted, and Gabriel exclaimed with joy. He didn't know where he was, where he'd been. They were alone, and he focused only with his inner sight.

I love you!, he prayed, and God assented.

This was the Divine throne room, where you and God met alone no matter how many people accompanied you there. No sight, no smell, no hearing, only light. Total focus. Awareness of only one thing permeated Gabriel. It was everything. It was more than everything.

He was home. Home. With his Father again, loved.

He grew conscious of God easing him back into himself.

Like a sleeper attempting to cling to dreams, Gabriel protested, but God reassured him he could return.

Gabriel blinked, and the world resolved around him.

You can let go now, God said.

Gabriel unlocked his arms and looked up at Satan.

He found Raphael.

With a gasp, he leaped up to hug him, and Raphael's wings got tangled in his as they each attempted to enclose the other. Fire swirled from Raphael even as Gabriel felt his heart churning out rings of calm, smooth like steel.

Twelve months of worry that Raphael would be angry melted like snowflakes in the sun. Gabriel closed his eyes and stayed, keeping his inner eyes trained on God but his senses trained on the Seraph.

When he let go, Raphael shifted back a little, and Gabriel scanned the area to find his other bonded Seraphim, plus Michael and Uriel, Raguel and Remiel.

His sight flickered to God, then back to Michael, familiar again with God's power flooding him. Gabriel said, "This shouldn't be. I had another day left."

Michael laughed out loud. "You fraud! I told Saraquael to make sure you hadn't counted the days!"

"You resisted just long enough for Satan to realize what we were doing," Raguel said.

Gabriel slipped backward so he sat with his wings against Raphael's.

"We learned what Satan had planned for the final day," Uriel said. "You'd probably have withstood it, but at great personal cost not only to you, but to Tobias's household as well. Fortunately, you'd written a letter asking for mercy. Using that, we interceded with God to get you reinstated sooner."

Gabriel projected his gratitude. He looked back at God, then at Michael again.

"When you resisted me, that gave Satan a window to attack." Michael sighed. "He seized hold of your senses. You saw me and thought I was him, and heaven only knows what you thought I was saying."

Gabriel turned to Raphael. "That was you?"

"God told me to go to Michael. I had no idea what I'd find." The Seraph still looked stunned. "When you grabbed me, I was just as surprised as everyone else. I thought you wouldn't be able to see me, and I knew I shouldn't be able to see you."

"I thought—" Gabriel shivered. "So the bond— It was really you?"

"Your soul recognized his," Uriel said. "Satan could blind you, but he couldn't numb your heart."

"But Satan attacked full-out because he knew then he'd lost you," Michael said.

"I thought God was punishing you because of it," Raphael said. "But you wouldn't let go, so Michael made me drag you here."

Here, Gabriel realized belatedly, was the Ring. He looked at God, then back at Raphael. "Satan had me thinking you were him. I thought the fire—that I'd been winnowed."

Raphael's heart in Gabriel's acknowledged the fear. Gabriel closed his eyes and looked at the Vision again.

When he looked back up, Michael was talking, but he didn't follow it. He looked back into the Vision, then back at Michael.

"Enough for now." Raphael turned Gabriel back to face the throne. "Do what you need to. We'll be here when you're ready."

Gabriel grasped his hand, took a long gaze at the Seraph's eyes, and then relaxed back into the Vision of the glory of the Father he loved, and who still loved him.

Children In Hell

576 BC

Atop Jerusalem's main gate, Michael screamed at God. With the Babylonians surrounding the city, he begged, he yelled, he insisted, and then no matter how he listened, God didn't reply.

Anything. Just anything, anything that resembled permission and Michael could save them. They'd saved Jerusalem before. He could save them again – but this time God was silent.

Kneeling at Michael's side, Uriel prayed for mercy. Gabriel prayed too. At the other gates, Remiel, Saraquael, Raguel and Raphael stood guard and prayed for reprieve. But after a thirty-month siege, God met their pleas with only silence.

Half of Hell is here, Michael prayed. *Please don't let them win. These are your people. They'll give glory to you eventually. Somehow. They've fouled it up, but you've been merciful before. Why not now?*

The Babylonians smashed into the gate, then smashed again. Beneath his feet, the structure shuddered. Michael whispered, "Please have mercy."

The gate crumbled. Stone toppled out from beneath Michael's feet, but there he remained in midair, hands clasped at his chest, head bowed.

The Babylonians roared with triumph as the first group of soldiers scaled the fallen stones. Others cleared the rubble to make a faster passage for the rest. Jerusalem's army met them at the gates, but that trickle of soldiers was about to become a tsunami, and Michael could do nothing at all.

Demons crowded the sky. Michael crumbled, and in the next moment Gabriel wrapped him in soft grey wings, pulling him into one of the houses and shielding him from their enemies.

"You might as well let them have me," Michael choked. "I can't protect my own people. I failed them."

"You're obeying God," Gabriel murmured, holding him closer. Michael yanked away, but Gabriel added, "You would save the nation if you could."

Michael snapped, "I can't. Maybe back at the beginning of time I should just have shut up and let Satan do whatever he wanted then, too. We'd have survived. And it's not like I stopped him. I'm useless."

"You're not useless." Gabriel took his hand. "If you're up to it, we need to get to work."

Michael opened his hands. "You're going to force God to save them?"

Gabriel said, "We can't save the nation. But the people – those are fair game. The nation came under judgment. God didn't condemn every individual soul."

Michael stared into Gabriel's eyes where they gleamed in the dark. "We can?"

Gabriel said, "I intend to until God tells me no."

And God hadn't told him no yet. That meant—

Michael flashed them to the top of the palace. "I need you to go through the building and tell me how many of the royal family are still in there. The Messiah will come from the House of David, so let's make sure there's still a lineage for him to come from."

Gabriel vanished. Saraquael appeared. "They're marching on the Temple with torches. I think they're going to burn it."

Michael's eyes gleamed. "Good. The Presence of God already vacated the Temple, so let's give them something interesting to do that isn't going to mean anything. Can you slow them down a bit?"

Startled, Saraquael said, "I think I can—"

"Bring Remiel. She can suppress the flames so it burns, but not too quickly."

Gabriel reappeared. "I've marked fifteen people for rescue."

"Raguel!" Michael called, and when the Principality appeared, he pointed to Gabriel. "Work with him. Get the royal family to safety. Even if they're taken prisoner, try to convince the Babylonians to keep them alive."

The palace and the Temple: the two main targets for an army bent on sending up a signal to a conquered people. And in addition to being large targets, they were hard-to-destroy targets. "Make it take a while," Michael kept ordering Archangels. At his side, Raphael helped guardians and other ministering angels hurry people out the holes Babylon had made in the walls while inside, the Babylonians made a god of chaos.

Hours into the battle, long after sunset, Uriel appeared. "Camael is here."

Michael called, "Remiel!" and when she answered, he said, "I need you out at the Babylonian encampment, where they're bringing the prisoners. Make sure they stay calm and don't get slaughtered."

From a distance came her reply: *Acknowledged.*

Michael turned back to Uriel. "Anything else?"

"Yes. You." Uriel frowned. "Raphael, you're needed."

Before Michael could ask why, Raphael appeared: shaking, pale. Raphael said, "You're worn to the core." He put a hand on Michael's forehead and fed strength into him. "I can't mend you completely, but—"

Michael took a deep breath, feeling strength return. He hadn't realized how tired he'd become with the constant battling, constant delegating and decision-making. "Get Gabriel to strengthen you."

Raphael said, "All my bonded Cherubim have given me everything they have. Gabriel's a curious shade of olive right about now. Get some rest before you do anything else, so the healing will take."

"You rest yourself." Michael listened with surprise to how tinny his own voice sounded, as though he had lost all the bass and tenor and could only rattle his vocal chords. "You've probably been busiest of us all."

"This is a nightmare," Raphael said. "You've been great, though. Thanks."

Raguel called for help, and both Uriel and Raphael answered. Michael summoned Saraquael. "You're in charge."

Saraquael bowed. "Sure, now that the worst is past, I'll take credit." Michael forced a smile, and Saraquael sent him off with a blessing.

Michael flashed himself someplace quiet, someplace dark where he could take Raphael's advice. He landed in the palace's lightless abandoned basement.

Opening his gaze to include non-visible light, he sat on a wooden box and rested his forehead on his palms and raised his wings like a jade tent. His heart instinctively reached for God's, inviting Him under that canopy, into a Holy of Holies the invasion hadn't destroyed. So tired. God accepted his invitation and remained there with His own wings folded in, making Himself small enough to be contained and large enough to fill that ragged hole. Neither spoke, each included within the other in layers as deep as desert sand.

A door banged and a child shrieked.

Five children pelted down the steps and right through Michael, unable to see him. A sixth doubled back to hide beneath the staircase.

A Babylonian charged in pursuit, a sword in one hand and a torch in the other. He barked a laugh that smelled suspiciously of alcohol before stalking into the darkness.

Halfway down, the hidden boy stuck a wooden bar through the steps and tripped the soldier across his ankles. The soldier tumbled, and as he went down, the torch landed on the steps.

Michael gasped. The child streaked from beneath the stairs and disappeared into the dark, the soldier lunging for him. He left the torch on the dry wood, instead picking up his sword. His anger blew through Michael like a flame-thrower.

Michael looked for another way out, but there wasn't one. *God, he'll let himself burn with them!*

The steps ignited. Michael tried to draw the soldier's attention to the only way out, but the man hunted for the children. He swung his sword into the darkness, shouting, threatening. He hit a support, grazed the wall, but never turned back toward the staircase. A palpable evil clung to him, a smoky aftertaste surrounding a hardened heart.

One of the children ran for the staircase, but it was already burning. The child stood, wide-eyed, then darted back into the darkness.

They can't hide forever, Michael prayed. *Please. Please give me permission. So many people died today. Please don't start the new day with new deaths.*

Michael paced the basement, feeling his way through the walls, the beams, the boxes. Behind him, the stairway crackled as it was consumed, but Michael opened his ears to hear everything else. Two children crouched very close to him. One child whispered, "There's a window. We'll stand on the boxes."

Even Michael had to look upward at that window. They'd need at least four boxes.

The boy and girl slid over a box, but the soldier heard the scraping and ran to them. They scattered.

Okay. At least now the kids had hope. Michael tried to distract the soldier, drawing him away from the window to the far side of the basement.

The boy and the girl found their friends where they hid and told them their plan. When the Babylonian heard their whispers and came after them, two ran noisily to the other side and three went to work stacking boxes, the last beating out any flames that came close.

By now the basement had filled with smoke. Shadows flashed one way and the other, revealing the children's profiles as the little ones moved. The Babylonian shouted as he charged after the children. Michael stood in a veritable hell.

The children stacked four boxes but then scattered as the soldier returned and knocked them over again.

Michael drew his sword. "Stop!" he shouted in Akkadian. "Why are you doing this? Leave these children alone!"

The Babylonian could not see what had called him, but he struck at Michael anyway. Parrying the blow, Michael felt the Lord making him more solid than before, the sword more dense, his body flesh-and-blood. He retained his wings, and their added balance gave him an advantage.

The children gasped at seeing a bonafide angel come to their rescue, but immediately resumed making a stack of boxes.

Swordplay had earned Michael his position, a sword forged from a will Lucifer himself had not shattered even after he'd shattered the sword. Michael checked out the children. Four boxes, and they worked on another. They had moved crates to either side to form a pyramid.

Michael disarmed the Babylonian; while the soldier groped for his weapon, Michael looked at the children—the last box was the most difficult. He wondered if he ought to help them, but then the soldier retrieved his sword, and Michael knew that if he helped them stack boxes he would be as much good as just another child. They needed him for his specialty, for his sword and his skill, and whatever remained of his strength.

Michael turned on the Babylonian in one strong swing that knocked the soldier into the far wall. The children stacked the last box and reached the ground floor. One by one they slipped upstairs.

The Babylonian regained his feet and attacked Michael with full force, not letting the barrage ease at all. His heart raced, and every muscle strained as he tried to stave off an attack driven by utter frenzy, by an unreasonable lust to kill Israelites: this Babylonian hated these children because of their birthplace, but Michael defended them for their faith. The soldier swung and swung and struck in a definite rhythm, and Michael concentrated his fatigued senses on the battle.

Then one blow came that surprised him, and it knocked him to the floor.

The last child to climb lost his balance, disloding the top box as he fell. He gasped as the Babylonian caught sight of him. Disregarding Michael, he closed in for the child.

Michael launched himself. In heat thicker than blood, he might have been a demon, and his wings scissored as he thrust his sword. Like blue needles through the smoke, his eyes pierced the power-madness of the Babylonian and forced him away from the child.

That's when the solider realized he was fighting an angel.

With his wings pressed against the basement ceiling, Michael made one blow that took the soldier's life.

The child huddled on the floor, hiding from whichever soldier had won. Michael left his sword sheathed in the body and replaced the top crate, then helped the child to a stand. The last child was about to crawl outside when he turned around.

"Thank you," he said.

His friends pulled him out, and the six children fled.

Michael felt God call him back to angelic form, and he yielded. He sat in the basement flames with his sword encased in a dead body, and he cried for Jerusalem.

An hour before sunrise, the soldiers had calmed down, but the air stayed smoky. Remiel reported King Zedekiah in flight to the plains of Jericho, but Babylon had many of the upper class and priests in chains, readied for a trip to another land.

Where the Temple used to be, Michael stood in the soot and closed his eyes. He remembered the altar, remembered the tapestry and the ornaments and the incense. Remembered the prayers and the people and the mercy.

Gabriel shuffled through the charred remains, focused into the ground. He paced, then paced back, and finally he plunged down one hand and came up with a burnt stone carved in the shape of a pomegranate. His focus altered, and Michael felt him asking a question, felt him receive an answer. Head bowed, Gabriel cradled the stone in both hands. "Thank you," he murmured.

Michael said, "Why are you keeping that?"

"I paid too much learning this lesson to chance forgetting it. Stone pomegranates have no taste." Gabriel turned. "How are you holding up? You did so well. You helped everyone."

Michael opened his hands and took in the city. "Everyone." He scanned the horizon: the smoke, the rubble, the dead in the streets. "Why?" His voice broke, and then he had his face in his hands and his wings all around himself, and he dropped to his knees in the Temple's cremains. "Why did it come to this?"

Gabriel wrapped around him, and Michael braced for a Cherub's onslaught of answers: the Will of God and the future and the coming Messiah and God's Plan...only Gabriel said none of that. Michael relaxed, and Gabriel rested his head against his.

Gabriel sang, "By the rivers of Babylon, the rivers, we sat and wept, remembering Zion. We hung up our harps on the willows."

Michael fought tears.

Gabriel sang, "For there our tormenters demanded a melody, a song of Zion."

Michael swallowed hard, then sang in a lower register, a different song, a psalm from a better time: "Our feet are standing in your gates, Jerusalem. Jerusalem, the city, so close and tight, where the tribes go up, the tribes of the Lord, to praise the name of the Lord."

Gabriel continued, "How can we sing of the Lord in a foreign land?"

When he faltered, Michael took the counter point to Gabriel's tune: "There stand the thrones of Judgment, the thrones of the house of David."

Gabriel went on: "If I forget you, Jerusalem, let me forget my right hand."

Michael couldn't sing aloud. He just projected it: *Pray for the peace of Jerusalem. May those who love you be secure.*

"Let my tongue stick to my mouth if I don't remember you, if I don't treasure Jerusalem as my joy."

May there be peace within your walls and security in your citadel.

"Remember, Lord, remember the day of Jerusalem, those who said 'Raze it! Raze it to its foundation.'"

For my friends and family, to them all, I say peace be with you.

Gabriel stopped singing. He looked stricken.

Michael whispered, "It's just a city. We helped the people."

Gabriel shook his head. "It was a city. A city is made of people."

The moon set. Michael intoned the morning prayer while Gabriel listened. And then, as Michael readied himself to check on Remiel and a fleeing Zedekiah, Gabriel spoke, his voice a mix of tenor and soprano. "There will be a new Ark and a new Covenant."

Michael's wings flared. "What?"

Gabriel gave a little shake of his head. "What?"

"What did you just say?"

"I..." He sat up, focused, then exclaimed, "A new Ark and a new Covenant?" He looked at Michael, then held the stone pomegranate to his lips. "Thank you."

Michael closed his eyes too. *Thank you for hope.*

He took a deep breath and touched his sword.

Gabriel said, "Do you want to go look over what they've done?"

Michael shook his head. "I'm heading to the Babylonian camp. I still have a people to protect."

The Epilogue

Watching the sun set over the Galilean hills, Gabriel sat on a roof and prayed in union with the family below. Uriel had become a guardian angel to a woman, and Gabriel often came for the evening and morning prayers because Uriel had been so present for him.

Raphael slipped onto the roof edge beside Gabriel and joined the prayer. The Seraph's fire flickered around him, and Gabriel thrilled at the beauty of the normal lives in Nazareth: the homes, the lamps, the routine, the prayers. This wasn't greatness as much as God present in the moment, and he opened his soul to Raphael to show him the wonder of ordinary time. *And look,* he sent to Raphael, drawing to his attention the long shafts of light piercing the sky, *see that? Air is still a colloidal suspension.*

Raphael chuckled.

The prayer in the house tugged at his soul, and Gabriel made himself docile to the pull. The woman was meditating, Uriel all around her and through her.

Raphael murmured, "What's going on?"

The pull increased. Gabriel said, "I'm being drawn inside."

Raphael kept his voice low. "Not that. Michael's set up a perimeter."

Gabriel absorbed the silence and felt an utter absence of demonic activity through the entire town. Michael, Raguel and Saraquael had taken positions at strategic points on the border, Remiel hovering. The demons didn't seem to be fighting, just elsewhere, as if they'd all forgotten this town at the same moment.

The tug grew in strength, and Gabriel released himself to its draw.

He found himself inhabiting the woman's prayer with Uriel, their intense contemplation of God as protector and king and guide. The hope of a promise made hundreds of years ago.

Gabriel became aware that the woman was aware of him. She grew wary. He remained present but silent.

God moved within Gabriel: it was time to speak. Gabriel reached his soul toward the woman's so they could hear one another. The woman's name was Mary.

She was paying full attention to him now. Uriel thrummed in her heart, gave her strength, and then backed off. It was just Gabriel and Mary.

Gabriel opened his hands and projected, *Hail, Full of Grace!*

As the words emerged, her soul opened up to him, and he realized what he'd said: *full of grace*. Full, as in containing nothing else. No other desires than God. No sin. Nothing other than total intensity of purpose for God alone. Full of grace. Uriel had cloaked this soul so he'd never seen it before, but now he could, and in that moment, Gabriel saw she was as God had made her to be, everything and nothing more.

The feel of her prayers hung around them both, but she was scared. He projected. *The Lord is with you. Don't be afraid.*

Her attention remained riveted to him. Gabriel's voice flowed into a mixture of tenor and soprano. "You have found favor with God. Listen: you will conceive in your womb and bear a son, and you will name him Jesus. He will be great, and he will be called Son of the Most High. The Lord God will give him the throne of David his father, and he will rule over the house of Jacob forever. Of his Kingdom there will be no end."

Gabriel focused on her alone, aware he was throwing off light and leaving a shadow, but at the same time she was looking into him without blinking. "How can this be?" she whispered. "I have no husband."

She was betrothed – surely she'd get the child in the usual way? Unless...unless she'd already promised that part of herself to God. Unless she'd already consecrated her body and made an agreement with her intended, and for Gabriel's words to be true meant she would sin, something she'd never want to do. Sin...or the impossible.

There will be a new Ark, God had told him. *A new Ark and a new Covenant.* He was speaking the message of a new Covenant, and here he stood, now, in front of the new Ark. The one who would bear the priesthood, the totality of the law, the bread that would feed the Lord's people. The Ark had contained the Spirit of the Lord, and it would again. The Ark was pure. No man could touch it.

The message flowed from Gabriel like a dream: "The Holy Spirit will come upon you, and the power of the Most High will overshadow you: therefore the Holy One who is to be born will be called the Son of God."

Gabriel shivered as he said the words. His soul whirled like a kaleidoscope.

"Elizabeth your cousin has conceived a son in her old age, and this is the sixth month for her who was called barren. For with God nothing will be impossible."

Mary clasped her hands at her chest: *Behold the maidservant of the Lord.* She murmured, "Let it be it done to me just as you say."

Gabriel felt himself eased back, still within her prayer but no longer within her vision. As he remained, he witnessed that kiss from the Holy Spirit, that breath where a new soul sparked into being within a human woman, and now here before him stood the Ark of the Covenant imbued with the Glory of the Lord, the fulfillment of every prayer the Jewish people had ever prayed.

Gabriel dropped to his knees. He formed a flower out of his soul material and laid it on the floor before Mary, who remained in prayer with tears streaking her cheeks. And he watched the glow of the second soul in the second body within her own.

Beside him, Raphael drew close, compelled, attracted. Gabriel reached for him. *Did you hear? Did you hear what I said?*

But Raphael remained focused on Mary. His confusion swirled through Gabriel, but also need. Determination.

Raphael bit his lip. "What's going on?"

Gabriel kept silence because he'd just had his moment, so Raphael should have his own, should cherish the wonder of realizing what Gabriel could already see. The little one conceived in Mary, the Messiah and the Son of God, was a human being. And humans had guardian angels.

Gabriel moved closer to Raphael, wing to wing, and took his hand. Squeezed. Then backed away.

Without even noticing Gabriel, Raphael stepped forward, and then a thrill shot through him. His attention flashed to God, one huge question, and then a surge of joy at the answer. He turned to Gabriel, beaming, and Gabriel extended his hand toward Raphael with a blessing.

Raphael turned back to Jesus, his human charge, and dissociated into the space around him.

In the corner, Gabriel tucked up his knees and waited. Mary emerged from her meditation looking shocked. She found the flower on the floor and set it in a pitcher of water, then paced. Nervousness rolled off her. Gabriel could feel Uriel's reassurance, could feel Raphael when he reached for the Seraph.

So many mysteries, so many wonders. It would take the Cherubim years to finish dissecting everything that had just taken place. Years. But he was no longer needed here, so he drifted up to the roof.

Michael had taken down the perimeter. Demons seemed to have remembered the town, as if they'd never forgotten to notice it.

Thank you, Gabriel prayed. Then, watching the multicolored sunset, Gabriel sent God a question.

God said, "You did it perfectly."

Gabriel's eyes reflected the sunset. "Was that my purpose? Was that why you created me?"

"Gabri'li," God said, "you still don't understand. I didn't create you for just one thing. You don't have one goal in life that's your ultimate purpose. None of you does."

Gabriel raised his wings. "But you said we had a purpose."

"True," God said.

Gabriel's brow furrowed. A purpose. Not one thing. Based on this conversation, not two things either.

The fading light curved through layers of sky, reflecting off the curled bodies of vapor and particulate ice carried by winds that were created by the heat of the sun and spun by the planetary rotation. The distorted light bent into a myriad of hues, and Gabriel allowed his angelic sight to recognize each one individually, then merge them back into the paintbrush blur that composed a sunset.

Gasping, he sat straight.

God laughed.

"You made us all to fit together," Gabriel said, "to work together, to be together. Life isn't a series of assignments and check-boxes. It's a continuum. We're gears that fit together like a machine to work in Your name."

Gabriel's mouth opened. "And—" He shifted his sight so he saw exclusively the Vision, looking at God face to Face. "And my ultimate purpose—?"

"You're fulfilling it now."

Gabriel opened his hands. "Anyone could have delivered that message."

"Anyone could have delivered that message, or no one. I could have done it myself. But no one else could fit into the community of angels like Gabriel ben Adonai, with your soul, your beauty, your power, your understanding, and your heart. Now not just a teacher of facts, but a teacher of life."

Gabriel bit his lip, and he hugged his knees to his chest.

"Come on home," said God to Gabriel, and the Holy Spirit wrapped him in a hug, carrying him to God's heart while the sun finished setting over the Judean hills.

Acknowledgments

2014

I wrote the first draft of this book in 1992, and I rewrote it about every five years until it stopped feeling not-quite-right. I have no idea how many people I've consulted, subjected to early drafts, or otherwise relied upon. I'm sorry. It's a problem of chronological sprawl.

Back in high school, I used to spend lunch breaks in the school library reading Gustav Davidson's "Dictionary of Angels." It was amazing to sort through all the myths and stories, but the book was out of print and I couldn't find a copy. Right before graduation, the librarian Arthur Stein handed me a copy he'd tracked down in a used book store. I especially want to thank him because having my own copy was an incredible inspiration.

While putting the finishing touches on "A Fish Story," I found by accident an article in the Catholic Biblical Quarterly, Geoff Miller's "Raphael the Liar: Angelic Deceit And Testing In The Book Of Tobit" and it helped clarify a number of issues.

Also, much thanks to the prophet Ezekiel, who in 16:49 spelled out the sin of Sodom (yes, some have scolded that I softened it for this story, but no, Gabriel's quoting the Bible) and recounted the vision of the wheels of the Cherubim in chapter 10. Where yeah, Gabriel does exactly what this story said he did.

Of the pre-readers I remember, in no particular order, I want to thank Maria Franzetti, Kenneth Elwood, Pauline Griffin, James Lebak, Ivy Reisner, Wendy Dinsmore, Kaci Hill, Sarah Begg, Evan, Madeline, Nicole Grimes, and Liz Grimes.

I want to thank my fans and followers who have offered me encouragement all the way through. I love hearing from you guys, and I hope you love this book too.

Thank you so much for reading *An Arrow In Flight*! Please consider leaving a review at Amazon or Goodreads (or both.) Forget what your 4th grade teacher said about book reports: leaving a review is as easy as finding the book's entry and clicking on a number of stars, then writing a couple of sentences about what you liked or didn't like. Authors will love you for it! (Well, I can't speak for all authors. This author will love you for it.)

I have an author page at http://facebook.com/JaneLebakAuthor if you'd like updates on new books and sales. But for right now, here's what we've got:

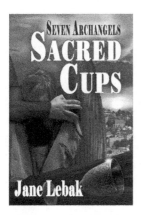

In Sacred Cups, the seven Archangels of the Presence have a new assignment: guard the Messiah during his childhood and ministry. Gabriel struggles to synthesize the lessons for his year as a man, and he carries that shame into his relationships with the other angels. When created beings kill the Son of God, mortal enemies suddenly become allies while close friends become enemies, and Gabriel finds himself on the battlefield of a war he never wanted to fight.

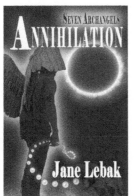

And in Seven Archangels: Annihilation, Satan thinks he's figured out how to destroy an angel's immortal soul. He starts with Gabriel.

Who's next?

Tabris is a guardian angel who killed the boy he vowed to protect.
Only instead of condemning him, God gives him a second chance
– another assignment. Another guardianship.

Although he struggles to help this new child, a ten-year-old girl
named Elizabeth, Tabris can't escape what he did with Sebastian.
Elizabeth's co-guardian doesn't trust him at all, which makes
sense because even Tabris doesn't trust himself. Everywhere he
goes, the angels all know what he's done, and the only angel who
seems to want him is a friend from long ago, now a demon.

Shame and guilt follow Tabris like a shadow, but it's only the
memory of the dead boy, and even though Sebastian still needs
him, Tabris cannot face him. After what he's done, there's no way
he can make it right. But his bright spirit is growing darker, and
the other angels have realized that if Tabris can't accept the mercy
he's been given, then he's going to fall forever.

Made in United States
North Haven, CT
23 August 2023

40682791R00173